# ashes OF YOU

## THE LOST & FOUND SERIES

# CATHERINE COWLES

Copyright © 2023 by The PageSmith LLC. All rights reserved.

No part of this book may be reproduced in any form or by any electronic or mechanical means, including information storage and retrieval systems, without written permission from the author, except for the use of brief quotations in a book review.

This is a work of fiction. Names, characters, places, and incidents are either the products of the author's imagination or are used fictitiously. Any resemblance to actual persons, living or dead, businesses, companies, events, or locales is entirely coincidental.

Editor: Margo Lipschultz
Copy Editor: Chelle Olson
Proofreading: Julie Deaton and Jaime Ryter
Paperback Formatting: Stacey Blake, Champagne Book Design
Cover Design: Hang Le

*For Rebecca.*

*Who loves single dads and G-Wagons. I gave you both in this series because I'm such a good friend. Sorry it wasn't in the same book. Nevertheless, Lawson is for you.*

*Thank you for the gift of your epic voice memos, horrible TV play-by-plays, puzzling updates, pep talks, and, most of all, your friendship. I know you don't like feelings, but I love you—a whole lot.*

# ashes
OF YOU

## Prologue

### Halston

### FIVE YEARS AGO

"Keep moving. Keep moving. Keep moving."

I said the words over and over, even though they were barely audible anymore. They'd become my mantra. The steady beat forced me forward, even if the howling wind swallowed the words, and my lips barely moved.

My teeth chattered violently as I struggled to get my legs to continue their motion. The fresh cuts on my stomach stung as the wind whipped against the thin sheath I wore. I wanted to tear it from my body and rip away everything that *he* had tainted.

I squinted into the night, trying to see through the thick trees and falling snow to…anything.

A whimper escaped my lips as my bare foot hit an especially sharp rock. I'd thought my limbs had lost feeling in the freezing snow, but I was wrong.

I told myself that was good. It meant they weren't frostbitten—yet.

I glanced over my shoulder at the night behind me. I didn't hear him. Not anymore. At first, he'd screamed my name into the night, but then he'd gone quiet.

Quiet was always worse. I'd learned that on day four. But then twenty-nine days followed. Days where I was sure I'd die in that damp, dark cave. Days where I sometimes wished I had.

"Keep moving."

I clenched my fists as my body trembled, pressing my fingernails into my palms and hoping the pain would spur me on. My nails were long now with nothing to cut them with. But I'd gotten used to pain, had a higher tolerance for it, and my nails cutting into my flesh did nothing.

My stomach cramped in a vicious twist. My joints felt stiff, like the Tin Man in that movie. *What was it called?*

A wave of dizziness swept over me, followed by a surge of heat. I suddenly felt like I was sweating, burning up from the inside out. The urge to pull the flimsy shift from my body was so strong.

Everything hurt, from the tips of my toes to the ends of my hair. My flesh felt as though it were cracking open.

I stumbled, falling to my knees. The chill of the snow was bliss on my overheated flesh. I let myself topple and roll to my back. Blessed snow. The cold seeped into my skin, soothing.

A voice lifted on the wind. I thought I heard my name.

Tears leaked from my eyes. It was *him*. He'd found me.

I needed to get up. Run. Fight.

But I couldn't. Maybe I'd be lucky, and he'd finally kill me.

Movement swam above me—a figure.

"Halston?"

The voice was deep with grit, as though sandpaper coated it. But there was also something comforting about it; it had a gentleness. It wasn't like the man's.

"Holy hell," another voice rumbled. "Is she wearing a nightgown? It's nine degrees."

"Call it in," the voice above me snapped.

The figure swam above me again, his face coming in and going out of focus. In and out. But every time my vision cleared, beauty struck me: dark hair and thick scruff around an angular jaw. A nose that looked as if it had possibly been broken at one point. And his eyes…

There was something about the deep blue. I wanted to drown in the pools. They were kind. Not mean. Not like the man's angry brown ones.

"Halston, you're safe now. We're gonna get you out of here. Can you tell me where you're hurt?"

I heard the other man calling off numbers and then the crackle of a radio.

I opened my mouth. Tried to speak. But nothing came out.

The man above me shifted, pulling something from a backpack. "Need to get you warm."

As he moved to cover me with a blanket, he froze. His head jerked up, and he looked at the other man. "She's bleeding. Been cut."

The second man cursed. "The rest of the team is still thirty minutes out."

"We gotta get her warm. She's hypothermic."

They moved around me.

Blue eyes hovered above me. "We need to move you. It might hurt. But we have to get you warm."

"No," I croaked. "Hot."

Pain streaked through those beautiful blue eyes. "I know you feel hot, but your body's lying to you right now. We're going to move you. On three. One. Two. Three."

Fiery agony ripped through me as the men lifted me onto something. But I didn't make a sound. It was instinct. *He* always liked when I screamed. I'd learned to stay quiet and not give him the power.

Darkness wavered at the corners of my vision.

A hand gripped mine. "Halston, stay with me."

Those fathomless eyes filled my vision. So beautiful. "Blue," I whispered.

He squeezed my hand harder. "Halston!"

But I was already slipping under. I didn't mind. At least I'd be drowning in kindness when I went.

# Chapter One

*Lawson*

## PRESENT DAY

I blinked against the early morning sunlight streaming through my bedroom window and tried to shift the weight off my bad shoulder—the one I'd hurt playing ball in high school—only I couldn't move. Hell, I could barely breathe with the tiny foot shoved into my diaphragm.

A six-year-old shouldn't have that kind of strength. But Charlie slept wild, like some wildebeest trapped in a cage. He kicked and punched. He'd even given me a black eye one night. *That* had been interesting to explain at the station.

Currently, he'd twisted himself sideways in my California king, so I had less than a foot of space and had his heel planted firmly in my gut. At least, it wasn't the face this time.

My alarm blared on my nightstand, and I reached over the small lump in my bed to shut it off. My eyes burned as if someone had poured acid into them.

Coffee. I needed coffee. Preferably an IV drip I could carry around with me all day.

As I shifted to lay back on the pillow, Charlie jerked, his legs lashing out, one striking me directly in the balls.

The strangled noise that escaped my throat sounded like a wounded animal going through puberty. I bit the inside of my cheek so hard I tasted blood.

Charlie stretched, oblivious to the fact that he had just ended all possibility of me having any future children. Good thing the three I already had were enough.

He smacked his lips. "Morning."

I breathed in through my nose and out through my mouth, waiting for the pain to pass.

Charlie's brow scrunched. "You've got a funny face, Dad."

I let one last breath out. "Just tired, bud."

He grinned at me. "I slept great."

Of course, he had. Even though I risked injury and possible death, I couldn't say no when my six-year-old appeared at my door after having a nightmare.

I studied my little man, his dark hair sticking up in all directions. He had more nightmares than his older brothers seemed to have. A weight settled in my gut, worry that past events had somehow embedded the nightmares there.

Charlie flicked my nose. "Stop staring."

I chuckled, tickling his sides. He squealed and jumped out of bed, a flash of color in his pajamas. They were his favorites, the ones covered in frogs. I'd had to order two more pairs because he refused to sleep in anything else.

"Daaaaaaaaad," Charlie whined, but I heard laughter in his voice.

"Do me a favor and go wake up your brothers."

A glint lit Charlie's eyes—irises a blue so similar to mine. "Can I jump on them?"

"Whatever it takes, Charlie Bear."

His grin was huge, and he let out some sort of war cry as he ran from my room.

I flopped back down on the mattress, my balls still aching. That kid would be the death of me.

My head throbbed, trying to think about the last time I'd gotten a full night's sleep. I honestly couldn't pull it from memory. Maybe the miracle would come this weekend. *If* Charlie was exhausted from his uncle's wedding, and Drew and Luke didn't pull something stupid.

I would sell a kidney for a good twelve-hour stretch of rest.

"Get the hell out of my room," Luke bellowed from down the hall.

*Shit.*

I sat up, swinging my legs over the side of my bed. Twelve hours wasn't coming anytime soon.

"You killed the Fruit Loops," Luke growled at his younger brother.

Drew looked up from his phone with a shrug. "I was hungry."

Luke turned his thunderous look at me. "And let me guess, we don't have any more."

My back teeth ground together as I moved toward the pantry. I'd known the teenage years wouldn't be easy, but it was as if Luke had morphed into a different human being when he turned sixteen. He mainly communicated in grunts and scowls and never told me what was actually going on in that head of his.

It cut more than he'd ever know. He'd made me a father, and we'd always had a special bond. Fishing, hiking, camping. We did it all. Until he suddenly wanted nothing to do with me, seemingly overnight.

I scanned the pantry shelves: Cheerios. Cocoa Pebbles. Shredded Wheat. Cap'n Crunch. Kix. No Fruit Loops. I winced as I saw that while we had a world of cereal, we didn't have much else. I needed to get to the grocery store. Stat. I grabbed all the boxes and headed back into the kitchen.

Depositing them onto the island, I met Luke's pissed-off stare. "Bad news. No Fruit Loops. Good news? We've got every other cereal known to man."

Luke shoved back his stool. "I'll get something at school."

I opened my mouth to argue but then closed it. I'd learned that I needed to pick my battles with Luke. And whether or not he ate breakfast at home was not the hill I wanted to die on.

Drew and Charlie didn't seem to even register their eldest brother's outburst. It happened so often that it was just background noise to them now. Charlie had his nose shoved into a book about reptiles, and Drew's fingers flew across his cell phone screen. I'd gotten him the damn thing so he could let me know where he was or if one of his various sports practices ran late, but it was now permanently attached to his hand.

I turned around and scanned the counter. The bananas were way past their prime, but there was a lone orange in the bowl. I reached for it, removed the rind, halved it, then quickly put the pieces in bowls, shoving them at the two kids who still spoke to me.

"Do me a favor and eat something that isn't just sugar and carbs so I don't get fired as a dad, okay?"

Charlie giggled and popped a wedge of orange into his mouth. "Not fired."

Drew made a face like he smelled something bad. "Oranges are gross."

I stared at my thirteen-year-old. His hair swooped into his face in a way I knew the teen girls loved. It was a touch lighter than mine, closer to his mother's color. Just that flicker of thought had anger surging, even after all these years. And quick on its heels came the guilt.

I did what I always did—shoved it all down to that place that would never be opened.

"Since when?" I probed.

Drew let out an exaggerated shiver. "Since I realized how gross all the strings are. It's like chewing on one of Gran's knitting projects."

Charlie's chewing slowed, and he spat the piece of orange back into the bowl. "Yuck."

I sent Drew a withering stare. "Thanks for that."

He just laughed. "Can't help if I'm always right. It's one of the main reasons the babes love me."

I bent my head and pinched the bridge of my nose. If we made it through high school without a pregnancy scare, it would be a miracle.

"Dad, can Cady come over after school for a playdate?" Charlie chimed in.

"I think they've got a lot going on with the wedding tomorrow, bud."

Charlie frowned. "Since Uncle Roan is marrying Cady's mom, does that mean I can't marry Cady?"

Drew choked on his cereal. "It's kind of incestual, little dude."

"What's in-in-ses-tal?" Charlie asked, struggling with the word.

I glared at his older brother. "Remember what we talked about? Not all words are meant for little ears."

Charlie's face scrunched up. "I'm not little!"

Drew rolled his eyes. "If you're still crawling into Dad's bed because you had a bad dream, I'd say you're little."

Charlie's face went red, and he dropped his spoon into his bowl. Sliding off the stool, he bolted for his room.

A muscle beneath my eye began to flutter. "Drew."

My middle son met my stare. While his hair was more like his mother's, his eyes were mine, through and through. "It's true. You gotta stop babying him, or he's gonna be sleeping with you until he's twenty."

I sighed. "He had a nightmare."

"That doesn't mean he can't sleep in his own bed. And he wakes me up, tromping down the hall and turning on every light known to man because he's scared."

"I'm sorry he woke you up, but that's no reason to make him feel bad about being scared. We've all been there. As I remember, you had a bout of being frightened of a green monster you thought lived under your bed."

A little bit of guilt slipped into Drew's expression, and his shoulders slumped. "Sorry. I'll go talk to him."

I clamped a hand on Drew's shoulder. "You're a good brother."

One corner of his mouth pulled up. "Say that when you drop me off at school. Make sure the babes hear. They eat that big-brother stuff up."

I smacked him lightly on the back of the head. "Don't call women and girls *babes*."

Drew's mouth curved into a full grin. "It's a term of endearment. They love it."

I bet they did.

I pinned him with a stare. "We treat women with respect, and we don't toy with their emotions."

Drew held up both hands as he slid off his stool. "Total respect, bruh."

"I'm your dad, not your *bruh*."

Drew just chuckled. "Okay, Daddio. Where are my pads? I need to load my gear bag."

A curse slipped free. I tried my best to keep my language clean for my kids, but every now and then, no other words worked. Like when you were supposed to wash your kid's lacrosse pads and completely forgot.

"Dad," Drew groaned. "Those pads reek, and Coach has a thing about doing our conditioning runs in them."

I started toward the laundry room. "I'll wash them now and drop your gear bag at school."

Drew frowned. "Don't you have work?"

"I've got interviews here this morning," I said as I ducked into the laundry room.

"We don't need a fucking nanny." I heard Luke's deeper tone from outside the room.

My spine stiffened, and I strode out, Drew's pads in hand. "You say that word again, and I'll take your electronics away for two days."

Luke's expression went hard. "You can't do that."

My brow rose. "It's a privilege, not a right."

"Everyone has a phone and computer. Taking them away is like putting someone in prison."

I wanted to laugh. This kid had no idea how good he had it. I tried hard not to let the fact that we had a lot of money spoil my kids. They didn't get everything they asked for and had to do chores for allowance, but they also had everything they *needed*.

I made a good living as the Cedar Ridge chief of police, but my dad's previous outdoor company made it so my four siblings and I never had to worry about money. He'd sold it when I was in high school, which had set us all up for life. But the truth was, I rarely dipped into my trust fund.

It was one of the things that had annoyed my ex, Melody, the most. She hadn't understood why I wanted to work. Why we didn't go on lavish vacations every month or drive Lamborghinis.

I'd used some of my portion to buy this house. And I'd use it to send the boys to college. But other than that, I didn't need it. I liked living simply.

My family had taught me time and again that it wasn't physical belongings that mattered but the people you had around you and the experiences you shared.

"Whatever," Luke mumbled, shoving something into his backpack.

He was the spitting image of me, but it was like looking at a stranger. He'd taken to wearing only black, and I'd caught him texting with a friend that he wanted to get a fake ID so he could get a tattoo.

A knock sounded on the door, but Luke ignored it. That muscle beneath my eye fluttered faster, but I didn't say a word; I simply crossed the vast, open-concept living and kitchen space to get to the front of the house.

Balancing the gear in one arm, I barely managed to grab the knob. A light laugh greeted me as I opened the door.

"You okay there, big bro?" Grae asked as she slipped inside.

"Just fine and dandy," I grumbled.

"Aunt G!" Charlie yelled, running down the hall.

He launched himself at her, and she caught him easily. "How's my guy?"

"Good. What are you doing here?" he asked with a grin, his earlier hurt clearly forgotten.

"I'm taking you to school today, but I don't think you can go in your PJs."

I glanced at the clock on the wall and bit back another curse. They were going to be late. "Gotta hurry, Charlie Bear. Get changed and brush your teeth. I'll come help, but I gotta get these in the wash."

"I've got him," Grae assured me. "You handle the laundry."

Luke strode toward the door. "Can I wait in your car?"

Grae's brow furrowed. "Sure. It's unlocked."

Luke was out the door without another word or even a backward glance at me. "Is he okay?"

Pain lanced me. "Teenager."

But I wasn't so sure that was it anymore. Something was off with Luke, and for the life of me, I couldn't get him to tell me what it was.

Lately, it felt like I was failing more than I was succeeding with him, and it killed me. But I'd fight with everything I had to make sure my kids were safe, healthy, and whole. I'd battle to the death to ensure I never failed them again.

# Chapter Two

### Hallie

I SPREAD MY HAND OVER THE COMFORTER, SMOOTHING IT. It was a little shabby-looking, fraying at the corners and faded from the sunshine that streamed through the window. If my brother knew where I was staying, he would not be pleased. He'd demand that I change to a nicer, more expensive place.

But I didn't want that. Emerson and his husband, Adrian, had done more than enough for me over the past five years—more than anyone should have to. And they weren't exactly rolling in it.

They were both teachers in Chicago. They'd met in grad school and had fallen head over heels for each other. My parents had already been displeased about Em's career choice, but when he told them he was marrying a man, they'd cut him off completely.

As if I'd summoned evil by simply thinking about it, my phone dinged.

> **Mother:** *I called Emerson's apartment. He said you weren't there. Where are you, Halston?*

I worried my bottom lip as I gripped my arm, my fingers tapping out a beat.

> **Me:** *I have a job interview.*

Not a lie. I did have an interview. It was just hours away from where she thought I was.

> **Mother:** *What kind of job? I thought we agreed that the art world was your future. You know I have connections in several important galleries. That's where you should be putting your focus.*

I stared down at the phone, my vision going a little blurry. My fingertips tingled, a telltale sign I was headed for a panic attack.

*No. Not today.*

I focused on the space around me. *Five things you can see.*

"Nightstand. Lamp. Pillow. Book. Water bottle."

I took a deep breath, and the tingling abated a smidge. *Four things you can hear.*

I listened carefully, picking up the faint strains of more than a few things. "Traffic. A door. The TV. A faucet dripping."

*Three things you can feel.*

"Slippers. Sweater." I let my hand drop to the bed. "Comforter."

*Two things you can smell.*

"Musty." I strained to smell anything beyond the old motel room. "Pine."

Something about that hint of wood gave me a sense of peace, pushing back the panic trying to grab hold.

One final long breath escaped my lungs. I stared at the phone. If I got this job, maybe I would finally be brave enough to change my number and be done with her—with *them*.

My cell rang in my hand, making me jump. I cringed, expecting my mother's number to flash across the screen. The pressure in my chest eased as I took in *Emerson* and that familiar Chicago area code.

Panic quickly followed when I saw that it was a video call. I scanned the room, looking for the best place to accept the call, a spot where he wouldn't instantly be on alert that I was staying somewhere he wouldn't consider safe.

I sat on the bed, kicking off my slippers. The headboard seemed pretty standard and undamaged.

Swiping my finger across the screen, I forced a bright smile. "Em."

His familiar face greeted me. His blond hair was a few shades darker than my nearly white locks, but our gray eyes were practically identical. Unfortunately, worry filled his now. "Mom called."

I winced.

He sighed. "I thought I'd beat her to you."

One corner of my mouth pulled up. "She wants to know why I'm not going on interviews with the galleries she suggested."

Emerson groaned. "Maybe because you think the gallery world is as interesting as watching paint dry?"

I grinned, the action easing some of the tension thrumming through me. On the drive out here, everything inside me had spun, constricting tighter and tighter. By the time I reached Washington, I'd felt like a spool of fishing line.

My brother studied me for a moment. "Are you okay? I could come out there. And you know you can always come back here."

"Em—"

"I mean it. You're our family. We love you more than anything. It's okay if you're not ready."

I let out a slow breath, tracing one of the flowers on the comforter with my finger. "You're starting your own family. You need the space to do that."

Emerson and Adrian's apartment was nice but not exactly spacious. It was crowded with the three of us, no matter how much I tried to stay out of their way. And if you added a baby into that mix, it would be too much.

"Adrian and I talked. There are a few suburbs we could move to—"

"No." My voice was stronger than I'd heard it in a long time. "You love the city. The energy. The people. The *food*. You're not moving to the 'boring ol' suburbs' as you call them because of me."

Em loved city life in a way that I never had. I'd always been partial to our family's vacation home a few towns from here. The mountains had always made me feel like I could breathe and had the freedom to be who I truly was.

After my ordeal, everything set off my anxiety. Loud noises, crowded spaces. It didn't make living in a city easy. I'd worked hard on all my triggers, but that didn't mean I didn't long for the peace of the mountains.

Emerson's expression gentled. "I'm just not sure it's healthy for you to be back there. There are a million places you could consider living. Illinois has plenty of lake communities—places that are only a couple hours' drive from us."

I heard what he didn't say: *Places where they could get to me quickly if I had a meltdown from being on my own.*

I pressed my lips together, biting the bottom one as I tried to choose my words carefully. "I want to face it."

I'd been working hard in therapy for the past five years. Doing every exercise my therapist recommended and slowly increasing my tolerance for difficult things. I'd managed to finish college, get a good job as a nanny, and even take a trip on my own. These mountains had been my favorite place in the world. I wanted to reclaim them.

And the truth was, when I first saw them again through my windshield, I hadn't felt anxiety. I'd felt wonder.

"That's very brave of you, but—"

A dark brown hand clamped down on my brother's shoulder in a squeeze, cutting off Emerson's words. The gesture was affectionate and a warning all at once.

Adrian's face filled the screen, then a wide grin spread across it. "How's our girl?"

I sent him a grateful smile. "Good."

"Have you explored the town at all yet? I looked it up yesterday, and it's absolutely adorable."

My fingers gripped the comforter, twisting. "Not yet. I'm pretty tired from all the driving."

Or scared.

I'd order pizza and have it delivered to my room when dinner rolled around, and would have my pepper spray in hand when it arrived.

"I'm just going to rest tonight, but I'll go out to get some breakfast tomorrow." I'd give myself today, but if I stayed in this room much longer, I knew I'd never leave. Which would mean I'd miss my interview, and Emerson might really have to come and get me.

"I saw an adorable little coffee shop and café online called The Brew. Has all the *Alice in Wonderland* feels," Adrian suggested. "It's right downtown."

I nodded my head for far too long, probably looking like some deranged bobblehead doll. "I'll check it out and report back."

Adrian's amber eyes glowed with pride. "Try one of the double chocolate muffins for me. They look like heaven."

My mouth curved in a hint of an authentic smile. "I think I can handle that."

"What time is your interview tomorrow?" Emerson cut in.

"Ten." My stomach did a series of somersaults. All I knew about the family was that they had three boys aged six, thirteen, and sixteen and needed help Monday through Friday with an occasional emergency thrown in.

"I don't know if this is a good idea—"

Adrian cut Emerson off again. "The agency fully vets all their clients. And Hallie is amazing with kids. She was born to do this."

Warmth spread through my chest at his words. There were times when I felt more comfortable around children than adults. There was no pretense. No pretending to be something you weren't. No hiding the dark sides.

"If it's meant to be, I'll get it. If it's not, then I'll keep looking." It was what I'd told myself time and time again. But the fact that my savings were limited kept me from fully believing it.

Emerson let out a long breath. "Okay." He met my gaze through the screen. "They'd be lucky to have you."

"Thanks, Em," I whispered.

"Call us as soon as you're done," Adrian insisted. "We want to hear *everything*."

The corners of my mouth pulled into a full smile. "You'll be my first call as soon as I get back to my hotel room."

"Knock 'em dead," he said as a sign-off.

Emerson just waved.

I hit *end* on the call and let the phone drop.

I pulled my knees to my chest and hugged them hard. Sometimes, it helped keep the anxiety at bay, the hard pressure against my chest.

"You can do this," I whispered into the room.

Releasing my legs, I picked up my phone again and opened the internet browser. I typed in *The Brew, Cedar Ridge*. The photos that popped up on my screen were beyond cute, and the menu had my mouth watering.

My heart began to hammer against my ribs, and my breaths came faster.

My eyes burned, tears of frustration trying to break free.

"One step at a time. What's the next step?"

My voice was shaky, but the words helped. My hand trembled around the phone. Opening my maps app, I typed in *The Brew*.

Directions populated the screen, and I traced them with my gaze. It was only three blocks from here.

I surveyed everything I would pass along the way and envisioned the streets I'd seen when I drove in yesterday with their quaint shops and picturesque restaurants.

New was never easy for me. It was even worse if someone tried to push me into it. Precisely why I'd left my parents' home and went to live with Emerson and Adrian. I needed to go at my own pace, and I'd found that if I practiced something in my mind before I did it, it wasn't quite as scary.

I ran my gaze over the route twice more. "Tomorrow, you just take the next step."

I surveyed what I'd need in the morning: the leather boots, my puffy jacket, and the hat from the chair in the corner. My focus shifted to the pepper spray on my nightstand. It wasn't as if I thought someone would attack me on a Saturday morning in the downtown area of a small community.

I wanted to believe that thought. But I knew that bad things could happen when you least expected them.

# Chapter Three

## Lawson

I shoved the pads and some of Drew's workout clothes into the machine. The smell that wafted from it had me fighting a gag. I knew I shouldn't try to fit everything into one load, but I didn't have a choice. I didn't have time to wait for two.

The three nanny candidates I planned to interview today wouldn't take more than an hour and a half—two, tops. Then I had to get to the station to catch up on a mountain of paperwork. Pouring detergent on top of the rank gear, I slammed the lid closed and hit start.

"What'd that washer ever do to you?"

I spun at the sound of Grae's voice.

"Charlie—"

"Is brushing his teeth, and his outfit is already laid out. It won't be the end of the world if they're five minutes late to school."

Except they'd been late more often than on time this year, and I knew the teachers and schools noticed.

Worry lined Grae's face. "Are you okay?"

An invisible fist ground into my gut. "I'm fine. Just a lot going on right now."

"Then let me help. You know Caden and I will take the boys if you need a break. My schedule is flexible now that I'm working at The Peaks. I can play chauffeur anytime you need."

Guilt pricked at my skin. My sister didn't need to be helping me. She was newly engaged and pregnant, working a new job with her fiancé at his family's resort. She should be enjoying that, not taking on *my* responsibilities.

"I'm fine. Really. And once I get a nanny in place, that'll help."

Grae sent me a skeptical look. "That means actually hiring someone."

I scowled at her. "This person will be taking care of my kids. It needs to be the right fit."

She leaned against the doorjamb. "And the last ten candidates were all atrocious?"

"One of them had a record," I growled. That was when I'd changed my strategy from simply placing an ad in the paper to using an agency. At least now, I wouldn't end up with someone convicted of possession with intent to distribute in my living room.

Grae winced. "Okay, that's fair. But every single one was awful?"

"There was no one I'd trust with my kids." Because those three terrors were my whole world. I'd almost lost them once and would never let them be at risk again.

Grae moved closer to me. "Then let us help. We're your family. That's what we do."

Except, all my younger brothers and Grae were moving on with their lives. Holt would welcome a baby any day with his fiancée, Wren. Grae was newly engaged and expecting, also. Nash was planning a wedding with Maddie. And Roan was marrying Aspen tomorrow. They didn't need my responsibilities weighing them down.

"The candidates today should be better. They're the ones from the agency," I assured her.

Grae's lips pursed. "Okay."

I pulled her in for a quick hug. "Thanks for taking the kids to school."

"I love doing it," she said, hugging me back hard. "I get to hear all about the soap opera that is middle school."

I chuckled as I released her. "See if you can turn Drew into a one-woman man."

She snorted. "That boy falls in love every other week."

I groaned as visions danced in my head. "I'm going to end up shot by some father."

Grae grinned as she patted me on the shoulder. "No one would come after the chief of police."

"I wish I had your confidence."

"Come on, munchkins," Grae called down the hall. "This bus is leaving the station."

Charlie ran down the hall, his backpack slapping against his back. "Don't leave me."

She bent and kissed the top of his head. "Never. I need to hear more about the golden dart frog."

Glee filled Charlie's face as he took Grae's hand. "If you just touch it, you could *die*. It lives in the Amazon and…"

Charlie continued listing the amphibian's many traits as Drew hurried down the hall.

"Gear is in the wash. I'll drop it at the school office. Sorry about that, D-man."

Drew nodded. "No big."

But it was. I was forgetting things left and right, dropping the ball. One of these days, those balls were going to shatter. I needed help, and I needed it now.

I pulled him in for a quick hug. "Love you. You know that, right?"

Drew reared back. "Do you have cancer or something?"

I made a face. "No. Can't your old man just tell you he loves you?"

"Sure…but you don't usually do it before I leave for school."

"Well, I should." Yet another ball I'd dropped.

"Dad," Drew said, his voice getting a little quieter, "I know you love me. You don't have to make a big thing about it."

"But it *is* a big thing. The biggest," I argued. "And I should make a point of telling you all the time."

"Okay," Drew gave in. "Just not in front of my babes, okay?"

I barked out a laugh. "Fair enough."

I followed Grae, Charlie, and Drew out of the house. As I stepped onto the front porch, the view stole my breath, even after all these years.

Cedar Ridge had something I'd never found anywhere else. A peaceful energy that grounded. The tiny mountain town hours east of Seattle had a beauty so pristine it almost hurt to look at.

My house was nestled in the foothills with a view of the lake surrounded by snow-covered mountains. And I never took it for granted.

The boys and Grae hurried to her SUV and climbed inside to join a scowling Luke. With a honk of the horn, they were off.

Just as I was about to turn back to the house, I caught sight of a truck heading up my gravel drive with two SUVs following it. I frowned as I recognized my brothers' vehicles.

They all parked and climbed out.

"What are you doing here?"

Holt grinned up at me as he beeped the locks on his fancy-ass Mercedes SUV. "You think we're gonna miss the show this time?"

I sent a glare in my youngest brother's direction.

Nash shrugged, pushing his dark blond hair out of his eyes. "You really think I could sit on the fact that someone you arrest on a regular basis applied to be your nanny?"

I groaned. "I really don't need an audience for this."

Roan's lips twitched. He was smiling a lot more now that he had Aspen in his life. It was still unnerving. I was used to seeing my brother with a perpetual scowl on his face.

"Well, you're getting an audience. This way, you can't cut perfectly good candidates," he muttered.

"And we get a couple of hours of amusement," Holt echoed, heading up my steps.

Nash followed him. "You got any snacks?"

I pressed my fingers to the bridge of my nose. "F my life."

Roan slapped me on the back. "Is that what the kids are saying these days?"

No, it was what *I* was saying. Because my interfering brothers were going to make this interview process hell.

The woman sitting across from me kept looking into the kitchen and frowning. Her hair was pulled back into a tight bun, highlighting the gray streaks running through it. "What do the children have for breakfast?"

She kept calling them that: *the children.*

"Depends on the day. But on school days, it's usually cereal," I answered.

Her frown deepened. "Sugary cereal?"

Out of the corner of my eye, I saw Nash freeze, his spoonful of Cap'n Crunch halfway to his mouth.

"That's no way to start the day," Mrs. Archibald continued. "They need a mix of protein, long-lasting carbs, and fruits."

I shifted in my seat. "I'm sure a warm breakfast would be welcome." I started to ask Mrs. Archibald about her previous placement when she cut me off.

"What about schedules? Children need strict schedules."

The word *strict* had my skin prickling. I mean, it was better than the first candidate, who had only asked what kind of cable package I had, if she could buy snacks with a company credit card, and whether I minded if she had an occasional beer while on the job. But I didn't want my kids with a drill sergeant either.

"Charlie, Drew, and Luke all have very different schedules." I stressed their names, annoyed that Mrs. Archibald hadn't used them once. "Drew is on several sports teams. Charlie has quite a few playdates. And Luke is sixteen, so he goes more his own way."

"It sounds like the children run the show around here," Mrs. Archibald said, her tone dripping with disdain.

Holt hid a laugh with a cough.

"They don't *run* anything, but they are my number-one priority, and I'll do anything to make sure they're happy, healthy, and safe." Annoyance began bleeding into my tone.

"They sound quite spoiled. We'll have to change that. I recommend waking them two hours before they must leave for school. They will help with chores around the house, make a *healthy* breakfast—there will be no more processed sugar in this home—and do calisthenics before we depart. Homework must be done as soon as they get home, and I will check it before they are permitted to do anything else."

The room went silent. I simply stared at the woman opposite me.

Roan grunted to my right. "Is this lady for real?"

"Excuse me?" Mrs. Archibald said, clearly affronted.

"On the upside, from the sound of things, you'd be building your own army of foot soldiers," Holt offered.

Nash frowned. "If there's no sugar in this house, I'll riot."

I let my head fall, pinching the bridge of my nose.

"If this is the influence you bring into the children's lives, I can see why you're having issues," Mrs. Archibald said with a huff.

My head snapped up at that. "Charlie, Drew, and Luke."

She looked puzzled at my words.

"My *children* have names. Charlie, Drew, and Luke. And I would rather they riot on a daily basis and be surrounded by family who *loves* them than be turned into robots at the hands of someone who can't even bother to use their names."

Mrs. Archibald's spine stiffened, and she gripped her purse tighter. "You're going to ruin your children."

I'd had enough. I might not be the perfect father, but I loved my kids. And I'd never leave them in the hands of a woman like this. "We clearly aren't a match. I'll show you out."

It was all I could do to keep a tight rein on my temper.

Mrs. Archibald's mouth went slack. "You're not hiring me?"

Nash's eyebrows hit his hairline. "Lady, you're about as cuddly as a porcupine. I wouldn't let you take care of my pet fish."

Holt glanced at Nash. "You got a fish?"

"No." Nash shook his head. "It's hard enough keeping up with the dog who's always stealing my shoes."

"A fish might be nice," Roan cut in. "As long as this one,"—he motioned to the woman on my couch—"isn't feeding it."

"Not helping," I muttered.

Mrs. Archibald shot to her feet. "I have never had such an atrocious interview in all my days."

"Well, that makes two of us," I agreed.

"And he interviewed an ex-con last week," Nash added.

Mrs. Archibald's eyes went wide. "I should've guessed that's who you'd be consorting with."

"They were definitely nicer than you," Holt called as I ushered Mrs. Archibald toward the door.

"Don't follow me," she snapped.

My jaw clenched with a vicious snap. "I'm not," I gritted. "I'm showing you out."

"I know the way, thank goodness."

She hurried toward the door and continued out it.

I stood on the front porch, watching her drive off.

A hand clamped down on my shoulder, squeezing. I glanced up at the brother closest to me in age. Roan shook his head. "I wouldn't let her watch Cady if she were the last person on Earth."

Just a few months ago, Roan had been the brother we could barely get to attend family gatherings. And when he did attend, he was stoic and surly. But meeting Aspen and her daughter, Cady, had changed all of that.

I let out a long breath. "I've got two other interviews. One in a few minutes, and then one first thing tomorrow morning."

Roan's brows rose. "My wedding's tomorrow."

I grinned at him. "Don't worry. I wouldn't miss your big day for anything. The interview's at ten."

He nodded. "Maybe the next candidate will be better."

Nash stepped up beside us, shoveling another bite of cereal

into his mouth. "We should ask her first thing how she feels about sugar."

Holt choked on a laugh. "It's good to have priorities."

Tires crunching gravel sounded before we caught sight of any vehicle. A second later, a cherry-red sportscar rounded my drive.

Holt let out a low whistle. "Nice car. But not all that practical for winters in Cedar Ridge."

It pulled to a stop in front of my steps. The driver's side door opened, and a woman stepped out. She wore boots with high, pointy heels, and a skirt that barely covered her ass. As she glanced up at the four of us on the front porch, her eyes lit up.

"Well, it's my lucky day. *Four* handsome interviewers. Don't worry, boys. I work for sexual favors."

Holt released a strangled laugh. Roan let out some sort of growl. And Nash started choking on his cereal.

"I know which one Drew would hire," Holt mumbled.

There was only one thing I could say. "F my life."

## Chapter Four

*Hallie*

I STARED AT THE DOOR AS IF WE WERE ABOUT TO DO BATTLE. And maybe we were. I'd done just as I'd said I would and had taken things one step at a time all morning. But this was the most daunting. The one it felt as though I couldn't turn back from.

Forcing my hand from my side, I rested it on the doorknob, but I couldn't get it to turn. I focused on the silver metal peeking through my pale fingers as if I could move it with my mind. I bit the inside of my cheek and twisted.

Bright sunlight hit my face, and the smell of fresh pine air filled my nose. They both helped. But it still took a beat of three for me to step outside.

I tapped my pocket, feeling the keycard there, and shut the door behind me. The click of the lock sounded like a cannon in my ears.

"Just three blocks," I told myself.

I started moving before I had a chance to rush back into my motel room. I picked up a brisk pace, knowing the sooner I arrived at my destination, the better it would be. There weren't a ton of people out—most were probably sleeping in. But there were enough to make me feel relatively safe yet not claustrophobic.

People lifted their hands in a wave or bobbed their heads in a nod, even though they didn't know me from Adam. It was jarring at first, but memories swept back in from time spent in the nearby area growing up. I remembered how warm and welcoming people were.

I missed that. Wondered what it would've been like to grow up in a place like this, where everyone knew your name and looked out for you.

Rounding the corner, I caught sight of the sign for the café. A burst of pleasure and pride swept through me. My therapist had drilled into me that I needed to celebrate every win, no matter how small.

I'd driven halfway across the country. I'd stayed alone in motels. I was interviewing for a job that I thought I'd absolutely love. And I was trying a new coffee shop in what could potentially be my new home. I deserved a damn double chocolate muffin.

The bell over the door tinkled as I opened it. There were a handful of patrons inside, but it wasn't overly crowded. A small line had formed at the register, and a woman stood behind it, moving between taking orders and grabbing coffees and food.

I crossed the warm and inviting space to stand behind three women who looked a few years older than me. They huddled together, talking and laughing.

"Do you really think Aspen wants food from her workplace on her wedding day?" a petite blonde asked.

"These are the best baked goods in town, G," a raven-haired woman argued.

The third woman laughed, swiping a hand over her pregnant belly. "I'm so hungry, I might hurt you if you make me go somewhere else right now."

The blonde grinned. "I know that hangry feeling. Thankfully, Caden fed me before I left."

The dark-haired woman shot the pregnant woman a smile. "Is Holt falling down on the job, Wren?"

She shook her head. "He left early to get the hotel suite ready with Caden. They've got a whole spread up there."

The blonde straightened. "We can't let them outdo us. We're getting one of everything."

The other two women burst into laughter.

My heart ached as I watched them, all continuing to laugh as they ordered. How long had it been since I'd had that easy camaraderie with anyone? A weight settled in my stomach. More than five years now.

I bungled things every time I tried to make a friend. I'd have an anxiety attack, or people would get annoyed that there was so much I didn't feel comfortable doing. Eventually, I just stopped trying.

"Can I help you?"

A woman's voice from behind the counter broke into my spiraling thoughts.

"Sorry, I, uh… Um."

The blonde I'd seen earlier glanced over at me as they waited for their food. She sent me a kind smile. "It's pretty overwhelming, isn't it?"

I nodded.

"I come here all the time. I recommend the cheddar scallion biscuit and the double chocolate muffin."

I nodded once more, resembling a deranged bobblehead yet again. "I'll do that. And tea, please. Something decaffeinated."

The last thing my anxiety needed was caffeine.

The blonde shot me a wider smile. "I hope you like them."

"Thank you," I said quietly, trying to force my mouth into an answering grin. I wasn't sure I pulled it off.

"That'll be eleven-fifty," the barista said.

I fumbled with my wallet, finally grabbing my debit card on the second try. I offered it to the woman, and she quickly swiped it, then handed it back, moving with expert ease as she gathered my order.

I typed in a generous tip and shoved everything back into my purse. By the time I had that sorted, the barista was sliding a plate and cup across the counter. "Here you go. Just bring the mug up if you want more hot water."

"Thank you." I could feel the line forming behind me, so I hurried out of the way and toward a table in the corner. One side of it was against the wall, and the other a window, so I felt protected on both sides.

I sank onto the chair with the wall to my back. It gave me a view of the street with the lake across the way and the rest of the café. The lake was completely frozen over, creating a gorgeous, light blue surface. My mouth curved as I saw a couple of kids skating near the shore.

Turning back to my meal, I broke off a piece of the biscuit and popped it into my mouth. Flavors burst on my tongue. The cheese, the scallions...and I thought maybe a hint of garlic, too. It was incredible.

My stomach rumbled, demanding more. I pulled out my book and lost myself in good food and a young adult story about a battle between angel races. Before long, I'd drained my tea and finished both pastries.

I checked my watch, and my eyes widened. It was almost nine-thirty. I had to be at my interview by ten. I stood quickly, grabbing my plate and mug to take to a bussing station.

"Was the book good?" I started at the deep voice, whirling and almost sending my dishes flying.

The man chuckled. "Sorry. I didn't mean to scare you."

My mouth went dry, and I struggled to swallow. He was older than me by five years or so. Definitely around thirty. He wore a police uniform that should've put me at ease.

"Way to go," the man beside him chided as he fought a grin. He, too, wore a police uniform and balanced a to-go cup of coffee in his hand.

The first man scowled at his friend but then turned back to me. He extended an arm, his brown gaze scanning me from head to toe. "I'm Reed. Reed Hall."

I stared down at the proffered palm as if it were a snake. Forcing my gaze up, I lifted my dishes as an excuse not to take the offered hand. "Hallie."

Reed grinned. "Nice to meet you, Hallie. You visiting, or—?"

The barista bustled into our space. "Oh. Here, let me take those."

I wanted to weep with appreciation. "Thank you."

The second she took my dishes, I grabbed my purse and coat and bolted for the door, not giving a damn that I was likely the rudest person Reed had ever met.

Hurrying down the street, I focused on my breaths. I zeroed in on the feeling of my lungs expanding and contracting inside my ribs and tried to make sure no movement was too quick. As I approached the motel's parking lot, I felt for my keys in my purse and beeped my locks. Within seconds, I was in my old-model sedan.

Locking the door behind me, I gripped the steering wheel. "You're fine. He was only being friendly."

The burn was back behind my eyes. A nice stranger—a police officer, no less—had sent me running. A single tear slipped free, and I quickly wiped it away. Two steps forward and one step back.

But it was still progress. At least, that was what my therapist would say. Still, I hated those bursts of weakness.

"Focus on what's next. What's the next step?"

I released the wheel and twisted toward the file folder on my passenger seat. I'd printed out directions to everywhere I needed to go, just in case service wasn't great, my phone died, I lost it, or—it didn't matter. They were my backup.

Pulling out the directions to the Hartley home, I scanned the sheet. I'd already gone over it at least a dozen times, but once more wouldn't hurt. The house was up the mountain a bit but not too high. Thankfully, there was no snow on the roads.

I shivered as a memory slammed into me. *Cold. So cold, it hurt. The wind whipping against my mutilated flesh.*

No. Not now. Not ever. I wasn't going back there.

I quickly typed the address into my phone—my car was too old for a GPS—and started the engine. I didn't give myself a chance to descend into anxiety. Instead, I carefully backed out of the parking spot and headed on my way as the navigation's British voice called out directions.

The drive itself was stunning. I had to force myself to keep my eyes on the road and not get distracted by the scenery. It only took about fifteen minutes to make it to the driveway. A mailbox had *Hartley* and the house number printed on it, so I knew I was in the right place.

Turning onto the gravel drive, I gripped the wheel tighter. When the house came into view, I sucked in a breath. It was gorgeous. All dark wood and glass, as if someone had taken a rustic farmhouse and brought it into the modern day.

There was a massive porch at the front of the house with an array of chairs and a swing. A child's bike leaned against the steps, and a few other toys and sports paraphernalia lay around. It looked beautiful but lived in. Not like the museum Emerson and I had grown up in.

Behind the main house and higher on the mountainside was a large barn in the same dark wood. To the right of the house sat a small guest cottage that I figured would be mine if I got the job. It was quaint and well-kept, and I knew it must have a lake view.

Hope bubbled up inside me. It had been so long since I'd felt it. The sensation was utterly foreign. But I would hold on to it with everything I had.

I shut off my car and flipped down the visor. I quickly checked my teeth for chocolate—that wouldn't be the first impression I wanted to make.

When I saw I was safe, I snapped the visor up and grabbed my purse. This was it. I squeezed my eyes closed. "Please, don't let me mess this up."

As I opened my eyes, I released the car door and stepped out. My boots crunched on the gravel as I headed for the steps. When I made it to the top, the front door swung open.

I had no time to prepare or steel myself. It wouldn't have made a difference anyway. Because when I saw the man filling the doorway,

I gasped. The familiar dark hair, with just a little silver at the temples. The strong, stubbled jaw. The nose that still looked as if it had been broken once.

And those eyes.

The eyes that had shown me kindness after enduring thirty-three days of brutal cruelty. The eyes that had given me hope. The eyes that had saved me.

"Blue."

## Chapter Five

*Lawson*

I STARED AT THE WOMAN ON MY FRONT PORCH. HER PRESENCE was a sucker punch to the gut. She had the kind of beauty that grabbed hold and scalded. White-blond hair cascaded in waves around her shoulders. Plush lips parted on an intake of breath. Her cheeks were flushed, whether from cold or shock, I didn't know.

It took me a beat to recognize her, longer than it should've, but she was older now. Changed.

The gray eyes did it. Ones that almost seemed silver as the sun caught her irises. They froze me to the spot.

Her face had haunted me for years. I'd wondered what'd happened to the young woman I'd found half-dead in the snow a county over. The one a madman had held.

It was the most twisted case I'd ever worked on. And it still taunted my memory. Maybe because it was so dark. Maybe because the hope I'd seen in her eyes had nearly broken me, hope that I would save her. I hadn't been sure I could.

But here she was, standing on my front porch—a walking miracle.

The search shouldn't have gone on for as long as it did, but her parents had held sway. The kind of connections that only came with wealth and politics. But I'd been glad they'd kept our search and rescue team on the case because she'd still been out there. Alive. Many of the other women hadn't been so lucky.

"I-I had no idea it was you," she said.

I hated the tremble in her voice and how it spread to her hands.

"I didn't either. The agency sent over the résumé of a Hallie Astor."

She bobbed her head in a nod. "That's what I go by now. It's easier…"

Her words trailed off, but I knew what she meant. It was easier to keep people from making the connection. Easier to try to forget the past.

The press had been all over her back then. A twenty-year-old college student missing in the dead of winter after half a dozen others had already disappeared that year. The daughter of a federal judge, no less. When we'd found her alive, it'd been mayhem. And when the sick bastard who'd taken her remained at large, the media had gone feral in their search for him.

Hallie's hands shook harder, making her whole body vibrate with the force of it.

Guilt swept in. Of course, this was hard for her. I was a reminder of the worst moments of her life. "We don't have to do this. I'm sure you don't want—"

Her eyes widened, that gray turning even more silver in the sunlight. "No."

Her hand moved, seemingly without her permission, and landed on my forearm. She barely made contact, and it was through my damned flannel, but it burned.

Hallie's eyes flared again as she jerked her hand back and stared at her fingers. "I'm sorry. I just meant…I'd like to still interview for the position. Unless you're not comfortable with me—"

"No, I'm fine." I wasn't. Hell, my arm *still* tingled where she'd touched me. It was the shared past. Trauma bonding. That was all. I cleared my throat. "It's just that I know a lot of victims would rather not have relationships with the people involved in their rescue. Especially when the cases are..."

"Messed up?" she offered.

A gentle smile pulled at my mouth. "Messed up is a good term for it. I just don't want to make things worse for you."

It was one of the reasons I'd never sought her out after the rescue. It wouldn't have mattered if I had, though. I'd heard that her parents flew her back to their estate in the Chicago suburbs the moment she was well enough to leave the hospital.

Hallie quickly shook her head, sending those blond strands into her face. "You're not making anything worse. I promise."

I hated that the action hid her eyes from me. "Good. Come on in."

Hallie tightly laced her fingers together as she followed me inside. I couldn't help but watch her as she took in my home, her laser focus absorbing every detail.

She stopped her gaze on things I didn't expect: a drawing Charlie had made in school, one of Drew's lacrosse sticks leaning against the wall by the door, the blankets in a haphazard disarray on the couch.

Her eyes finally landed on a photo of the boys and me from a couple of years ago. "These are your sons? Charlie, Drew, and Luke?"

She already had one up on the drill sergeant from yesterday simply by using their names.

"Those are the hellions. They're a lot bigger now."

A smile played on Hallie's lips, but she didn't look away from the photo. "You can tell they love you."

The photograph was from a family camping trip. Nash had snapped it after we'd had an epic water fight in the river. All four of us were soaking wet but wearing huge grins. It was before Luke had turned to his stony silence. Before Drew became consumed with sports and his *babes*. The only one who still smiled at me like that was Charlie.

"They love me some of the time," I said honestly.

Hallie's gaze flicked to me. "That's being a parent, I think."

I nodded. "True."

She opened her mouth, then closed it as if she wanted to say something but wasn't quite brave enough. She swallowed, twisting her fingers tighter. "Is there another parent in the picture? A wife or husband?"

I grinned, fighting a chuckle. "No wife or husband." The humor slipped away. "The boys' mom isn't in our lives."

Empathy swept over Hallie's expression. "That must be hard."

"I need help. Things have gotten a little squirrely trying to keep up with all the boys' activities and work."

"What do you do?" Hallie asked.

I was reminded that the agency left it to their clients to share personal details with the prospective candidates. "I'm the chief of police for Cedar Ridge."

Hallie's lips parted on a silent O. "They never said…when I was in the hospital, they just told me that a volunteer search and rescue team found me."

"That's true. I volunteer with SAR on the side. Sometimes, the gigs overlap."

She nodded. "That makes sense. Being a police officer must be a rewarding job."

"I love it, but it also means that whoever takes this nanny position has to be okay with middle-of-the-night emergencies. I can usually get my family to help on the weekends, so you'll have those days free to do whatever you want with friends, but—"

"I don't mind. I can be on call on the weekends, too." Her cheeks flushed. "I'm kind of a homebody."

I studied her for a moment, an ache settling somewhere deep as questions flooded me. Was she a homebody because of her personality? Was it what she wanted? Or was she scared to go out into the world?

The latter had that ache inside me burning brighter. In so many ways, Hallie's life had been stolen from her—her innocence cut short. Everything about it was wrong.

But as much as I felt for her, I couldn't help but wonder if she could handle taking care of my three boys. They were rowdy and loud, and Luke would test her at every turn.

I shoved the concerns to the back of my mind for now. "I appreciate your willingness to be available."

"What do you and your boys need, Mr. Hartley?"

The question was earnest as if she really wanted to make our lives easier.

"Call me Lawson. Or Law."

Hallie nodded slowly. "Okay, Lawson."

It was rare that I heard my formal name these days. And Hallie said it as if it were some extraordinary foreign language.

I forced my focus back on her question. "Getting the boys to and from school. Drew has sports practices. Charlie has playdates."

Hallie nodded. "And your eldest? Luke? Does he drive?"

The muscle at the apex of my jaw tightened. "Luke hasn't been allowed to get his license yet." I paused momentarily, trying to choose my words carefully before simply going with blunt honesty. "He's had some behavioral issues lately. He needs to rebuild some trust before I'll let him get behind the wheel."

Taking my department SUV for a joyride hadn't helped things in that department.

Hallie frowned. "He's sixteen?"

I nodded.

"That's a hard age. Trying to figure out who you are, needing your parents but also wanting to spread your wings. It can be uncomfortable. Like outgrowing your own skin."

I stared at her for a few beats as we stood in my entryway. None of the other candidates had sought to understand my boys—where they were at and why. Maybe what Hallie had been through had given her a more finely tuned empathy and a better understanding of others.

"I think you're right." I squeezed the back of my neck. "I probably haven't done the best job navigating it either."

"You're trying," Hallie said quietly. "That's what matters."

I had to move. Her kindness was almost too much to take. "How about I show you around, and we can talk more about what I'm looking for?"

Hope flared in her gray eyes. It was the same expression I'd seen five years ago. Something about it slayed me.

I forced my gaze away from her and headed deeper into the house. As I showed her the kitchen, living room, bedrooms, and even the gym in the basement, I told her more about each of my boys. Hallie asked insightful questions but mostly listened.

"Do you need housekeeping help?" she asked as we headed back upstairs.

I barked out a laugh. "What gave that away?"

Hallie flushed. "I didn't mean—"

I held up a hand. "I'm not insulted. We're drowning. I'll take any help you feel comfortable offering. If you're willing to do some cooking and laundry, I'd be happy to adjust your salary."

She quickly shook her head, her hair covering her face again. "The pay is more than generous. Since the boys are in school for most of the day, I'm happy to clean or run errands for you." She worried her bottom lip, bringing my gaze there. "I'm not the world's best cook, but I'm happy to try."

"I make three things well, so I'm sure just having a little variety would make the boys happy," I told her. Charlie, Drew, and Luke were beyond sick of steak, pasta with meat sauce, and chili.

Hallie interwove her fingers with one another again and squeezed hard. "I'll do my best."

I had no doubt.

"Do you want to see the guest cabin?"

"I'd like that." A flicker of excitement passed over her expression. It lit all her features, making her even more beautiful somehow.

I tamped that down in a flash. Hallie's attractiveness wasn't something I needed to be thinking about. The woman was a potential nanny and someone with whom I'd witnessed her worst moments. Not to mention, she was thirteen years my junior.

I forced my gaze away from her face and headed for the door.

Hallie followed silently behind me.

The bite of winter air helped, shocking my system and forcing me back to reality. "The place is furnished, but you're welcome to make it yours. I'm happy to put anything you don't want in storage."

I pulled my keys from my pocket and unlocked the door, stepping inside. The cabin was small. A bedroom area with a tiny bathroom and then a living and kitchen space with a large window that overlooked the lake below. There were bookshelves and cabinets for storage and a wardrobe that could serve as a closet. But there definitely wasn't space for a ton of belongings.

Hallie didn't make a sound as she explored the guest house. Her fingers ran over a quilt on the end of the bed, one my grandmother had made before she passed. Her gaze tracked over every inch of the space, stilling on the large picture window.

"It's perfect," she breathed. Her eyes shone, unshed tears glistening in them.

The reverence in her tone and the emotions running over her face were more than I could take. And it had me doing something reckless.

"Do you want the job?"

## Chapter Six

### Hallie

My stomach did a seriously impressive series of acrobatics as I zipped up my suitcase. Pulling it off the bed, I set it near the door. My belly did another dip and roll.

"It's a new beginning," I whispered to the walls.

One somehow tied to my past.

As the morning light streamed in my motel window, Lawson's face filled my mind. His strong jaw and kind eyes had been a staple in my brain for the past twenty-four hours.

I'd never known his name. He'd always only been *Blue* to me. I'd begged my parents to find him so I could thank him, but they'd never understood what his kindness had meant to me that night. They'd simply wanted to forget the whole ugly thing ever happened. When I was finally well enough to call, the county told me they couldn't release the information.

Everyone else wanted to move on. But I couldn't forget.

My fingers moved to the raised flesh near my hip bone. Scars riddled my body, but most of them were thin. Razor-sharp slashes where the man's blade had sliced into me.

The mark on my hip was different. The brand made it so I had no prayer of forgetting. Somehow, even after breaking free, I was still his.

My vision went blurry, and I blinked to clear it. My fingernails had pressed so hard into my palms that I'd drawn blood.

I hurried into the bathroom, turning the water as cold as it would go. I soaped my palms, not caring about the sting, and then submerged them in the freezing liquid. The cold took away the worst of the sting, and I washed and washed until no evidence remained except tiny half-moons dotting my skin.

If Emerson could see my hands, he'd say I was pushing myself too far. Maybe I was. But if I didn't, then I had no prayer of finally living a somewhat normal life.

My throat tightened as I tried to keep the welling emotions at bay. I wanted normal. I wanted friends. To be able to wander down the street without bracing for an attack. I wanted to feel safe being out past dark. To go to dinner parties or out dancing. I wanted to be free.

"What's the next step?" I whispered.

To get in my car and drive to my new beginning.

I walked through the motel room one last time, checking under the bed and in the closet. I'd already checked every nook and cranny at least four times, but I didn't want to risk needing to come back.

When I saw no stray belongings left behind, I slipped on my coat and slung my purse over my shoulder. Then, opening the door, I wheeled my suitcase outside.

As I stepped into the cold air, I came up short. A man nearly crashed into me. He had a scruffy beard and a brown gaze that jumped around from thing to thing until it zeroed in on me.

"Excuse me," I mumbled, hurrying to my car.

He didn't say a word, just stared at me hard as I walked away, almost as if he were trying to place my face.

He probably was. People didn't recognize me often anymore. But it still happened occasionally.

There'd been countless newscasts, several *Dateline* specials, and even a Lifetime movie about my story. Only it wasn't the real one.

The police and FBI had kept some facts from the media. Things that would haunt me forever. But the little they had gleaned felt like being victimized all over again.

I shoved my suitcase into the trunk and hurried to the driver's door. Slipping inside, I pressed the lock button.

The man was still standing there. Staring.

My hand shook as I struggled to get my key into the ignition. On the fifth try, I finally got it. Starting the car, I backed out of my parking spot.

I didn't look back at the man, didn't want to know if he was still staring with that perverse sense of curiosity. I kept my gaze locked straight ahead as I turned onto Main Street.

I let glimpses of the frozen lake soothe me as I drove through downtown. There were countless restaurants I wanted to try, and I promised myself then and there that I'd go to each and every one and report back to Adrian about the food. I'd make a list of the ones I wanted to take him to when he and my brother came to visit.

The drive to Lawson's went by in a flash. I parked in front of the guest cabin, wondering how my car would fare getting up his steep drive in the snow. I rarely drove in Chicago, and definitely not when it was snowing. Now, I'd have the most precious cargo: Lawson's children.

I worried my bottom lip. I'd practice the moment it snowed—over and over until I got it down.

Turning off my car, I slid out. I left my belongings inside and headed for the main house. I wasn't due to start until tomorrow, but Lawson wanted me to have some time to get settled and meet Charlie, Drew, and Luke while he was around.

A fluttery feeling took root in my chest. Not the one I used to get around a childhood crush, but one comprised of all the terrifying what-ifs. What if the boys hated me? What if one of them got really sick while I was taking care of them? What if someone took one of them?

I squeezed my lids together and balled my fists. When I opened my eyes, I focused on the space around me. *What do you see?*

"Gravel. Bike. Steps. Trees. House."

I let air fill my lungs, then exhaled. *What can you touch?*

"Jeans. Jacket. Sweater. Zipper."

Another breath. *What do you smell?*

"Pine. Smoke. Snow."

That phantom energy still buzzed through me, but I forced my legs to move. They felt heavy, a sign my breathing hadn't returned to normal. I focused on making sure the inhales and exhales were even and not too rapid.

I climbed the steps slowly, and as I reached the top, a peal of laughter lit the air, followed by thunderous footsteps. "You'll never catch me!" a child's voice called from the other side of the door.

The happy innocence had my mouth curving and a little of my anxiety easing. Still, my palms were damp as I lifted a hand to knock.

More shrieks of laughter came, but no sounds of someone coming to the door.

I licked my lips as my heart pounded, then pressed a finger to the doorbell.

"She's here!" that same young voice yelled.

"I'll get it," Lawson's voice boomed, deep and gravelly.

A second later, the door swung open, and my mouth went dry. Lawson stood in a white T-shirt pulled tight across a muscular chest. He wore dark jeans that hugged his hips and thighs and had nothing on his feet.

Something about his bare toes felt intimate, like a sight I shouldn't be witnessing.

I forced my gaze back to his face. "Hi."

He smiled, warm and welcoming. That same kindness oozed out of him. "Welcome to the zoo, Hallie."

A young boy skidded to a stop next to his dad and looked up at me. His hair and eyes were very similar to Lawson's, but his wide smile had a big gap. It only made him more adorable.

His lips parted, and his eyes went wide. "Whoa, you're pretty. Like one of the princesses in Cady's books."

A laugh bubbled out of me. "Thank you. I don't think I've ever been called a princess."

Lawson ruffled his son's hair. "This charmer is Charlie."

"Hi, Charlie. It's very nice to meet you."

"Dad, did you get a babe for a nanny?" another voice called from deeper inside the house.

Lawson groaned. "Drew…"

"It's a compliment," the boy said, exasperation filling his tone as he rounded the corner.

Drew was lanky and tall for thirteen. His hair had that artful disarray I was sure made him incredibly cool, and his blue eyes shone brightly against his tan complexion.

He shot me a grin. "Total babe."

Lawson pinched the bridge of his nose. "Please, don't make Hallie quit before her first day."

Drew only grinned wider. "Never. I'm into this. I'm Drew. Whatever you need, just let me know."

I pressed my lips together to keep from laughing as I sent Lawson a sidelong look.

He shook his head and clamped a hand on Drew's shoulder. "I apologize. My son is still learning manners where women are concerned."

"Don't let him get in your head," Drew said, his grin not faltering in the slightest. "I'm a total gentleman."

I managed to keep my laughter at bay. "That's good to know."

"Come in, please. It's freezing out there," Lawson said.

I stepped inside, letting the warmth of the space swirl around me.

A small hand grabbed mine, tugging me. "Do you like frogs, or do you think they're icky?"

I glanced down at Charlie. "I like frogs. They eat flies, and flies are annoying."

He grinned up at me. "Lizards?"

"My brother had a bearded dragon growing up."

"No way! I got to pet one when the reptile guy came to class last month. It was the best. It would be so amazing to have one every single day."

Charlie kept chattering on as Lawson sent me an apologetic smile, but I didn't mind in the slightest. I let the little boy tug me toward the living space as more of my nervousness slipped away.

I came up short when I was met with a glare. The teen I knew had to be Luke looked up from the sandwich he'd been eating at the kitchen island. Unlike his younger brothers, there was nothing warm or welcoming in his demeanor.

He shoved back his stool, leaving the half-eaten sandwich on the counter. His eyes narrowed on me. "What is she? Barely out of college? Didn't want to spring for a nanny who actually had experience?"

"Luke," Lawson barked.

My hands balled at my sides as I tried to hide the shaking. I'd only get this moment once, and if I let Luke steamroll me, he'd do it every time.

"Actually, I nannied for a family for three years before this and have taken several child development classes." I didn't think you could hear the tremble in my voice, but I could feel it.

Luke snapped his mouth closed, but his glare only intensified. "I don't need a fuckin' nanny."

Charlie sucked in a breath at my side. "That's a bad one."

Lawson's expression hardened to granite. "Go to your room. I'll come talk to you in a minute."

Luke didn't say a word; he simply stalked off.

"I'm so sorry, Hallie. I knew he wasn't crazy about this, but I didn't think he'd be that rude." Worry creased Lawson's brow as he waited for my reaction.

"It's okay," I assured him. "I'd rather know how he really feels than have him hide it."

"Well, he certainly shouldn't be using that language," Lawson said.

Drew sent his dad a worried look. "You taking his gear?"

A muscle beneath Lawson's eye fluttered. "Actions have consequences."

Drew kicked at the floor. "He's gonna be a nightmare."

Charlie bobbed his head. "Super grouchy."

I looked at Lawson in question, unsure if I had a right to ask, but at the same time, needing to know if I had to be his backup.

He ran a hand through his dark hair. "I warned Luke I was taking his electronics if he used the f-word again."

I winced. It wasn't that I thought Lawson was doing the wrong thing; it was just that I knew how much teenagers loved their devices. One of the two girls I'd nannied for previously was only twelve and already had a cell phone permanently attached to her hand.

"I need to talk to him," Lawson said softly. "Make yourself at home. Drew, get Hallie something to drink."

Lawson headed out of the living area, tension evident in his shoulders as he went. I didn't envy him for that conversation. Luke had been out of line, but this was a huge change for them, especially if their mother hadn't been around for a while.

I wondered for the countless time what the story was there. Lawson hadn't said she'd passed away, so I assumed it was a separation. But I couldn't imagine not seeing my kids at all.

"Soda, juice, water?" Drew asked as he pulled open the fridge. He'd lost the cocky charm from earlier. His brother's actions clearly weighed on him.

"Water would be great. Thanks, Drew."

Charlie grabbed my hand. "Can I stir the pasta sauce?"

I was confused by the question until I saw the pot on the stove. As I walked closer, I took in the bubbling red sauce. It smelled amazing.

A pang of longing hit my chest. Adrian was an amazing cook and had been teaching me the basics back in Chicago. No one made Bolognese like him, but this smelled close.

I glanced down at Charlie and his sky-blue T-shirt. "I'm thinking we should find you an apron first."

Drew chuckled as he set my water on the island. "Smart move. The munchkin can get dirty doing just about anything."

Charlie scowled at his brother. "I'm not a munchkin."

I pivoted quickly, knowing how fast sibling rivalry could escalate. "I'm completely hopeless at staying clean in the kitchen, so I'm gonna need one, too. One time, I tipped an entire saucepan on myself. The tomatoes made my hair pink for a week."

Drew's lips twitched, and a giggle escaped from Charlie.

"Pink hair?" Charlie asked, disbelieving.

I shrugged. "Some people thought it was a fashion statement."

Drew bent and opened a drawer in the island. He handed Charlie an apron and then one to me. "Wouldn't want any more fashion statements."

I grinned and took the garment. As I slid it over my head, raised voices sounded down the hall. Each one struggled to top the other.

"She's a joke!" Luke yelled.

I winced.

Apparently, my fresh start wouldn't be as smooth sailing as I'd hoped.

## Chapter Seven

### Lawson

I stared at my son, sensing the anger coming off him in waves. "I know you're not crazy about the idea of a nanny, but—"

"We don't need one," Luke snapped, his dark hair flying across his brow.

I took a deep breath, making an effort to lower my voice. "Maybe you don't, but *I* do. You guys have a lot going on, and I'm working long hours. I need someone to give us a hand."

Luke's jaw worked back and forth. "If you're too busy to take care of your kids, maybe you should let us go live with Mom."

My spine snapped straight as blood roared in my ears. The idea of them in Melody's care had ice running through my veins. I struggled to keep my voice even. "You know that's not an option."

"No, I don't. You won't even tell us why we can't see her."

I bit the inside of my cheek. Hard. First, their mother would have to *want* to see them. But even if she did, the courts wouldn't allow it, not after what had happened.

I should've guessed they'd start to have questions. Ones I couldn't answer with half-truths and non-responses. Maybe this had been wreaking more havoc on Luke than I realized. Or maybe he just knew how to hit me where it hurt.

"Your mom isn't in a place to take care of you."

The truth was, I didn't know where the hell Melody was these days. And I didn't want to know. The only way I could deal with everything that had happened was to shove it down. Force it so far down that it didn't exist for me.

Luke's jaw clenched. "It's not like you are either. You're pawning us off on some stranger."

I lowered myself to Luke's desk chair, staring at my son. "You and your brothers are the most important people in the world to me."

He scoffed.

"It kills me that you don't feel that from me, but it's true. Bringing someone on is to help me be the best possible dad. So the time we get together is quality time and not me stressing over schedules and laundry and grocery shopping."

Luke stayed silent as he sat on his bed, focusing on his shoelaces.

"I miss you, Luke. Miss talking to you. Going fishing and camping."

Heat filled his blue gaze. "I'm too old for that kid crap."

Pain dug deep. "It's not *kid crap* because those are some of my favorite things to do. And you need to watch your language."

"You curse. I've heard you."

"You're right, I do. But I'm an adult. And I try not to do it in front of you and your brothers. Do you want to explain to Charlie's teacher why a first grader is dropping F-bombs left and right?"

I'd hoped the question would get a smile out of Luke, maybe even a laugh. But his mouth didn't move even slightly.

"Whatever," he mumbled.

I sighed. "I need your phone, iPad, and laptop."

Luke's eyes went wide. "No way."

I pushed to my feet. "I warned you, Luke. I told you what would happen if you kept using that language."

"This is bullshit."

My back molars ground together. "That's three days now."

Luke snapped his mouth shut.

I picked up his laptop from the desk. "Phone and iPad."

Luke stood, yanking his cell out of his pocket and slamming it on the desk. Then he jerked open a drawer and grabbed the iPad.

I hated this. Hated my kid being mad at me. Hated that he wouldn't have the few things that seemed to make him happy now and then. But letting him get away with murder wouldn't help either.

I gathered up the electronics and headed for the door. "Dinner should be ready around six."

Luke didn't speak at all. It was his form of retaliation. It worked, too. Cut deep.

I slipped out of his room, shutting the door behind me. I walked to my office and deposited his gear in my desk drawer before moving in the direction of the living area.

Charlie's voice reached my ears before I saw him. "What would you pick, gecko or African bullfrog?"

"Hmm," Hallie said as I paused at the threshold, taking them in. "Frogs are cool, but geckos have those toes that help them stick to everything. I'm going gecko."

Charlie beamed at her as he knelt on a stool, stirring my pasta sauce. "Those toes are the coolest. I wish I had them. Then I could walk on the ceiling."

Drew chuckled from his spot on a stool opposite him. "You'd completely turn into a lizard if you could."

Charlie's mouth pressed into a thoughtful line. "Only if I could turn back. I'd miss chocolate too much."

A laugh escaped Hallie, light and almost musical. It caught on the air, sending a shiver over me.

"I'd miss chocolate, too," she admitted. "But I do think it would be cool to turn into a bird. Then I could fly wherever I wanted."

There was a wistfulness to Hallie's voice. A longing. For what? Flight? Freedom, maybe?

"I'm going monkey," Drew said. "You could climb trees crazy high and eat bananas all day."

Hallie grinned at him. "And hang upside down using your tail."

She was different with my boys. More at ease. Relief swept through me. Hallie seemed to be in her element with them. As if she'd truly come alive for the first time since our interview. And Charlie and Drew seemed to revel in her attention.

I pushed off the wall, rounding the corner. "Is Chef Charlie making us dinner?"

He grinned, that gap between his teeth on full display. "Hallie's helping me. This is gonna be the best sauce ever."

Drew glanced at Hallie. "Will you be cooking for us?"

A faint pink hue deepened on her cheeks. "Yes, to the best of my ability."

Drew stretched his arms across the kitchen island in a dramatic plea. "Please, tell me you know how to make more than pasta, steak, and chili."

I crossed to my middle son, ruffling his hair. "Trolling your father?"

He knocked my hand away. "Not the hair, bruh!"

Hallie laughed softly. "I promise to avoid those three things."

Drew lifted his hands skyward. "There is a God in heaven."

I just shook my head. "Sorry you got thrown right to the wolves."

"I don't mind. And this pasta sauce smells amazing."

A bizarre sense of pride filled me.

Drew grinned at Hallie. "This is his best meal. He wanted to impress you for your first night here. When you've had it every week for years, it's a little less exciting."

I barked out a laugh. "Geez, Drew, tell me how you really feel."

Hallie shrugged. "I don't know. Mac and cheese is my all-time favorite meal, and I could probably eat that every other day for the rest of my life."

Charlie bounced excitedly on the stool. "Mac and cheese is my favorite, too! Can we have that tomorrow?"

Hallie glanced at me in question.

I held up both hands in surrender. "If you want to make it, we'll eat it."

She seemed to let out a breath at that as if she'd expected me to disapprove.

"Dinner won't be ready for another couple of hours. Do you need to go get settled?" I asked.

Hallie shook her head, those blond locks sweeping around her face. "I don't have that much, and I'm happy to help here. Unless you'd rather I get out of your hair."

"No," I hurried to say. "You're welcome to stay. I just didn't want to hijack your settling-in time."

"She's staying," Charlie said definitively.

Drew snorted at that. "You have to ask *her* that, little man. Babes don't like when you're controlling."

Hallie's lips twitched. "Very true."

Charlie tipped his head back. "Will you *please* stay?"

She smiled down at him, the expression wide and uninhibited. The action lit up her entire face. "I'd love to stay."

I didn't blame my son for demanding she stick around. Her presence seemed to bring a new warmth to the house, shifting the energy somehow. It just would've been a hell of a lot easier if she wasn't so damn gorgeous while she did it.

## Chapter Eight

*Hallie*

I slipped the last of my hanging clothes into the wardrobe and shut the door. Turning, I took in the space. My new home. A thrill of excitement swept through me.

This was mine. Lawson had said I could make it completely my own. I'd never change the furniture or anything like that, but I could see where little additions might be nice.

A vase of fresh flowers on the kitchen table. Books on the empty shelves in the living area. Maybe a framed photo or two.

I stared out the massive window at one end of the cabin. Moonlight shone on the ice-covered lake, making it glitter in the dark. Everything was quiet. Still. There were no honking horns or loud sirens to rachet up my anxiety. There was only peace.

God, I hoped this worked out. I wanted it so badly it almost hurt.

Worry gnawed at me. Luke hadn't come out of his room for dinner. When Lawson sent Drew to tell him the food was ready, Drew had returned, saying that Luke said he wasn't hungry. I'd seen that tiny muscle beneath Lawson's eye twitch.

I knew I'd have to win Luke over for Lawson to keep me around.

But I also knew I had to stand my ground with the surly teen if I wanted him to respect me. It would be a delicate balance.

A wave of fatigue swept over me as I stared at the starry sky outside. The day had been a long one, and I hadn't exactly slept well the night before. I made quick work of brushing my teeth and washing my face in the tiny but adorable bathroom with its clawfoot tub and antique fixtures. Then, after changing into pajamas, I slipped into bed.

I sighed with relief. The mattress and linens were a million times more comfortable than the bed at the motel. No matter how much I'd needed to budget while living with Emerson and Adrian, I'd always splurged on soft sheets. I told myself it was because I liked being cozy, but deep down, I knew it was more.

Memories pressed in, trying to break free, but I shoved them down. Not now. Not the first night in my new home. I wanted this place to be my haven. Somewhere I felt totally and completely safe. Having the chief of police on the premises definitely wouldn't hurt in that quest.

I let out a long breath and turned out the lamp on my bedside table. The soft glow of several nightlights illuminated the cabin. Two in the bedroom. One in the living room. One in the kitchen. And one in the bathroom. There wasn't anywhere where I was in darkness.

Never again.

---

*I shivered against the cold, my teeth chattering as I waited. This was the worst part. The waiting.*

*I would've thought it would be the agony I knew was coming next, but it wasn't. It was waiting for the pain.*

*Turning my head, I tried to see under the blindfold, but I never could. He always tied it too tightly. The material was thick, black silk—nothing I could see through.*

*The fact that he'd chosen such a soft material almost made me laugh. Why care about our comfort when all he wanted was our pain?*

*No, it was more than that. He wanted our submission.*

*But I'd heard what'd happened to the other women he'd taken when they gave in. I knew he hurt them in ways that went far beyond the scars that now littered my skin.*

*A hum began somewhere to my right, and my head jerked in that direction, my body following. My wrists and ankles pulled at the bindings. It had taken me days to identify the tune.*

Ring of Fire *by Johnny Cash.*

*Always that song.*

*The man kept humming as he circled me. I bit the inside of my cheek until the coppery taste of blood filled my mouth. Anything to keep the tears away.*

*I wouldn't have thought it was possible to have this many tears. But they just kept coming.*

*"Are you ready, Halston?"*

*I didn't say a word, but my body shook. Fear and being clad in nothing but a flimsy white sheath would do that.*

*He chuckled. "I like your fire. That stubborn streak will make your acquiescence that much sweeter."*

*His footsteps sounded against the stone as he picked up his circling.*

*"Say yes, Halston. I'll honor you as my wife."*

*Saliva pooled in my mouth. I'd let him kill me first.*

*"Say, yes." Anger slipped into his tone.*

*I didn't utter a word. I knew what happened when we said yes. I wouldn't let him hurt me like that. Not ever.*

*"Have it your way."*

*The humming started again. He jerked at the sheath, hauling it up, and then the knife slashed across my belly.*

*I couldn't hold in my scream.*

I jerked upright, that same scream caught in my throat. I hauled my legs up to my chest and bit my knee to keep the sound at bay. I hugged my legs with everything I had in me, rocking to steady myself.

Tears filled my eyes and tracked down my cheeks. He always won.

I might have escaped, but he still had me in my dreams. He was still out there somewhere, walking around free. I had to look at every man that passed and wonder if it was him.

I'd never seen his face. Not once. Not even when I escaped.

He'd always worn a mask when he came to get me for our *sessions*. Only his dark brown eyes peeked through. Then he would cover my face with a blindfold. I wasn't sure I even truly knew his voice. It had sounded slightly different during my escape, almost like it was deeper than he'd made it out to be at other times.

I quickly shoved to my feet, struggling to get free of the sheets. They were damp with sweat, and my pajamas were practically soaked.

The tears morphed then. Turning from ones of fear to those of frustration. I yanked the comforter back and carried it to the small couch in the living room. I jerked the top sheet free and then the bottom, before roughly pulling the pillows out of their cases.

Bundling it all up, I stalked toward the stackable washer and dryer next to the bathroom. I shoved everything inside and poured in the soap. Slamming the washer closed, I hit start and stepped back.

I watched as water began to fill the machine and suds started to form. In thirty minutes or so, all evidence of my torment would be cleansed away. I wished it was as easy to do the same for me.

I pressed my palms to my eyes and then ran my fingers through my hair. It, too, was damp with sweat. I needed it all off. Gone.

Slipping into the bathroom, I shucked my pajamas and turned on the water. I set it as hot as I could stand and stepped into the tub-shower combo.

I let the stream of scalding water cascade over me to wash away every remnant of cold and pain. Lifting the shampoo bottle, I filled my palm with soap. My fingers dug into my scalp, cleansing every strand, and then I conditioned it.

Bodywash came next. I scrubbed every inch of my skin as if I could erase the thin scars crisscrossing my flesh. My fingers stilled on the brand.

I stared down at the burn—a permanent mark not even a laser could erase. It was some sort of multi-faceted gemstone. And it had been burned into eight women.

But only one had survived. Me.

I jerked my hand away from the mottled skin and stepped back under the spray. I rinsed the soap from my body and turned off the water. Pulling back the shower curtain, I stepped out of the tub and quickly grabbed two towels. I wrapped one around my hair and dried my body with the other.

Letting out a long exhale, I stared down at the pile of nightclothes on the floor. It felt like just another piece of evidence of my weakness.

I squeezed my eyes closed. "You're not weak. You're stronger than anyone knows."

## Chapter Nine

*Lawson*

I KEPT GLANCING OUT THE WINDOWS AT THE FRONT OF THE house as I sipped my coffee, my thumb tracing circles on the mug. When I got up at five for my workout, lights had been blazing in the guest cabin. And I hadn't missed that a soft glow emanated from the windows well after midnight last night.

A million different questions swirled in my mind. Could Hallie not sleep? Was she scared of the dark? Was it hard for her being in a new place?

"Not things you need to be worried about," I growled aloud, forcing myself back into the kitchen.

I didn't miss the dirty dishes in the sink caked with tomato sauce. Luke had clearly come out for leftovers after we were all asleep. I was relieved that he hadn't gone to bed hungry, but beyond frustrated that he'd left a mess behind.

Maybe I needed to get him into therapy. Cedar Ridge had a decent therapist that treated a variety of patients. I should give her a call.

A soft knock sounded on the front door.

My body jolted, coffee sloshing over the rim of my mug. I muttered a curse and grabbed a towel as I headed for the door.

Opening it, I stilled, gray eyes freezing me to the spot. Hallie stood holding a towel-covered bowl. Her hair fell in loose waves to frame her face, and she wore a sweater that shouldn't have been enticing but somehow was. It skimmed her curves, falling to mid-thigh, where it met with black leggings that left little to the imagination when it came to those long, toned legs.

I forced my gaze back to her face. *Hell.* The last thing I needed to be thinking about was my twenty-five-year-old nanny's legs. "Morning."

My voice sounded like I'd just woken up, not as if I'd been up for two hours already.

"Morning," Hallie echoed, shifting her weight from one foot to the other.

I quickly stepped back. "Come in."

Hallie moved into my space, the scent of something sweet but somehow smoky weaving around me.

"Thanks for stocking my fridge. I made sunshine muffins as a thank-you," Hallie said, extending the bowl to me.

My lips twitched. "Sunshine muffins?"

It was fitting for a woman who was pure light herself. I had to fight a laugh.

She worried her bottom lip. "My housekeeper used to make them when I was growing up. They're orange-flavored, but they're pretty healthy, too."

"Just as long as they don't have gross orange pulp in them," Drew grumbled as he stumbled down the hallway in his sweats, his hair sticking up in every direction.

"Drew," I clipped.

Hallie just laughed. "No pulp. I promise."

"Sweet," Drew said, pulling back the towel and grabbing one. He broke off a piece and popped it into his mouth. His eyes went wide. "These are amazing."

His words were barely discernible since his mouth was full, but Hallie grinned. "I'm glad you like them."

"Will you wake up your brothers, Drew?" I asked.

He nodded, turning back to the hallway and yelling, "Charlie, Luke, get up. Hallie brought sick muffins. If you don't hurry, I'm gonna eat them all."

I pinched the bridge of my nose. "Not what I had in mind, D-man."

He shrugged. "I've got muffins to eat."

Drew grabbed another one and headed for the kitchen just as Charlie bolted out of his bedroom. He ran down the hallway, crashing into me. "I want muffins!"

I grinned at Hallie. "I'd say you're a hit."

That pretty pink stained her cheeks again. "I'm easily won over by food, too."

I'd have to remember that.

---

"Let's go," I called as I headed for the door. I glanced over my shoulder at Hallie. "Ride with me today, and I'll show you the drop-off ropes. Drew has lacrosse conditioning after school, so you don't have to pick him up. One of his teammates' parents will drop him off at the house."

"She doesn't need to pick me up either," Luke muttered as he grabbed his backpack by the door.

I sent a glare in his direction. I hadn't missed how Luke refused to call Hallie by her name. He hadn't done it even once. "It's a little too far to walk."

He slid his backpack over one shoulder. "I have a science study group after school."

I examined Luke for a moment. I hated that I wasn't sure if he was lying or not. "With who?"

"Someone in my science class."

"Who?" I pressed.

Luke's jaw clenched. "Violet Hooper. I'll get a ride home after."

It could've been a lie, but I knew the girl's name. She was the daughter of a local pastor and not exactly a part of Luke's usual crew.

"I can pick you up after the study group," Hallie offered. "It's no problem."

Luke just scowled at her and headed for the door. "Whatever."

The door slammed behind him, and Hallie winced. "I'm sorry he's not my biggest fan."

Worry lined Hallie's features, and she tied her fingers into intricate knots.

I gently touched her shoulder. "It's not you."

She tugged on her bottom lip with her teeth. "Seems like it might be."

"He's not happy with anyone these days," I admitted.

Hallie's expression gentled. "I'm sorry, Lawson. I know that must be hard to see."

A burn lit along my sternum at her kind understanding. "It hasn't been the easiest lately."

"I'm ready!" Charlie called as he hurried down the hallway, Drew following behind. He grinned at Hallie. "You're gonna meet Cady. She's my bestest friend. Do you like ballet? Ballet's her favorite, and she's really good. But she also likes animals like me. She has a bazillion of them. Even an emu."

I clamped a hand on Charlie's shoulder. "Let's fill Hallie in on the way. How about that?"

She pressed her lips together to keep from laughing. "I am quite curious about this emu."

Charlie chattered the entire way to the high school, telling Hallie all about Cady and Aspen's makeshift animal rescue. Luke didn't say a word as he slid out of my department SUV and headed for school, but I didn't push.

Charlie kept right on talking as we headed for the middle school to drop off Drew, who at least had a wave for Hallie and me. By the time we reached the elementary school, I was pretty sure we'd covered every animal on Aspen's property. Well, I guessed it was

Aspen and Roan's now that they were married and combining their adjacent homes.

Hallie twisted in her seat as I pulled to a stop in front of the elementary school. "That sounds incredible. I'd say you lucked out when it comes to best friends."

Charlie bobbed his head in a nod. "I'm the luckiest."

I shut off the engine. "Better hurry. I see your bestie over there."

Charlie's face lit up as he saw Cady, and he unhooked his booster seat. "Can I get out? Please, Dad?"

I nodded, and he quickly hopped out next to the sidewalk.

"He's amazing," Hallie said softly.

"A ball of energy, that's for sure. Come on. He'll want you to meet Cady."

We climbed out of the SUV and headed in their direction as they talked rapid-fire.

Aspen stood next to them and lifted a hand in a wave. "You'd think they'd been apart for a month instead of two days."

I chuckled. "I can't believe you're back to drop-off duty the day after your wedding weekend."

She gave me a sheepish smile. "Cady has another recital at the end of the week. Roan and I didn't want to miss it, so we're doing the honeymoon a little later."

Aspen's red hair swished around her shoulders as she turned to the woman next to me. "You must be Hallie. I'm Aspen, Cady's mom. And, I guess, Law's sister-in-law now."

"I really hope my long line of new sisters doesn't give me as much grief as Grae does."

Aspen laughed. "I don't think any of us could hold a candle to mountain-climbing, knife-throwing G."

Confusion swept over Hallie's expression.

"All three of my younger brothers are engaged or newly married, so I'm gaining a brood of sisters," I explained.

"And Grae, his actual sister, is kind of a bad—" She cut herself off, glancing at the kids. "A bad-A."

Hallie smiled, but I saw the lines of tension bracketing her mouth. "I didn't know you had such a big family. That must be fun."

"Sometimes, it's fun. Other times...mayhem," I told her honestly.

Aspen chuckled. "Very true." She turned to Hallie. "How are you settling in?"

"Good. Everything's really good." Hallie's hands trembled a bit, and I saw Aspen's gaze zero in on the movement.

"That's great. If you're up for it, you and the boys should come over after school. You can meet the animals," Aspen offered.

I shouldn't have been surprised at her kindness. Everything she'd been through had given her a radar for others who might have pain in their pasts.

"Yes!" Charlie cheered, zoning in on our conversation. "It'll be so fun, Hallie. The funnest! You'll meet Emmaline."

Hallie's mouth curved at that as though Charlie's mere excitement eased her somehow. "I have always wanted to meet an emu."

Cady grinned at Hallie. "She's super sweet." The grin slipped. "Well, she doesn't like my dad, but she loves me and Mama."

My chest constricted at Cady calling Roan her dad. That little girl had worked a miracle where my once-broody brother was concerned.

"Well, hopefully, she likes me, too." Hallie turned to Aspen. "I'd like that. Should I get your address or...?"

Aspen waved her off. "We'll just meet here after school. You can follow me home."

"Sounds good. Thank you."

"Anytime," Aspen said, turning back to her daughter. "Hugs, Katydid."

Cady launched herself at Aspen, who laughed as she hugged her tightly.

I ruffled Charlie's hair. "See you tonight. You can have Hallie call me if you need me."

Charlie nodded, but he was already heading for school.

"He used to not want me to leave him," I mumbled.

"This just means he's healthy and well-adjusted," Hallie said as we made our way back to my SUV.

"True, but I miss him needing me a little."

Hallie climbed inside as I rounded the vehicle. "I think I'd be that way, too. Sometimes, it's nice to be needed."

I heard a longing in her voice that had me glancing over at her. Every tiny detail about Hallie pulled me closer and had me wanting to know more. It made sense. I'd always wondered what had happened to the woman I'd rescued on the mountain. With the case being as brutal as it was, it had stuck with me. It was all natural curiosity.

I forced my gaze away from her and toward the parking lot as I started the engine. "I've got one more stop to make if it's okay with you."

"Of course."

"I ordered a new SUV for our nanny to use. Figured it would be easier for wear and tear and gas mileage. I need to pick it up. I've got a credit card for expenses, too."

My statements weren't entirely true. When I first saw Hallie's sedan, a pit had formed in my stomach. It didn't look like it should've survived the trip out here, let alone stay on the road during a winter storm in Cedar Ridge.

Hallie's eyes widened. "Oh. I guess that makes things easier."

"You're welcome to use it all the time. It'll probably do better in the snow than a sedan, given the specialty tires and four-wheel drive."

She toyed with her seat belt. "I did kind of wonder about my car's ability to make it up your driveway in the snow."

I grinned, grateful I wasn't facing a battle. "It's definitely a bit more rustic than Chicago."

"I should probably trade in my car for an SUV."

I tapped my fingers on the steering wheel as I turned onto Main Street. "There's plenty of time for that. And this will give you a chance to test one out."

The truth was, I wasn't sure Hallie's sedan would get much as a trade-in. But I knew that living in the guest cabin with the salary I was paying her, she'd probably be able to save up for a safe, reliable car in a matter of months.

Her fingers released their hold on the seat belt. "True. I've never driven a big car before."

"It only takes a couple of days to get used to. And it comes in handy with three boys who start brawling if they're in too close of proximity to one other."

I caught a flash of a smile out of the corner of my eye. "They actually seem like they get along pretty well."

I grunted. "Sometimes."

Her smile widened. "Siblings."

"So very true." It was a miracle that my brothers and sister and I had made it through childhood relatively unscathed.

I glanced over at Hallie as I slowed to a stop at a red light. She stared out the window at the passing scenery. It seemed to hold her captive as if she'd never seen anything more beautiful.

"Is the guest cabin treating you okay? Heat good? Bed comfortable?" I wanted to kick myself the moment the word *bed* left my lips. The image of white-blond hair splayed across a pillow filled my mind. Of Hallie tangled in those sheets.

Her gaze flicked to me. "It's perfect."

"I just saw your light on pretty early." It was none of my business, but I couldn't help but wonder why she'd been up before dawn.

Shadows swirled in Hallie's gray depths, her expression closing down. I wanted to take back my words, erase every syllable. Anything to get back the look of wonder that had been on her face moments ago and clear away the pain that filled it now.

She forced a smile. Everything about it was fake. Wrong. "I guess I was just excited for my first day. Woke up before my alarm."

It was a lie. I'd been working in law enforcement long enough to know. I hated the deception between us, but she didn't owe me the truth. She didn't know me. Not really. I was her boss. And someone she'd barely met years ago. "Better get to bed early tonight. Don't want to get run-down. Trust me when I say that the elementary school germs are vicious."

A hint of a laugh escaped Hallie's lips. "I am very familiar with those from my last job. So, hopefully, I've got a bit of immunity."

I kept the conversation light as we traveled the rest of the way to Brookdale—anything to avoid seeing that pain on Hallie's face again. As I pulled into the Chevrolet dealership, Hallie's fingers tightened around her purse straps. Her gaze jumped around as if she expected someone to pop out and attack her.

Knowing she lived with that every single day killed something in me.

I pulled into a parking spot but left the engine running. "You okay?"

Hallie bobbed her head. "Good." But her voice was strangled as if she could barely get the word out.

I shifted in my seat and turned to face her. "It's okay if there are things you aren't comfortable with. We'll just pivot."

Her eyes glistened, and she swallowed hard. "How did you know?"

I reached over and gently tapped the fingers that had her purse straps in a death grip.

A laugh bubbled out of her, and she released the bag. "I guess I'm not going to win an Oscar anytime soon."

I grinned. "Might want to take a few classes before you head to Hollywood." My smile slipped. "What's got the anxiety humming?"

Hallie's tongue darted out, licking her lips. "Everything."

My brow furrowed.

"Anything new. Unknown. It's hard. But that doesn't mean I don't want to do it. I just need to run through it in my head first."

"Run through it in your head?" I asked.

She nodded. "It's a trick I learned with my therapist. If I picture what I'm about to do in my head, imagine all the possibilities, it helps. That probably makes me sound crazy."

"No," I insisted. "It makes you sound smart. You've figured out a way to make life work for you, even though you've been through something incredibly traumatic. Something that changed you. It makes you smart as hell."

Hallie stared at me for a long moment. "Thank you."

"We all have scars. Things that we think might make us weak. But, in reality, they're usually the source of our strength."

Her eyes shone as they bored into mine. "I like thinking of it that way."

"Me, too. Now, let's do a practice run of what's about to happen."

The corner of her mouth kicked up. "Really?"

"Really. The SUV has already been ordered. Paperwork should be ready, and I've faxed in all the information they need. So, we'll go in, the salesman will try to schmooze us, I'll sign the papers, inspect the vehicle, and then we'll be on our way."

Hallie let out a slow breath as she stared at the building. I watched as her eyes tracked over the exits and realized she was planning her escape routes.

"I'll be with you the whole time."

That steely gaze flicked to me. "Let's do this."

I nodded, and we both slipped from my SUV. Heading for the doors of the dealership, I had the bizarre urge to take Hallie's hand. To sweep my thumb back and forth across her knuckles to reassure her. I told myself it was because I'd been the one to find her years ago. Because I'd seen her in the aftermath of the horror she'd endured. That was all.

Opening the door, I held it for Hallie, and she cautiously stepped inside. I quickly followed, wanting her to feel my presence.

A man with a too-white smile was striding across the showroom floor in seconds. "I'm guessing you're Lawson Hartley."

The fact that I was in my police uniform was likely a dead giveaway. "I am. Chip?"

He nodded, extending his hand for a shake. As he did, his gaze tracked to my right and swept over Hallie. "And who is this lovely lady?"

*Hell.* The last thing Hallie needed was some smarmy bastard making her feel uncomfortable.

Chip offered Hallie a hand, but she just nodded at him. "Hallie."

I stepped forward, cutting Chip off from Hallie. "How about we tackle that paperwork? I don't have long before I need to head to the station."

"Uh, sure thing. Of course." Chip gestured for us to follow him down the hallway.

I moved in closer to Hallie as he started in that direction. "You okay?"

She bit her lip but nodded. "Men make me a little uneasy."

It made sense. She'd suffered the worst kind of pain at the hands of a man. It would change how someone viewed the entire gender.

"I never saw his face," she whispered. "Every man I meet, I wonder if it's him."

My eyes flared, my gut tightening. "You didn't seem wary around me that first day. For the interview."

Hallie's hypnotic gaze lifted to mine. "You're different. You saved me."

## Chapter Ten

*Hallie*

My fingers ghosted over the massive SUV's leather steering wheel. Everything about it was fancy. The screen in the dashboard with its eighty-two million controls. The spaciousness. The finishes.

It wasn't that I'd never been in a nice car; my parents drove a BMW and a Porsche. It was just that it had been a while. Years. And the idea that I might do something to harm a high-end vehicle that Lawson had just paid his hard-earned money for made me sick to my stomach.

"What's that look about?" he asked as he took me in from his spot in the passenger seat.

"What if I hurt your car?"

A laugh burst out of him. "Hallie. Don't worry about the damn SUV. If you wreck it, I'll get another one."

I frowned in his direction. "Easy as that?"

He twisted in the seat so he fully faced me. "I'm not hurting for money. My dad had an outdoor company that he sold when I was in high school. It set us all up pretty well. I'm never going to be reckless or ridiculous with that money, but it does mean that I don't have to worry about damage to a vehicle."

Everything I learned about Lawson made me want to know more. He was this enticing mix of things I couldn't quite pin down. Strong yet gentle. Protective yet able to let those around him find their way. Stoic yet laughed easily.

"You don't have to work," I surmised.

"No," he admitted.

"So, why do you do it?"

Our parents always held Emerson's and my trust funds over our heads like a carrot. They tried to use them to get us to do what they wanted. And I had for a long time. Not because of the money, but because I didn't want to lose them. Until I finally realized that the quest to keep them was killing me.

Lawson swept his thumb back and forth across his knee. "I love my job. I like that I get to help people, try to keep them safe, and make my community a better place."

My eyes burned. He was one of the good ones—someone who wanted to help just because he could. "You do. All of that."

I knew because he'd been and done that for me. A blinking light of kindness on my darkest night.

His expression gentled, going soft in a way that made my insides flip. "Thank you. I try. Don't always get it right, but I'll never *stop* trying."

"It's all we can do." I'd learned that the hard way. When you stopped trying, you stopped living.

A ding sounded, and Lawson pulled out his phone. "I need to head to the station. Will you be okay to get back to the house?"

I gripped the steering wheel and nodded. "Yes."

My voice didn't waver, and I was glad for it. I didn't want Lawson to know that I was scared out of my mind.

He reached out as if he might squeeze my shoulder but then stopped himself.

The course correction was a knife to the gut. He'd halted because of what I'd said: that men made me nervous. I knew it wasn't logical, not all men were evil, but it was just how my mind worked.

Anytime I met a man, a part of me wondered if he could be

the one. Was he the person who'd kept me for thirty-three days? Was he the one who'd carved a kaleidoscope of scars into my flesh?

Even in the dealership just now, I'd pictured douchey Chip in that black balaclava, hovering over me, ready to inflict the maximum pain. Even when the body type and voice didn't match, I could still see them as the man.

But never Lawson. He was the first male who wasn't family that I'd felt comfortable with since the incident. Even in the hospital, they'd had to switch my care team to one entirely made up of females. Maybe that was why Lawson's retreat hurt so much. But I didn't blame him either.

Lawson dropped his hand back to his lap. "I'll have my phone. Call if you need anything at all. I don't mind. I know school pickup will be new."

*Crap.*

He was worried about me doing my job. I didn't blame him, but it still stung. "I've been to all three schools now, so I'm good." I forced as much brightness into my tone as possible.

Lawson nodded. "All right. But I'm just a phone call away if you need me."

"Thanks. For everything." That was so much less than I wanted it to be—a six-letter word for everything that Lawson was. But it would have to do for now.

He nodded, pausing for a moment as if he might say something else, then he finally slid out of the SUV. I watched as he climbed into his police-issued vehicle, praying he wouldn't wait for me to pull out. The last thing I wanted was an audience.

The air left my lungs in a whoosh as Lawson's taillights illuminated, and he backed out of his parking spot. The moment he pulled out into traffic, I turned back to the SUV. I released my death grip on the steering wheel and ran my palm over the leather. "We're going to be friends. I am going to speak to you only with loving words, and you aren't going to spin me off into a ditch."

My therapist had told me once that if you spoke lovingly to a plant, it would grow infinitely faster and healthier than any that were put down and demeaned. She used the story to illuminate the ramifications of my relationship with my mother, but I figured it applied here, too.

The SUV didn't say anything in return.

"I feel like you need a name. But maybe we should leave that to Charlie. He seems like he'd be good at that."

Yet again, the car didn't reply.

I put my foot on the brake and pressed the button to start it. It purred to life, the vibrations sweeping through my body.

"You can do this." I plugged the address of Cedar Ridge's grocery store into the navigation system. Gripping the wheel yet again, I stared out the front windshield. "Just the one next thing."

---

By the time I pulled into the elementary school pickup line, I felt like I'd done one of the extreme boot camp workouts I saw advertised on late-night infomercials. No wonder Lawson had needed help.

I'd driven the brand-new SUV back to Cedar Ridge like a grandma. When I finally parked at the grocery store and released the wheel, my hands ached from how tightly I'd been grasping it. But I was already getting more used to it. I wasn't completely at ease yet, but it was better.

I'd jotted out a meal plan for the week, second-guessing every choice, then I'd done the shopping. When I got back home, I breathed a sigh of relief at being truly alone for the first time all day. I unpacked the groceries and started some laundry. I didn't think I'd ever seen so many clothes in my life.

Between the six loads I'd managed to get in before having to leave for pickup, I scoured the kitchen and organized the pantry. I'd also cleaned the bathrooms and picked up the living room. I needed to check with Lawson to see if I should tidy bedrooms as well, but I didn't want to overstep.

My mother would've been appalled at how much joy it

brought me. There was just something about cleaning. You saw the impact of your work right in front of your eyes like nothing else. It helped me feel like some tiny things in this world were, in fact, under my control. And after a few days of endless *firsts*, I needed a little of that.

I caught sight of Charlie looking around for me and realized he didn't know this vehicle. I quickly shut it off and hopped out. "Charlie!"

His head flicked in my direction, and a huge grin spread across his face. "Hallie!"

He ran at me, hitting me with a force that nearly sent me falling backward. But I'd take the easy acceptance and kindness of children over and over again. There was nothing like it.

I ruffled his hair the way I'd seen Lawson do. "Good day?"

"Really good. I got to feed our class fish today."

"That sounds like a very important job. It says a lot about how amazing you are that your teacher entrusted you with it."

Charlie's little chest puffed up as he released me. "I measure real careful."

"Who are you?" a high-pitched voice snapped.

I stiffened, turning to face a blonde who was absolutely stunning except for the twisted scowl on her face. "Excuse me?"

"Who are you?" she bit out again. "I've never seen you before, and I highly doubt Law would entrust his child to a stranger."

A little girl about Charlie's age hovered behind the woman, looking embarrassed.

Charlie glared at the woman. "This is Hallie, my new nanny. You better be nice to her, or my dad'll be real mad."

I rested a hand on Charlie's shoulder. "It's okay. She just wants to make sure you're safe." Though she could've been a hell of a lot nicer about it.

The woman gaped at me. "Nanny?"

Her voice went up an octave on the word.

I nodded, extending a hand. "I'm Hallie."

She stared at my palm for a second before taking it. "I'm

Katelyn. I'm *really* close to Law, so I'm just surprised he didn't say anything. He knows I'd always help out with the kids if he needed."

My stomach twisted in a vicious squeeze at her words. I was unsure how to answer.

Footsteps sounded to my left, and Aspen appeared. She sent a sharkish grin at the woman next to me. "Katelyn."

The blonde's mouth thinned into a hard line. "Aspen."

Aspen turned to me and gave my arm a squeeze. "You ready to go?"

I nodded. "You have everything, Charlie?"

"Yup! I didn't forget my lunchbox this time." He held up the cloth satchel as if to prove his point.

"I'd say that deserves a gold star," I said.

Aspen glanced at the little girl hovering behind Katelyn. "Does Heather want to come home with us? I'm going to show Hallie the animals."

Katelyn opened her mouth to object, it was written all over her face, but her daughter spoke up first. "Please, Mom? I want to see Mabel."

Katelyn's nose wrinkled in distaste, but she acquiesced. "All right." She glanced at Aspen. "What time should I pick her up?"

Aspen glanced at her watch. "How about four-thirty?"

Katelyn jerked her head in a nod before turning back to her daughter. "Be careful. I don't want you getting mauled by a herd of goats and donkeys."

Heather giggled, but her mother hadn't sounded like she'd meant it as a joke. "Mabel loves me. She'd never do that."

Katelyn looked doubtful but headed for the parking lot with one last scowl in Aspen's direction.

"That was…" My words trailed off.

"Something?" Aspen offered.

"Definitely something," I agreed.

The three kids were happily chatting away now, so Aspen moved in closer. "Don't take Katelyn personally. She's an unhappy soul." She glanced at the retreating woman, wincing. "She's got a thing for Law, though, so she might make your life a little difficult."

"Are they dating?" The question popped out of my mouth before I could stop it. Who Lawson was involved with was none of my business.

Aspen burst out laughing. "Oh, God, no. And don't ask him that. He'd be insulted you thought it was even possible."

I flushed but couldn't deny the relief washing through me. "Oh."

She studied me for a moment. "Law hasn't dated anyone for as long as I've known him, which is a few years now. Haven't heard of him dating anyone since his divorce, actually."

That twisting sensation in my stomach was back. Was he so in love with his ex that he couldn't move on? I wanted to ask Aspen but swallowed the question. *None of my business.*

Her eyes shone with mischief. "I think he's just waiting for that one right person, ya know?"

"Sure. He'd want to be careful with kids involved."

"It's more than that. He's not someone who's in it for instant gratification. He wants real. That's hard to find."

It fit the man I'd seen a glimpse of all those years ago, and it fit the man I was growing to know now. "That's good."

Aspen's lips twitched. "Yes, it is."

Cady pulled on her mom's hand, her red pigtails swinging with the action. "Let's gooooooo."

Aspen booped her nose. "The princess is ready for her carriage to depart?"

Cady giggled. "Yes!"

"Then let's hit it." Aspen glanced at me. "You good to follow? I'll drive slow."

A little anxiety bled out of me. "Slow would be great because I'm driving a brand-new car that Lawson bought, and I really don't want to crash it."

Aspen laughed. "There's nothing like the pressure of new wheels. No problem. I'll drive grandma-style."

"That's exactly my speed."

"Dad got a new car?" Charlie asked, excited.

"He did." I pointed to the massive black SUV. "And I think it needs a name."

Charlie was already running toward it, his tiny backpack thumping against his back. When he reached the vehicle, he ghosted a hand over the side. "Batman. It has to be Batman."

"Okay—"

"No, wait. The batmobile!"

I laughed as I opened the back door to help him in. "I think that's perfect."

Charlie grinned as I got him situated in his booster seat. "We should add rocket launchers so it's really a batmobile."

"I'll make sure to add that to the list."

"Yes!" he whisper-shouted as he bounced in his seat.

I made my way around to the driver's door and climbed in. I tried my best to listen to Charlie talk about his day while paying close attention to the road, traffic, and Aspen. Luckily, Charlie didn't need much prodding to keep chatting.

Aspen's house was somewhat in the same direction as Lawson's; you just turned off on a different road. The lane quickly turned to gravel, and I spotted an adorable farmhouse in the distance. As we got closer, I saw it needed a little work, but the bones were great, and it had an amazing front porch.

A truck was parked in front of it with an emblem for Washington Fish and Wildlife, along with another SUV with no moniker, but I didn't see anyone in sight. I followed Aspen's lead and parked next to her station wagon.

The moment the engine was off, Charlie was unbuckling himself. "Can I get out? Can I?"

"Wait just a second. This car is pretty high." The last thing I wanted was for Charlie to fall and break a bone.

"Hurry!" he pleaded.

My lips twitched as I climbed out and rounded the vehicle. I quickly lifted Charlie down, but he was already running toward a pasture where two donkeys and a herd of goats grazed. As I turned around, I came face-to-face with a massive man, maybe half an inch shorter than Lawson and slightly broader. They had similar features, but this guy's hair was lighter, and his expression was definitely less welcoming.

I instinctively took a step back, tripping over my feet and nearly falling. I managed to save myself by grabbing the SUV's side mirror.

The man's eyes narrowed on me, but then a ball of motion hurtled itself at him. "Daddy!"

The man's face completely changed as he caught Cady in mid-jump. "There's my Tiny Dancer. I thought you ditched me to join the circus."

She giggled. "I told you, never. I love our circus too much."

Aspen hurried over to us, a look of worry on her face as she took in my expression. "Hallie, this is my husband, Roan. Also known as Lawson's brother and Charlie's uncle. Roan, this is Law's new nanny, so stop scowling and scaring the crud out of her."

Roan looked a little sheepish as he turned back to me. "Nice to meet you, Hallie."

"Y-you, too."

"I swear he doesn't bite, even when he looks like the abominable snowman," Aspen assured me.

That last part confused me, but I just went with it. Seeing Roan's gentleness with a daughter I surmised wasn't his by birth was enough for me to give him the benefit of the doubt.

"I really am glad to meet you," Roan said. "You're honestly a miracle."

"A miracle?" I parroted.

He set a wiggling Cady down, and we followed her, Charlie, and Heather toward the fence line. "I didn't think Law would ever settle on someone to hire."

Aspen pushed into her husband's side, and he wrapped an arm around her. "Cut him some slack. Law had some real doozies for applicants."

Roan chuckled, the sound deep and rich. "My favorite was the one who only cared about the cable and snacks."

Aspen arched a red brow. "What about the one who offered to have a five-some with all of you?"

My jaw went slack. Was she for real?

Roan grimaced, then bent his head to brush his lips against hers. "You know you're the only one I'm interested in taking to bed, Tenderheart."

Pain streaked through me at the sweetness of the moment, the intimacy. You could see the dance of emotions between them as clear as day: care, love, respect, heat.

What would it feel like to experience just one of those things, let alone all of them at once?

Aspen kissed him back, then sent him a look. "There are children and company, Roan."

He just grinned at her. "There's always the barn."

My cheeks flushed at the insinuation.

She smacked his stomach. "You're incorrigible."

"That's how you like me."

Aspen shook her head but extricated herself from her husband's hold, moving to my side. "Sorry about him."

"I'm not," Roan called as he helped the kids into the pasture so they could greet the animals.

I pressed my lips together to keep from laughing. "He seems nice."

"*Nice* is not a word I've ever used to describe Roan. He's far too honest for that."

I glanced up at Aspen. "Honest is good. Way better than nice."

People hid behind niceness. It could be fake. Honest kindness, the type I'd seen from Roan with Cady and Aspen, people would give anything for that.

"I agree."

"Aspen," a deep voice called from behind us.

I hadn't heard someone come up, even on the gravel. I'd been paying too much attention to the show between Aspen and Roan. I jerked, whirling around, my heart hammering.

The man's footsteps faltered as he took in my reaction. I instantly ducked my head, embarrassed. Twice in a span of five minutes, I'd overreacted and made a fool of myself. Which was why my friendships were short-lived. People didn't know what to do with me.

Aspen's hand pressed into the small of my back gently. "Hallie, this is our vet and friend, Damien Miller. Damien, this is Hallie, Lawson's new nanny. She's new to Cedar Ridge."

I didn't want to look up and would've paid a million dollars not to, but I'd only seem odder if I didn't. I forced my gaze up to the man a handful of feet away from us. His expression was curious, but there was also kindness in his green eyes, and he made no move to come closer even though the distance was awkward.

"Hi, Hallie. It's nice to meet you."

I nodded. "You, too."

My palms were more than damp, and my heart thudded against my ribs. Too many new things, too close together. I struggled to rein it all in.

Damien turned to Aspen. "I'm all done with the inoculations. You know the drill. Some fatigue and upset stomach are normal, but if anyone seems extra out of sorts, just give me a call."

She didn't move from my side, her hand still on my back, letting me know she was there. "Thanks, Damien. I really appreciate you coming out."

He dipped his head in answer. "Anytime." His gaze flicked to me. "Welcome to Cedar Ridge, Hallie."

My mouth was so dry my tongue stuck to the roof of my mouth. "Thank you. Nice to meet you."

My words sounded robotic, as if I were some sort of AI. But at least they came.

Damien waved and headed for his vehicle. When he shut his door, I let out a breath. It was only then that Aspen moved her hand from my back.

I expected her to say something, maybe prod into my reaction or at least ask if I was okay. She didn't say a word, simply turned around and began pointing out the animals to me.

Pressure built behind my eyes. Frustration. Despair. Anger. I only wanted one thing: normalcy. But I wasn't sure it would ever be mine. All because of *him*. He'd stolen that chance from me. Of all the scars he'd left behind and the pain he'd inflicted, that was the worst of all.

## Chapter Eleven

*Hallie*

"And then Emmaline tried to eat your hair!" Charlie said, practically bouncing in his booster seat.

I grinned back at him. Charlie was so easy to love, full of life and kindness. So easily accepting of me and anyone else in his orbit. "She must've been extra hungry. Unless emus usually eat hair."

Charlie laughed harder, shaking his head. "Good thing we had treats."

"Good thing," I agreed as I turned onto Main Street and headed toward the high school. I was beyond grateful for the size of Cedar Ridge. And the fact that it created a sort of easily remembered grid.

But it was more than that. The town being so small made it easier for me to push my boundaries and dive into the *new*.

"I wish we could've stayed longer," Charlie said wistfully as he turned to look out the window.

"I bet Emmaline wished you could've, too." It was the best I could give because, after my second freak-out of the afternoon, all I'd wanted to do was run back to my cabin and hide.

My cheeks heated just thinking about it. Aspen's kindness said so much about who she was, but I was sure she wondered what was wrong with me. Everyone did. And I didn't blame them. It generally didn't come from a bad place, but it made me feel like a freak all the same.

Charlie let out an epic sigh, his shoulders rising and falling with the action. "I wish Dad would let us get a puppy or kitty."

I glanced in the rearview mirror. "I always wanted a pet growing up, too."

His eyes sparked with hope and a bit of mischief. "You could get one now! And then I could play with it all the time. Dad couldn't say no because it would be yours, and you're a grown-up."

I couldn't help the laugh that bubbled out of me. "Has anyone told you how smart you are?"

"Not today."

I grinned at him. "Since I'm living in your dad's guest cabin, I don't think it would be very fair of me to get a pet without his permission."

Charlie's shoulders slumped. "He's never gonna say yes. He says we're too busy, and pets make a mess."

The dejection in Charlie's tone killed me. I thought of all the times I'd begged for a dog. But they shed and might've left hair on the floor of the museum disguised as a house. It hadn't been possible. Not for a second. Maybe I could broach the subject with Lawson once things were a little more under control at the Hartley house.

Flipping on my blinker, I turned into the high school parking lot. There were still a fair number of cars around. I saw two groups practicing soccer in a far field, some runners from the cross-country team stretching, and a handful of students heading from the main school building to vehicles parked in the lot.

My hands grew clammy as I pulled to a stop in front of the school. This would be my first time around Luke without Lawson present. Part of me hoped that not having his father around would help Luke's acceptance of me, but another part feared his behavior would be far worse.

I put the SUV in park and gripped the steering wheel as we

waited. I was five minutes early, not wanting Luke to think I'd forgotten him if he got done before we planned.

"Luke's *always* late," Charlie grumbled.

"Actually, we're early. And it's okay if we have to wait for a bit. He's working on his schoolwork."

Charlie let out a harumph that made him look and sound like a tiny grandpa. "Doubt it. He and Dad are always fighting about his grades."

I worried the corner of my lip. One thing had been clear in the few interactions I'd had with Luke. He was in pain. Some might think he had an attitude problem or was just a typical teen, but I knew it was more than that.

There was real anger stewing in Luke. And anger like that only came from one thing: hurt. Something was causing him pain. I hated the idea of it. I'd only known the boy for a single day and wanted to fix it. But I knew he'd never open up to me the way things were now.

*One step at a time.*

And the next one was to simply be here. To not let him get a rise out of me.

Charlie kicked the seat as we waited. I asked him questions about his favorite frog and lizards—I'd need to look up reptile facts to keep him entertained.

A beige minivan pulled in front of me and parked as the minutes ticked by—fifteen past when Luke had said to pick him up.

My stomach churned. What if he'd already left? What if I'd lost Lawson's son on my first day of work?

My mouth went dry as I gripped the steering wheel tighter.

Then the school doors opened.

Luke walked out, clad in a black tee and black jeans, a backpack slung over one shoulder. A girl kept pace next to him and was his complete opposite. Golden-blond hair where Luke's was so dark it looked almost black, a petite frame next to his tall one. She wore light blue jeans and a floral top and beamed up at him.

She smiled at Luke as if he'd hung the moon. But the real miracle was how he looked at *her*. His mouth curved with the hint of a grin. It was the most positive emotion I'd seen out of him yet. His whole body tilted slightly in her direction as if she were the sun, and he orbited around her.

A woman got out of the minivan in front of me, not looking especially pleased. "Violet. We need to go."

The girl's head jerked up, but then she quickly nodded, giving Luke a quick wave and hurrying toward the woman.

I rolled down the passenger window to flag Luke down. His hint of a smile disappeared, replaced by that familiar deep scowl.

Instead of getting into the front seat, Luke opted for the back. The message was clear. I was the help and nothing else. He slammed the door behind him to punctuate the statement.

"How was the study session?" I asked.

Luke didn't answer; he simply glared at me through the rearview mirror.

I fought a sigh as I started the engine. This would be a marathon, not a sprint, but what Luke didn't know was that I'd had to live through what felt like a lifetime of agony. A few death glares from a teenager were nothing.

---

Charlie watched me from his perch at the kitchen island as I pulled an array of ingredients from the cupboards and refrigerator. "Whatcha making?"

His voice held a bit of skepticism, and it echoed the doubt rolling around inside me. My mother's words swirled in my head. *"Enough with these juvenile eating habits. It's embarrassing and ridiculous. Eat something normal for once. You're not five."*

I rested my hands on the counter, squeezing the edge. "I was thinking mac and cheese and a salad with roasted chicken. Do you think everyone will like that?"

A grin split Charlie's face as he bobbed his head. "Mac and

cheese is me and Drew's favorite." A little of the smile slipped. "I don't know about salad. I don't always like that."

My lips twitched. What kid enjoyed greens? "Well, you can try it and tell me what you think. Maybe you can help me with the recipe."

Charlie brightened at that. "Really?"

"I could use a sous chef."

His face scrunched. "What's a soush chef?"

I bit the inside of my cheek to keep from laughing. He was too adorable. "It's a second-in-command."

Charlie's doubt slipped away at that. "I wanna help with the recipe! I don't like olives or peppers. Or broccoli or spinach. Or—"

"How do you feel about corn, onion, cucumbers, tomatoes, and avocado?" I asked, thinking it might be simpler this way.

He paused for a moment. "I don't know about cucumbers…"

"That's fair. Why don't you try one bite, and then you can tell me whether they make the cut or not."

Charlie nodded, sliding off his stool. "Sure. I'm a real good taste tester. I gotta get my chef's hat first, though."

He was running down the hall before I could ask how—and why—he had a chef's hat.

I moved to the sink, rinsing the cucumber with some veggie wash before placing it on the cutting board. As I began dicing it, I heard a door slam down the hall. I expected Charlie, but Luke entered the living area.

"Do you need anything?" I asked.

I'd made Charlie a snack when we got home, but Luke had gone straight to his room. Now, he ignored my question and crossed to the fridge. He grabbed a soda and then turned, entering my space as he bent to pull a bag of chips out of the drawer next to me.

I focused intently on my chopping and breathing. The quicker Luke knew he wouldn't get a rise out of me, the better.

Luke paused, hovering near me. "Jesus. Did you do that to yourself? Did Dad hire some sick freak cutter or something?"

I stilled, my knife halfway through the cucumber. So stupid. I hadn't thought. I was so used to being around Emerson and Adrian, and they knew all about my scars. I'd pushed my sleeves up to wash the cucumber and hadn't pulled them back down.

My heart hammered in my chest. Memories slammed against the walls I rebuilt on a daily basis. I swallowed the bile surging up my throat and looked up at Luke. "No. I didn't do this to myself. But if I had, it would mean I was hurting. And needed help. I doubt your response would've inspired me to seek that help."

Luke's mouth snapped shut, and his cheeks flushed.

My goal hadn't been to embarrass him. It had been to make him pause and think. To remember that his words and actions had consequences.

I gentled my tone. "Everyone has a battle, an inner war they hide from the world. It's good to remember that."

Luke's Adam's apple bobbed as he swallowed. He didn't say anything, simply turned on his heel and stalked away. But he left the bag of chips on the counter when he fled.

## Chapter Twelve

*Lawson*

Each leg felt as if it weighed a ton as I trudged up the steps to my house. I'd sworn the day would never end. A mountain of paperwork. A town council meeting. Reed and Clint getting into it about something that didn't matter at the station and me having to soothe egos. Nash demanding that he wanted to meet the *new, mysterious nanny*. And a call from Luke's English teacher telling me he had failed to turn in the paper that was due today.

All I wanted to do was crawl into bed and sleep for a week. No, a month. A month might actually catch me up on what I'd been missing.

I slipped my key into the deadbolt and turned it. Opening the door, I stilled. Charlie's and Drew's voices came from the kitchen, and warmth blasted me. They were laughing as they debated who would win in a fight, a great white shark or a grizzly.

But it wasn't their laughter that knocked me sideways; it was my house. The living room hadn't been this clean since the place was built. Toys, books, and games had been put away. Blankets were folded on the backs of the sectional. The pillows were even fluffed, with that little karate chop thing you only saw in furniture showrooms.

When I stepped inside and closed the door behind me, the smell hit me. Chicken. And maybe bacon? Something else I couldn't identify, but it smelled damned amazing.

I rounded the corner to find Hallie mixing something in a small bowl with a spout. Where the hell had she found that? I couldn't remember the last time it had been used.

She had her white-blond hair piled atop her head in a bun that somehow stayed in place. But the look exposed her neck. Long and sinewy, I found myself wanting to trace a finger down it.

I gave my head a good shake. Since when did I find someone's *neck* attractive?

I cleared my throat, turning my focus to Drew and Charlie, who were perched at the island. "Did I come home to the wrong house?"

Charlie's forehead scrunched. "Of course, you're in the right house."

Drew snorted. "It doesn't smell like feet in the living room anymore. That's what confused you."

Hallie wiped her hands on a towel as she shifted her weight from foot to foot. Instead of dropping the towel back to the counter, she threaded it through her fingers and pulled it taut. "I should've asked what you wanted for dinner before you went to work, but I didn't think of it. And I didn't want to bother you once you were there, so I just kind of guessed—"

"Hallie," I cut her off as I moved into the kitchen. "Whatever it is smells amazing."

A little of the tension left her shoulders, but the towel stayed pulled tight in her hands. "It's a roasted chicken salad and homemade mac and cheese."

"I helped with the salad," Charlie said, sitting up straighter on his stool. "I added bacon. And also, I like cucumbers now."

My gaze flicked from my son to Hallie. "My kid likes cucumbers now? Are you some kind of sorcerer?"

Drew shook his head. "Don't get any ideas about me and oranges. That ship has sailed."

Hallie's lips twitched. "I solemnly swear not to try to sell you on oranges." She turned, seeming to check the timer on the oven but the towel stayed firmly in her grasp.

I followed behind her, lowering my voice. "You're nervous."

She pressed her lips together and shook her head. "I'm good."

"You're not," I growled.

Hallie jolted a bit, and I cursed myself.

"I can't help if you don't tell me what's going on."

Her gaze flicked up to me, the gray in her eyes seeming to swirl, pulling me in. "Is it really okay? What I made? Not too kiddish?"

I barked out a laugh. "Hallie, if you haven't noticed, I live with three kids. And I'm not exactly a gourmet foodie."

Her hold on the towel loosened, and stray tendrils of hair fluttered as she let out a breath. "Good. That's good."

I leaned in closer, not having a clue how to ease the worry that obviously had her in knots. "What's all this about?"

Hallie started to shake her head and open her mouth as if to say *nothing*, but my narrowing eyes stopped her. She huffed out a breath. "My parents are into the gourmet stuff. My mom was always telling me that I ate like a five-year-old."

"So what if you eat like a five-year-old? That's the privilege of being an adult. You can eat whatever the hell you want."

"You sound like Adrian," Hallie said with a smile.

I stilled. Adrian. Who the hell was Adrian? Friend? Boyfriend? I shifted to lean a hip on the counter. "Who's Adrian?"

My voice sounded light, casual, as if I didn't particularly care who he was. God, I was grateful I was a good liar.

Hallie's entire face lit up as if someone had flicked on a light switch inside her. "My brother Emerson's husband. He's an amazing cook. He's the one who taught me the basics. He's always saying I should cook whatever makes me happy."

I didn't want to look too closely at the relief coursing through me. "Sounds like a wise man."

"He's one of the best."

The oven timer dinged, and Hallie grabbed two oven mitts from the counter. Opening the door, she slid out a casserole dish, and the entire space filled with the scent of heaven.

Drew was off his stool in a flash, coming to peek over Hallie's shoulder. "Dang, bruh. That's fire."

Hallie sent me a puzzled look.

I chuckled. "That means he likes it."

"I need to brush up on my teen language," she mumbled.

"You'll get there in no time around here," I assured her.

I clapped Drew on the shoulder. "Will you go get your brother for dinner?"

He made a face. "Do I have to? He's been in a piss-poor mood ever since you took his phone."

I fought a groan but nodded. "You can yell it from outside his door, then run."

"If I get decked with a textbook, I hope you feel really guilty."

My lips twitched. "Fair enough."

Charlie slid off his stool as Drew headed out of the kitchen. "What about our dressing?"

Hallie grinned down at him. "I think it needs one more stir, and then it's ready to go."

She grabbed the bowl and a whisk from the island and held it out for Charlie. He took the whisk and gave it a few stirs. "Is that enough?"

"I think it's perfect." Hallie turned and poured a healthy amount over the massive salad.

"I'll get the drinks. What would you like?" I asked.

She glanced up as she tossed the salad. "I made some iced tea earlier. I'll take a glass of that."

"It's really yummy, Dad," Charlie added. "I helped."

"Then I think I'll have some of that, too." I grabbed the pitcher and poured five glasses, putting them on the already-set table. There were even placemats and cloth napkins I hadn't realized I had.

I glanced back at Hallie. "How did you do all of this?"

She looked confused.

"You cleaned, went grocery shopping, cooked," I explained.

"I didn't get all the laundry done, but I should have that finished tomorrow," she said.

I just shook my head. "Thank you. You're kind of a miracle worker."

"And Emmaline loves her," Charlie added as if that were the most important thing in the world.

I grinned at Hallie. "Well, that seals it. You're stuck with us now."

A smile lit her face, morphing her beauty from something that stopped you in your tracks to something you'd never forget. It was the kind of beauty that could change a man if he let it.

"I think I like being stuck with the Hartley fam."

Charlie grabbed Hallie's hands and started dancing around the kitchen with her. He was singing some made-up song about Hartleys and Emmaline and Hallie. She laughed as he spun her in circles. It was the kind of life this house had been missing for far too long.

Drew came back and stared at the scene and then at me. "Bruh, I wanna smash that mac and cheese while it's hot."

I fought the urge to roll my eyes. "Then bring it to the table, *bruh*."

He just grinned and headed for the food. Hallie took that as her cue and extricated herself from Charlie's dance moves. We were all sitting down in a matter of minutes, Luke included.

He was quiet at dinner, which was typical, but the tone of the silence tonight had a different quality to it. Every now and then, I caught him stealing glances at Hallie. Only it wasn't with derision this time. It almost looked like worry or guilt.

I knew something was really wrong when he didn't argue when I asked him to do the dishes with Drew. Pushing back from my seat, I glanced at Hallie. "Do you have a few minutes before you head home?"

A hint of apprehension passed over her features, but she quickly rose. "Of course."

I led her toward my office, slipping inside and closing the door after us. I motioned to a large couch opposite my desk. Hallie sat and immediately twisted her fingers into a series of intricate knots.

"You're not in trouble, I swear," I said quickly.

Hallie nodded but didn't seem entirely convinced.

I blew out a breath, wondering how long it would take her to be completely at ease around me. "Did something happen with Luke today?"

Hallie stiffened, and I had my answer.

"What did he do?"

Her fingers tightened, knuckles going white.

The instinct to touch her was so strong I had to bite the inside of my cheek to stop myself. "Hallie."

Her gaze flew to mine. "I might've messed up."

I doubted that. "Whatever it is, we'll deal with it."

She swallowed hard. "I wasn't thinking, and while I was making dinner, my sleeves were pushed up."

My brow furrowed.

Hallie took a deep breath and pushed up one sleeve of her sweater and then the other. Thin scars crisscrossed her forearms. So many there was no way I could count them all.

Bile churned in my gut. I'd known the man who kept her had cut her. After I'd found Hallie half-dead in the snow, I hadn't been able to let go of the case. I'd read everything I could get my hands on, which hadn't been much since I wasn't on the state investigation team. But I'd read enough. I knew he'd tortured her—hurt all the women he held.

Hallie stared down at her arms. "Luke made a comment about me being a cutter."

My body jerked, hands fisting on my knees. "He *what*?"

"He's angry, Lawson. It wasn't about me. I informed him that I didn't do this to myself, but if I had, I'd need help and not judgment. It might've been the wrong thing—"

"No, that's exactly what you should've said, but I'm damned ashamed that he said something like that in the first place. I'm going to talk to him and—"

I started to rise, but Hallie put a hand on my forearm to stop me. "Don't."

It was the first time she'd touched me since the interview. I'd thought for sure the jolt I'd felt that day was simply shock at seeing Hallie after all these years, but I'd been wrong. Because her fingers ghosting over my skin now felt like a bolt of lightning to the system. Every part of me was attuned to every part of her.

"We have to find our way, the two of us. If you step in every time, that'll never happen."

I stared at the woman opposite me. So damn brave. So damn strong. "I don't want my son to be cruel. That's not how we operate in this house."

Hallie's expression gentled. "I've been here forty-eight hours, and I already know that. I think Luke got the message. If it happens again, I promise I'll tell you."

"Or if anything else happens," I demanded.

"Okay. We can have check-ins about him and how he's doing."

I nodded, slowly lowering my hand atop hers. I searched her expression for any sign of discomfort, but there was none. Gently, I turned her wrist over so I could see the worst of the scars. I traced one with my finger. "I'm so sorry this happened to you."

Hallie's breathing grew ragged. "I got out. *You* saved me."

"I wish I would've gotten to you a hell of a lot sooner." She'd been missing for thirty-three days. Spent over a month with a madman. What did that do to a person?

"But you got to me. That's what matters. When I had what felt like endless cruelty, you gave me kindness. You gave me blue."

My gaze locked with hers. "Blue?"

The corners of Hallie's mouth lifted. "Your eyes. I thought I could drown in all that blue, but it would be okay because there was only goodness there. Safety. Peace."

Pain struck my chest, jagged and brutal. "I want you to have all of that."

Her smile widened. "I'm finding it. Because you're giving it to me all over again."

## Chapter Thirteen

### Hallie

"You really didn't have to make breakfast," Lawson said as he cut off a bite of the egg casserole.

"Shut it, Dad. This is amazing," Drew mumbled, his mouth full.

I pressed my lips together to keep from laughing. "I really don't mind. I need to cook for myself anyway, and it's hard cooking for one person."

Drew shot me a grin. "Marry me, Hallie. My babes will understand."

Luke snorted. "Like you could pull Hallie."

Drew sent his brother an affronted look. "I'm a catch."

"For one of your middle school sycophants, maybe."

"What the Hades is a syco-whatever?" Drew snapped.

"Children…" Lawson warned.

But just the fact that Luke had said anything in my presence gave me a bizarre sense of hope.

Drew turned to his dad. "That's a curse, isn't it? You should take his phone for another day."

Luke glared at Drew. "Pick up a book once in a while, moron."

Drew shoved back his chair to go at Luke, but Lawson caught him by the T-shirt. "No bloodshed before first period. Go get your books. You need to leave in five." Then Lawson turned to Luke. "Apologize to your brother for the name-calling."

Luke's eyes went hot. "Sorry," he grumbled.

Drew pulled out of Lawson's hold and headed for his room. "Real believable."

Charlie's gaze ping-ponged between all the participants of the altercation. "Is it a bad word?" he whispered to me.

"No," I assured him.

"What's it mean?"

I glanced at Luke. "It's a fancy word for a follower. Your brother must be reading some pretty advanced books to know what it means."

Luke pushed back from the table. "Gotta get my stuff."

Lawson sighed. "Never a dull moment."

I sent him an empathetic smile. "I'd think you'd be used to this with four younger siblings."

He squeezed the back of his neck, the movement making his biceps bulge beneath his uniform shirt. "I've certainly apologized to my parents for the he—Hades we put them through."

"I know the h-word, Dad," Charlie said as he took the last bite of his breakfast.

"Father of the year over here," Lawson said sheepishly.

He was way too hard on himself. He clearly loved his kids like crazy and would obviously do anything for them. Most importantly, he was present. He wasn't checking his phone at meals or skipping out to hang with his friends. His boys knew he was there for them, no matter what.

"I think you get more than a passing grade." I stood, gathering dishes, and Lawson followed.

"I've got these. I don't need to leave for the station for another thirty," he said.

My surprised gaze flicked to him. "You're paying me to do it."

Amusement filled his expression. "You're already going above and beyond. I can handle a few dishes."

I opened my mouth to argue, but Lawson just squeezed my shoulder. "You handle carting the ragamuffins. I'll take care of cleanup."

Tingles spread through me at his touch. I had no idea if that was a normal reaction since a man getting too close would usually send me into a panic attack.

I'd lain awake last night, tracing the same scar Lawson had, following the path his finger had taken. Echoes of the feeling still coursed beneath my skin, phantom energy I never wanted to lose.

"Okay," I whispered.

He squeezed my shoulder again and let go. I instantly missed the contact. The warmth. The comfort.

"Hallie, can you help me find my other shoe?" Charlie called.

That jolted me back to the present. I wasn't in some daydream. I was working a job. Lawson was *paying* me to be here.

I hurried to help Charlie with his shoes as Drew and Luke headed for the SUV. Charlie yelled goodbye to his dad, and we followed his brothers out. Drew had called shotgun, and I helped Charlie into his booster seat in the back.

When I rounded the SUV, Luke stood by the back passenger door. He shuffled his feet. "Hallie?"

I stilled at his use of my name, waiting.

He swallowed, his throat working on the action. "I'm sorry about what I said yesterday. It was a dick move."

I tried not to smile like a feral clown. "Thank you, Luke. Water under the bridge."

He looked up, his eyes locking with mine. "Whatever happened to you, it had to hurt. I'm sorry about that, too."

My chest burned. There he was. The *real* Luke. Tenderhearted and probably feeling too much. I wanted to wrap my arms around him and hug him tightly. Instead, I met his gaze and put every ounce of emotion I could into my words. "Thank you."

The Brew's sign beckoned as I headed down Main Street and away from the elementary school. I made a last-minute decision and pulled into a spot just in front of the café. I bet the boys would be thrilled with some of those double chocolate muffins for an afternoon snack. And I wouldn't mind a hit of caffeine.

Sleep had come in fits and starts last night. It wasn't exactly surprising. My system was on overload. The caffeine wouldn't help with that, but it *would* keep me upright.

I stared into the coffee shop, assessing. It wasn't overly full, but it wasn't empty either. I studied each person. No overt threats, but sometimes you couldn't see danger coming.

I squeezed the wheel hard. "You're safe. Just a coffee shop. You've done this a million times."

Shutting off the SUV, I slid out and headed for the café. The bell tinkled as I walked in. There wasn't a long line, but a woman was in front of me. When she stepped aside after ordering, I was greeted with a wide grin.

"Hallie! It's so good to see you," Aspen said, her green eyes shining with warmth.

"Hi. I didn't know you worked here."

"For over five years now. I know all the best items on the menu."

I couldn't help but smile. "I'm already pretty partial to the double chocolate muffins."

Aspen echoed my grin. "A girl after my Cady's heart. Would you like one of those?"

"Actually, can I get four to go? And a hazelnut latte?"

"Treat for the kiddos later?" she asked, already moving to the bakery case.

"Them and me," I admitted.

"Now that's a girl after *my* heart."

I chuckled. "I do have a sweet tooth."

Aspen rang me up, and I stepped to the side to wait while she made my drink.

The hair on the back of my neck prickled, a telltale sign someone had eyes on me. My muscles stiffened as I fought the urge to pull my pepper spray from my purse. I was safe. We were in broad daylight in a public place. Aspen was just feet away.

"We meet again," the deep voice said. Close. Too close.

I turned to see the police officer from the other day standing next to me.

"Hi," I croaked. The urge to bolt was so strong, but that would only give Aspen another reason to find me odd, and I liked her so much. I wanted to find friendship with her.

"Reed. Reed Hall," he reminded me.

I just nodded like a bobblehead again.

"So, you're either new in town or on an extended vacation," he said with a grin, moving a step closer.

I tried to back up, but the bakery case prevented me from getting any real distance. My heart hammered in my chest, and my breaths came quicker. Tiny black spots danced in front of my vision.

"Reed," a voice cut in.

Some part of my brain recognized the voice as Aspen's. Safe.

Reed took a step back, sending Aspen a grin. "Hey there. How's married life?"

She smiled at him, but I saw the strain around her mouth. "Everything's good. You've met Hallie? Law's new nanny?"

The second man from the other day appeared behind him. "The chief got a nanny?"

"He did. She's just here picking up a few things for him and the kids."

Something passed over Reed's expression. Annoyance, maybe? Whatever it was, he quickly covered it. "Well, nice to meet you, Hallie."

The second man gave me a warm smile, the expression lighting his dark eyes. He was probably a couple of years older than Reed and a bit taller, as well. "Welcome to Cedar Ridge. I'm Bryan, but everyone calls me Daniels."

I managed a nod, but that was all I could do.

Confusion clouded Daniels' gaze as if he didn't understand my reaction, and I knew heat suffused my cheeks. I could feel Reed's eyes, too, boring into me. It was all too much. My breaths came quicker, and my hands started to shake.

"You boys had better get going. Don't want to be late now, do you?" Aspen said lightly.

Daniels slapped Reed on the shoulder. "She's right. Can't piss off the boss."

Reed muttered something under his breath, his gaze cutting back to me before he turned toward the door.

Aspen moved in closer to my side as they made their way out into the sunshine. "You're safe. Just take some nice, steady breaths. Follow me."

She raised and lowered her hand so that only I could see. I tried my best to follow along, but it took me a few tries to get there.

My eyes burned as heat filled my cheeks. "I'm sorry, I—"

"The only thing that'll piss me off right now is you apologizing for a damn thing. Reed is pushy. Couldn't read a sign that a woman wasn't interested if she wrote it in red on her forehead."

A laugh wanted to push free, but it couldn't quite get there.

Aspen's expression gentled. "I'm going to tell you something I don't tell most people. I lost my sister to a monster that was supposed to love her. He almost killed me, too. I know what it's like to have darkness in your past. I know something's casting shadows for you. If you ever want to talk about it, I'm here."

I blinked back tears, trying to keep my emotions in check.

Aspen reached out and squeezed my hand. "And if you don't want to talk about it, just know I'm a safe place that will always understand."

My throat burned, fire scorching it. "Thank you, Aspen. Thank you."

It was all I could get out, but it would have to be enough.

## Chapter Fourteen

*Lawson*

Nash leaned back in his conference room chair, studying me as he ate a burrito.

"Stop doing that," I muttered as I flipped through some paperwork.

"Doing what?" Nash mumbled around a mouthful of food.

"Staring at me. It's creeping me out."

"I'm not staring."

I looked up, arching a brow.

Nash firmly set the front legs of his chair back on the floor. "You get good sleep last night?"

"Are you feeling all right? Since when do you care about how I slept?"

He set the burrito down. "Since you started looking like the walking dead. Those dark circles under your eyes were starting to swallow you whole."

I frowned at him. "It wasn't that bad."

This time, Nash arched a brow.

I fought the urge to squirm in my seat. "I'm fine." I hated being a source of worry for my family. It was the last thing I wanted. When everything went down with Melody, they'd rallied around me. They'd taken babysitting shifts, carted the kids to and from school and daycare, and dropped off meals.

And they'd worried about me. Afraid I would lose it. I could admit that I'd come damn close. But my kids needed me.

I never wanted to be the source of their anxiety again. I'd put them through enough.

"Really," I promised my brother. "Hallie is already helping a ton."

A smile played at Nash's lips. "Roan said she's smokin'."

My gut tightened as jealousy flared. It was beyond ridiculous. My *married*, madly-in-love brother had noticed that Hallie was beautiful. So what? "I highly doubt Roan called you up to say my nanny was smokin'."

Nash just grinned wider. "Mads and I were dropping off their wedding present. He was intrigued about how you were handling working in close proximity to her."

The muscle beneath my eye began to flutter. "She's thirteen years younger than me, not to mention the fact that I'm her boss."

"Age ain't nothin' but a number, big bro."

"Don't." My single word sliced across the space, and Nash's eyes flared. I struggled to gentle my tone. "I'm sure you and the rest of our family will meet her soon. I don't want anyone making her feel uncomfortable. She's..."

I wasn't sure what the right word was. I had intended to go for *sensitive*, but that could make Hallie sound weak when she was anything but.

"Hallie's been through a lot. She doesn't need you or any of our siblings giving her a hard time."

Nash straightened, going on alert. As much as he was a jokester, he had a fierce protective streak. He didn't stand for anyone hurting women. Especially after everything his fiancée, Maddie, had been through.

"You said you knew her from your past. A case?" Nash probed.

My fingers tightened reflexively around my pen. Hallie was trying to make a fresh start. I knew she wouldn't want people to know everything she'd been through. But I needed to let it out. Talk to someone. And Nash would recognize her when he saw her anyway.

"This stays between you and me. Don't even tell Maddie."

Nash's expression was stony. "Okay."

I forced my fingers to release the pen, letting it drop to the table. "You remember the search about five years ago over in Shallan County? The twenty-year-old college student at her parents' vacation home for winter break? She went to a bonfire party and was abducted on her way back to her car. Held."

"Sure. Most messed-up case we've ever worked—" Nash's words cut off as his eyes widened. "No way."

My expression was grim, but I nodded.

"But the name was different," Nash argued.

"Halston. She goes by Hallie now. Trying to get some distance from it. A fresh start."

Nash blew out a breath. "Holy hell. What're the chances?"

One in a million, it felt like. That she would be the one to show up on my doorstep. The one who was the perfect fit for my family.

"I never forgot her," I admitted.

"Of course, you didn't. You saved her life. Didn't the doctors say that she might not have made it had it been another hour?"

Just the thought had my insides turning to granite. Hallie was light. Goodness. I'd only really known her for a few days, and I already knew that was true. The world would be a hell of a lot dimmer without her in it. "I don't know," I lied. "I'm just glad that didn't happen."

Nash had that thoughtful look on his face as he studied me again. "How is she?"

What a loaded question. It was one I wasn't sure I had the answer to.

"She's got scars—mental and physical. But she's stronger than anyone I've ever met. And there are some powerful women in my life."

Nash made a noise of agreement.

"Like I said, she wants a fresh start. But everything new is a struggle. I'm pretty sure she has PTSD and anxiety."

"Who wouldn't after everything she went through?" Nash muttered.

I met his gaze. "But she never stops trying. Even when she's terrified."

Emotion filled Nash's eyes. "Sounds like a hell of a woman."

The corner of my mouth kicked up. "She's great with the boys. Charlie's made her his second best friend. Drew already proposed."

Nash let out a bark of laughter at that. "Good. Maybe he'll stop hitting on Maddie."

I chuckled. "She even has a way with Luke. No matter what he throws at her, she just keeps calm. Steady."

"Sounds like you scored on the nanny front."

"No question." But I knew it was so much more than that.

Footsteps sounded on the linoleum, and I lifted my gaze to see Daniels and Reed coming in from patrol.

Daniels lifted his chin in greeting. "Met your new nanny this morning, Chief."

Reed let out a whistle. "The body on her. Think I could get her to tuck me in at night?"

Nash muttered a curse as he shoved his chair back.

But I was already on my feet, striding toward Reed. "What did you say?"

His eyes went wide. "Shit, boss. I was just joking around. She's hot, that's all."

"Think that's information you should've kept to yourself," Nash said.

"We don't talk about women like that in this station. Especially not those taking care of my children," I growled.

But I knew that wasn't the whole of it, not even close. The idea of this asshole creeping on Hallie was enough to get my blood boiling.

Nash clamped a hand on my shoulder, squeezing hard. "He heard you. Isn't that right, Reed-y?"

Hall was only a handful of years younger than me, so having

Nash put him in his place wasn't exactly welcome. His eyes went hot, and he opened his mouth to say something stupid, but I stopped him.

"Don't," I clipped. "You say something else, and I'm writing you up."

Reed snapped his mouth closed as his partner gave him a little shove.

"Come on," Daniels said. "Let's fill out that paperwork and grab lunch."

Reed jerked his head in a nod but gave me and Nash one last glare as he stalked away.

Nash squeezed my shoulder one more time. "Breathe. I really don't want to have to bury a body in the woods today. Ground's frozen. It'd be a real bitch."

I knew he wanted me to laugh, but I couldn't quite get there. Because my mind was running in circles. Where had he met Hallie? What had he said? Had he scared her?

The urge to call her was so strong my fingers twitched. But what the hell would I say?

I clenched and flexed my fists. "No gravedigging today."

Nash slapped me on the back. "Good. Because that burrito is damn good, and it's getting cold."

Daniels turned back to me. "Sorry, Chief. He doesn't mean any harm."

Anger surged again. "If he doesn't mean it, then he should catch a clue and not say moronic things. And if I find out he's bothering Hallie—"

"He won't," Daniels assured me. "I'll talk to him."

"Good," I clipped.

But Daniels made no move to follow his partner. "What's her story anyway?"

I stiffened. "What do you mean?"

"She's really skittish. I just wondered."

He was fishing, and I wasn't about to betray Hallie's secrets.

"She's shy, that's all. Don't overwhelm her."

Daniels' eyes narrowed, and I knew he didn't believe me. Still, he nodded. "Sure. We're taking lunch. Be back in sixty."

I just nodded in agreement, but some movement caught my attention. Wren, Holt's fiancée and one of our dispatchers, moved through the sea of desks with one hand on her pregnant belly. She'd be on maternity leave any day now, but she wasn't letting it slow her down.

"Everything okay?" I asked as she got close.

"Not sure. We've got a missing hiker. I already called Holt. He's getting the word to SAR, too, but I told him I'd grab you and Nash."

I muttered a curse. "He calling in everyone?"

Wren nodded, her light brown hair swishing around her with the movement. "It's already below freezing. He doesn't want her out there overnight."

Her. Below freezing. Overnight.

It brought back too many memories already humming at the surface: a terrified girl cut to hell but so determined to fight for her freedom.

I shoved all that down, locking it away with everything else I couldn't let myself think about. "Give me the details. I want every officer on the lookout, too."

Wren nodded, handing me a pad of paper. "I thought you might say that. Everything's right here. I'll get an APB out."

I nodded in thanks, already moving toward my office and maps, Nash on my heels.

I'd have to call Hallie and tell her I might be late. And I'd need to tell her why.

What would news of a missing woman bring back for her?

## Chapter Fifteen

### Hallie

I teased open the door to Lawson's bedroom but didn't enter. He'd said it was fine to go into all the rooms, but something about crossing the threshold to his made me pause. Being in the place he slept each night felt intimate somehow.

*Dumb. Dumb. Dumb.*

I was getting his dirty laundry, not waiting for the man in sexy lingerie. Just the thought made my cheeks heat. I wanted that with someone. To feel so safe I could let myself be completely free.

But seeing as I'd had a freak-out when a man had simply tried to talk to me today, surprising someone with sexy lingerie was a long way off.

I forced myself to walk into Lawson's room. The minute I was inside, I realized my mistake. His scent wrapped around me: sage, bergamot, and something else I couldn't quite put my finger on that was achingly familiar.

The feeling of being engulfed by it all was too good. I never wanted to leave.

My phone buzzed in my back pocket, jerking me out of my spiraling thoughts. As I tugged it free, I expected to see Emerson's or Adrian's name. Instead, *Lawson* flashed on the screen.

My gaze darted around the room as if I were looking for a camera. Some paranoid part of my brain wondered if he somehow knew where I was and what I was thinking.

I forced myself to take a deep breath and slid my trembling finger across the screen. "Hello?"

I said it like a question instead of a greeting. As though I wasn't sure he'd meant to call.

"Hey, Hallie. Everything going okay today?"

Lawson's voice was calm, steady. The reassurance I was quickly beginning to realize was simply *him*.

I cleared my throat. "Sure, kids made it to school, and I'm just working through the mountains of laundry."

A deep chuckle reverberated across the line. "I bet we could keep you on laundry duty for a month straight."

The corners of my mouth tipped up. "I don't mind. There's something meditative about doing laundry. I might solve world hunger if I'm at it long enough."

"I look forward to hearing all about that Nobel Prize-winning idea."

I could hear the smile in his voice. It was heady, knowing I'd put it there. I wanted more of that. More of the knowledge that I made Lawson smile. Made him laugh.

The sound of a drawer opening and closing came across the line. "Listen, I got a search and rescue callout."

I stilled. Someone was missing. Or injured. Or worse. "Oh." It was all I could get out.

"I never know how long these things will last, so I might be late. Would you mind staying late tonight?"

I straightened, steeling my spine. "Of course, not. Take all the time you need."

Anything to help someone who desperately needed it.

Lawson shifted the phone, making a static noise. "There's a guest room opposite mine that you're welcome to sleep in if things go really late."

"Okay. Just…be careful."

It was freezing out there. I couldn't imagine tromping around in the wilderness for hours with little to go on. Not to mention the wildlife and other dark things that could hide there.

"I always am. If I have service, I'll text when I'm on my way home."

I nodded and then realized he couldn't see me. "Sure. Don't worry about the boys. We'll play a game or watch a movie after dinner."

"Sounds perfect. Thanks, Hallie."

"Of course."

"Talk to you soon."

"Soon," I echoed.

Lawson paused for a moment before hanging up, his even breathing sounding across the line. And then it was simply gone.

---

"Can you believe it?" Charlie asked as he all but bounced on his bed in his adorable frog pajamas. "I kicked both their butts!"

I pressed my lips together to keep from laughing. "Are you allowed to say butt?"

Charlie gave me a sheepish smile. "Dad says booty is better."

"Then I think it's freaking awesome you kicked both your big brothers' booties."

He grinned widely. "Yeah, it is."

I'd been shocked speechless when Luke had agreed to play Sorry! with the rest of us. He wasn't chatty, except occasionally bantering with his brothers, but I didn't miss how he watched me. It was as if he were trying to put the pieces of a puzzle together. But that was far better than the alternative.

"When's Dad getting home?" Charlie asked, cutting into my thoughts.

I pulled out my phone, checking it for approximately the fiftieth time today. "I'm not sure. But he'll be here when you wake up."

"Sometimes not. Sometimes, they stay out overnight in tents."

My stomach cramped. Surely, they wouldn't be doing that in below-freezing temperatures and in the snow.

Charlie showed no such apprehension of the possibility, beginning to bounce again. "I'm gonna be on SAR just like my dad and uncles and Aunt G. I'm gonna help people who get lost and hurt. But I don't want to be a policeman. I want to be an animal scientist."

My heart clenched as I stared down at the boy with a heart of gold. "That sounds like a great plan to me. But it means you'd better get to sleep so you can study hard tomorrow."

"Aw, man," he mumbled as he flopped back onto the pillows.

I laughed as I switched off the light, leaving only a small frog nightlight on. "It'll be worth it."

"It better be."

"Goodnight, Charlie. Sweet dreams."

"You, too," he said, his voice already slurring with sleep.

I slipped out of the room, closing the door behind me. I moved down the hall and paused at Drew's open door. He was bent over his desk, scribbling in a spiral notebook.

"How's it going?" I asked.

His head lifted, brown hair all askew. "I hate pre-algebra."

I laughed. "I don't blame you. Do you need any help? It's been a minute since I've conquered that particular beast, but I bet I can brush up."

Drew shook his head but grinned. "Naw, I FaceTimed one of my babes. She helped me."

I bit the inside of my cheek to keep a second round of laughter at bay. "I hope you thanked her."

"Duh. Babes love words of affirmation."

My brows lifted at that. "Do they?"

Drew nodded. "I read all about it."

"Just make sure you're using your powers for good, not evil. And don't stay up too much later."

Drew sent me a salute, and I closed the door behind me. I kept going down the hall, hovering outside Luke's shut door. I worried my bottom lip and then finally lifted my hand to knock lightly.

"Come in," Luke called, his voice gruff.

I opened the door to find Luke propped against his headboard, a familiar book in his hand. I couldn't help the smile that tipped my lips. "You're reading *The Way of Kings*?"

Luke's brows rose. "You've read it?"

I nodded. "I loved it. I usually go more for YA fantasy or paranormal, but I loved that one."

"The battle scenes are pretty sick."

"I'm glad you're liking it. You might try *Fourth Wing*. Epic dragon riders."

Luke's eyes flared. "I'll check it out."

I shuffled my feet. "I just wanted to check in and see if you need anything before you call it a night."

Something passed over Luke's face. "I'm good. I'm used to him bailing on us for whatever."

I stilled, tension wrapping around my shoulder blades. "He's on a search and rescue call."

Luke shrugged. "Whatever. I just mean I'm used to strangers being more important than us. That's all."

My fingers curled into my palms, nails digging in deep. "I know for a fact that no one on this planet is more important to him than you and your brothers."

Anger flashed in Luke's eyes. "You don't know him."

"I *do* know him."

Luke stilled, curiosity winning out. "Whatever."

"I know that he saves people. He finds them when they're alone and lost and close to dying. He gives them back their lives. And that's what he's doing tonight. But it doesn't mean he loves you any less. It just means he's trusting me to make sure *you* aren't alone or lost or dying while he helps someone who might be."

Luke stared at me for a long beat, his throat working as he swallowed. "Sorry."

"Your father is a good man. Probably the best I've ever known. You just have to give yourself the chance to see it."

His fingers tightened on the book, but he didn't say a word.

I didn't force it. All I could do was plant the seed. "I'll be in the living room if you need anything."

I didn't wait for an answer. I knew there wouldn't be one. Instead, I headed for the door and shut it behind me.

The moment I reached the living room, I got to work picking up the remnants of a brutal Sorry! game and our evening snack. The tornado of destruction three boys could wreak in just one afternoon was amazing.

I grabbed the bowl of mostly demolished popcorn and began picking up stray kernels. How some had landed in a chair across the room, I didn't want to know. It was probably a miracle there weren't pieces stuck to the ceiling.

Packing up the game board, I slid it back onto its shelf. As I folded blankets, a wave of tiredness hit me. Maybe it was the long day or the concern for Lawson, but I suddenly felt as if I'd been hit by a Mack truck.

I flopped onto the sectional that was as comfortable as a cloud and pulled out my phone. Still nothing from Lawson. But there was a text from Emerson.

> **Emerson:** *How's everything going? I haven't heard from you much.*

I could read the underlying message. *Are you spiraling?*
I quickly typed out a text.

> **Me:** *I'm good. Things have just been super busy. Apparently, taking care of three boys is a lot. Who knew?*
>
> **Emerson:** *I think Adrian and I are sticking with one for that very reason.*
>
> **Me:** *I don't know. These three were pretty adorable playing Sorry! tonight.*
>
> **Emerson:** *You used to kick my ass in Sorry!.*
>
> **Me:** *Don't worry, I took it easy on the kiddos.*
>
> **Emerson:** *You sound good.*

I was quiet for a moment before I responded. It wasn't as if things had been easy since I'd arrived in Cedar Ridge, but they'd most certainly been good. And I guessed, at the end of the day, the two weren't mutually exclusive. You could have the achingly difficult with the profoundly beautiful. Sometimes, the hard made you appreciate the good more.

**Me:** *I am. Really good.*

**Emerson:** *No one deserves it more. Love you, Hallie.*

My eyes burned, chest cracking with the force of my love for my brother—the one who had always been there, no matter what.

**Me:** *There aren't words, Em. Love you more than I loved kicking your ass at Sorry!.*

**Emerson:** *Retribution is coming.*

I laughed as I kicked off my shoes. Curling up on the couch, I opened my e-reader app and started back into the world of fallen angels. But it wasn't long before my eyelids were drooping, and the world faded away.

---

A hand curved around my shoulder, shaking me gently. "Hallie."

The voice was deep, coated in sandpaper, but somehow, I only wanted to get closer. "Hmm?"

I blinked against the low light of the living room. Lawson's face filled my vision. His scruff-covered jaw, his piercing blue eyes. I jerked upright. "You're okay?"

His lush mouth curved. "Still gettin' feeling back in my toes, but I'm just fine."

"How did it go?"

All hint of humor fled Lawson's face as he lowered himself to the couch. "We didn't find her. We'll reassemble tomorrow after first light."

It wouldn't be light until at least seven in the morning. "Will she make it through the night? It's freezing."

Lawson stared down at his hands before looking at me. "If she found shelter, she has a chance. The friend she's in town with says she always hikes with an emergency kit."

"Why wasn't the friend with her?"

Lawson's fingers worried the seam of a couch cushion. "Not much of a hiker. One went to hike this morning, the other set off to poke around town, then they were going to meet for lunch and an afternoon at the spa."

A painful ache settled in my chest. "It was supposed to be a fun trip."

Lawson nodded.

"Do you think you'll find her?"

He stared back at me, not breaking the connection. "We'll keep trying for as long as we can."

I knew they'd looked for me for far longer than they should have. My parents had made donations and pulled strings to ensure it. The initial search had lasted over a week. After that, they'd sent out teams every few days to check different areas of the wilderness near where I'd disappeared.

"But, usually, they won't let you search for long," I surmised.

Empathy filled Lawson's expression. "Resources are limited. But Holt does everything he can to give us our best shot."

"Holt?"

"My brother. He's the head of search and rescue for the county."

"I'm glad he's trying to help," I said, breaking our stare.

I couldn't help but think about the woman. Alone. Scared. Freezing. Had she found somewhere to hide from the elements and animals? Was she already gone?

Strong fingers linked with mine, creating a woven tapestry of comfort and something so much more.

"Hallie."

I stared at our joined hands, the miracle that was a simple touch. A closeness that didn't send me spinning into anxiety and panic.

"Look at me."

The command was somehow gentle yet forceful all at once.

My head lifted as if I had no choice.

Emotion swirled in Lawson's blue eyes. A million different things morphed from one to the next, moving so quickly I couldn't pin any down.

"Stay in the now," he said.

"She's scared and alone."

That muscle beneath Lawson's eye fluttered. "And it reminds you of being scared and alone."

"No one should feel that way. No one," I whispered.

He tightened his hold on my fingers. "But you're not alone now, are you?"

I stared into those deep blues again, watching the emotions swirl faster. "No. I'm not."

## Chapter Sixteen

*Lawson*

Footsteps sounded behind me as sunlight streamed through the kitchen window. I glanced up to find a skeptical-looking Drew standing there.

"You're making…breakfast?"

I sent my son a droll look. "I can make eggs and bacon."

"Bruh, the last time you made a hot breakfast was when you told us that Great-grandma died." Drew was suddenly alert. "Is someone dead?"

I winced. Apparently, my lack of devotion to my culinary skills had scarred my children. "No one's dead. I just woke up early so I could make my family breakfast while Holt draws up plans for the day."

*Woke up early because I tossed and turned all night long.* My hand tightened around the skillet handle. I could still feel Hallie's fingers in mine, her skin like silk. The pressure. The heat.

A simple, innocent touch had turned my blood to fire.

"Isn't Hallie making breakfast now?" Drew asked hopefully, cutting off the thoughts sure to send me straight to hell.

I stirred the eggs and added some cheddar cheese, peppers, and onions. "She doesn't have to make something every day."

"But she *could*, and then I wouldn't have to risk missing practice or seeing my babes because I have food poisoning. Bruh, having the shits is not sexy."

My focus flicked to my teenager. "Help yourself to the cereal, then. And watch your language."

A knock sounded on the door.

"I'll get it," Luke's voice boomed as he strode down the hallway from his bedroom.

Drew and I shared a look. When was the last time Luke had offered to do anything?

There were muffled voices, and then he and Hallie appeared. I couldn't help but stare, taking in her cheeks rosy from the cold, bright berry lips, and shining gray eyes.

"Morning," she greeted with a hesitant smile.

"Thank God," Drew called. "Dad's trying to kill us."

Hallie's brows flew up. "Kill you?"

"He's making breakfast. Food that requires heat and ingredients that spoil."

"Drew…" I warned.

Luke covered a laugh with a cough.

Hallie fought a smile. "That's nice of your dad."

"It's not nice if he kills us," Drew whined.

Hallie's teeth bit down on the lip I wanted to tug and taste. "What if I supervise? Would that help?"

Drew stared at her as he debated. "I guess it's better than nothing."

Hallie laughed as she headed in my direction, the movement accentuating her long legs in another pair of those damned leggings. She might as well have worn nothing under that sweater. The thought had me hardening against my zipper.

*Fuck.*

I tried to think of something—anything—else as she approached. Baseball. Nope. Paperwork. Not even close. Drew's rank-as-hell lacrosse pads? That did it.

"Drew, go make sure Charlie's getting ready while I add a little extra poison to your food."

"Not cool, bruh," he called as he headed out of the kitchen.

Luke just snorted.

Hallie sent me a nervous smile. "Can I help with anything?"

"Want to handle toast and drinks?" Anything to put some distance between us so her orange-blossom scent wasn't teasing my nose.

"You got it." Hallie turned and smiled widely at Luke. "Can you grab me some juice glasses?"

Luke opened his mouth as if to argue but simply nodded instead.

Was I in the *Twilight Zone*?

I gave the eggs one more stir, then put them on the platter with the bacon. My phone buzzed in my back pocket as thundering footsteps sounded from the hallway.

Roan's name flashed across the screen, and I frowned as I answered it. "Everything okay?"

"Why do you always answer the phone like that?" he groused.

"Because when people call, there's usually a problem."

Roan was silent for a moment.

Hell. "What happened?"

"One of our guys found a body."

---

The cold sliced into me as I walked up the trail, a silent warning of what was to come. A bird called overhead, and the wind rustled the pine branches. It should've been peaceful, calming. It was anything but.

I rounded a curve, and the first hint of voices sounded from up ahead. My team had beaten me here, but they were already on duty. I'd had to explain to Hallie that I had a call and say goodbye to the kids.

I'd seen the silent question in her eyes. The way her face had paled. But I hadn't been able to give her any reassurance. Not when the worst was likely to come.

Roan's large form came into view. His hands were shoved into his jacket pockets, and he looked pissed as all hell. His chin lifted in greeting.

"It her?" I asked. Kimber Anderson. Twenty-four years old. Here on damned vacation.

A muscle in Roan's jaw ticked. "Looks like it. Luisa won't say officially until there's a DNA match, but—"

"It looks like her," I finished for him.

I'd seen the woman's photo; we'd sent it far and wide, hoping to find her. Her red hair and freckles were fairly unique.

I moved closer to the scene.

Roan shifted slightly, blocking my path. "It's a bad one."

I didn't take offense at the warning. Roan didn't say it because he thought I couldn't handle it. We'd both seen things that would be burned into our memories forever. He'd said it so I could steel myself. Prepare the best way I knew how.

By locking everything down. Turning off all emotion. Going blank.

I took a deep breath and let the pine air fill me. I'd hold that scent in my lungs the best I could to fight the smell of death.

Moving toward the group of crime scene techs, I nodded at Luisa. "Thanks for getting here so quickly."

She glanced up at me with amber eyes, her dark brown hair pulled back in a bun. "I was already in town. Getting a scone and some coffee at The Brew. This really put a damper on my morning treat."

I turned my gaze to the body and had to bite the inside of my cheek to keep from showing my reaction. Pain helped. It kept you from cursing or puking or whatever other reaction surged to the surface.

Kimber Anderson lay sprawled across the trail as if she were nothing but a piece of trash a hiker had carelessly left behind. She was missing her jacket and her pack. Her shirt was torn, and so many stab wounds covered her torso I lost count.

An angry, dark blue mark across her neck said she'd been choked or strangled. As my eyes narrowed, I could see the impression of a rope, the tiny lines branded onto her skin.

My gaze flicked to Luisa. "What killed her?"

Luisa's expression went hard. "The petechial hemorrhaging in the eyes suggests it was strangulation, but I need to confirm back at my office. It looks like some of the stab wounds were inflicted perimortem, others post."

"Rage," Roan said from my left.

Rage was an understatement. This kind of fury wasn't easily quenched.

I glanced at Roan. "This feels personal. But she's a tourist."

"Someone could've followed her from home," he suggested.

"True. I'll get in touch with the PD in her hometown and talk to the friend. Maybe there's a partner or ex in the picture."

Luisa leaned forward on her knees. "There's something else you should see."

With a gloved hand, she lifted Kimber's shirt a fraction, exposing her hip bone. There was a wound there. I squinted but couldn't quite make it out.

Leaning over the body, the injury came into focus. A series of tiny cuts that formed a pattern. One that was familiar. The same design I'd seen in crime scene photos from a case five years ago. Only then, they weren't cuts. It was a brand.

Something I knew had been burned into Hallie—that gemstone shape with its intricate design.

And now it was here. On this woman's body.

## Chapter Seventeen

### Hallie

"I'm starving," Drew complained as we pulled away from the middle school.

Luke grunted. "You're always hungry."

Drew patted his stomach. "Gotta fuel the six-pack. Babe—"

"If you say *babes* one more time, I'm going to hurt you," Luke cut him off.

"Let's try to hold off on the violence before we've even made it home," I said as I flipped on my blinker. "I'd really rather not have to take someone to the emergency room."

Charlie giggled at that. "Drew's had to go four times, and Luke three. But I've *never* had to go."

I could only imagine what shenanigans had landed the older two Hartley boys in the ER.

"It's no big," Drew said. "Babes dig scars."

Luke smacked Drew upside the head, and he whirled on his older brother. "Not the hair, bruh."

"How about we grab an after-school snack downtown?" I quickly suggested before I had a WWE match in the back seat.

"Dockside!" Charlie cheered.

Drew turned back around. "I could go for some french fries and a milkshake."

I glanced at Luke in the rearview mirror. "I'm good with that."

The tension in my shoulders eased a bit. Luke was softening. He wasn't warm and fuzzy, but he wasn't rude either. I was taking it as a huge win.

I kept going on Main Street instead of taking the turn toward home. *Home.* The word had warmth swirling deep because that was exactly what it had started to feel like. Somewhere safe and comforting.

It didn't take long for us to reach downtown. I turned into the parking lot next to Dockside and grabbed an open spot. The kids were out of the SUV in a matter of seconds.

Drew and Luke were still needling each other, but Charlie came straight to my side, grabbing my hand. He swung our arms back and forth. "This is the bestest day."

I grinned down at him. "Well, that's fabulous news."

I wished I felt the same, but I'd been on edge since Lawson left this morning. A million questions had been on the tip of my tongue, but none of them were things I could ask in front of the kids. And I hadn't heard a word from him all day.

My fingers had itched to text him more times than I could count. I wanted to know what was happening, but I also wanted to make sure he was okay.

Drew paused to pet a passing dog, crouching low to scratch its ears.

The owner grinned at him. "She loves you."

Drew answered with a smile of his own. "She's awesome. Is she part Husky?"

The woman nodded. "Good eye. We think she's a Husky-shepherd mix."

Charlie moved to pet the dog. "She's so pretty. We want a dog, but Dad keeps saying no."

The woman's eyes softened. "They are a big responsibility."

I sent her a grateful smile. I had no idea if a dog was even on the table for the boys, and I didn't want anyone to get their hopes up.

Drew straightened. "Thanks for letting us pet her."

"Anytime," the woman said with a wave, heading down the street.

Drew sighed. "A dog would really up my game with the—"

"Don't even say it," Luke growled as he grabbed the door to the restaurant and pulled, holding it open for all of us. We filed inside. Dockside was warm and inviting, with a counter to the right, booths lining the left wall, and windows straight ahead. An assortment of tables were arranged in the center of the room. The space was only about a third full, but it wasn't exactly mealtime.

A woman with a warm smile walked up to us. "Well, if it isn't the three most handsome faces I've ever seen."

Drew sent her his most flirtatious smile. "I've missed you, Miss Jeanie. You're looking beautiful today."

She shook her head as she waved him off. "You charmer."

She turned to me. "You must be the new nanny. Hallie, right?"

I squirmed in place, uneasy that people were clearly talking about me. *Small town*, I reminded myself. A small town where people would, of course, take an interest in the person working for the chief of police.

I did my best to force a smile. "That's me."

Charlie grabbed my hand and gave it another swing. "She's the bestest."

The woman laughed. "Well, that's lucky for you." She glanced back at me. "I'm Jeanie. Staple at Dockside. You need any menu recommendations or takeout orders, you come to me."

Her genuine warmth lessened my unease a fraction. "Thank you. I really appreciate that."

She waved us on. "Come on. I've got a booth just perfect for you."

Jeanie led us to a table at the windows. The view of the frozen lake and mountains was majestic.

I couldn't help but stare. There was nothing like it. The area my family had a vacation home in had a slightly different view, but it had been no less breathtaking. Something about it had always put me at ease, brought me peace. I'd missed it like a limb when my parents sold the home after the incident.

But that was what they did. They erased anything unpleasant or imperfect. They didn't talk about my kidnapping or my torture. They pretended like nothing had happened at all. If I wore something with short sleeves that revealed my scars, my mother would tell me to change. Not in a cruel way, but enough to tell me she couldn't handle seeing the truth.

I didn't blame her, but I died a little inside each time she did it. Emerson had seen me fading away into nothing. He had done everything he could to help, finally insisting that I come to live with him and Adrian. And that had changed everything.

"Can I get you drinks while you look at the menu?" Jeanie asked, breaking into my thoughts.

"Shirley Temple, please! Then a milkshake!" Charlie cheered as he slid into the booth.

"Coke," Luke said.

Drew sent her another of his signature smiles. "How would you feel about making me a Cherry Coke and a shake?"

Jeanie just chuckled. "For you? Anything."

She turned her focus to me.

"Get a Cherry Coke," Drew urged. "Jeanie makes 'em with cherry syrup."

"They're pretty darn good if I do say so myself," Jeanie agreed.

"How can I say no?" I said with a smile.

Jeanie clapped her hands together as she turned to leave. "Coming right up."

The boys told me their favorite things on the menu, which ranged from grilled cheese to the burger. I ended up going with chicken fingers, Drew's favorite. We ate and laughed, and it felt good. Normal.

Heat flared on the side of my face, and my skin felt itchy and too tight for my body. All telltale signs that someone was watching me.

I swallowed hard and glanced around the room. My gaze landed on a man sitting alone. The same one I'd practically run into at my motel—the one with the scruffy beard and the jumpy eyes. Only now, those eyes were fixed on me.

My fingers curled into my palms, nails pressing into my flesh. I spoke reassurances to myself over and over. I was safe. People were everywhere.

I should've gotten used to the staring. The fixation. My face had been plastered all over newspapers and TV screens. While five years had passed, there was a surge of specials every year around the anniversary, and now was that time. He'd probably seen some *Unsolved Mysteries* episode or read a true crime blog.

I focused on my breathing. In and out. In and out.

"Hallie?" Luke's voice snapped me back to the present. Concern lined his face. "You ready to go?"

Heat hit my cheeks. "Sorry." I forced a chuckle. "Lost in dreamland."

I thought my voice sounded normal, but I felt the tremble in my vocal cords. Just a handful of minutes, and we'd be home. I could excuse myself to the bathroom and do my breathing exercises. Ground myself in the safety of Lawson's house.

Grabbing my purse, I stood and clasped my hands in front of me so no one could see them shaking.

Charlie ran ahead, and Drew followed. But Luke stayed near me. I wove through tables toward the door. The bearded man's seat was directly in our path. If I avoided him, it would be extremely obvious. Awkward, even.

I kept my focus on my breathing. In and out. Not too long, not too short.

As we neared his table, he stood. "It's you. You're here."

I stumbled to the side as the man tried to get closer.

Luke was there in a flash, pushing the man back. "Dude. Not cool."

Anger flashed in the man's dark eyes. Eyes that sent me spiraling back to another time. Where a masked man tore me from sleep to send me into a sea of agony.

I hurried toward the door, tripping over my feet and struggling to breathe. As I stumbled outside into the cold, fresh air filled my lungs. It helped to ease the worst of the panic.

I squeezed my eyes closed, battling the memories and pushing them back. It was as if I fought a mental war every day, positioning my soldiers in places I thought there might be an assault. But, sometimes, there were sneak attacks. Ones I could never prepare for. Like now.

It took more than a few moments to get my breathing under control. When I opened my eyes, Luke's worried face filled my vision.

"Are you okay?" he asked softly.

I nodded, swallowing hard. "Charlie and Drew?"

My voice was raspy, as if I'd just smoked a pack of cigarettes and chased it with a shot of whiskey.

"They ran to the car."

Good. That was good. Then I hadn't scared them with my freak-out. "I'm sorry, Luke, I—"

Luke shook his head. "That guy was being a creep. You didn't do anything wrong."

God, he had a good heart. It was just hidden beneath pounds of armor. "Thanks for your help."

He nodded, and we started walking. But he still kept close, the silence wrapping around us.

"What happened to you?"

Luke's question was so quiet I almost couldn't hear it. But it was there all the same.

Blood pounded in my ears. I didn't want to lie to Luke, not when the progress we'd made was tenuous at best. But even at sixteen, I didn't want to fill his head with the darkness out there.

I settled for the simple but broad truth. "Someone took me."

That was all it was at the end of the day. Someone took me. Ripped me from a carefree night at a bonfire with friends. Tore me from the innocence and wonder of new adulthood. He took me from my life and made it so I was never the same.

Luke's steps faltered, and his jaw turned to granite. "They hurt you."

It wasn't a question, but I answered just the same. "They did. But I got away. I got out. And then someone amazing found me."

Luke's brow furrowed. "Who?"

"Your dad."

## Chapter Eighteen

*Lawson*

Night curled around me as I drove, and each revolution of the wheels twisted my gut tighter. I hadn't wanted to be this late. Hadn't wanted to leave my kids and Hallie alone in the dark. Not with everything going on.

When I texted Hallie to tell her I'd be late, I'd asked her to make sure all the doors and windows were locked. Told her to set the alarm—one I needed to have Holt give a once-over because it hadn't been upgraded in years. And there wasn't even one in the guest cabin. That was a problem.

I hated that I'd probably scared Hallie with the request. I'd probably ratcheted up her anxiety to a ten. But safety was more important.

My house glowed as I rounded the curve in the drive. The boys' rooms were dark, but the living room and kitchen were blazing. I pulled into my parking spot next to the SUV and pulled out my phone.

> **Me:** *It's me who just parked. I'm coming in. Didn't want to startle you.*

Maybe Hallie had already fallen asleep in the guest room or on the couch. Maybe she wouldn't notice my entrance at all.

I turned off the engine and slid out of the SUV. Beeping the locks, I headed up my front steps. It only took a matter of seconds to unlock the door and disarm the system. But as soon as I was inside, I relocked the doors and reset the alarm.

Turning, I saw Hallie. She hovered in the living room as if she'd been pacing. She still wore those damned leggings, but she'd switched the sweater for an oversized sweatshirt, and her hair was piled in a haphazard bun on the top of her head.

She didn't say anything, nor did I. We just stood there, staring. I had the intense urge to go to her, wrap her in my arms, and not let go.

Hallie was chipping away at my defenses, bit by bit. I tried to make repairs every night, but it was proving futile.

I forced my legs to move, to walk. The motion seemed to jolt Hallie out of whatever haze she was in. She instantly headed for the kitchen. "I saved you dinner. We had something light because I took the boys to Dockside after school, and we feasted. I hope that's okay. They loved it."

She pulled a covered bowl from the fridge, unwrapping it to reveal some sort of soup. "I've got rolls from the bakery, too. I need to reheat the soup—"

"Hallie." I gently took her arm to stop her movement. "We had pizza at the station."

"Oh." She deflated as if she were lost without a task.

"But thank you for saving me some. I'll take it for lunch tomorrow. It'll be a hell of a lot better than cold pizza."

Hallie nodded, a few strands of blond hair falling from her bun. "I'll just put it back in the fridge, then."

She moved from my hold and headed back to the refrigerator. As she straightened, those gray eyes found me. "Are you okay?"

"Not really," I answered honestly.

Pain and empathy filled Hallie's expression, but she didn't look away. "What can I do?"

The question was so simple, but it meant everything.

I let out a long breath. "I need to talk to you about a few things."

Hallie stiffened. "Did I do something wrong? I can fix it. I—"

"You're perfect." The words slipped out of my mouth before I could stop them.

Hallie's eyes went wide, and her lips parted as she sucked in a breath. I wanted to tease and taste those lips. Wanted to feel them wrapped around me—*hell*. I shut those images down.

"You're doing an amazing job. Better than I thought possible. Even Luke seems…"

I wasn't sure what the right word was. Gentler, maybe? Not as filled with rage?

Hallie's entire demeanor softened. "Luke is an amazing kid. I think he just feels more than the average person. It makes everything hit him harder."

My throat constricted. I'd known that about him. I'd felt it on the first day of kindergarten when he hadn't wanted to let me go. Saw it as he wept uncontrollably when my parents lost their dog. But I'd somehow forgotten along the way.

"He is. A feeler, I mean. He always has been."

Hallie twisted her fingers together. "He needs to learn to take care of himself. To not let others' emotions overwhelm him. But he'll get there."

I loved how she saw my boy. Loved it so much that the knowledge hurt, causing my chest to crack the way ice did when it thawed. "He will."

She worried her bottom lip. "You wanted to tell me something."

Hell, she'd pulled me under again. I got lost in the Hallie spell. I cleared my throat. "Yeah, let's sit. Do you want tea or anything?"

As if that would help what I needed to tell her.

Hallie shook her head. "I had some hot chocolate earlier."

I nodded and headed for the sectional.

She sat an appropriate couple of feet from me. I wanted to close the distance, hating that it was there at all, but I stayed where I was.

"A body was found today."

Hallie sucked in a sharp breath. "The missing woman?"

I nodded. "Someone killed her."

Hallie's face went blank. It was as if someone had erased all hint of emotion from her. "Someone killed her."

She echoed the words robotically. Her gaze was locked on me, but I knew she didn't see me. She was somewhere else entirely. Her hands trembled in her lap, the force of it making her entire body shake.

I hated everything about it. It was so completely wrong.

I moved instinctually, closing the distance and taking her hands in mine. "Come back, Hallie. Come back to me."

I squeezed her fingers, trying to remind her that she wasn't alone. That I was right here.

Hallie blinked, the movement jerky and rapid, but then her eyes seemed to focus. The gray had a bit more life. "Sorry—"

"Don't apologize. That kind of news always hits hard."

"How?" Hallie whispered.

I didn't want to tell her any other details. Didn't want to fill her mind with the trauma I'd seen today. "Are you sure you want me to keep going?"

"I need you to."

I read between the lines. She didn't *want* to hear, but she had to. I understood that. "She was stabbed and strangled."

Her hands started shaking again in mine, but I held on.

"There was a mark on her hip bone."

Hallie's gray eyes flashed. "Her hip?"

I nodded. "It wasn't a brand. It was made up of a series of tiny cuts, but it looked similar…"

"To what's on me," Hallie finished. "To what was on the rest of them."

Them. The seven women who hadn't made it out. Who'd been found one at a time over the course of several months, each in a different location somewhere in the woods, clad in those disturbing white nightgowns and covered in flowers. All their bodies were littered with scars and fresh cuts, and each had a ring of bruises around their neck.

"Yes. It looks similar. It's likely a copycat. Someone who followed the case and is either using it to cover their tracks or has developed an obsession." The only way we would know for sure was if another body showed up—or didn't.

Hallie swallowed hard. "Why do you think it's a copycat?"

I heard the unasked question in her words. "The original unsub kept women for much longer."

Unshed tears welled in Hallie's eyes. "Or it could be him, and he's gotten impatient."

I hadn't let myself go there today. Hadn't let myself consider that the man who had terrorized Hallie and seven other women and girls might be back.

When the case went cold five years ago, the FBI had believed the unsub had either committed suicide, ended up in prison on an unrelated charge, or changed his hunting grounds and MO. My friend, Anson, who'd been a profiler at the time, doubted it could've been the latter. He believed the unsub was too compulsive for that.

My fingers wove through Hallie's. "Let's not go there yet. This is only one case, but I think we need to take extra precautions. I'd like you to move into the main house. You can take one of the guest rooms. Even if this is a one-off, I'll be working long hours. I want you to have a place to sleep while keeping an eye on the boys."

My voice was even as I said it. The idea of Hallie in the cabin alone was like a blowtorch to bare skin. Too much for me to bear.

She instantly began shaking her head. "I can't."

I frowned. "Why not?"

Hallie swallowed hard, averting her gaze. "I have nightmares. I could scare the boys, wake you all up."

Nightmares. Of course, she did. My mind flashed back to the first night she'd stayed here. The lights on in the cabin at five in the morning. I wondered how Hallie slept at all.

"I'll explain it to the boys. They've all had bad dreams at one point or another. Charlie still ends up in my bed every other week with one. And I've got the bruises to prove it."

Hallie's brows rose. "Bruises?"

"That kid is tiny, but he's a violent sleeper."

Her lips twitched, a little lightness entering her expression. "I don't want to disrupt things for you guys."

My thumb swept back and forth across her hand. "You won't. Things will hardly change at all."

I'd just have a walking temptation living right across the hall.

## Chapter Nineteen

*Hallie*

The sky was still dark as I pulled a sweater over my head, but a faint glow in the distance promised the sunrise. I crossed to the bed, pulling the covers up and tucking them neatly into place. Somehow, I caught a hint of Lawson when they moved, maybe in the sheets themselves—that scent of bergamot, sage, and something else.

I'd slept with the smell curling around me like a warm embrace and managed the miracle of only having one nightmare. Of a dark-eyed man hovering over me with a branding iron. But I'd caught myself before a scream left my lips.

As I pulled up the covers on the other side of the bed, I checked my watch—a few minutes before six. I couldn't stay in this room a moment longer. I needed to move and escape the feeling of my skin being too tight for my body.

My book hadn't been holding my interest, and the silence and stillness just made room for Lawson's words from yesterday to fill my mind. *Killed. Stabbed. Strangled.*

I shoved it back. Pushed it all away. I couldn't go there. Not now. Not ever.

Tossing the last pillow into place, I headed for the door. I'd make a breakfast feast. Potato pie, homemade biscuits, maybe even something sweet to finish it all up.

My slipper-clad feet were practically silent on the wood floors. I opened the door and headed into the hall, only to crash into a wall with an *oomph*.

Strong hands encircled my arms. No, not a wall. A very broad and muscular human being. Heat flared as I pulled back.

The only thing I saw was skin. Lightly tanned skin pulled taut over hard muscles. Skin that gleamed in the low light with a sheen of sweat. Sweat that somehow smelled...good. That wasn't possible.

"You okay?"

Lawson's deep and raspy voice had my gaze jerking to his face. "Sorry," I whispered, even though the boys' rooms were on the opposite side of the house.

I couldn't help but let my gaze dip again. Broad shoulders. Muscular pecs dusted with dark hair. Defined abdominals that seemed to clench at my gaze. They all pointed to a V of muscle that had my mouth going dry.

"You...were...working out?"

A low chuckle skated over my skin. "Gym in the basement, remember?"

I nodded, the motion going on for far too long.

"You're welcome to use it if you'd like. Helps with anxiety sometimes. The physical exertion."

I forced my gaze back to his. "Thanks. I haven't spent a lot of time in a gym."

Before I was taken, I'd been a runner. Every day, rain or shine. But after...I just couldn't. It had me feeling too exposed. And going to a crowded gym wasn't even an option.

Lawson's eyes tracked over my body, making everything tighten. It wasn't with the usual fear, though. It was as if his gaze lit a million tiny sparklers beneath my skin, and I could feel him *everywhere*. As if he were bringing my body back to life after years of hibernation.

"I'd be happy to work you up a routine if you want."

My breaths came quicker, but again, not in panic. "Sure. That'd be good." It was too much. Too much feeling. Sensation. Everything. "I'm going to get started on breakfast."

I tore myself out of Lawson's grasp and raced down the hall. I was sure I looked ridiculous. But I'd do whatever it took. Because Lawson Hartley was dangerous on a good day. Lawson Hartley shirtless and touching me? That was lethal.

---

I pulled into the high school pickup line, Charlie chatting away from the back seat and Drew scoping out freshmen he thought he might have a shot with.

"It's gonna be so fun," Charlie said, bouncing his feet up and down. "Like a sleepover every night."

Drew grunted. "Careful, Hallie. Charlie will end up trying to sleep with you when he gets scared, and he gave Dad a black eye once."

Charlie's face screwed up. "I didn't mean to."

The boys had taken me moving into the main house in stride. Lawson had said it would make things easier when he had to work nights. Luke was the only one who seemed to know there was more to the story. But he hadn't said anything.

I knew the reason behind it all, though. And I couldn't help but think about the woman who'd lost her life. No, the woman whose life had been *stolen*.

The brand on my hip burned as if someone were searing the flesh anew. I knew it was all in my mind, the same way I'd felt eyes on me all day when there was no one there. Even now, my shoulder blades itched. I refused to look around to try to find the source because I knew no one would be there.

"Is Dad working late again?" Drew asked, putting his socked feet up on the dash.

I turned in my seat. "He might have to. He wasn't sure yet."

"Because someone got killed?" Drew pushed.

"Someone got *killed*?" Charlie gaped.

*Crap.* I sent Drew a warning look. I did not want Charlie's nightmares on my conscience. "Your dad's working an important case," I hedged.

I guessed word spread fast around a small town. It made sense but twisted my insides just the same.

Charlie's feet began bouncing again. "Sometimes, they can't save people on their SAR trips. It's really sad."

"It is sad," I agreed. "But they do save lots of people, too."

Charlie's head bobbed in a nod. "Sooooo many. That's why I want to do it. Dad says when I'm in high school."

"Me, too, Little Man," Drew agreed. He shot me a grin. "When I save a life, it's really going to drive the babes wild."

A laugh burst out of me; I couldn't help it. But the release of the pressure, nerves, and fear felt like heaven. "It's good to have your priorities in order."

I caught sight of Luke striding toward the SUV, the girl I'd seen him with before at his side. She bit her bottom lip as they walked, glancing up at him every so often. He looked supremely pissed.

I grabbed the keys from the cupholder and slid out of the driver's seat. "Stay here, guys."

Rounding the vehicle's hood, I watched as Luke and Violet parted ways. But she glanced back at him as she slowly walked in the direction of a station wagon.

I was so focused on Luke that I didn't even notice the uniformed man to my right.

"Well, if it isn't my lucky day. Never been happier to be on high school duty," Reed greeted.

I couldn't help my jump as his gaze raked over me. The intense focus made me shiver, but I refused to make a fool of myself yet again. "Hi, Officer Hall."

He frowned. "Call me Reed, Hallie." He stressed the use of my name.

"Okay," I said. "I need to go—"

"Do you ever get time off, Hallie? Or is Law working you to the bone?"

I bristled at that. "I work normal hours."

Reed grinned. "That's good. I'd hate to have to report him for overworking his employees."

I didn't say anything in return. What was there to say?

"How about I take you to dinner tomorrow night?" he offered.

My blood went cold, but my hands started to sweat. I knew dating was part of the normalcy I was reaching for, but just thinking about going to dinner with Reed had dark spots dancing in my field of vision. "I'm not really in a place to date," I croaked.

Reed studied me for a moment. "As friends, then. A welcome to Cedar Ridge."

"Hallie," Luke said as he moved to my side. He glanced down at me, a silent question in his eyes.

I forced a smile, trying to tell him I was good. "We have to get going," I said, avoiding Reed's question.

He scowled but quickly covered it. "Sure. Good to see you, Hallie."

I simply nodded and headed away from him with Luke next to me.

"That guy's a douche," Luke muttered.

I pressed my lips together to keep my reaction in check. "Is douche a curse word? Should I be making you put a dollar in a swear jar?"

Luke just grunted.

I glanced up at him. He tried for an impassive mask, but I saw the tension in his jaw.

"Everything okay?" I asked quietly, not wanting the other kids to hear my question.

"Fine," he clipped.

My gaze flicked to Violet. "Do you want to invite your friend over? She's welcome."

A muscle ticked in Luke's cheek. "Like her parents would let her hang with me."

His words lit an ache in my chest. Below the annoyance was hurt. Rejection. I got why Luke might give another parent pause with his black attire and scowls, but they only needed to get to know him a little to see the amazing heart beneath.

I glanced at Violet, who approached a man who shared her light hair and green eyes. He was a bit imposing. His expression wasn't harsh per se, but it wasn't overly warm either. And he was quite large, tall *and* broad.

As an idea entered my mind, my heart began pounding against my ribs. I could do this. For Luke.

"Wait here a second."

I was moving before my brain could stop me, heading toward Violet and the man I assumed was her father. Each step made my heart hammer harder. By the time I reached them, my breaths were coming in pants, but I forced a smile to my lips.

"Hi, I'm Hallie," I began.

The man's expression didn't warm, and Violet gave me a curious look.

"I'm the Hartleys' nanny. I was wondering if Violet would like to come over to study. I was going to make cookies with Charlie while Drew and Luke did their homework, and Luke mentioned how helpful Violet has been with his science." I smiled at her. "Luke said you are incredibly smart."

Violet's cheeks flushed, and she turned to the man. "Can I, Dad? We have a ton of homework tonight."

The man's expression softened a fraction as he looked at his daughter. The slight gentling had me breathing a little easier.

"I don't know, pumpkin. We have family dinner, and—"

"We have family dinner *every* night," Violet argued.

The man turned to me, assessing. The attention had a pins-and-needles sensation taking root in my fingers. He extended his hand. "I'm Thomas Hooper."

The tingling intensified in my hands. I didn't. I couldn't. But when I thought about how much Luke needed a friend, I knew I had to. I forced my hand into Thomas's. "Hallie Astor."

The contact was only for a beat of three, but I nearly collapsed when Thomas released my hand.

He gave me a slightly puzzled look. "You'll be with the kids the whole time?"

I nodded, not able to get my voice working again quite yet.

"And they'll be in common areas, not a bedroom or basement?" Thomas pushed.

"*Dad,*" Violet said, her face flaming.

"We'll all be in the living room and kitchen." My voice sounded a bit raspy, but at least I'd managed words.

Thomas was silent for a moment as Violet and I waited.

"I'll pick you up at five-forty-five. I don't want you missing family dinner," he said finally.

Violet beamed, and her whole face lit up. She threw herself at him for a hug. "Thank you!"

He chuckled as he patted her back. "I expect an A on that science assignment."

She just rolled her eyes. "I always get an A."

Thomas simply grinned.

I exchanged phone numbers with him so he could call if any plans changed and to make him feel better about the whole thing, and then Violet and I started back toward the SUV.

"Thanks for talking to my dad," she said quietly. "He's really overprotective."

"I think it's nice that he cares so much," I told her honestly.

She nodded. "Most of the time. But sometimes, he's protective about things he shouldn't be."

I followed Violet's gaze toward Luke, who was staring at us as if we were a walking miracle.

I dropped my gaze to my feet, grinning at my shoes. I might not be able to fix everything for Luke, but I'd done *something*. And I'd faced a fear to do it. That knowledge made me feel stronger, braver.

But maybe it shouldn't have because there was still someone out there who had stolen a woman's life. And there was a chance it was *him*.

# Chapter Twenty

## Lawson

I pulled into a makeshift parking spot in front of my house. I had a garage if I needed one, but it felt like one extra unnecessary step on long days. And today had been one of the longest.

My temples pounded as I stared at the light streaming beyond the windows, but I didn't make any moves to shut off the engine. I needed a minute to pull it together. To try to release the dark cloud hanging over me.

My phone rang in the quiet space, and I glanced down at the cupholder. Luisa's name flashed across the screen. More darkness.

Grabbing the phone, I tapped *accept*. "Isn't it past your cutoff time?"

Luisa was religious about not working past five unless she got called to a crime scene. She said it helped keep her healthy, both mentally and physically. I could probably use some of those boundaries.

"She wouldn't leave me alone, so I needed to finish," Luisa said, and I could hear the exhaustion in her voice.

But I understood it. Cases like this dug their claws in, and this one, in particular, had me in a chokehold.

"She tell you anything?" I asked.

"Quite a bit. One piece was that she suffered."

My gut soured. I knew there was no way she hadn't, but it sickened me to know for sure.

Luisa kept talking. "Contusion to the back of the head suggests a blitz attack from behind. My guess is he incapacitated her, then tied her wrists and ankles to keep her from fighting back."

An acidic taste filled my mouth. "Sexual assault?"

I hated even asking the question, but I needed to know. The man who'd taken Hallie had assaulted the majority of his victims. Only one hadn't been violated in that way. I didn't know about Hallie. It was far too personal and invasive for me to try to find out.

"There are no signs of sexual trauma," Luisa answered. "But there were far more cuts and stab wounds than I initially saw. Her arms, legs, and torso were covered with them."

Like Hallie.

"You said there was a mixture of peri and post-mortem?"

The sound of papers shuffling came across the line. "Yes. From what I can tell, he used the initial cuts to bring her back to consciousness. She fought him to the best of her ability, which made him mad. He started stabbing instead of slicing and finally strangled her. But he was so angry. He had to get a little more rage out."

"So, he kept stabbing," I surmised.

"That's my best guess."

God, I hoped the family didn't ask for details. I'd already had to tell them they'd lost their girl in the worst way imaginable. Sometimes, next of kin thought the details would give them closure. But they never did.

"Thank you for taking care of her, Luisa."

"It was my honor." The coroner was quiet for a moment. "Get this bastard, Law. We can't have someone who's capable of this running around our county. We just got rid of one psychopath."

"I won't stop until I do."

"Good. Now, go home and hug those babies."

"Already here, just gotta make it inside."

"Glad to hear it. Talk tomorrow."

"G'night." I ended the call and shoved my phone into my pocket. As I slid out of my SUV, headlights rounded the curve of the drive.

My hand instinctively went for the holster at my side, given everything going on lately. But my Glock was locked away in the gun safe in the back of my SUV.

The station wagon pulled to a stop, the engine cut off, and a man stepped out. "Evening, Lawson."

The tension flowing through me eased, but surprise followed on its heels. "Reverend Hooper. Everything okay?"

"Just here to pick up Violet. Your new nanny invited her over for cookies and a study session."

I glanced up at the glowing house. Not just because of the lights but because of Hallie. "That's great. I really appreciate her helping Luke with his science."

Thomas nodded. "My girl's smart as a whip, and she's got a good heart to boot."

"Luke could use a friend like that."

Thomas didn't say anything to that. Likely because he wasn't thrilled about his daughter's friendship with my son. I understood, but it killed me.

I led him up the stairs and inside. "Reverend Hooper's here," I called.

The only thing that greeted me was hysterical laughter. As I moved into the space, I found my boys, Hallie, and Violet crowded around the coffee table, a board game on top of it. The only one not sitting was Charlie, who was up on the couch, doing some sort of booty-shake dance.

"I'm the Sorry! king! I'm the Sorry! King!" he half-chanted, half-sang.

Hallie's head tipped back, her blond hair cascading down as she laughed full-out. The sight stopped me dead. There was no inhibition, no reservations, no fear. Just pure joy.

As she straightened, our eyes locked. Her laughter eased, but her smile didn't. Just that tip of her lips lit a fire within me.

"We finished homework, and Charlie decided to crush us in Sorry!," she explained, getting to her feet.

I glanced at Thomas, who surveyed the scene. Something in him shifted slightly at the sight. "I was always good at Sorry!," he said.

Violet laughed as she stood. "Dad, I kicked your butt every time."

The skin around Thomas's eyes crinkled. "I think we need to get your memory checked."

Violet just shook her head and then glanced at Luke. The look she gave him, one of shy adoration, had me mentally cursing. "Thanks again for having me over, Luke. Ms. Astor."

"Hallie," she said as she moved to give the girl a quick hug. "You're welcome anytime. It's nice not to be the only girl around here."

Violet grinned at her. "Next time, we team up to destroy them at Sorry!."

Hallie laughed. "I like the way you think."

Luke got to his feet and met Thomas's gaze. "Thanks for letting Violet come over, Mr. Hooper."

Thomas's eyes flared in surprise and begrudging respect. "You're welcome, Luke. We'd be happy to have you over for dinner one of these days."

Violet's entire face lit up as she grinned at Luke.

Luke swallowed. "I'd like that, sir."

*Sir?* Maybe I really was in the *Twilight Zone*.

I watched, thunderstruck, as Violet and her dad made their way to the door.

Hallie came up to me, her arm brushing mine. "I told him that a little show of deference might get him further than he thought."

I tipped my head to meet Hallie's gaze. "You do realize that if my son starts dating the pastor's daughter, I'll have to start sleeping with a shotgun under my pillow. Drew's bad enough."

Hallie laughed, another of those completely uninhibited ones that hit me like a damn meteor. "Shouldn't have birthed such charming boys, then. It's really your fault. Their dad has the same problem."

She moved off before I had a chance to say a word, but I couldn't take my eyes off her.

---

I balanced the beer on the arm of the Adirondack chair as I stared out at the dark forest. The cold was grabbing hold and digging in, but I needed it. It was the only thing that had a prayer of clearing my head.

Dinner was done. The dishes were washed. All the kids had headed to bed. And I needed to breathe.

Hallie had made lasagna, garlic bread, and salad. The kids and I scarfed it down. And Luke had talked at dinner. About the *book* he was reading. An epic fantasy that Hallie had also read. Their conversation flew back and forth as if they were speaking another language.

I had simply sat there in awe. Because Hallie was slowly but surely giving me my family back. Charlie hadn't had a single nightmare this week. Drew was getting his homework done before I had to ask five times. And Luke was talking. There'd even been a smile or two.

I should've been happy. And I was. But I was also on edge.

The door sounded behind me, and I glanced up. The lights from inside backlit Luke's lengthening frame.

"I thought you'd already hit the hay," I said.

He shook his head. "Why did Hallie really move into the main house?"

*Shit.* I'd known by his expression this morning that he had questions. "Like I told you guys, I'm working a case. There might be some late nights. It'll be easier this way. Hallie can go to sleep instead of waiting up for me."

Even through the dark, I felt Luke's glare. "I'm not six like Charlie, Dad."

I bit back a curse. "I know you're not—"

"So, tell me the truth for once."

This was a little more of the son I'd grown used to. Combative, angry. The difference was he was speaking outright. I could respect that. But I also couldn't give him the details regarding what was going down for a million different reasons.

"That is the truth," I said, searching for my calm.

"Bullshit," Luke clipped.

"Language," I warned.

"I might be cursing, but at least it's honest. Do you ever tell us the truth about anything?"

Luke turned on his heel and stalked into the house, slamming the door behind him.

I stared at the spot where my son had been. Sure, I did what I could to protect my boys, but I always tried to level with them, as well. They knew what I did. They knew that the outcomes of my cases or searches sometimes weren't good. I just didn't go into detail.

I had no clue what Luke was talking about.

Another slam sounded from deeper in the house, and I winced. Turning back around, I stared at the trees as if they had the answers. They never did.

I took a pull from my beer. The answer wasn't in a bottle either, but at least it tasted damn good. But I'd never have more than one. I wouldn't let myself. Not when I was the sole parent.

The door squeaked as it opened, but I didn't turn around. I didn't have the energy for whoever it was. There was nothing for a few beats, and then a blanket wrapped around me.

Hallie lowered herself to the chair next to me, cocooned in a massive parka, but she still didn't speak.

I stared down at the fuzzy blanket. It was one from the couch. It seemed fluffier than it had been, smelled better, too. She'd switched something in the laundry. And just like everything else she touched, it was magically…better.

My fingers ran over the soft fabric. How long had it been since someone had taken care of me? I didn't even know. Probably because I didn't let them. My family tried. Did what I allowed them to do. But Hallie? She'd snuck under my defenses. And it was reckless as hell that I wasn't shoving her out. Because when it came to women, I hadn't made the best choices. It was better to steer clear altogether.

"Want to talk about it?" she asked finally.

I took another pull from my beer and stared out at the forest. "Luke's pissed at me."

"The slamming doors kind of gave that away."

My lips twitched. "He knows there's more to you moving in here than I told them."

Hallie pulled her legs up to her chest and wrapped her arms around them. "You want to protect him."

"Of course, I do. He's my son."

"A son that's growing up. A sensitive and empathetic one, who reads people extremely well."

My gaze flicked to Hallie in the moonlight. So damn beautiful. "So, he knows when I'm not telling him everything."

"Probably. He also noticed when a panic attack was edging in for me."

I straightened in my seat. "When did you have a panic attack? Why? Was someone bothering you?"

I fired off the questions like a barrage of bullets.

"Just someone I think recognized me from past media coverage. They got a little too close, and I got a bit wobbly."

"No one should be invading your personal space," I growled.

"Your son agreed with that point because he gave the guy a nice little shove and told him to move along."

I wanted to get Luke a new video game for that one.

Hallie hugged her knees harder. "Then he made sure I was okay. Wanted to know what had happened."

"What'd you tell him?"

"I told him that someone had taken me. Didn't give him any

details, but he figured out they'd hurt me. He's seen the scars on my arms. But I told him I got away and someone amazing found me."

A burn lit deep—agony and pleasure all wrapped into one. It didn't matter how dangerous it was. I wanted to be the person who always showed up for Hallie. "How'd he handle it?"

"Didn't ask a single other question, but he watches. When Officer Hall was talking to me at school today, Luke hurried right over like he knew I wasn't totally comfortable."

The muscle beneath my eye began to flutter. "What did that douchebag want?"

Hallie barked out a laugh. "That's what Luke called him, too. You guys are far more alike than you are different."

I was proud of Luke for being that kind of person, one who would step in for someone who might need it. But Hallie shouldn't have needed it at all.

"Has Reed been bothering you?" I gritted out.

She lifted a shoulder and then dropped it. "I wouldn't say *bothering*."

That meant he was.

"He asked me to dinner—"

"He what?" I snapped.

"He asked me to dinner. I told him I wasn't really in the headspace to date, but that wasn't entirely the truth."

I stared at Hallie through the dark. "What is the truth?"

Maybe it was the darkness that made Hallie bold. Perhaps it was the cold and the quiet. "I don't want to date him. But I want that with someone. To know what it's like to have a person want you more than their next breath. To feel safe enough to want them, too. To crave them so badly it hurts."

My breaths came quicker, shorter. "And you haven't…had that…"

It wasn't a question, but it wasn't quite a statement either.

Hallie tugged her lip between her teeth, her cheeks flushing. "I'm not a virgin or anything. I had a boyfriend before everything…

happened. But it was never like that. And when I was such a mess after, he couldn't handle it."

"Limp dick," I muttered. What a piece of shit.

Hallie choked on a laugh. "Definitely, a two-pump chump."

Oh, hell, I did not need that kind of imagery in my head. I didn't need to want to show Hallie what sex could be like. To make sure she came so hard, she saw stars. There'd be no hurry. I'd worship every inch of her skin. Taste her. Make her quiver and beg for release.

"What about you?" Hallie asked.

I took a long swallow of beer. "What about me?"

"Aspen says you don't date much."

Now that Aspen was married and happy, she would likely make it her mission to get me to settle down, too. "My life doesn't really allow it." I'd learned that lesson the hard way.

Hallie stared at me through the darkness, and I wanted to know what she saw. "It obviously did at one point."

A weight settled in my gut as my fingers tightened around the bottle. "I was young and stupid."

Hallie's eyes flared. "We've all been there. Young and stupid. If you ever want to talk about it—"

"I don't," I clipped, pushing to my feet and letting the blanket fall.

Hurt flashed in Hallie's expression, but I couldn't let it land. Couldn't let myself take it in. I had to keep moving.

Because I was a coward who couldn't face that it was so much more than being young and dumb. Because I'd believed pretty lies once. And keeping Melody in my life had nearly cost me everything.

## Chapter Twenty-One

### Hallie

I rubbed my eyes as I sat in the elementary school pickup line. They burned as if they'd been repeatedly doused in acid. I guessed going on five or so hours of sleep each night would do that.

It had been a while since I'd had to function like this, but the past two weeks had done it to me. It was a mixture of nightmares and missing Lawson. Because while he was physically present, he was a million miles away mentally.

He'd put up an invisible forcefield between us. I'd touched on a sore spot, and he'd cast me out.

Everything about it hurt—the distance and the fact that he had obviously cared deeply for the boys' mom. You didn't have the sort of reaction Lawson did if you *didn't* care.

Just the thought made me nauseous. And that made me foolish on top of it all. More than that, it made me feel naïve and silly, like a little girl whose crush had rejected her.

The doors to the school opened, and Charlie was one of the first kids out. I slid out of the SUV and met him on the other side as he launched himself at me. "I missed you!"

My heart squeezed. "I missed you, too."

He tipped his head back and grinned at me. "Are you excited to see Emmaline?"

"I can't wait. I put my hair in a braid just in case she's hungry."

Charlie laughed. "Don't worry. I'll bring extra treats."

Aspen waved at us from down the pickup line. "See you in a few?"

I nodded. "Need me to bring anything?"

She shook her head. "I brought extras home from the bakery."

I'd never argue with that.

I got Charlie settled in the car, and we headed for Aspen's house. Charlie bounced his feet up and down in a rhythm that was only his. "Do you think Dad'll get Drew a puppy for his birthday?"

I winced as I made the turn onto Aspen's street. "I don't know, buddy. A dog is a big undertaking."

"I'll help! Promise. I'll even pick up the gross poop."

A laugh bubbled out of me at that. "That's really nice of you."

Charlie grinned. "I'm really good with animals."

"You are the best."

And I wished the kids could have that puppy they wanted so much. I hadn't broached the subject with Lawson. Mostly because he hadn't seemed very open to conversation at all with me lately. It stung more than I wanted to admit.

"Maybe I'll be a vet instead of a scientist," Charlie said thoughtfully.

"That would be an amazing job. Think about all the animals you could help."

His whole face lit up at the idea, and his little legs bounced harder. "Vet and SAR searcher!"

Warmth spread through me at what a great kid Charlie was. "You make the world a better place, buddy."

Charlie stilled. "Really?"

My gaze flicked to the rearview mirror. "One hundred percent. You're kind and caring. You want to help people and animals. That's the best kind of person in my book."

His chest puffed up with pride. "Thanks, Hallie."

"I'll always tell you how awesome you are."

I pulled into a makeshift parking spot next to Aspen's station wagon and an unfamiliar SUV. Charlie was unbuckling himself before I could even get out of my seat. "Can I go? Can I?"

"Be free," I said with a laugh.

Charlie launched himself from the SUV. I followed behind him, not even coming close to keeping up. He ran ahead toward Aspen, Cady, and a taller figure. It took me a second to recognize the vet from my first day at Aspen's.

Heat hit my cheeks as I remembered my freak-out. As I walked, I worked on keeping my breaths even and steady. When I reached the group, Charlie was peppering the man with questions.

"What school do you need to be a vet? Can I come work with you now? What kinds of animals do you take care of?"

The man let out a warm laugh. "That's a lot of questions. Do you want to be a vet?"

Charlie nodded, his head bobbing so fast he was a blur. "I just decided. I'm gonna be a vet and a SAR searcher."

"Sounds like a great combo to me. I think being a vet is pretty darn fun." He glanced up at me, green eyes shining in the sunlight. "Hi, Hallie. How are you settling in?"

My hands fisted. "Hi. Everything has been really good, Dr…"

"Damien," he reminded me.

"Right. Sorry, I'm meeting a lot of new people."

He chuckled. "I bet. Even in a small town, there are endless introductions." He turned to Aspen. "I think we should put Gertie on an antibiotic and a probiotic. That should help even things out. If she doesn't improve in forty-eight hours, let me know, and I'll come back."

"Sounds good. Thanks, Damien." Aspen glanced at me. "Goat with an upset stomach."

"Poor Gertie," I mumbled. That did not sound fun for any of the parties involved.

Damien nodded, empathy filling his expression. "Usually, antibiotics help within twenty-four hours. Sometimes, even sooner. Hopefully, she'll be right as rain tomorrow."

"That's good."

"I'm going to check on Mabel and Phineas," Damien said, heading for the pasture.

"I wanna watch!" Charlie yelled.

They were already moving before I could stop them. Damien was good with the kids, explaining what he was doing while Aspen held the animals steady, and I watched from the fence line. The Hartley boys needed a pet. That was clear as day. I just needed to figure out a way to make it happen.

Damien closed his medical bag after finishing his exam and headed back toward me and the fence.

"Thank you for showing Charlie what you were doing," I said.

He waved me off. "It's nothing. It's nice to have helpers."

"If you're not careful, Charlie will start showing up at your office."

Damien chuckled. "Might not be so bad if his nanny comes with him."

I bit the inside of my cheek, unsure what to say.

He studied me for a moment. "Would you like to grab coffee sometime? I could show you around Cedar Ridge."

My stomach flipped and twisted. Damien was handsome with his dark hair and piercing green eyes, but I didn't feel that pull. The only person I'd felt that pull with was my boss. Despite the fact that he didn't want anything to do with me and was clearly still in love with his ex.

"It's totally okay if you'd rather not," Damien quickly assured me.

"I, um, can I think about it?" If I wanted normal, I needed to reach for it. That meant friends and dates and everything that went along with it.

He grinned at me. "Of course." He pulled a card from his pocket. "This has my cell at the bottom."

"Thanks."

Damien gave me another smile and headed for his SUV.

"What was that about?" Aspen asked, sidling up to me as the kids brushed Mabel.

"He, uh, asked me to get coffee."

A smile split Aspen's face. "A date with Dr. Hottie?"

I laughed. "What a nickname. I told him I needed to think about it."

Concern filled Aspen's expression. "That's fair. You want to talk it through?"

I shook my head. I wasn't ready to explain my past, and I certainly didn't want her to know I was hung up on a certain boss of mine.

"Drew wants a puppy for his birthday," I said, trying to change the subject.

Aspen leaned against the fence. "He and Charlie have been asking forever. Luke will even get in on the action sometimes. Think Law'll do it?"

I bit my lip. "I'm going to talk to him about it. I'm home for most of the day, so it seems like it might be feasible."

"Never hurts to ask, and Damien has a litter of puppies right now. Someone found a stray, and she ended up being pregnant. Gave birth a month or so ago, so I think the puppies will be ready in another couple of weeks."

The boys would be thrilled. And I wouldn't mind having a cute, cuddly thing around either. I just had to find a way to get Lawson to talk to me. *Really* talk. But that might take a miracle.

---

Drew opened the door to the house, holding it for me with a smile.

"Well, thank you. Such a gentleman."

His grin only widened. "The babes love chivalry."

I laughed, ushering Charlie inside. As we made our way into the living room, I found Luke and Lawson in the kitchen, pulling dinner together. The sight stopped me in my tracks.

They were chopping up vegetables for what looked like stir-fry. They looked so much alike, especially working in tandem. Luke glanced up. "Dad's trying to cook something new. Everyone beware."

Lawson sent him a wan look. "Have a little faith in your old man."

"Bruh," Drew started. "You only know how to make three things. Maybe Hallie should oversee this."

Lawson's gaze flicked to me. As our eyes locked, they held. His attention being on me while I felt the distance hurt.

"I can—"

I cut Lawson off before he could cast me out again. "Let me just wash my hands."

I set my coat and bag down and headed for the kitchen.

"You can take over for me," Luke offered. "I need to call Vi."

"Charlie, want to play some Xbox?" Drew asked.

Charlie grinned. "Yes!"

"Homework?" Lawson asked.

"Finished it in afternoon study hall," Drew called as he and Charlie raced for the den.

Turning on the water, I dipped my hands in the stream before soaping them up. Once I'd rinsed, I dried them on a towel and donned an apron. "What can I do?" I asked Lawson.

His throat worked as he swallowed. "Snap peas would be good."

I took Luke's place and began chopping as Lawson sliced the red pepper. He didn't say a word. Didn't ask about my day or the boys. Everything about it felt wrong. The silence was oppressive.

My mind swirled with what to say, something to close the distance.

Lawson started to hum. The tune wasn't familiar, but just the faint musical trill had my palms dampening. My breaths came quicker, turning into short pants, one tripping over the next. Black spots danced in front of my vision as memories assailed me.

The bite of a knife slashing my skin, digging into my flesh. The burn of the branding iron on my hip.

I dropped the knife. "Please, stop."

My words were barely audible, but Lawson froze.

"What? What happened?"

My hands shook violently, and I had the urge to sink to the floor. "He hummed when he hurt us."

## Chapter Twenty-Two

*Lawson*

"He hummed when he hurt us."

Hallie's words echoed in my head, pinballing off my skull with brutal pain. She'd been hurt. She'd listened to others enduring the same torture. And the monster had hummed a merry tune while doing it.

I'd been doing everything I could to keep my distance from Hallie. Not to let her into my fucked-up past. Or be tempted by everything about her. That night on the porch had been the reminder I needed that my judgment was far from stellar when it came to women, and my life wasn't built for a relationship.

But I'd been so damn focused on myself that I'd ignored what Hallie was going through. What the murdered woman had brought up for her.

Hallie's entire body trembled. Her legs shook so hard it looked like they might give out.

I moved then, unable to stand her fear and pain. My arms went around Hallie, pulling her to me and practically holding her up. She burrowed her face in my chest, her hands fisting my tee.

Her scent wrapped around me, the hint of orange blossom digging into me in a way I knew I'd never get out. But I didn't want to.

"You're safe." I whispered the words against her hair. "No one's going to hurt you."

I didn't know how long we stayed like that. Slowly, Hallie's shaking subsided, her fingers unknotted from my shirt, and she pulled back. "I'm sorry, I—"

"Don't." I brushed the hair away from her face. "The last thing you need to do is apologize."

"I freaked out. I practically climbed you like a spider monkey."

I barked out a laugh. "I don't think things went that far." My hands framed her face as though moving on their own. "You okay?"

Hallie stared up into my eyes. "I'm okay. Are you?"

There were a million questions in those gray depths, but worse, there was hurt. I'd inflicted more pain on the woman who had already endured far too much. And I wanted to gut myself for it.

"I'm sorry." My words were a rough whisper, my hands still cupping her face, thumb stroking her cheekbone. "So damn sorry."

"I crossed a line. I shouldn't have—"

"You didn't. I just—I've got some baggage." Understatement of the century.

"You still love her. I get that—"

"Fuck, no," I bit out.

Hallie jerked back, not in fear but in surprise. "You don't?"

"Not even close." I scrubbed a hand across my stubbled jaw as I leaned against the counter, my hands missing the feel of Hallie's face. "Things with her went bad. Really bad. And I've got a lot of guilt for putting my kids in that situation."

Hallie was quiet for a moment, studying me. "I'm so sorry. That's why you haven't dated much," she surmised.

I met her gaze. "I'm not sure I have it in me anymore. Too many mistakes. Too much distrust. It's easier—better—if I just focus on my kids, my job, and my family."

The words hurt as I spoke them. But they needed to be said. I'd caught some of the looks Hallie had sent my way. Ones of interest, of want. Ones I couldn't let take root and grow, no matter how badly I wanted them to.

Grief played across her face. "I understand wanting to just turn it all off. It would be so much easier."

"But you haven't," I said quietly.

"If I gave up, he would win. It would've been like he killed me, along with the others." Determination filled her expression. "He doesn't get to win."

Hallie's eyes sparked silver as she looked up into mine. "You shouldn't let her win either."

---

I handed Hallie a dish to put in the dishwasher as the kids argued about what movie to watch.

"Whose turn is it?" I yelled over the noise.

"Mine!" Charlie called.

"He wants to make us watch *Cars* for the millionth time," Luke complained.

"I can practically recite it by heart," Drew echoed.

Hallie lifted her head. "I've never seen it."

"See?" Charlie defended.

Luke groaned and flopped onto the couch.

"Your betrayal hurts," Drew grumbled.

Hallie pressed her lips together to keep from laughing. "They are brutal."

I handed her another dish. "You have no idea."

She smiled up at me, the action hitting me straight in the gut. "We need to talk about Drew's birthday," she said, her voice lowering to a whisper.

This time, I groaned. Kid parties, especially at Drew's age, required a delicate balance. His aunts, uncles, and grandparents would all want to come. But he would want his friends here and to play things cool. "I don't have the first idea where to start," I admitted.

Hallie straightened, rolling to the balls of her feet. "I can do it.

I already have some ideas for games and a cake. I could order food from his favorite place or make some, and—"

"You're hired."

She laughed, the sound wrapping around me and digging in. "Awesome. I have one more question for you."

"Shoot."

Hallie clasped her hands under her chin, looking nervous but far too hopeful. "What would you think about getting Drew a puppy?"

I blinked a few times. "A puppy?"

"He wants one so badly, and Charlie and Luke would love it, too. It would teach them responsibility and caring."

"You've seen the chaos we live in. You really think adding a puppy to the mix is a good idea?"

Hallie rolled her lips over her teeth. "Your family is busy, but I'm helping now, and I'll be here most of the day to help with the potty training and all that."

I stilled, shutting off the water and looking down at Hallie. "You want a puppy?"

Her gaze slid to the side. "I wouldn't mind having a wriggly ball of joy around." She sighed, looking back at me. "My parents never let Emerson and me have a pet growing up. They were too concerned with keeping their house pristine."

Half a dozen curses flew through my mind. "Okay. Let's look for a puppy."

Hallie's eyes went wide. "Really?"

"Really. We can try the shelter in—"

"I already found some."

The corner of my mouth kicked up. "She comes prepared."

Hallie just grinned as she pulled out her phone to show me a photo. "Damien has a litter of puppies that should be ready soon. They're some sort of mixed breed. Look how cute."

I glanced down at the photo. They were certainly adorable, even though their giant paws spoke to how big they might get. But my mind was stuck on something else. "Damien?"

My tone was far too casual.

Hallie's cheeks flushed. "Dr. Miller, the vet. I met him at Aspen's."

A sick feeling swept through my gut. "You like him."

Her eyes flared. "No. I mean, yes. I mean, he's nice. Good with the animals and Cady and Charlie. He asked me to get coffee."

That muscle beneath my eye began to flutter. "You going?"

Hallie twisted her fingers together. "I told him I needed to think about it."

Think about it. She might not be ready now, but she would be someday. And I'd have to watch her leave for dates. Come home from them. Or worse, not come home at all. I gripped the edge of the counter as the torturous images filled my head.

"Dad! Hallie! Come on!" Charlie called. "It's starting."

Hallie shut the dishwasher and headed for the living room.

And I just watched her go, hating every second of her walking away.

## Chapter Twenty-Three

### Hallie

I was floating in a sea of warmth. Everything about it was wonderful. Like a cocoon of safety, comfort, and heat. I let out a moan, trying to burrow deeper.

An arm tightened around me, and I froze. *An arm?* My eyes flew open. The living room filled my vision, credits rolling on the screen. But Charlie, Drew, and Luke were nowhere in sight.

I shifted slightly and realized why I was so warm and comfy. I was lying on Lawson. Practically using him as a mattress and blanket all in one.

Slowly, I pulled back, meeting his gaze. "I'm so sorry."

He chuckled. "Don't worry about it. You're cute when you sleep. You burrow like a kitten."

I flushed. "I practically accosted you."

A grin spread across Lawson's face. "I've taken self-defense. I could've extricated myself if I wanted."

*What the hell did that mean?* I knew what I wanted it to mean. What his hands on my face had meant in the kitchen. But I feared it was simple kindness and nothing more. He'd told me straight out that he wasn't equipped for relationships. Only I knew there wasn't anyone else I'd rather try to find normal with.

Lawson's thumb glided up and down my arm, sending pleasant shivers coursing through me. "Good nap?"

"I don't think I've slept that deeply in years." Not since I took pills to knock me out in the hopes of getting a single decent night's sleep.

He frowned. "Have you been having nightmares?"

I shifted in place, but it only brought me closer to Lawson. Too close. That scent of sage and bergamot wrapped around me.

Lawson lifted his hand, sliding it along my jaw until his fingers tangled in my hair. He tipped my head back, so I was forced to meet his gaze. "Talk to me, Hallie."

"They've been worse since the missing woman was found," I admitted.

A curse slipped out, almost under his breath. "I'm so sorry."

"It's not your fault. It's just the way things are."

But I could see from the look on Lawson's face that he was taking my nightmares on the way he took on everything else. As if it were his personal responsibility to fix it.

I shifted my hand, placing it on his chest. His heart beat in a steady rhythm through the muscle. "Don't take this on."

Lawson's jaw clenched. "I hate the idea of you being scared and hurting."

My breaths came quicker, but not because of anxiety. Because Lawson cared. Because he was so close, it would only take the smallest of movements to close the distance between us. To finally know what he tasted like.

"I'm not scared now," I whispered.

It was an invitation and a challenge.

Lawson's gaze dropped to my mouth, his eyes tracing my lips. He moved the slightest bit, coming closer, so close I could practically feel the heat of his mouth and taste the promise of him.

"Daaaaaaad! I can't find my toothpaste," Charlie yelled.

Lawson dropped his hold on me as if he'd been burned. He quickly stood, clearing his throat. "Better go find that before we have cavities on our hands."

Disappointment coursed through me, my body still tingling from his touch. "Go on. I'll clean this up."

I got to my feet as soon as Lawson disappeared. I tidied the living room and turned off the TV, but the whole time, I did it imagining what it would be like to kiss Lawson Hartley.

---

Laughter came from down the hall as I pulled a baggy sweatshirt over my leggings. The sun was streaming through the window, bright and strong. I'd tossed and turned all night, my dreams alternating between ones that had me fighting not to scream and others that left a throbbing pressure pulsing between my legs.

The latter were always of Lawson. His face. His hands. His tongue.

I buried my face in my hands. "Get it together, Hallie."

Pulling my hair into a topknot, I blew out a breath and headed toward the sound of chaos.

"*Daaaaaad*, come on," Charlie whined.

"We're waiting for Hallie so she can have first pick," Lawson chastised.

"This is cruel and unusual punishment, bruh. Isn't that against the law?" Drew asked.

I rounded the corner to find all four Hartleys converged on the kitchen island, hovering over two bakery boxes.

"We can't have anyone going to prison," I murmured.

Drew raised his hands to the sky. "Hallelujah! Please come pick a donut so we can eat."

Luke stifled a chuckle. "Drew might never forgive you for having to smell donuts a full fifteen minutes before he could eat them."

"It's brutal," Drew shot back.

"You didn't have to wait for me." I glanced at Lawson and immediately regretted the move as images from my dreams filled my mind.

Lawson moved in closer to me so his heat seeped into my side. "Wanted you to have first pick."

Charlie opened one box and then the second. "The chocolate sprinkles are my favorite!"

My eyes went wide. There had to be almost two dozen donuts in various shapes, sizes, and flavors. "Who is going to eat all of these?"

"These'll be gone in probably an hour or two tops," Luke informed me.

"Pick one! Pick one!" Charlie chanted.

Lawson leaned in closer, his breath ghosting over my ear. "What flavor do you want?"

A shiver coursed through me, one I never wanted to end.

I scanned the options and settled on a pink frosted donut with rainbow sprinkles. Plucking it from the box, I straightened. "This one."

"How'd I know you'd be strawberry?" Lawson asked with a grin.

"Good guesser," I mumbled, nearly dropping my donut.

"Me next! Me!" Charlie yelled.

Lawson chuckled. "Pick a number between one and ten but don't say it," he instructed me.

"Okay…"

Drew immediately shouted, "Five!"

"Nine!" Charlie cheered.

Luke grinned. "I'm going with…two."

"It was three," I admitted.

"Aw, man!" Charlie complained.

Luke snatched up a Boston cream. Then Drew went for double chocolate. And Charlie got his chocolate sprinkles.

I turned to Lawson, who wasn't touching me but was still closer than he normally was. "What about you?"

He reached in and snagged a bar with golden frosting. "Butterscotch all the way."

"Gross," Drew muttered.

"Your tastebuds are malfunctioning," Lawson shot back.

"I don't think I've ever had a butterscotch donut," I admitted.

Donuts hadn't exactly been a staple around the Astor home. French pastries, sure. Donuts, never.

Lawson held it out to me. "Try a bite."

I sucked in a breath as my eyes locked with his. I leaned forward, taking a small bite of the confection. Sweet and almost caramelly flavors played on my tongue. "That is delicious."

Lawson's gaze heated. "Told you." And then he took a bite right from where I had eaten.

My stomach dipped and rolled as heat pooled low. I forced my gaze away and back to my donut but didn't miss the look Luke gave me and his father. Crud.

A phone rang, and Lawson pulled his cell from his pocket. "Hartley."

He quickly straightened, setting his donut on the counter. "When?"

There was another pause. "Okay. Call in everyone else and get Roan, too. I want word getting out to Fish and Wildlife in case they spot something. I'll be at the station in fifteen."

He tapped the screen, ending the call.

"You gotta work?" Charlie asked, sounding bummed.

Lawson ruffled his hair. "Sorry about that, bud. I'm still going to try to make dinner at Grandma and Grandpa's."

"I can take them and drop them off if you're late," I offered.

"You sure you're okay watching them on your day off? I could call Grae and see if she and Caden can come over."

I shook my head. "I'm fine. I don't have any plans today. We'll figure out something fun to do."

Something passed over Lawson's eyes. "Stick close to the house or in town."

My stomach dropped. "Okay."

Lawson moved then, grabbing his wallet and keys. I followed him to the door, pitching my voice low. "What happened?"

His deep blue eyes locked with mine. "Another woman's missing."

## Chapter Twenty-Four

*Lawson*

"FILL ME IN," I CLIPPED THE SECOND I HIT THE DEPUTIES' desks.

"Harriet Johnson called thirty minutes ago," Clint began, reading from a notepad. "Thought it was weird her daughter, Adrienne, wasn't up yet since she's an early riser. Knocked on her bedroom door, no answer. Opened it, and the room's empty, bed hasn't been slept in."

Nash's expression was hard as he leaned back in his chair. "Adrienne's home from college for winter break and picked up some shifts at Dockside. She usually walks to and from since they live close, but she worked the late shift last night."

I cursed, an ominous feeling sweeping over me.

Reed shifted in his chair. "She probably went out partying with friends after work. That's what I'd be doing at her age. Probably just forgot to text her mom that she was staying with a friend."

I stared at the man, understanding why he'd never made it past officer rank in all his years on the job. Reed had moved to Cedar Ridge from Idaho about six years ago and was more of a headache than any help.

"Do you really think we should *assume* that a young woman

around the same age as our murder vic just went to hang out with friends and forgot to tell her mom?" My voice vibrated with fury.

Reed grimaced. "I'm just saying she might be fine."

"And I hope to God she is, but we are going to get all of our asses out to look for her," I snapped.

Daniels sent his partner a quelling look. "Hope for the best but prepare for the worst, right?" He turned to Nash. "No one saw her on the way home? Getting into a vehicle? Anything?"

Nash shook his head. "No one from that last shift saw her after she headed out. So far, no one that lives on her route has either."

Daniels drummed his fingers on his desk. "God, I hope this sicko doesn't have her."

"Law." Roan's voice cut in from behind me.

I turned, my back molars grinding. "Thanks for coming in."

"Of course. You got a photo I can send to our officers?" he asked. While Fish and Wildlife mostly dealt with poachers and wildlife issues, it wouldn't hurt to have them out looking.

Nash stood. "I pulled a recent one from social media. Texting it to you now. And I have Wren putting together some flyers."

"Thanks, man."

Nash clamped a hand on my shoulder and squeezed. "We're gonna find her."

We would. I just hoped we weren't too late.

---

Worry and unease gnawed at my gut as I tromped up the steps to my front door. We'd combed through downtown and the surrounding areas and found only one sign of Adrienne. Her cell phone, cast alongside the road, presumably where she'd been walking home.

No twenty-one-year-old just casually tossed their cell onto the ground. And there'd been marks in the dirt that could've indicated a scuffle. Nothing good.

We'd pulled every available officer in to search, and local

volunteers had gotten to work handing out flyers and talking to their neighbors. Nothing.

At this point, I knew something bad had happened. It felt beyond wrong to go home. But darkness had closed in, and there was nothing else we could do. The officers patrolling tonight were on alert, and we'd all be back at it first thing tomorrow.

Sliding my key into the door, I turned the lock. Charlie's and Drew's laughter met my ears as I stepped inside. I quickly plugged in the alarm code and locked the door behind me.

The boys were moving around the living room, playing battle with what looked like pool noodles, blissfully unaware of the darkness swirling just outside their door. My gaze kept moving, searching.

I found Luke and Hallie sitting at the dining room table, working on a puzzle. Hallie's hair was piled in a bun atop her head, and my fingers itched to pull it loose. To watch the blond locks tumble down her back.

Luke looked up at my approach, concern lighting his features. He pitched his voice low. "Did you find her?"

My brows lifted.

"Vi told me. Her dad's helping organize the civilian search."

Of course. Normally, I would've made the connection much sooner, but I was exhausted. "We haven't found her yet."

Hallie's face paled as her fingers curled around a puzzle piece. "Poor girl," she whispered.

I moved then, not caring if my son was sitting right next to her. My fingers curled around her shoulder, squeezing and kneading. A silent promise that I was there. That she was safe.

"Can I do anything, Dad?" Luke asked.

I glanced at my son. "I'll show you her photo. You can keep an eye out. And you can get your brothers ready to head to your grandparents' for dinner."

Luke sent a look in Hallie's direction. "Maybe we should just stay home tonight."

God, I loved my boy. I'd forgotten he could be this way.

Protective. Always looking out for his people. "We're going. All of us. Hallie, too."

Hallie's body jerked at that. "I don't know—"

"Mom and Dad have been dying to meet you, and this will take all our minds off what's going on."

She bit the corner of her lip but nodded. The fact that she'd given in so easily meant she was scared to be here alone. Damn, I hated that.

Hallie pushed to her feet. "I need to freshen up. I'll be quick."

I watched as she headed for her bedroom, long, leggings-clad legs carrying her down the hall.

"She's tweaked," Luke said, bringing my focus back to him. "She covers it pretty well, but I can tell. I don't think she should be here alone when it's dark."

I nodded. "Thanks for looking out for her. Hallie's lucky to have you."

Luke shifted uncomfortably in his chair and then stood. "Gotta get my jacket."

I guessed we weren't at the praise part of our reconnection. "Hey, warriors, grab your stuff for dinner."

Charlie's head popped up. "Can we bring our lightsabers?"

I had to fight a chuckle. I guessed that was what the pool noodles were. "Let's leave the weapons at home."

"Aw, man," Charlie complained.

"You know your grandparents have approximately eighty-two million toys for you to play with at their house, right?"

My parents spoiled the boys. I didn't mind because it seemed like a grandparent's right.

Drew dropped his noodle onto the couch. "What's for dinner?"

"Not sure. We're gonna have to go over and find out."

Drew gave me a chin lift that made him look ten years older. "I could eat."

I couldn't hold in my chuckle this time. I clamped a hand on his shoulder. "Then let's go. Get your coats. It's freezing outside."

Footsteps sounded in the hall, and I looked up, suddenly

wishing I hadn't. I would've done anything to erase the image that would now be forever implanted in my brain.

Hallie walked toward us wearing jeans that hugged every curve and dipped into leather riding boots, a soft pink sweater molded to her body like a second skin, giving me a peek of the swells beneath—swells I wanted to trace with my tongue.

Her hair cascaded around her in soft waves from being tied up in a bun all day. Her gray eyes were deeper somehow, lined with kohl and pulling me in. And her lips... They were coated in some sort of gloss that I wanted to lick off.

I was fucked.

"You look so pretty, Hallie! Like a princess," Charlie said in wonder.

She flushed but smiled. "Thank you, Charlie. That's very kind."

Drew grinned at her. "Total bae status."

Luke hit him upside the head.

"Bruh," Drew clipped, whirling on him. "That was a compliment."

"Don't make her feel uncomfortable," Luke shot back.

"He didn't," Hallie hurried to assure them. "I know that's Drew-speak for the ultimate compliment."

Drew's chest puffed up. "See? Hallie gets me."

Her orange-blossom scent wrapped around me, stronger than before. "Let's go."

My voice was gruff, a few tones deeper than usual as I motioned everyone toward the door.

The kids led the way, but Hallie was close behind them. I let her get a ways ahead of me. Establishing distance so I didn't have to be tempted by her scent. But that got shot to hell when we got into the SUV. I was half-tempted to roll down the window.

I tried to focus on Charlie's chatter about seeing Cady, their plans for next week, and the animals at Aspen's.

Hallie was quiet on the drive, but I was grateful. The sound of her voice on top of her scent would've been too much.

As we pulled up to the gate, I rolled down my window and sucked in a deep breath, trying to wash her out of me. It was no use.

I punched in a code, and the gate opened.

As we headed up the drive, my childhood home came into view. Built into the mountainside, the blend of stone, wood, and glass felt as if the mountain itself had birthed the house.

"It's beautiful," Hallie murmured.

"It was a great place to grow up," I admitted.

A smile played on her lips as I parked next to the other vehicles. "I'm glad you had that."

But she hadn't. I'd figured that much.

"We're here!" Charlie yelled, unbuckling his booster seat and jumping out of the SUV.

The other two boys followed him.

Hallie met me around the front of the vehicle. "You're sure it's okay that I'm here?"

I glanced over at her as she pulled her coat tighter. So damn beautiful. "They'd be pissed if I didn't bring you. And Aspen will be here, too. If it gets to be too much, just let me know."

She bit the corner of her lip and nodded.

Luke waited for us at the bottom of the steps, taking Hallie's other side. The door above opened, and Grae's tiny form filled it. "My favorite boys."

Charlie's arms flew around her instantly. "Aunt G!"

You could just see a hint of a bump on her stomach if you looked closely enough. The thought had my chest squeezing. I was happy for her but scared as hell that her type 1 diabetes might create complications for her pregnancy.

She ruffled Drew's hair. "How's my heartbreaker?"

"Bruh, not the hair."

Grae just grinned. "Get inside."

Her smile widened as she took us. "Hallie! I'm so glad you came. Aspen's been saying how amazing you are, and I've been more than a little jealous that she snagged you as a friend before I could."

Hallie smiled back, but the action wavered a bit. "It's so nice to meet you. Grae, right?"

She nodded. "I hope these hooligans haven't been too hard on you."

"Only when we're playing Sorry!."

Grae laughed. "Charlie?"

Hallie's smile turned more genuine. "He's a shark."

"Completely." Grae glanced at Luke. "Want to go a round on the Xbox?"

"Maybe a little later," he mumbled.

Grae's eyes flared at that. Luke always opted for video games over family time. But now, he followed us inside and stuck close as we hung up our coats.

Loud voices beckoned from the living room. We made our way deeper into the house, Luke and I sticking close to Hallie.

"Finally!" Nash called from the couch. "I swore he was lying about your existence, Hallie."

Maddie's dark hair shifted around her as she smacked her fiancé. "Don't put her on the spot." She glanced at Hallie and smiled. "Excuse Nash. He never did learn his manners, no matter how hard Kerry tried. I'm Maddie."

Hallie gave a little wave.

Charlie raced back over to us, squeezing in and taking her hand. "This is my Hallie. She's the bestest. She makes cookies and plays games and she's real good at the voices with bedtime stories."

Holt grinned from his spot next to Wren on the other couch. "Sounds like a winning combination to me. Hi, Hallie. I'm Holt, and this is my fiancée, Wren."

Wren smiled widely. "I'd get up, but this basketball is making it a little hard these days."

Caden's lips twitched as he glanced at Grae. "I can't wait until you're basketball status, Gigi."

Grae rolled her eyes. "That charmer is my fiancé, Caden."

"Don't forget baby daddy," he cut in.

Hallie's smile came more easily now. "Nice to meet you all."

Aspen waved from the kitchen where she worked with Roan. "Welcome to mayhem."

My mom crossed the space, my father at her side. "It's so nice to meet you, Hallie. I'm Kerry, and this is my husband, Nathan. I'm so glad you could come."

"Pleasure to meet you, Hallie," my dad said, extending his hand.

Luke moved before I could, stepping in to give my dad a hug and block the shake. "Hi, Grandpa."

Dad's eyes went wide as he thumped Luke on the back. "It's good to see you, too."

My mom's gaze tracked from the two of them to Hallie and back.

"Thank you so much for having me. I would've brought something, but—"

"But let me guess, my boy told you two seconds before you were leaving that your attendance was requested?"

I winced, rubbing the back of my neck.

Mom just shook her head. "You'll never learn."

Aspen appeared then, putting an arm around Hallie's waist. "Want to help me in the kitchen? We have drinks."

Relief washed over Hallie's face. "I'd love to."

"I'm helping, too," Charlie hurried to say.

"Me, too," Luke grunted.

Aspen led them all into the kitchen, and I watched Hallie relax a fraction.

My mom hooked her arm through mine. "And you're coming with me."

"I should stay and—"

"Five minutes," she promised.

I knew it would take less time to just go with the woman and let her say whatever she needed to, so I nodded.

Mom guided me down the hall toward Dad's office. "The boys are protective of her."

"She's good with them. They've bonded," I explained as we stepped inside.

My mom closed the door behind us. "You're protective of her, too."

My spine stiffened. "Mom..."

"And she's stunning."

"Yeah, and a good thirteen years younger than me, not to mention my employee."

I said the words as a reminder to myself as much as to her.

Mom waved me off. "Your father and I have a few years between us."

"Don't."

The single word was low but firm.

Pain flashed across my mother's face. "Lawson."

"I can't go there." Pain sliced through my chest.

She moved in closer, lifting a hand to my cheek. "When are you going to stop punishing yourself?"

"I'm not punishing—"

"You are. Just because you had a partner who made poor choices doesn't mean you don't deserve to be happy."

I jerked out of her hold. "I don't want to talk about it, Mom. I'm fine. We're good. Hallie makes our lives easier, but I'm not interested in her like that."

*Lies, lies, lies.* So many lies I was starting to smell the bullshit on my breath. But it was the only thing that my mom would understand because she was wrong. I didn't deserve happiness. Not when my choices before had almost ruined us all.

# Chapter Twenty-Five

## Hallie

"I wanna try some of these cookies," Nash said with a serious expression.

I fought a laugh as I nodded. "Come by anytime. Or I'll have Lawson bring some to the station."

It had become clear that Nash was highly food motivated, and the moment Charlie had gone on and on about my chocolate chip cookies, Nash had been determined to get some.

"Lawson'll eat them before they even make it halfway," Nash complained.

Maddie pinched his side. "He will not. You're the competitive eater in this bunch. Heck, you've been jealous of a six-year-old for half the night."

Nash frowned down at her. "He said they're ooey-gooey *and* crunchy. That combo shouldn't be possible."

Maddie rolled her eyes. "I'm so sorry, Hallie. You'll never get rid of him now."

Holt strode up, his arm around Wren. "I wouldn't mind trying some either."

Nash glared at his brother. "Stay away from my cookies."

"Dear God," Wren muttered. "It's going to be a blood bath."

I laughed then. Not one of my polite ones, a real one. Because the Hartley family was hilarious, warm, and welcoming. You could feel how much they loved one another, even when they were giving each other a hard time. After the first thirty minutes, I'd eased into simply being around them. The effortless friendship I'd seen between Grae, Wren, and Maddie at The Brew my first day in Cedar Ridge spread through the entire group. And a part of me wondered if I could find a place among it, even if it wasn't at Lawson's side.

Kerry moved in and gave me a quick squeeze. "Please come next week."

"Mom," Lawson warned.

But she just waved him off. "Don't listen to the big bad wolf grumbling over there. Please, come. And bring those chocolate chip cookies."

"Thank you for having me," I told her noncommittally as I glanced at Lawson.

His face was a stony mask. He'd been tense through dinner, but I hadn't been able to tell if it was the case or something else.

The boys said their goodbyes, and we piled into the SUV. The drive home was only a stream of Charlie talk, while Lawson didn't say a word.

The second we got home, Lawson charged up the stairs, muttering something about getting in a workout.

I glanced at Luke as we made our way up the steps. His jaw clenched. "He gets like this sometimes."

What did that mean?

It was already late, so I got Charlie moving toward bed and made sure Drew and Luke didn't need anything. Once Charlie's light was out, I headed back into the living area. It was empty, but I could hear the faint strains of music from the basement below.

Steeling myself, I opened the door to head down. The music got louder as I went, but it wasn't until I opened the second door that it hit me full bore. I didn't recognize the song, but it was a heavy rock beat with angry guitar riffs.

When the gym came into view, I stopped dead.

Lawson sent punch after punch into a heavy bag with nothing but wrapped hands. The punching bag swung back and forth violently with each connection. His bare torso already glistened with sweat. His muscles bunched and flexed, making my mouth go dry.

But as I watched him move, I saw the anger beneath each motion. The rage. Normally, that kind of emotion would've sent me running back up the stairs. But Lawson didn't scare me. He never would.

Lawson moved around the heavy bag with blow after blow until I came into his line of sight. He jerked upright, chest heaving. He simply stared at me for a long moment, then stalked toward me.

I swallowed hard but stayed exactly where I was.

He hit a button on the wall, and the rock music cut off. "Something wrong?"

The anger was still humming there, below the surface.

"Yes."

Lawson's deep blue eyes went on alert. "What's going on?"

I stared at him for a moment. "Something's eating you alive."

That muscle beneath Lawson's eye fluttered. "You don't have to worry about me. I'm not in your job description."

It was a blow intended to hurt, but I wouldn't let it stop me. I knew how he operated now. When you got too close to a vulnerability for him, Lawson shoved you back. But I wouldn't let him do that this time.

"You saw me at my worst possible moment. Sliced to hell. Freezing to death. Scared out of my mind."

The muscle fluttered more wildly now.

"Trust me to hold whatever's tearing you up."

Lawson didn't say a word, but his eyes never left mine.

"Please, Blue."

He sucked in a breath at the name I'd only called him two other times.

He moved in closer. So close I could smell the sweat clinging to him. "I'm trying to keep my distance, Hallie. For both our sakes."

My heart hammered against my ribs. "What if I don't want you to keep your distance?"

Lawson's jaw clenched in a vicious squeeze, but his hand lifted. His knuckles skimmed across my cheek. "I don't deserve to be close to you. To touch this skin."

Blood roared in my ears. "Why?"

His hand dropped away. "I don't love my ex-wife."

My head spun at the turn of conversation.

"Thought I did once. Turned out I was just an early twenties walking hormone being led around by my dick."

I stayed quiet. Watching. Waiting. Hoping he would explain.

"She was beautiful. So damned fun. Always looking for the next adventure. The next high." Lawson shook his head. "Not drugs, but I guess that didn't matter. It was a high all the same. Parties, daredevil stunts, trips at the drop of a hat. I think growing up in a small town made her feel stifled, trapped."

He let out a long breath. "When Melody got pregnant, we weren't expecting it. Hell, we hadn't even talked about marriage. We were still young, barely twenty-two. But I wanted to do the right thing and have our kid grow up in a real family. So, I asked her to marry me."

Of course, he had. Lawson would always do whatever he could to give his kids the best life possible. Even if it meant him losing out on that once-in-a-lifetime type of love.

"Melody wasn't sure she wanted to get married, but I convinced her. She settled down for a bit once Luke was born, and we had Drew, too. She wanted me to quit my job so we could use my trust fund to travel the world. Wanted us to take off and leave the kids with my parents every weekend."

"But that's not you," I whispered.

"No. I like work, purpose. I like my life here, and I love my family." He squeezed the back of his neck. "When I wouldn't go, she started taking off alone. Just weekends at first, then longer. She said that I worked too much, and she felt like a single parent."

My stomach twisted. Lawson would've taken that accusation

like a punch to the gut. "I know you, Lawson. I know you would never put your job before your family. But that doesn't mean your career isn't important."

His jaw worked back and forth. "It was an escape. From her. From a marriage I knew in my gut didn't work."

"Which means you're human."

He shook his head. "It means I failed. I finally suggested couples therapy and thought it had worked. Things seemed to get better. We were never close like we'd been when we were young, but I thought things were working."

Lawson laughed, but it was an ugly sound. "Turned out she was racking up tens of thousands of dollars of credit card debt and having affairs with guys she met on a dating app."

"Lawson," I croaked.

His hands fisted and flexed. "It wasn't that I even thought I loved her. I'd realized that what we had was young infatuation. But I wanted my boys to have a mom. What I gave them was a selfish, reckless imitation of one."

My eyes flared as I watched Lawson's breathing go ragged.

"I worked longer shifts then. A lot of nights because I was lower in the ranks. Melody hid it well. I didn't realize what she was doing."

That nausea flared again as panic set in.

"I got a call from an unknown number. It was Luke. Ten years old and scared out of his mind. Drew was crying in the background. Charlie, only a few months old, was bawling uncontrollably."

My hands fisted, fingernails digging into my palms.

"That bitch took them to a party with one of the guys she was seeing and shoved them in a room. It was loud as hell, and they were so damned scared. Had no adult watching them. And that fear turned to terror when they heard gunshots."

"Lawson…"

His eyes reddened, tears gathering there. "Luke snuck out of the bedroom and found a cell phone. I stayed on the line with my boy while I had the number traced. Got a location, and we rode out. Turned out the guy Melody was fucking was a well-known dealer in the area. Someone had shown up thinking they could rob him. Two people were killed. Three more wounded."

I wanted to strangle the woman. I couldn't begin to imagine how Lawson had felt.

"Got up to the room, and my boys were shaking and sobbing. Drew had wet his pants, too scared to find a bathroom. Charlie's diaper was full and soiled. He hadn't been fed and was so dehydrated he needed an IV. Luke didn't talk for a week."

Tears filled my eyes, spilling over and tracking down my cheeks.

"I don't love my ex-wife. I hate her with everything in me. The only person I hate more is me, for not seeing her for who she truly was."

I didn't think. I just moved, launching myself at Lawson and wrapping my arms around him. I gripped him as hard as I could, trying to comfort the man who took everything on his shoulders. But Lawson didn't move at all.

## Chapter Twenty-Six

### Lawson

My breaths came in ragged pants as Hallie's arms wound around me, her slight form pressed against me, her arms far stronger than they looked.

"It wasn't your fault, Lawson."

Those words on her lips, my name on her tongue were almost too much to bear. "Hallie," I croaked.

"It wasn't. You were trying to make it work, to give your boys a family. You didn't know."

"I knew that Melody was flighty, that she'd take off for a weekend at the drop of a hat," I argued.

Hallie pulled back, but her hands held my arms tightly. "Did she ever leave your children without appropriate supervision?"

"No. She'd drop them at my parents' or wait until I was home—"

"See?" she pressed.

"I should've known."

Hallie scowled at me. "Are you a psychic and didn't tell me?"

I wanted to laugh but couldn't get my mouth to obey. "Not a psychic."

"Then it wasn't your fault."

Any hint of humor slid away as I stared down into Hallie's face.

"I could've lost them. One of those bullets could've gone through the ceiling or they could've come out of that room and been caught in the crossfire."

Hallie gripped my arms tighter. "And I can't imagine how terrifying that was. But you have to stop punishing yourself for something that isn't yours to atone for."

"You sound like my mom."

Hallie's brows rose at that.

"She said something similar tonight," I explained.

Hallie's hold on me released. "And that set you off."

"Maybe..." I admitted.

Her finger skated across my wrap-covered knuckles. "And this is how you process."

"It's the only thing that seems to keep the demons at bay." The self-hatred.

Hallie's expression softened. "You hurt yourself because you think you deserve it."

"I'm not *hurting* myself."

Her fingers tugged the end of the wrap free and began unwinding. The fabric dropped to the floor. She moved to the other hand and did the same thing, then lifted it. There were tiny tears in the skin along my knuckles.

I didn't usually hit hard enough to bleed, but tonight had been especially bad.

Hallie lifted my hand and pressed her lips to my knuckles.

I sucked in a sharp breath. "Hallie..."

Her eyes shifted to mine. So innocent and trusting.

"I can't," I rasped. "It doesn't matter how much I want to."

"But you do want to?" There was hope in that voice. So much of it.

And I found that I couldn't extinguish it. I could've lied and told her I wasn't attracted to her, but that would've hurt her, and I couldn't stand to cause Hallie any more pain.

"Hallie, you're the most stunning woman I've ever laid eyes on.

Your kindness and empathy only make you more beautiful. But your bravery? It steals my breath."

Her eyes turned molten silver. She stretched up onto her tiptoes, her mouth getting closer and closer to mine. Blood roared in my ears as my breath caught. Then she stopped.

I realized why. She was giving me the choice. She knew far too much about choices being ripped away. She'd never do that to me, even though I could've stopped her with one single step.

Hallie hovered there, just shy of my mouth, her scent wrapping around me. It was too much. She'd been pulling me in since the moment she stepped out of her car. Pulling me under. And I wanted to drown in her taste.

I closed the last of the distance and took her mouth. Not forcefully, but not all that gentle either. The need was too great.

Hallie's lips parted, welcoming me in and letting me take.

My tongue stroked hers, teasing, toying. And God, her taste. It was unlike anything I'd ever experienced. I never wanted any other flavor.

My arms encircled her, pulling her into me, and she let out a tiny moan that had my dick hardening. My hand slid to her ass, and she stiffened slightly.

The tension had me yanking myself out of the haze of lust.

Hallie's gaze was wide, her fingers going to her lips. "That was…"

"I'm sorry. I shouldn't have pushed."

She looked confused.

"You tensed when my hand moved."

Hallie bit her lip. "I liked it."

I studied her for a moment. "But it made you nervous."

She was quiet for a moment and then nodded. "He never touched me. Not like that. He wanted us to submit first. To say we'd *marry* him."

Rage flared somewhere deep. That monster might not have assaulted Hallie in that way, but the threat was there. Anything sexual had to be confusing as hell for her. "I'm so damned sorry."

Hallie's eyes flashed. "I don't want anyone to be sorry. I want to be normal. I want to know what it's like to turn someone on. I want to feel sexy in my body and powerful. I want to know what it feels like to break apart."

"Hallie," I began.

"I don't want your pity," she spat.

"The last thing I feel for you is pity. Take a look at my goddamned shorts."

Her gaze dipped, and her mouth fell open in an adorable O-shape. "Oh."

"Yeah. So, I'd say you can cross turning someone on off your list."

The smile that split her face socked me right in the gut. "I can?"

"You can." I moved in closer, pulling her into my arms. "I don't know the *right* way to go about this. Hell, I'm your boss—"

"And my friend," Hallie cut me off.

"And my friend. But this is complicated, and I don't ever want to push. I think you need to be in the driver's seat. You need to be in control."

Hallie nibbled the corner of her lip. "Okay." Her gaze lifted to mine. "What do you want?"

I stared down at her, knowing I would likely go to hell for admitting it, for tasting her just once. "I want you, Hallie. But I'm the last thing you need."

## Chapter Twenty-Seven

### Hallie

CHAOS REIGNED IN THE KITCHEN AS THE BOYS PRACTICALLY tripped over each other to cram breakfast into their mouths and get ready for school. I hurried to pick up plates and stack them in the sink, but my gaze kept going to Lawson. The way his uniform shirt pulled taut over broad shoulders, how his forearms flexed as he washed a plate.

I could still feel his lips on mine. Could still feel his heat and taste his flavor on my tongue. But Lawson hadn't said a word about the kiss.

He'd left me with that cryptic warning and headed up the basement steps. Meanwhile, I'd basically been a puddle on the floor.

But knowing that I affected him? It made me feel powerful. Helped me regain a little of what I'd lost.

I just wished it seemed like that kiss haunted Lawson a fraction as much as it haunted me.

I understood. He had more important things on his mind. A missing woman. A killer to find. Just the thought had me fighting a shudder.

Lawson had worked for more than twelve hours the day before, and he'd be back at it today. And I knew he'd feel every dead end like a weight on his shoulders. God, I hoped they found whoever had done this. Prayed they located Adrienne Johnson safe and unharmed. It was a naïve hope, but I'd hold to it anyway.

"We need to go, guys, or you're all going to be late," I warned, turning to Lawson. "Don't worry about those. I'll get them once I'm home."

He stilled, his blue eyes finding mine. "Be careful. I want you parking in the garage up here and not getting out of the car until the door is closed."

My mouth went dry, but I nodded. "I'll be careful."

"Call me if anything tweaks you," Lawson ordered.

I nodded, studying him. "Are you okay?"

His jaw clenched, somehow illuminating the dark circles under his eyes. "I'll be okay once we find Adrienne."

That meant he was far from all right.

"Ready!" Charlie called.

I forced myself to walk away from Lawson, even though it was the last thing I wanted to do.

---

The bell over the door of Gifts 'n' Things jingled as I ducked inside. I hadn't been in here before, and my jaw dropped as I took in the space. It was crammed full of all sorts of gifts and party supplies. There were piñatas, a wall full of every kind of balloon, an entire shelf of streamers, and another display with items for goody bags.

Picking up a basket, I started selecting items in colors I thought Drew would like as more of my idea came into focus. I pulled out my phone and typed out a text.

> **Me:** *Sorry to bother you at work, but would it be okay if I cleared out the barn for Drew's birthday?*

The structure set back on Lawson's property housed a snowplow, some ATVs, and other larger equipment and sports paraphernalia. But it would also be the perfect place to create a Nerf gun obstacle course. I could move in bales of hay and create targets. And it wouldn't be hard to order two dozen Nerf guns for Drew and his friends.

My phone dinged, and I looked down.

> **Lawson:** *My brothers and I can do it next weekend.*

I bit the corner of my lip.

> **Me:** *I don't want to make extra work for you.*

> **Lawson:** *You're strong as hell, but I don't think you can get a snowplow out of there on your own.*

He made a good argument.

> **Me:** *Point taken. Thank you.*

> **Lawson:** *No problem. Remember, stick close to the house today. No exploring the barn.*

I frowned at my phone. That was exactly what I'd planned to do after I got home.

> **Lawson:** *Promise me. I'll check it out with you tonight, and you can tell me what you're thinking.*

Damn him, knowing exactly what I was planning.

> **Me:** *I promise.*

"Hallie, right?" a sugary-sweet voice asked.

I looked up to see the woman I'd met the first day of drop-off. "Katelyn?"

She smiled, swinging the bag in her hands, but it was all sorts of fake. "That's right. How are you settling in?"

"Well. Thank you."

Katelyn's gaze dipped to my basket. "Having a party?"

"Drew's birthday," I explained. "Just getting some decorations."

Her mouth thinned. "Law plans his boys' birthday parties. He always has."

Oh, hell. I did not want this to turn into some weird sort of pissing contest. "He's got a few cases on his plate right now, so I'm just helping out."

Katelyn forced a smile to her lips. "That poor man. I was just going to head over to The Brew to get him something. He never eats properly when he's working so hard."

My stomach twisted in a vicious squeeze. The urge to pop her one in her perfect nose was almost too much to take. That wasn't me. I didn't get jealous or possessive. I was the one who couldn't care less about any man unless it was to make sure he kept his distance.

But I did care about Lawson. Wanted to claim him as mine for the entire world to see. Only I wasn't sure he felt the same. Attraction? Sure. But being willing to reach for more? He might have too much past hurt.

As if she smelled blood in the water, Katelyn's grin widened. "Don't get too used to playing house up there. You're not their mother, and you're not Law's wife. The truth is, he won't need your help for long."

She tossed her honey-blond hair over her shoulder and sashayed out the door.

I stared after her, my insides wringing themselves out like a wet towel. It wasn't that I thought Law would jump at her offer; his waters ran deeper than that. But the *playing house* remark landed. Hit harder than I wanted to admit.

Because daydreams were all I'd allowed myself to have for so long, maybe I'd let them go too far. Maybe I was seeing the glimmer of *more* with Lawson because I wanted it so badly.

I forced those thoughts out of my head, quickly filling my basket and paying at the counter. I dropped the bags in the SUV and rounded the corner to the Cedar Ridge Veterinary Clinic. A bell jingled as I walked inside, and a full-faced woman grinned warmly at me.

"Hello, how can I help you today?"

I answered her smile the best I could. "I wanted to see if I could talk to someone about the litter of puppies."

The woman clasped her hands together. "Wonderful! They're snoozing right back here."

I couldn't help but peek over the reception wall. The second I did, my heart completely melted. The little balls of fur were a mix of grayish tan and black and were currently snoozing in a puppy pile.

"Want to come back and take a peek?" The woman held a swinging gate for me.

"Thank you." I crossed behind the desk and crouched low. The second one of the puppies scented me, he lifted his head and sniffed the air. Letting out a little yip, he hurled himself at me.

I caught the little guy and gently cradled him to my chest. He rewarded me with a bite to the chin. I couldn't help it, I laughed.

"Looks like you've been claimed," a deeper voice said.

I looked up to see Damien standing nearby in a lab coat. "He's a love."

"That he is. Of the group, that one is full of the most mischief. You considering a puppy?"

I shook my head. "Well, kind of. Lawson wants to get one for Drew for his birthday in a couple weeks."

Damien smiled, the action lighting his green eyes. "This fella would be perfect. But let me guess. You'll be taking on puppy daycare?"

I laughed. "That I will. But I'm also in charge of picking one out, and I think this guy has sold me."

The puppy batted at a strand of my hair and bit it.

The woman to my side laughed. "He's going to make a great pet with a little training. Want me to mark you down for Red?"

I saw then that the puppy had a red string as a collar. "Sure." I kissed the puppy's head and set him back with his brothers and sisters. "When will they be ready?" I asked Damien.

"Right around Drew's birthday. They just need another week and change with their mom."

"That's perfect. Thank you so much." I relayed my phone number to Susan, the receptionist.

Damien guided me toward the door. "Put any more thought into that coffee?"

I couldn't help the wince that surfaced.

I expected him to be annoyed, but he surprised me by laughing. "I'm taking that as a no."

"I don't want to waste your time. And right now, my heart's somewhere else."

Damien's eyes flared in surprise. "Left someone behind?"

"Not exactly. It's complicated."

He waved me off. "You don't owe me an explanation. I'll have Susan call when Red's ready to go. Give us a ring if you have any questions when getting all the puppy gear."

"Thanks, Damien."

He held the door for me, and I stepped out into the crisp sunlight. A smile played on my lips, thinking about the sweet puppy and how happy Drew would be. Distracted, I almost ran into someone.

I skittered back on my heels. "Sorry. I didn't see you there."

The familiar man with the beard stared down at me, his dark eyes blazing. "It's you."

"Sure," I mumbled, trying to skirt around him.

His hand snaked out and grabbed my arm. Hard. "It's you. Lost you. Need you back."

My heart hammered in my chest, and black dots danced in front of my vision. I tried to jerk my arm free, but his grip was too strong. "Let go!"

"Lost you, but now I found you. Not letting you go now."

## Chapter Twenty-Eight

*Lawson*

KATELYN BATTED HER EYELASHES AS SHE HANDED ME THE box of pastries. "I know how hard you and the boys have been working. Just wanted to get you something to show my appreciation."

Nash made a strangled noise from deeper in the conference room where we'd spread out to go over the cases from top to bottom.

"That's very thoughtful. Thank you." I tried to take the box from her, but she held firm.

"We're so grateful you're looking out for us. Especially us single gals who live alone. Maybe you could come over and check out my security alarm? Make sure it's running smoothly?"

This time, Daniels made a noise. He let out a series of coughs that sounded like he was desperately trying to cover a laugh.

"Sorry, Katelyn. We're swamped. But I'm sure the local company that installed it will be happy to do a check."

She pulled a full-on pout so similar to my six-year-old that I fought not to grimace.

"I need to get back to work, but thanks so much for this." I stepped back, closing the conference room door in her face.

"Harsh, bro," Nash muttered.

"I think you might've broken her heart," Daniels added.

Reed just shook his head. "She's smokin'. I'll never know why you'd turn that down."

Adams looked up from her stack of papers, giving Reed a withering stare, then turned to me. "I hope she at least brought the good stuff."

I chuckled as my phone buzzed in my pocket. Pulling it out, I hit *accept* on the local number. "Hartley."

"Chief." A panicked voice came across the line. "It's Susan. I'm at the office, and there was an attack. Dr. Miller has the guy on the ground, but your nanny's in a state. I don't know if he hurt her or not. Oh, shoot, I should've called 9-1-1, but I just thought of you and called."

Everything around me slowed. A million horrible what-ifs. Had she been stabbed like the woman a few weeks ago? Had he touched her?

My feet were moving before my brain registered it. "We're on the way."

Nash was standing in a flash. "What's wrong?"

"Hallie."

It was all I could say. I'd already picked up a jog, heading for the station door. But Nash was hot on my heels. I slammed into the door, making it fly open, and then broke into a run.

Four blocks. Not far at all. But the trip felt like it lasted a lifetime. Each vision that filled my head was worse than the last.

My lungs burned as the scene came into view. Dr. Miller wrestled with a man on the sidewalk, but Hallie was pressed against the side of the building, her knees pulled to her chest, rocking back and forth.

Nash immediately dove in to help Dr. Miller, but I only had eyes for Hallie. I approached her slowly, crouching to get to her level. "Hallie. It's me. It's Lawson."

She didn't register anything, just kept rocking, her breaths coming in quick pants.

I couldn't take it. I moved, scooping her into my arms and sitting right there on the pavement.

"No!" Hallie shrieked, beating at my chest. "Don't take me! It hurts!"

Her violent outburst broke something in me. I wrapped my arms tightly around her. "It's me, Hallie. You're safe."

My words seemed to get to her. As she fought, she sucked in air, suddenly freezing as if she knew my scent.

"Blue?" she croaked.

The broken desperation in that one word shattered whatever was left of the contents of my chest.

I lifted a hand to her face. "I've got you, Hallie. I've got you."

And then she passed out in my arms.

---

I pulled up to the front of my house, glancing at the woman in the passenger seat. Hallie stared out the front window, her face pale. Doc had briefly checked her out, telling me she'd had an intense panic attack where she wasn't getting enough oxygen. Now, Hallie was almost in a hungover state. Doc had recommended rest, food, and a follow-up with her tomorrow.

"Do you think you can make it up the stairs?" I asked softly. "I can carry you."

Hallie just nodded robotically.

I wasn't sure if that was a yes to walking or to me carrying her, but I got my answer when she climbed out of the SUV. Hallie moved as if she were the Tin Man but in need of oil in her joints.

I hurried to meet her at the front of the vehicle, bracing an arm behind her. The last thing she needed was to take a tumble down the stairs. We made our way slowly up and then paused at the front door. I unlocked it and quickly deactivated the alarm, but Hallie just stood on the front porch.

Fury and agony battled within me, each reaching for dominance. But I forced them both down. "Come on, let's get you into bed."

I guided her down the hallway but not into her bedroom. Instead, I took her to mine. I wanted her in my space. Safe. Tucked away in my massive bed.

Hallie didn't register the unusual space as I guided her to the mattress. She stared over my head as I knelt to untie her shoelaces. I slipped off one sneaker and then the other. She wore athletic socks with purple polka dots—fun and whimsical, just like Hallie herself. But so different from the woman sitting in front of me now.

I pulled back the covers and helped Hallie in. Rounding the bed, I kicked off my shoes and settled on top of the blankets, just needing to be near her. To smell that orange-blossom scent and know she was safe.

Hallie instantly rolled into me, pressing her face against my chest. "Don't leave, Blue. Don't leave me."

I pressed my lips to the top of her head. "I'm right here. I'm not going anywhere."

## Chapter Twenty-Nine

*Hallie*

MY EYELIDS FLUTTERED AGAINST THE GOLDEN afternoon light. Everything felt hazy, almost like a dream. As my surroundings came into focus, I registered that I was lying against a hard chest, and fingers ran through my hair.

That was when I recognized the room. Lawson's *bedroom*. His bed. I had to be dreaming. There was no way this was—it all came rushing back. The man outside the vet's office. Damien rushing out to help. Me completely falling apart.

"I'm so sorry," I whispered.

The fingers in my hair stilled, then trailed down to cup my face. Lawson tipped my head back, forcing me to look into those blue eyes. "For what?"

"I freaked. I—please don't fire me."

Lawson's expression went thunderous. "Why the hell would I fire you?"

I averted my gaze. "I'm not sure I would want my kids with someone who can't keep it together."

Lawson was quiet for a moment, and then he bent his head and pressed his lips to my temple. "You make Charlie laugh like crazy; you make him feel safe. You've made Drew want to be present instead of on his damned phone so much. And you've *healed* something in Luke that I haven't been able to. You're a gift, Hallie. Don't doubt that for a goddamned second."

My heart hammered viciously against my ribs. "I'm a mess," I said, a sob clogging my throat.

Lawson pulled back to meet my gaze, his hand still on my cheek. "You're human, Hallie. In an extremely charged and triggering situation. Anyone would be shaky after getting grabbed on the street."

I swallowed down my tears. "I'm usually better at fighting back the panic attacks. Five, four, three, two, one."

Lawson's brows drew together in question.

"A grounding technique. You name five things you can see, four things you can hear, three things you can touch, two things you can smell, and one thing you can taste."

"And it helps?" he asked.

I nodded. "Usually, it brings me right back. But that was…"

"Something that never should've happened," Lawson growled.

"Who was he?" I whispered.

Lawson's breathing grew more ragged as if he were fighting for control. "Len Keller. Name ring any bells?"

I shook my head.

Lawson's hand trailed down my neck to my shoulder, then my arm, before he finally twined his fingers with mine. "We haven't been able to get much out of him. He needs a psych eval, and we're waiting on a doctor from the county and a public defender."

My body trembled slightly. "Do you think he's—? Do you think he's the one who hurt that girl and took Adrienne?"

I couldn't even bring myself to say the word *killed*, let alone bring up the idea that he could've been the man who took me. They had similar dark eyes—the kind of brown that was so deep it almost looked black.

"It's too soon to say anything, but we'll be looking at him hard." Lawson's thumb traced circles on the back of my hand. "Can you tell me if he said anything to you?"

My body shook harder.

Lawson wrapped his arm tighter around me. "You don't have to if you're not ready."

"No. I want it over. I want to forget."

"Okay." He kept a tight hold on me as if he knew I needed it.

"I've seen him around town. Maybe twice? He's the one who acted weird at Dockside."

Lawson stiffened but didn't say anything.

"Today, I almost ran into him. I tried to walk around him, but he grabbed my arm and said something about me being *her*. I started to panic and hyperventilate. I tried to break away, but he was strong. The last thing I remember was him saying that he'd lost me, but now he'd found me. Then Damien came out. I must've screamed. I don't remember. I remember you, though. Sage and bergamot and blue."

Lawson pulled me closer, brushing his lips over my hair. "I don't know what I'd do if anything happened to you."

My heart leapt and twisted, hope and fear in equal measure. "I'm okay."

"You are," he whispered. "You are." Almost as if he were reassuring himself.

We stayed like that for a long moment.

"I might have to ask you more. Ask you things again. I'm sorry. I know it hurts."

"I can do it." I tried to pour as much strength into my voice as possible, even if I didn't feel it.

Voices sounded from down the hall.

"It's just us," Grae called.

My gaze flew to the clock. It was after three-thirty. "I missed pickup. The boys—"

"Are fine," Lawson said with a squeeze. "Aspen and Grae grabbed them."

"I'm so sorry—"

Lawson moved in so close our noses were almost touching. "No more sorries, okay?"

I swallowed hard.

Lawson closed the distance, brushing his lips across my temple and then pulling back. "Will you be okay if I run to the office for an hour or so? Aspen and Grae will stay—"

"They don't have to."

He pinned me with a stare. "They're staying."

"Okay," I whispered. "What do the boys know?"

Lawson sighed. "Drew and Luke know what happened, but only the broad strokes. It was too public; they'd find out anyway. Charlie thinks you aren't feeling well."

I gripped Lawson's fingers tighter. "Okay."

"You up for heading out there, or do you want me to bring food back here? You need to eat."

Not facing everyone would just make things worse. I forced myself to sit up. "I'll go out. I want to see the boys and let them know I'm all right."

Lawson nodded slowly as he rose. He stayed close as I pulled my hair into a topknot but didn't bother with shoes. We made our way down the hall and toward the living room. Charlie's and Grae's voices lifted as they talked about the lizard he'd get to help take care of in his classroom next year.

As Lawson and I entered the space, Charlie's whole body swiveled in our direction, then he was running. He skidded to a stop right in front of me. "Are you okay? Aunt Aspen said you were sick but not constageous. Did you get the pukes? I hate the pukes more than anything."

I couldn't help the smile that stretched my lips. "No pukes, thank goodness. And I'm feeling much better."

Charlie threw his arms around me. "I'm so glad. I didn't want to hug you till I knew because I didn't want you puking on me. I'd throw up for sure then."

Grae laughed. "True love right there."

I glanced at her. "Thanks for getting Drew and Luke."

She waved me off. "Anytime. I'm just glad you're feeling better." She sent me a meaningful look as Charlie released me.

Aspen's gaze swept over me from the kitchen. "Katydid and I are making you some soup. Law said you haven't had lunch."

"Oh, you don't have to—"

"Yes, I do. And you're going to eat it and not fight me on it." Aspen pinned me with a total mom stare.

"I will eat it and love every bite. Promise."

"That's better," she said with a huff, turning back to a pot on the stove as Cady stirred while standing on a stool.

Drew and Luke were perched at the island, but both watched me carefully. I crossed to them, trying to make my smile bigger. "Hey, guys."

Drew met my gaze, swallowing hard. "You're okay?"

I reached out and grabbed his hand, squeezing. "Totally fine. Promise."

He nodded but didn't look completely convinced. "I'm glad. I didn't really want a nanny, but you're fire. I like having you around."

"Fire?" I asked, my brows lifting.

"Awesome, cool, something like that," Grae explained.

I laughed. "Thanks, Drew. I'm really glad I get to hang out with you all the time, too."

The legs of Luke's stool scraped on the floor as he stood. His jaw was granite like as he stalked toward me, but his eyes shone with unshed tears. He pulled me into a hug, careful not to squeeze me too tightly. "I'm glad you're okay, Hallie."

My heart shredded as I hugged the sensitive boy with his big heart. "Thanks, Luke."

Luke held on tightly as my eyes met Lawson's over his shoulder. A million things passed between us in that moment. And I knew then that I'd fallen for all of them, my heart be damned. I just needed to know if Lawson would make the leap with me.

## Chapter Thirty

*Lawson*

I strode into the station and gave Daniels a chin lift. "How'd you pull desk duty?"

Something passed over his expression. "Smith wanted to take an hour to check on Adrienne's mom. I told him I didn't mind covering."

My gut twisted. Smith was one of our younger officers, around the same age as Adrienne, both of them having been born and raised here. They'd probably gone to school together, might've even been friends.

"Hell. Poor kid."

Daniels nodded. "Small towns. Everyone has a connection."

"You're right there." I'd have to check on Smith later and make sure he was hanging in there.

Daniels glanced over my shoulder to the street. "You hear anything new?"

He knew I would've gotten word to the station if I had, but I didn't blame him for asking. We were all desperate for news, clues, *anything*. "Nothing yet."

Daniels grimaced. "Seems like this guy could be good for it."

My back teeth ground together. "Let's hope so. And let's hope he can lead us to Adrienne."

I made my way deeper into the station. The last thing I'd wanted to do was leave my house and *Hallie*. But this was where I needed to be. And I had to get my head in the game.

The station was fairly empty, but Nash waved me over to his desk. There was none of his typical humor on his face. "How is she?"

I swallowed hard, an image of Hallie pale and shaking in my arms filling my mind. "She's better. Shaken, but better. What's the deal with our guy?"

A muscle in Nash's jaw ticked. "They transferred him to the psychiatric facility in Brookdale. Lawyer wouldn't let us talk to him until he was evaluated. Shrink said he needed to be put on a hold."

I let out a stream of curses.

"It'll be at least a few days before we get a crack at him," Nash said.

"I still want charges filed. He's guilty of assault, at the very least." I didn't want to think about what else. If he had been the one to kill Kimber and take Adrienne, he might know where Adrienne was.

Nash leaned back in his chair. "I've already got the county prosecutor on it. I knew you'd want to move."

"And tell that damned public defender that his client may know where an innocent woman is."

He tapped his fingers on the arm of his chair. "I tried to make that point. Lawyer wasn't all that moved."

"Of course, he wasn't," I muttered.

"I tried talking to Len before the lawyer got here. He wasn't in his right mind. Just kept mumbling about finding *her*."

Rage flared, hot and bright. He wasn't getting anywhere near Hallie.

Nash was quiet for a moment, watching me. "You think there's a chance he's the guy who took her? Took all those women?"

I scrubbed a hand over my jaw. "I don't have a clue. Seems

almost too easy. That unsub hid his kills for a long time. This guy doesn't seem like he could hide anything."

"Could be devolving," Nash suggested. "His mental illness taking its toll."

"Maybe," I hedged.

Nash went quiet again but was still watchful.

"What?" I clipped.

"You care about her."

I stiffened. "Who?"

Nash sat up straight again, his chair letting out a loud squeak in the mostly quiet room. "Don't play dumb. You know exactly who I'm talking about. Hallie. The gorgeous nanny your boys are already half in love with."

No, the boys were already there. How they'd all reacted today was proof of that. Vicious claws dug into my chest as panic set in. My boys were attached, and no matter which way I moved, I could screw this to hell, making them lose her. *I* could lose her.

"Why do you look like I just said you have a month to live?"

"It's complicated," I muttered.

Nash pushed to his feet and got in my face. "Law, it's me. I know exactly how complicated this kind of thing can be. How terrifying. But be honest. With yourself, at least."

Blood roared in my ears. "I care about her. So much it scares the hell out of me."

A shit-eating grin spread across Nash's face.

I gave him a shove. "Don't be an asshole."

Nash didn't care at all. "It's about damn time, brother."

"It's not time for anything. She's thirteen years younger than me. She's my *employee*. There are a million reasons I shouldn't go there." But I couldn't stop touching her, wanting to be close enough to bask in her light.

"She feels safe with you," Nash said, the humor leaving his expression. "For someone who has been through what she has? Nothing says more about what she feels for you."

That twisting sensation was back, low in my gut. "I made so many mistakes before."

Nash's expression darkened. "*You* didn't make mistakes. Melody did."

"I made the mistake of trusting my kids with her."

"She was their *mother*." Nash stilled. "Are you scared to trust Hallie with them?"

"No." The answer came quickly and with complete certainty. Something that should've surprised the hell out of me. "She'd do anything for them. They love her. I just—" I couldn't find the words for the sick feeling that lived in my gut.

"You don't think you deserve it."

My gaze jerked to Nash's.

"You think because you believed Melody's lies that you need to pay some sort of ultimate price and never be happy again. That's bullshit, Law. You've been taking care of everyone your whole life. It's okay to reach for some happiness."

My mind whirled. Was that what I was doing? Punishing myself for my past mistakes?

"I—" My ringtone cut off whatever I was going to say, and I pulled my phone out of my pocket.

"Hey, Roan."

He didn't waste any time on polite greetings. "One of our officers found a body."

---

The parking lot of the trailhead was already packed with vehicles. As Nash and I slid out of my SUV, I caught sight of Luisa and her assistant getting out of the coroner's van.

"We gotta stop meeting like this, Law," she said as she slung a bag over her shoulder.

I grimaced. "I'd take a beer and pizza over this any day."

"You have any leads?" Luisa asked, falling into step next to Nash and me.

"One possible, but he just got put on a 5150, so we won't be talking to him anytime soon."

Luisa let out a few muttered Spanish words. "At least he won't be able to hurt anyone if he's in a hospital."

If it was him.

As we headed up the path, Roan met us. His expression was harder than anything I'd seen on him in a long time, and his gaze was locked on me.

"You need to brace."

An electric current raced through me. "Tell me."

Roan just shook his head. "You need to see."

I wanted to deck my brother for his cryptic statements, but I picked up my pace. A burn lit in my muscles as I rounded a bend in the trail. And then my blood went cold.

Crime scene techs had already put up lights since the sun was sinking low in the sky. Their forethought meant every inch of the visual assaulted me.

Adrienne lay sprawled across the trail but arranged as though she might've been sleeping. Flowers were woven through her hair, and she was clad in one of those damned white nightgowns. Only you could see the blood seeping through it from too many wounds. Dark, angry bruises littered her throat.

Nash muttered a slew of curses behind me.

I jerked my gaze to a tech. "You get all the photos?"

He nodded, his face pale.

My back teeth ground together. "Lift the edge of the nightgown so we can see her hip."

The man crouched low, carefully lifting one side of the gown.

There weren't any cuts this time. There was an angry red brand.

The same one that had been burned into Hallie.

## Chapter Thirty-One

*Hallie*

THE SOUND OF A VIDEO GAME BATTLE FILTERED IN FROM down the hall. Grae just shook her head as she tucked her legs up on the couch. "They get vicious."

Aspen grinned. "I just hope Drew doesn't end up teaching Cady the F-bomb. She's already calling me *bruh*."

A laugh bubbled out of me. "It drives Lawson nuts, but I think it's kind of cute."

"You and my brother seem pretty close," Grae said in a falsely casual tone.

Heat hit my cheeks. "We're together a lot."

Aspen grinned into her mug of tea. "He watches you whenever you're in the same room."

My heart picked up its pace. "He was worried about me today."

"Not just today," Aspen argued. "At dinner the other night. Even the day he first introduced us."

I worried the inside of my cheek, unsure what to say. Just hearing Aspen's words had that fickle hope flaring to life in my chest again.

Grae sighed as she turned to face me. "Do you like him?"

"Of course."

Her gaze narrowed on me. "I mean want-to-rip-his-clothes-off like him." She made a gagging noise. "That is so sick to say about my brother."

My face burned now. "Grae…"

"Good, I'm taking that as a yes. Then you have to make the first move."

I blinked a few times. "Grae—"

"Trust me," Grae said. "My brother hasn't dated for a long time. He clearly has feelings for you, but it's going to be hard for him to make the jump. The fact that you work for him will only make that tougher. He's a rule follower."

Aspen nodded. "You need to tempt him into making the jump."

I bit my lip hard. "I'm not good at that sort of thing. I don't have a ton of experience, and—"

Aspen reached over and squeezed my hand. "I don't think you have to do much. He already looks like he's ready to crack."

I averted my gaze as my lips tingled at the memory of the kiss Law and I had shared in the basement.

Aspen jerked upright, nearly sloshing her tea. "Something happened already."

I buried my face in my hands. "We might've kissed."

Grae let out a hoot. "Then now it's time to just sit back and watch him crumble."

I lifted my head. "I don't want him to crumble. I want him to choose me."

Grae and Aspen went quiet.

"Hallie," Aspen said softly. "He is. I see it every time you guys are together."

Grae set her mug on the coffee table. "He's been through a lot."

I nodded. "I know Melody hurt him, and that he blames—"

Grae's eyes went wide. "He told you about Melody?"

I glanced between her and Aspen. "Yes…should he not have?"

"He's never even spoken her name to me," Aspen said, "and we've been friends for years. The little bits I know are from Roan."

Grae grabbed my hand. "That kind of trust and vulnerability? It's him choosing you."

My throat burned. I so badly wanted that to be true.

A key sounded in the lock, and the door opened a second later. "It's me," Lawson called as he plugged in the alarm code.

"We should go," Aspen said, leaning forward to give me a hug. "I'm always here if you need to talk about *anything*."

"Thank you," I whispered, a burn lighting behind my eyes. This was the kind of friendship I'd dreamed of but had always felt was just out of reach.

"I am, too," Grae echoed, giving my arm a squeeze. "Well, except the sexy stuff with my brother because that's just gross."

I choked on a laugh. "Fair enough."

As the women stood, Lawson entered the living room. One look at his face told me something had gone terribly wrong. My skin went clammy, and my blood ran cold.

"We found Adrienne."

---

I hovered in the hallway, listening as Lawson read Charlie a bedtime story. It was such a simple and pure thing. All about the runaway bunny and the shenanigans he got up to. So different from the cloud I knew was hanging over him.

I hadn't gotten much information about Adrienne before the kids descended. I'd heated up some leftovers for Lawson while Charlie chatted about his day, and Drew and Luke stuck close. There hadn't been a single moment where I could talk to Lawson alone. But I needed to.

Lawson's deep, gravelly voice faded, and then the light switched off. As he stepped out of Charlie's room and spotted me, he stilled. He held up a finger, and I nodded.

Lawson poked his head into Drew's room and then Luke's, saying goodnight. His eyes locked on me as he walked in my direction, so much swirling in those dark depths—emotion and need.

I swallowed hard, but Lawson didn't give me a chance to say anything. He wrapped an arm around me and guided me down the hall to the other side of the house. He didn't stop at his office but kept going toward his bedroom.

Once we were inside, he shut the door. The moment it clicked shut, he pulled me into his arms.

Lawson held me tightly, breathing me in. "Just need a second."

I wrapped my arms around his waist, my fingers fisting in his uniform shirt. But I didn't say anything. Whispers of apologies didn't come close to being enough.

"Need to know you're safe. Feel you breathing."

My heart broke for this strong, beautiful man with the best heart.

"I'm right here, Blue. I'm right here."

He pulled back, his thumb ghosting along my bottom lip. "You are, aren't you?"

"What happened?" I whispered.

Shadows played across his eyes. "I don't want to tell you. I know I need to. But, God, I don't want to."

My heart hammered against my ribs. "I can take it."

"She was held. Dressed in a white nightgown. Had a brand on her hip."

My body began to shake in the same staccato rhythm of my heart. "He's back."

My words were barely audible, but Lawson heard them. He pulled me back into his arms. "We don't know anything yet. This could be a copycat. It could be the man we arrested today. We're searching for DNA, and we'll test him when we find it."

"What if it's not him?" I croaked.

"Then I'll find the bastard and put him away."

My eyes burned. "I don't want him to hurt you."

"He's not gonna get to me. I promise."

But Lawson couldn't make that vow. No one could.

He held on to me, stroking my hair and surrounding me with

his warmth, until my shaking subsided. Slowly, he loosened his hold to meet my gaze. "Stay with me tonight?"

My lips parted on an inhale.

"Just need to hold you. That's it. Need to feel you close and know you're safe."

I tugged on the corner of my lip with my teeth. "What about Charlie?"

"He hasn't had any nightmares since you moved in."

My brows lifted. "Really?"

A corner of his mouth kicked up. "You put him at ease."

God, I loved that.

Lawson stared down at me, gaze heating. "Stay?"

"I'll stay."

His shoulders relaxed a fraction. "Do you need to get changed or…?"

I glanced down at myself. I already had my pajamas on with a large hoodie over the top. "I'm good, I just—" I took off my sweatshirt.

Lawson grinned, moving closer and tugging at my top. "I like the polka dots."

I ducked my gaze. "They make me happy."

His fingers caught my chin, lifting it. "Anything that makes you happy." Lawson brushed his lips over mine in a featherlight touch. "Get in bed."

My skin flushed, heat at the contact rushing through me, but I forced myself to move toward the mattress. I slid under the covers, inhaling Lawson's scent that clung to them.

He moved to his dresser, unbuttoning his uniform shirt as he went. I watched in fascination as he shucked it and tossed it into the hamper. Then he pulled off the white T-shirt beneath. His back and shoulder muscles bunched and flexed.

I knew I should look away, but I couldn't.

Lawson opened a drawer and grabbed a pair of flannel pajama pants, laying them on the top of the dresser. As his fingers went to the fly of his pants, my mouth went dry.

I still didn't avert my gaze.

He pulled down his pants and boxer briefs in one smooth move. All I could see was a tight, round ass. My fingers itched to touch it. To know what his skin felt like against mine.

Lawson pulled on the flannel pants and turned toward the bed. He didn't say a word as he rounded it and climbed in. His arm encircled mine, and he gently tugged me against him. "You like watching, Little Minx?"

My breaths came quicker. "You?"

"Yes," he growled.

"Always."

Lawson's Adam's apple bobbed as he swallowed. "You're going to be the death of me."

## Chapter Thirty-Two

*Lawson*

I woke surrounded by scent. Smells that pulled me in and under and merged with the heat wrapped up in it. My dick pulsed, wanting to get closer. Something pressed against me. No, some*one*.

A little moan sounded, and my eyes flew open.

*Hell.*

Hallie's pale blond hair teased my bare chest as my cock nestled between her ass cheeks. She let out another little mewl.

Yup, hell was exactly where I was going.

I forced myself to roll to my back.

"Hmm?" Hallie mumbled, slowly waking.

She shot up at the unfamiliar surroundings, sending the covers flying. Her hair was a wild mane around her, and her nipples poked out through the thin cotton of her pajama top.

My dick practically wept at the sight of her.

"Morning," I said, my voice beyond raspy.

"M-morning. Did you, um, sleep okay?"

I thought about it for a moment. "Better than I have in years."

Her expression softened. "Me, too. No nightmares."

Perverse pleasure swept through me at those words. That I could be the one to keep her nightmares away. I lifted a hand, my thumb ghosting across her bottom lip. "Good."

Her lips parted on an audible inhale.

*Shit. Shit. Shit.*

I snatched my hand back and hurried out of bed. "I'm going to take a shower. A *very* cold one."

"Why would you take a cold—?"

Her words trailed off as I turned around. The tent in the front of my pajama pants was more than obvious.

Her cheeks turned the prettiest shade of pink. "Oh."

"Yeah. Ice baths from now on," I grumbled, heading for the bathroom. But Hallie's giggle followed me all the way.

---

Nash studied me as he handed me a coffee. "You look surprisingly good."

"Gee, thanks," I said, accepting the mug.

Nash wasn't bothered by my response and settled on the couch in my office. "Hey, it's an improvement from zombie Law. That's all I'm saying. I just expected it to be a rough night's sleep last night."

I shifted in my chair. "Well, it wasn't."

Nash was quiet for a moment and then jerked upright. "You slept with Hallie!"

"Would you shut up?" I barked.

My office door was closed, but the walls weren't exactly thick. "You did."

"No, we *slept* together," I corrected.

Nash's brow furrowed. "Dude, are you having a stroke?"

I sighed, setting down my coffee. "She slept in my room, but nothing happened." Unless you counted a raging case of blue balls.

He winced. "Rough."

"It was nice, actually. I slept better than I have in a long time. I feel like I can think today."

"And Hallie?" Nash pressed.

"Said she didn't have any nightmares."

A shadow passed over Nash's face. He knew what it was to love a woman with demons in her past. "If it helps, gotta keep sleeping with her."

I shifted again. The truth was, I didn't think I could sleep without her now. It felt too good to slip under while wrapped around her body. But I wasn't about to tell Nash that.

"You hear anything from the lawyer?" I asked.

He nodded. "Got an email from him. We should be able to ask some questions tomorrow. Not that I think he'll let his client answer them."

That muscle beneath my eyelid fluttered.

"You find anything yet?" Nash asked, gesturing to the map in front of me.

"Maybe."

He stood, crossing to my desk. "Walk me through it."

"No other bodies, but three women who fit the profile have gone missing in neighboring counties in the past nine months. Ages twenty to twenty-five, petite, blond hair."

Nash's gaze met mine. "Vics that have the same physical profile as the ones all those years ago. Women who look like Hallie."

I swallowed hard and nodded. I'd already asked Holt to make an excuse to be at the house today so Hallie wouldn't be alone. He planned to help her clear out the barn for Drew's birthday. But I could only pull that kind of thing for so long before she caught on.

"We've got a redhead in the victim mix now, though," I argued.

Nash nodded. "Could've been she discovered him doing something illegal. Could've been he was in a rage and couldn't wait for a vic that fit his type."

That last statement hit as the truth. The uncontrolled stab wounds, the lack of nightgown and flowers. My back teeth ground together.

"Your gut's saying it's all connected, isn't it?" Nash pressed.

*Hell.* "It is."

Nash pinned me with a stare. "I trust your gut over a signed confession any day. We follow that lead. You talk to Anson?"

I grimaced. An old friend I'd met at a law enforcement conference, Anson had once been one of the Behavioral Analysis Unit's best and brightest agents. But when a case took the worst of turns, he'd walked away from the FBI.

"Left him a message on my way home last night. He hasn't called back."

Nash sighed. "You're going to have to keep trying him."

"I know," I grumbled.

The truth was, I'd been worried about my friend. Giving up a life he loved in DC to work construction in a tiny town in Central Oregon didn't seem like him. And the fact that he'd been dodging my phone calls for the past year didn't help.

"Want me to pull the three missings' case files and go over them?" Nash asked.

"That'd be great. Let's see if there are any other similarities."

Nash jerked his head in a nod and moved to the door. "Call Anson."

"Yeah, yeah."

Nash shut the door behind him, and I stared at my cell phone. Muttering a curse, I picked it up. I hit Anson's contact and waited.

It rang and rang before one of those automated voicemails picked up that only read the phone number. I ended the call and tapped his contact again. This time, he picked up on the third ring.

"What?" he clipped.

"Well, it's good to hear your voice, too."

"I don't have time for tea and chitchat, Law. Heading to a jobsite."

I leaned back in my chair. "How's the building business treating you?"

"Fine."

"Please, don't talk my ear off."

"What do you want?" he grumbled.

"Maybe just to see how my friend who dropped off the face of the Earth is doing."

Anson was quiet for a moment. "It's more than that. You wouldn't call three times in less than twelve hours for a check-in."

I blew out a breath. Of course, he'd know that. Because Anson knew behavior and motivation better than anyone. "Need your help."

"You need someone to take on a reno for you, we can talk. Anything else, no dice."

"An—"

"No, Law. I'm done. You know why."

I did. And it killed me that a monster had destroyed my friend, taken away everything he cared about.

"It's a bad one. That serial from five years ago. Might be back—"

"Don't give a flying fuck. I don't want to know a damned thing about whatever sick-ass killer you're trying to find. Don't call me about it again, or I'll block your number."

The line went dead.

"Well, that went well."

Just as I was about to set my cell down, it rang in my hand. The high school's number flashed on my screen, and my gut tightened. I hit *accept*.

"Hartley."

"Hey, Law. It's Debbie at the high school."

The school secretary had been there since I was a student, and I still had no idea how old she actually was.

"Hi, Debbie. Everything okay?"

"No one's dying, but I'm afraid your boy's in with Principal Meader. Got into a physical altercation with some other boys. Principal Meader would like you to come down to discuss a few things."

That muscle beneath my eye fluttered again. "I'll be right there."

# Chapter Thirty-Three

*Hallie*

"Thanks again for helping me," I told Holt.

He smiled as he hefted random sports gear into the bed of a trailer to haul out of the barn. "Not a problem."

"He's better with a project," Wren said from her spot on an old truck bench seat where her dog, Shadow, was protectively curled into her side. "And I'm better when that project's not me."

Holt pinned her with a stare. "You are going to pop any day. I'm allowed to be a little protective."

Wren just rolled her eyes. "A little protective means trailing me everywhere I go? Yesterday, he tried to follow me into the bathroom. A girl needs to pee in peace."

He let out a huff. "You looked like you were in pain."

"I am. All the time. Because this little bundle of joy is doing a tap dance on my bladder twenty-four-seven."

I couldn't help it, I laughed. "You guys are cute."

"Trust me, Hallie. It gets old by day two," Wren mumbled.

Holt stalked across the barn toward his fiancée. He bent and took her mouth in a scorching kiss. "Old, huh?"

Her cheeks flushed. "You do have some perks."

I turned away, feeling like a voyeur. But it was more. It wasn't jealousy exactly. More like want. Desire to build a family with someone and create what I'd never had growing up.

A little flicker of guilt flared to life as I thought of my mother's unanswered texts and calls. I'd sent an email telling her I'd landed a job out west. She hadn't been pleased. But for once, I was simply silencing that noise.

My phone buzzed in my pocket, and I pulled it out.

**Emerson:** *Please think about coming home.*

I'd finally bitten the bullet this morning and told my brother what was going on here. He'd hit the roof, insisting I get on the next plane to Chicago. I'd calmly told him that I wasn't going anywhere, and he hadn't been pleased.

I started to type out a response when another text came in.

**Luke:** *Can you come to the school? I need you.*

My stomach plummeted, and I whirled to face Holt and Wren. "I'm so sorry. I have to go."

Holt was instantly on alert. "What's wrong?"

"I'm not sure. Luke just said he needs help at school." I was already grabbing for the keys I'd left on the bench.

"We'll follow you down. I don't think you should be going anywhere alone right now," Holt said.

I stilled. "Lawson asked you to check up on me."

Wren let out a snort as she pushed to her feet, Shadow following her. "Of course, he did. Told you. Protective. And it gets annoying. Most of the time, it's better to just go with it."

I muttered something under my breath but started jogging toward the SUV. I beeped the locks and hopped behind the wheel. If Holt wanted to follow me, fine. But I wasn't waiting around.

My heart hammered as I made the mountain turns toward town. I did the drive in half the time I normally did, screeching to a halt right next to a familiar police SUV.

Lawson frowned at me as I got out of my vehicle.

"Did Luke text you?" I asked, rounding to him.

That frown turned into a scowl. "No. The school called to tell me he got into a fight with some other boys."

My mouth fell open. "A fight?"

Lawson nodded, his jaw tightening. "A fight. Not his first scuffle, but if the principal's calling me in, this one's worse."

Panic flashed through me. "Is he okay? Hurt?"

"The secretary didn't say he was injured in any way."

The air left my lungs in a whoosh. Thank God for that.

Lawson's jaw worked back and forth. "Luke texted you?"

"He said he needed me."

Lawson muttered a curse. "Playing you. Trying to play me."

It was my turn to frown. "Playing us?"

He braced his hands on the back of his head and squeezed. "Luke knows I won't be as hard on him if you're here. Or he hopes, anyway."

"Lawson…"

"I know you two have a bond, but he's pulled more shit this year than I know what to do with. This has to have real consequences."

Anger bubbled from somewhere deep. "You haven't even talked to him yet."

Lawson stilled. "I talked to the secretary, and she filled me in."

"And you have a right to be upset, but you also need to take a breath and get Luke's side of the story."

"He's been lying and giving half-truths all year!"

"Stop it!" I yelled. "He's hurting. I don't know exactly why, but I know there's pain in him. I know what that looks like. I also know that your beautiful, amazing, kind, and protective boy is all of those things because it's who you raised him to be."

Lawson went stock-still. His blue eyes blazed.

Oh, hell. I'd done it now.

"You yelled at me."

I bit the corner of my lip. "I did."

I couldn't remember the last time I'd done that.

Lawson moved into my space, pulling me into his arms. "Love that you feel safe enough to yell at me."

Something shifted in me at that. Because he was right. Lawson made me feel so comfortable, I knew I could express anything to him. Except the one thing I needed to tell him most of all.

That I'd fallen in love with him.

## Chapter Thirty-Four

*Lawson*

My fingers itched to take Hallie's hand. I knew that just the feeling of her skin against mine would ease the edginess coursing through me. But I also knew the last thing we needed were tongues wagging about the two of us right now.

I opened the door to the school office and held it for Hallie. She stepped inside, her gaze sweeping the space.

"Hey, Law. Sorry I had to call you in. Know you boys are busy," Debbie said. There was worry in her expression, maybe even a hint of fear. Two dead bodies in a matter of weeks did that to a town. And as necessary as the public safety announcement had been, it just put everyone more on edge.

"Not your fault," I said. "Debbie, this is Hallie. Hallie, Debbie."

Debbie gave her the once-over but had a warm smile. "The nanny, right?"

Hallie nodded. "Nice to meet you."

"You, too, honey. You guys go right on in. The principal's waiting for you."

My gut churned as I lightly knocked on the office door.

"Come in," Principal Meader's voice beckoned.

I opened the door and gestured Hallie inside. She made a beeline for Luke, who had an ice pack resting on his knuckles. She quickly lifted it, assessing the damage as she sat. "Are you okay? Do you think you need an X-ray?"

"The only one who needed an X-ray was the boy whose nose he broke," Principal Meader said with a scowl.

Anger flared, sweeping through me. I'd taught Luke better than this. Taught him to solve his problems in ways other than violence. I stared down at my son. "You broke someone's nose?"

Luke's back teeth ground together, causing a tic in the muscles along his jaw. "He deserved it."

"Luke," I snapped.

Principal Meader turned his focus to me. "This is not the kind of behavior I expect from the son of our chief of police."

That muscle beneath my eye began to flutter.

"I didn't ask to be the son of the chief of police," Luke muttered.

His words hit, a harsh blow.

Hallie took Luke's uninjured hand. "What happened?"

"I can tell you what happened," the principal began.

"I didn't ask you," Hallie clipped.

Meader's eyes widened.

Hallie ignored his reaction and turned back to Luke. "I want to hear it from you."

Luke's jaw worked back and forth. "I was supposed to meet Vi at her locker between classes. When I got there, Henry Cleary had her backed against the wall. He was making fun of her, the way she dresses, that she's so freaking smart. She was crying. He made a move like he was gonna touch her, and she didn't want that."

Luke let out a shuddering breath. "I pulled him off her and told him to get lost. He got in my face, said some colorful things. But I don't care about that. Then he tried to make a grab for Vi again. So, I punched him."

That anger was back, but not at my boy. At this asswipe Henry Cleary.

"We have a zero-tolerance policy for violence at this school," Meader began.

"Good," Hallie interrupted. "Because it sounds like Henry needs to be expelled."

He gaped at her. "Luke is the one who punched another student. Henry didn't hit anyone."

"Backing a young girl up against a wall, threatening her, trying to *touch* her, isn't violence?" Hallie's whole body trembled, but not with fear. With fury.

Luke gripped her hand tightly, and I moved to her other side.

"She has a point," I said as I took the seat next to Hallie. "I could bring the boy in for sexual harassment and assault."

Meader's face grew red. "And then he could press charges against your boy."

I shrugged. "True. But if you put Violet Hooper, a pastor's daughter, on the stand, and she says how scared she was, how upset, I doubt a single jury in this county would come back with a guilty verdict."

"Well, this isn't a court of law. This is a school. And I am tasked with keeping the students here safe and healthy," the principal shot back.

"As you should," Hallie said calmly. "Then you'll make sure *Violet* feels safe. Did you even talk to her?"

Meader shifted in his seat. "She said she felt picked on."

"She said she was terrified. She was still crying when you got there. Had to call her dad to come pick her up," Luke snapped.

"She was overly emotional," Meader argued.

"I can't imagine the school board would be happy to hear that you called a girl who'd been assaulted '*overly emotional*,'" Hallie said. "I'll be happy to talk to Reverend Hooper about contacting them."

Meader's eyes narrowed. "Is that a threat?"

"No. It's a fact. If you let young men like Henry get away with things like this now, the cruelty will only fester and grow. What happens when he doesn't stop there? What happens when he rapes someone? Would you want that on your conscience?"

Invisible claws dug deep into my chest. Young men like Henry, if left unchecked, grew into the kinds of monsters that had taken Hallie.

I couldn't keep from touching her now. I took her hand, lacing our fingers.

"Hallie's right." I tried to keep my voice even and not tell this piece of work how I truly felt about him. "That kind of behavior is incredibly concerning. If you don't mandate counseling, I'll be forced to go to the school board."

Meader glared at me. "And what about Luke?"

My back teeth ground together. "He'll have consequences at home."

Luke muttered something I couldn't make out under his breath.

"He needs to have them here, as well," Meader snapped. "I can't have students thinking they can punch whoever they want."

"That's fair," Hallie said. "But nothing that goes on his permanent record."

The redness was back on Meader's face and neck. "You don't get to decide—"

"No, she doesn't," I cut in. "But we'll fight you on anything you do that would leave a permanent mark on Luke's record. I'm not sure you want people taking a closer look at *your* record."

Meader's face screwed up. "Suspension for the rest of the week. Not on his record."

"That's very fair," I said as calmly as possible.

"Get out of my office," Meader snarled.

"With pleasure," Hallie mumbled under her breath.

We all stood, making our way out of the office. Debbie gave me a wide-eyed look as we passed but flashed a thumbs-up. I was sure she'd heard the majority of what had been said in the meeting. I stole glances at Hallie as we walked. I expected her to be shaky, maybe freaked, but she just looked mad.

"You okay?" I asked quietly.

"That man needs to be fired before he does real damage."

"I don't disagree with you there." He'd always been a piece of work, grabbing hold of the little power he had and wielding it like a weapon. I held the door for Hallie and Luke.

We stepped into the chilly sunshine and headed for the parking lot. We came to a stop by our vehicles. I turned to Luke. "I expect you to get all your missed assignments and to stay on top of them. No phone, video games, or TV for the rest of the week."

I held out my hand for his cell.

Luke stared at me for a long moment. "You know what I did was right."

I let out a sigh. "I'm glad that you're the kind of kid who wants to step in to protect those who need it. It makes me so proud of you. But I also know that you could've detained that kid until a teacher got there, *without* breaking his nose."

"He needed a message, or he would've kept doing it," Luke argued.

I searched for calm. "Maybe that's true. So, you made a choice. And there are ramifications for that choice you need to be willing to deal with."

Anger flashed in Luke's blue eyes, ones so similar to mine. "Mom warned me you're like this. Said you have a stick so far up your ass you can't even see when something isn't a big deal. She said that's why you keep us from her."

And just like that, my entire world fell out from under me.

## Chapter Thirty-Five

### Hallie

SILENCE SWAM AROUND US, THE KIND OF QUIET THAT ECHOED in your ears. The kind that was so absent of sound it hurt.

"You've been talking to your mom?" Lawson's voice vibrated with emotion, so many different kinds I couldn't pin one down.

Luke lifted his chin, defiance shining in his eyes. "You can't keep me from talking to her."

"Wanna bet?" Lawson clipped.

"She said I could go to a judge. That I'm old enough, and they'll listen to what I want. I could ask to live with her."

Pain struck through me. For Lawson. For the agony I knew Luke's words inflicted.

"Have you seen her?" The emotion was gone from Lawson's tone now. His voice was completely empty. Devoid of everything.

"No. But she wants to come visit. You can't keep me away from her."

Lawson studied his son, and even though he was trying to hide it, I could see the brutal pain in those blue eyes. I wanted to go to him, to wrap my arms around him and give him a fraction of the comfort he'd given me.

"Did you go looking for her?" Lawson asked.

"She messaged me on Insta," Luke mumbled. "She misses me. All of us."

Lawson stared at his son for one beat, then another. "How long?"

Luke crossed his arms over his chest. "I dunno. Like a year. Is it a crime to talk to my *mom* now, too?"

A year. I remembered Lawson telling me that Luke had seemed to change overnight about a year ago. It couldn't be a coincidence. And I could only imagine what Melody might be filling Luke's head with.

"She told me that you screwed her in the divorce, too. That she's gotta work two jobs just to pay for a shitty studio apartment," Luke went on.

Lawson's jaw tightened, his back teeth grinding together. "She ask you for money?"

Luke's gaze jerked away, and I knew we had the answer.

"How much?" Lawson whispered hoarsely.

"None of your business," he snapped back. "It's my money."

"Money that you get in allowance from *me*."

Luke whirled back toward his father. "I do stupid-ass chores for that money, so it's mine. You hate her that much? She's our *mom*!"

Lawson stared, unseeing. "Gave her every penny."

My gut twisted, anger flaring again at Lawson's ex. A woman who would take all the money her kid had. Who would fill his head with lies and cause him untold pain.

Luke glared at his dad. "It's beyond fucked up that you told her she can't see us."

"A judge told her that," Lawson growled.

Luke blinked a few times as if this were new information for him, but then he brushed it off. "Yeah, 'cause you're the police. They'll always take your side."

"They didn't take *my* side, Luke. They took yours. They took Drew's. They took Charlie's."

"Not letting us see our mom isn't taking our side. That's stealing from us."

The muscle along Lawson's jaw fluttered as he struggled for words.

I reached out, grabbing his hand and squeezing. My message was a silent one, but I hoped Lawson could hear it. Luke needed to know the truth. It was the only way he'd truly heal.

It didn't surprise me that Luke didn't remember. It had been a trauma. He'd blocked it out, even being ten years old at the time. I understood that. There were still holes in my memory from my time in the cave. Things I'd never get back and didn't want to.

But this was different. Luke needed to understand what his father had been protecting him from all these years. Because it was clear that his mother was messing with his head.

The blue in Lawson's eyes darkened with emotion as I released his hand, and his throat worked as he swallowed. "Your mother went to prison for a year for child endangerment."

Luke's gaze jerked back to his dad. "No, she didn't."

"She did," Lawson said gently. "You can look it up if you don't believe me. The sentence is public record."

"You sent her to *prison*?"

"I didn't do anything." Frustration leaked into Lawson's voice. "She started taking you to parties while I was working nights. I didn't know it was happening. Had no damned idea until *you* called me."

Luke's brow furrowed. "I didn't call you from any party."

"You did. You were ten years old and scared out of your mind. Drew was beside himself. Charlie wouldn't stop crying. You had locked yourselves in a bedroom upstairs."

"You're lying!" Luke accused. "Mom warned me you would. That you'd make up crazy stories just because you want us to hate her like you do."

Lawson's hands fisted at his sides as he battled for control. But he pushed on. "You heard gunshots. Shouts. Someone crying. And you called me."

Luke shook his head angrily. "Shut up! I didn't. I didn't hear any of that."

"I had to trace the call to find the house. When I arrived with backup, a man had killed two people already, was threatening to kill more. Just so he could get drugs from the man your mother was having an affair with."

Luke's face screwed up. "Bullshit! I'd remember that. I was ten, not two!"

"Your mom didn't have one word of concern about you and your brothers. She just wanted me to fix it so she wasn't arrested. Wanted me to bribe my fellow officers."

"S-she didn't. I'd remember." Luke's voice trembled slightly as if he were battling with a memory.

"She'd completely forgotten she had kids to take care of. Drew had wet his pants. Charlie was so dehydrated we had to take him to the hospital."

"I-I'd remember."

Lawson moved in closer, slowly, gently. "You blocked out the trauma. You called me. You said—"

Luke stumbled back a step. *"Daddy, I'm scared."*

He said the words as if recounting a memory.

"Someone was pounding on the door after the shots…" Luke's words trailed off. "I didn't know how to get Charlie to stop crying."

"But you found a phone and called me," Lawson said, moving toward his son. "You were so brave. And you got help."

Luke's gaze shot to Lawson, his eyes filling with tears. "She forgot us."

Lawson pulled him into a hard hug. "You're okay."

"She left us there and didn't care. I told her Charlie was crying, and she said to go away."

Lawson gripped Luke harder. "But you got him help."

"You came," he croaked, his shoulders beginning to shake with the force of his sobs.

"I'll always come for you, Luke. Always."

Luke cried harder, and Lawson just held on as his boy let it all free. My heart broke into a million pieces. For all of them. For the damage Melody had wrought and the damage that had been done by trying to forget it had ever happened.

Lawson's ravaged gaze connected with mine. I tried to pour every ounce of love into mine. To somehow silently tell him that I was here for him, that he had me. Always.

"Dad," Luke croaked, pulling out of his hold. "She lied. She said you were mad because she didn't want to be married anymore. That you kicked her out of all our lives."

Lawson squeezed the back of Luke's neck. "Your mom lies. I don't know what happened, or how things twisted for her. But she's sick. It's not because she doesn't love you. She just can't show up the way we need her to."

"She doesn't love us. She just wants money and to not feel guilty," Luke snapped.

He'd hit the nail on the head there. It was just that, over the years, Melody's actions had caught up with her and they were now eating her alive. She'd concocted a whole other story to make herself feel better. Maybe she even believed it. But she didn't mind getting some cash out of it either.

Lawson dipped his head so he was looking straight into Luke's eyes. "I know one thing for certain. I love you. With everything I have. You and your brothers are the most important things in the world to me. And I'd do anything to keep you safe."

Luke's tears began again. "How can you even look at me? I've been such a dick. I thought you were keeping us from her."

Lawson pulled Luke into another hug. "There isn't anything you could do that would ever make me stop loving you."

My tears fell then. Lawson's love was a force unlike anything I'd seen. And it would bring Luke back, help him find his way again.

"I'm sorry," Luke whispered.

"Everything's forgiven. I just missed my boy." Emotion filled Lawson's voice as unshed tears glistened in his eyes.

"I missed you, too."

Lawson's throat worked as he swallowed. "Why don't we all go home?"

*Home.* The place Lawson had created for all of us. A haven of warmth and acceptance. But it was time for someone to give a little of that back to him.

## Chapter Thirty-Six

*Lawson*

I STALKED OUT OF MY HOUSE AND DOWN THE STAIRS, RAGE pulsing through my veins. Luke was calmer now but drained. There wasn't a single person I would've trusted him with more than Hallie right now. And I had to. Because if I didn't fix this, I would put my fist through a wall.

Jogging down the stairs, I pulled my phone out of my pocket. I didn't trust myself not to yell, so I needed distance. I wasn't about to traumatize Luke any further.

I strode toward the guest cabin and unlocked the door. Stepping inside, I slammed the door behind me. Scrolling through the apps on my phone, I found my digital file folder. I didn't keep tabs on Melody, but I'd asked Holt to. I wanted to have a current phone number and address for her wherever she was. Easy as pie for my brother with the security company.

Pulling up the file with her name, I grimaced. Her address was listed in Seattle—only a few hours from here. A cell phone number was noted below the address. I tapped it.

It rang twice before a familiar voice came across the line. "You've got Melody."

Her voice was bright, cheery. It didn't fit with a woman who'd put her kids through hell. Nothing about her had.

"This is Lawson, and I need you to listen—"

"Law, how are you?" she chirped.

"Shut up."

"Excuse me?" That familiar hostile tone took over.

"I just had my sixteen-year-old son crying in my arms for the past hour because the woman who was supposed to be his *mother* has been fucking with his head."

"I am his mother," Melody snapped back. "You're the one who kicked me out—"

"Bullshit. We both know what happened. So does the State of Washington. And now, Luke remembers it, too."

Melody was silent for a moment. "You blew it out of proportion. So, I took them to a party. They were upstairs the whole time. Totally fine."

"Melody." Rage made my voice shake as if someone had me by the throat. "Our kids were terrified. People were *killed*. It could've been one of them." Just saying the words had ice and fury surging through my veins. "You have a no-contact order from the state. I could report you now, and you might do a little more jail time—"

"You can't do that!" The whiny little girl was back.

"I'm going to give you one warning. Do not contact my children again. You're blocked on Luke's social media now and on his phone, too. I'm going to have Holt running checks on you regularly. You even blink in our direction, and I won't be so forgiving."

"Fuck you, Law!"

Melody hung up before I could get another word out. But I knew her. She wouldn't risk seeing the inside of a cell again. Especially for kids she couldn't pull her act together for anyway.

I let myself sink to the couch and dropped my head into my hands.

Pain and regret swept through me in angry, choppy waves. I couldn't have made more of a mess of things if I'd tried. All I'd wanted to do was protect my boys. The beings that were my whole world. I'd thought them forgetting what had happened was a good thing. Instead, it had only built secrets and lies between us.

The door to the cabin squeaked, but I didn't look up. It was as if my head was too heavy to even lift.

Light footsteps sounded, and then Hallie lowered herself to the coffee table in front of me. I smelled her before I saw her, that orange-blossom scent wrapping around me. She dipped low so my head dropped to her shoulder, her body taking the weight. Then she simply held me.

How long had it been since I'd had this? Never, I realized. I'd had elements of it when I was a little boy, and my parents would soothe a nightmare or illness. But that wasn't the same. That wasn't *this*.

I breathed Hallie in, letting her scent wash away the worst of everything that had happened. "Luke okay?"

Hallie's fingers ran over my scalp, stroking and massaging. "He passed out hard. Adrenaline dump."

That was good. He needed to sleep off whatever he could.

"Did you call her? Or someone who can talk to her?" Hallie asked.

She knew me so well. Knew I'd instantly need to try to fix this mess to the best of my ability. "I called. Haven't spoken to her in five years." The same year I'd rescued Hallie. Thinking back on it, she'd been a reminder that, as humans, we can handle far more than we think we can. She'd been a beacon of hope.

"How'd it go?" she asked cautiously.

"She told me to fuck off, but I think she got the message."

Hallie pulled back so she could meet my eyes. "I try not to let myself hate people, but I've got some strong dislike going for her."

My mouth tried to curve but couldn't quite get there. "You're damn cute, Little Minx."

Hallie's cheeks blushed that pretty shade of pink. "I'm scrappier than I look. I could take her in a fight."

"I have no doubt. But I think one broken nose today is enough."

She winced. "You might have a point there."

We were both quiet for a moment.

"Are you going to keep Luke's punishment in effect?"

I sighed. "I don't know. I don't want him decking kids, but I understand where he was coming from."

"We could split the difference. No cell, but he can use the house phone to talk to friends. No video games, but he can watch TV or movies with Drew and Charlie once they're home."

I reached out, wrapping a strand of her silky blond hair around my finger. "How'd you get so good at this?"

A smile tipped Hallie's lips as she shrugged. "Guess I'm learning from the best."

"Don't feel much like the best right now," I grumbled.

Hallie leaned forward, cupping my face with her hand. "You're the best man I've ever known."

Her lips ghosted across mine, featherlight, but a buzz lit beneath my skin, embers stoked somewhere deep.

I leaned into her, and Hallie's tongue stroked mine. The moment her flavor exploded on my tongue, I was lost. I could've drunk Hallie dry and would still be starved for her taste.

She let out a mewl, and my dick pressed against my zipper. I forced myself to pull back, not to frighten her.

I lay my forehead against hers, breathing heavily. "I want you so bad it scares me sometimes."

"I feel the same way," she whispered against my lips.

"I don't ever want to scare you."

Hallie pulled back. She lifted a hand, her fingers tracing the line of my lips. "You don't. What I feel does."

Those gray eyes swirled, sparking silver. "But maybe that fear is good. It means I'm alive. I've been frightened for so long, but I've felt the bravest since I came here. Since you reminded me of everything I'm capable of."

My rib cage gave a violent squeeze. "You're the strongest woman I've ever known. The bravest."

Hallie's chest rose and fell, the swells of her breasts peeking out of her sweater with each move. "I want to be brave now."

My mouth went dry. "Brave how?"

Hallie's tongue parted her lips. "I want you to touch me."

## Chapter Thirty-Seven

*Hallie*

My mouth went dry as I stared into Lawson's eyes. The deep blue blazed brighter with the kind of heat you knew would leave third-degree burns. I couldn't believe I'd spoken the words. But what I'd said was true. Lawson made me brave.

And I could be brave now.

I released my hold on him and stood. My legs trembled as I walked toward the bed. It wasn't fear. It was a whole tangle of emotions. Nerves, for sure, but the strongest was want, need. A craving so intense my body couldn't handle the force.

Lowering myself to the mattress, I focused on Lawson. That blue gaze swept over me, bringing heat to each place it touched.

"Hallie," he rasped.

"I trust you," I whispered.

A muscle along Lawson's jaw popped. "Tell me what you want," he said, grit coating his words.

I swallowed hard, my heart hammering against my ribs. "You. I want you to touch me."

Sparks danced in the blue depths. "Need you to be more specific."

Color hit my cheeks. "You know."

Lawson's expression gentled for a moment. "You're in control, Little Minx. You're going to tell me exactly what you want. And I'm going to give it to you."

My lips parted as I sucked in a breath. "I, um, you know my last partner wasn't all that…" I didn't know the words I was looking for. "I'm not sure what I want," I finally finished.

Admitting that had me wanting to crawl under a rock. The only boyfriend I'd had was in high school, and he had always been the one to lead things. The sex hadn't been what I'd call good, but I hadn't had to figure it out either.

Lawson leaned back on the couch, gaze roaming. "It's instinct. You *know* what feels good, don't you? Or what you might like to try?"

"Maybe…"

He ran his thumb along his bottom lip. "Do you touch yourself, Hallie?"

My face flamed.

A grin stretched across Lawson's face. "My girl touches herself. Good. That means you know your body. Know what you like."

I huffed out a breath. "It's not. It's never as good as what I think it could be."

Lawson's eyes hooded. "We're going to change that."

I licked my lips and nodded, my heart picking up speed.

"Tell me where we start." Lawson's voice was liquid smoke.

"You come here." My words held the slightest tremble, but Lawson did as I asked.

He prowled across the space, stopping just short of me. He was so much taller than me, but when I was sitting, he seemed like a giant.

As if he could read my mind, he sank to his knees. His hands wrapped around my calves. "It's you, Hallie. You're leading the show. Nothing happens that you don't want."

I nodded but couldn't get any words out.

Concern flitted across his features. "Why don't we take sex off the table for today?"

My brows flew up. "Isn't that the whole point?"

A husky chuckle escaped him. "Little Minx, we can have so much fun without crossing that line."

Heat pooled low in my belly. A hint of fearlessness swept through me. "Show me."

Lawson's hands slid up my legs, over my thighs, and came to rest at my waist. His fingers played with the hem of my sweater.

I knew he was waiting for me. "Take off my top."

My voice was barely audible, but Lawson heard me clear as day. "That's my girl."

Lawson lifted my sweater and shirt, pulling it up and over, tossing it to the floor. The cool air hit my skin in a rush.

He sucked in a breath. "So beautiful."

My breath hitched as my heart picked up speed. I couldn't help but let my gaze drop to the scars crisscrossing my torso. They were all thin, faint even, but they covered every inch of skin.

"Eyes on me, Hallie."

My gaze jumped to Lawson's face.

"Beautiful. Every single thing about you."

"Lawson," I croaked as my eyes burned.

Lawson's hands tightened on the edge of the mattress as if it were killing him not to touch me. That simple knowledge made me feel more powerful than I ever had before.

"Every. Single. Thing."

The burn dropped deeper.

"My bra," I whispered.

Lawson's hands lifted, his finger tracing the line of fabric against my breast. "You were born for lace. Delicate and beautiful, just like you."

He bent forward, his lips tracing the same line, his tongue flicking out.

My core pulsed, pulling in, wanting.

"Blue," I breathed.

His head pulled back. "Love when you call me that."

I lifted a hand, running it through his dark hair. "Blue…"

Those eyes flashed. He reached behind me, unfastening my bra. My breasts fell free, but Lawson's hands were there in a flash. He looked up for permission.

"Please," I whispered.

He palmed the swells, his thumbs ghosting across my nipples. They pulled into tight buds as if crying out for his touch. Lawson leaned forward, taking a peak into his mouth.

My back arched, my body seeking more of the sensation. It was as if it set off a chain reaction of sparks, leading from nipple to core.

My legs tightened around Lawson, needing pressure at the apex of my thighs. And I couldn't help the moan that slipped from my lips.

He released my breast, his eyes heating. "The sounds you make."

I sat up straighter, emboldened by the need in his eyes. I reached down, pressing a hand to the front of his uniform pants.

Lawson let out a groan as he pressed against my palm. Hard and thick.

My breath caught as his dick twitched. "Can I see?"

"You are going to kill me," he muttered. "Those innocent eyes ask such devilish things."

I bit my lip. "Please."

Lawson stood then, taking a step back. "Only because you asked so nicely."

His fingers made quick work of his uniform shirt, then he tossed it to the floor as he kicked off his boots. My gaze drank in the planes of muscle and the dusting of hair over his chest. Then those clever fingers were on his fly. They moved fast, and then he was shucking his pants, too.

I couldn't do anything but stare. I swallowed hard as I took in his length. Lawson's hand closed around it, and he pumped once, twice.

My core tightened, wanting so badly to know what it would feel like to be filled by him. "Blue," I whispered.

"Tell me what you need."

"I—I don't know. I just—I need." My words wouldn't come, but it was like my body was burning up, and only he could stop it.

Lawson stalked toward me. "You aching, Little Minx?"

"Yes," I breathed.

"Need me to help?"

I nodded.

"Words, Hallie. Give me your words."

"I need you," I whispered.

Lawson sank to his knees again. He pulled off one shoe and then the other, taking my socks with them. Then his fingers hooked into the waistband of my leggings, and his eyes met mine.

"Yes," I said before he could even ask.

My bottoms were gone in a flash, my panties with them.

"These fucking leggings have been driving me crazy," he growled, startling a giggle out of me. Lawson's eyes connected with mine as he tossed the clothing to the floor. "My girl loves torturing me."

Warmth spread through me at his words. "Maybe just a little."

His lips twitched, and it was only then that I realized he'd completely bared me to him. But I wasn't scared or nervous. All I felt was desire. A desperate need for Lawson. Whatever he could give me.

Lawson's fingers ghosted up my inner thighs, pressing them farther apart. His gaze dropped to my center. His thumb parted me, and Lawson sucked in a breath.

"So beautiful. Glistening. Aching for more. You want me to eat you, Hallie? To make you come so hard you see stars?"

My core spasmed. "Please."

I was begging, and I didn't even care.

It was all Lawson needed. Two fingers slid inside me as his tongue circled that bundle of nerves.

I cried out as my back arched, so much sensation. And I felt it everywhere. My fingers fisted in the blankets as Lawson's fingers stroked inside me. They twisted and curled, making me tremble.

"Blue," I whispered.

Lawson growled against my clit, the sound sending another wave of pleasure coursing through me. He added a third finger. There was the slightest hint of pain, but it melted into heat as he teased that bundle of nerves with his tongue.

My legs shook violently as black spots danced across my vision. "Please," I begged.

Lawson's lips closed around my clit, and he sucked deeply just as his fingers curled.

I fractured.

My walls clamped down on his fingers, taking all the pleasure Lawson had to give. Wave after wave crashed through me. But Lawson didn't let up. He took and took until I collapsed back on the bed, my vision blurry.

He moved then, lying next to me and curling around my spent body.

I turned into him, my eyes meeting those stormy blue ones. "I think I love not-sex."

Lawson's laugh boomed out of him. He bent forward, taking my mouth. "We're only just getting started."

## Chapter Thirty-Eight

*Lawson*

Waking up with blue balls was my new constant state. I groaned as I rolled to my back, reaching for the alarm.

"Too early," Hallie muttered, trying to put the pillow over her head but failing.

I chuckled as I leaned over and pressed my lips to her hair. "We gotta get up before we get caught having a sleepover."

"Mmm," she mumbled.

I pressed up on an elbow, looking down at Hallie. God, she was beautiful all mussed and sleepy. I swore I could still taste her on my tongue. My dick twitched at the memory, and I wondered if it was a horrible idea to pull her into the shower with me. I didn't regret making yesterday all about her, but my balls hated me just a little.

*Children in the house*, I reminded myself and pushed from the bed.

That had Hallie waking fully. She blinked as I turned on a light. "Showering?" she asked.

I looked down at my throbbing dick pressing against my boxer briefs. "What do you think?"

A strangled laugh escaped her. "Sorry?"

I shook my head. "You're not sorry in the slightest, Little Minx. You could at least feel bad for me."

She bit her bottom lip. "I could come help..."

"Killing me," I grumbled as I headed for the shower, her laughter following me.

By the time I was out of the bathroom and dressed, the scents of an amazing breakfast were filtering through the house. My stomach growled, but I ignored it and went looking for Luke first. His door was closed, and I knocked lightly.

"Yeah?"

I poked my head in. "Morning."

Luke looked up from his desk but quickly averted his gaze. "Morning."

I moved in and squeezed his shoulder. "How are you feeling?"

"Fine," he mumbled.

"Luke, look at me."

My son lifted his gaze. There was so much pain there.

"We're not brushing things under the rug anymore. We're talking about everything. Okay? I want to know how you're *really* doing."

Luke's jaw worked back and forth. "I'm worried you're pissed at me."

I took a seat on his bed and spun his chair around to face me. "Nothing in me is pissed. Not at you. Worried about you? Yes. Pissed as hell at your mom? Another yes. Hurting because I know that the kid I love more than life is in pain? Yes again. But I'm not mad at you. Not at all. I'm glad to know what's been going on."

Luke swallowed. "Vi said you weren't mad."

"Sounds like you've got a smart girl there."

Luke shifted in his seat. "She's really been there for me when I've needed to talk."

"I'm glad. We all need that."

He looked up at me. "I like her."

I grinned at him. "You'd be an idiot not to, and I'd like to think I didn't raise any fools."

Luke's lips twitched, and he looked down at his shoes. "Could I invite her over, even though I'm grounded? I want to make sure she's okay."

I sighed. "All right. Invite her for dinner this week. I want to get to know her better."

A smile split Luke's face. "Thanks, Dad."

How long had it been since he'd called me that? I didn't remember. He'd avoided using any moniker at all for me. And now I was *Dad* again. It left a burn, but it was the kind I loved.

⊕

I strode into the station, the wind swirling as I let the door close. Smith was back at his desk, and I greeted him with a nod. "You hanging in there?"

He swallowed hard as he nodded. "Who does something like this?"

I stopped in front of the desk. "A monster. But we're going to find out who's responsible and put him away."

"He's already killed two people, maybe more. Daniels said it's gotta be the guy you picked up."

My gut clenched at the thought of the missing persons that might be added to the unsub's list. I'd put a call in to the FBI team who had worked Hallie's kidnapping and let them know of the similar cases we were seeing. They'd promised someone would get back to me, but I hadn't heard a word yet.

"I hope it's him and we've got him locked away. But until we're certain, we're putting all our manpower behind it, and we've got a county meeting this morning," I assured him.

Smith nodded. "Just let me know what I can do."

"I will," I promised.

I'd have to do a check-in with all my people. I didn't want anyone playing vigilante. We needed focus and attention to detail.

A whistle caught my attention, and Nash motioned me toward

the conference room. I headed in that direction. His gaze was assessing as I approached. "How's Luke doing?"

I'd filled my family in via our text chain last night. To say they weren't happy with Melody was an understatement.

"He's a lot better today. I just dropped him and Hallie at the SUV. They're going to work on stuff for Drew's birthday."

"Good. I'd like to put ex-lax in Melody's coffee indefinitely," he grumbled.

"You and me both. But at least Holt's keeping a closer eye now."

Nash nodded, changing the subject. "Mads told me you gave in and are getting a puppy for D-man for his birthday."

I groaned. "I hope Maddie's dog-whispering ways are charged and ready for use because I really don't want to be picking up dog shit in my house for a year."

Nash chuckled. "She's great with puppies. She'll have your buddy in tip-top shape in no time. I just hope yours isn't a constant shoe-stealer like mine is."

"Let's hope."

"Chief." A voice sounded behind me.

I turned to see our crime scene photographer, Gibson, heading toward us. "Morning."

"I've got everything loaded. Want me to set up in the conference room?"

"That'd be great. I think we have coffee and donuts in there, too. Help yourself."

"Just don't take the Boston cream," Nash called.

I shook my head. "You can't call dibs on group donuts."

"I picked them up, didn't I?" Nash argued.

I pinched the bridge of my nose. "You need help."

Movement caught my eye as Reed wound through the desks toward his. "You feeling all right?" I asked as he passed.

"Huh?" Reed looked up, dark circles standing out under his bloodshot eyes. "Oh, yeah. Late night."

"Get some coffee. We're meeting in fifteen."

Nash let out a low whistle as he walked away. "Did he bathe in a vat of whiskey or something?"

I didn't want to know. I just hoped he got his head on straight with what we were dealing with.

"Come on, let's get set up." I motioned Nash into the conference room.

Copies of the case files were already at each seat. Coffee and donuts were set on a table off to the side. Gibson was hard at work setting up the projection screen.

I wanted everyone to go over the case together, talk it out. Because you never knew what would shake loose as you did.

I moved to my spot against the wall and set down my water and notes for the meeting. As I straightened, our county sheriff's frame filled the doorway.

"Lawson," he greeted.

"Morning, Bruce. Thanks for coming out." Thankfully, Sheriff Jenkins and I had a good working relationship. Neither of us was threatened by the other, and we always lent a helping hand when we could.

He didn't respond to my thanks; instead, he strode toward me. "I think we have a problem."

Gibson and Nash both glanced in our direction at that.

"Tell me," I clipped.

"I extended the parameters of the search to a few more counties north and south of us."

I nodded for him to continue.

Jenkins met my gaze. "Nine more missing persons that fit our profile. Ones that pick up six months after Halston Astor was found. He could be back. Hell, he may never have left."

## Chapter Thirty-Nine

*Hallie*

Luke glanced in the SUV's back seat. "Are you really going to use all this stuff?"

I grinned but kept my eyes on the road. "We've got to make targets and obstacles. And I think I can even make pop-up people we can manually trigger."

Luke just shook his head. "Drew's going to freak. He has no idea you're planning all this. He just thinks people are coming over for cake and to hang out."

My smile only got wider. I loved that I would get to surprise Drew. That he would feel loved and celebrated. "Fourteen's a big birthday."

Luke was quiet for a moment before he spoke. "It's really nice of you, Hallie. I know I wasn't stoked about you being here before, but I'm glad you are now. You're good for us. Good for Dad."

Cracks spiderwebbed through my chest. "That means the world, Luke."

His cheeks reddened, and he turned to the window.

"How much homework do you have today?" I asked.

Luke glanced back at me. "Not too much. Why?"

"I was thinking we could pick up sandwiches from the deli on the way home."

Luke grinned. "Totally. They have epic brownies, too."

"I never turn down chocolate," I said with a laugh.

Silence filled the vehicle again, and I took a deep breath. "How are you feeling today? You don't have to talk about it if you don't want to. But I'm always here if you do."

Luke toyed with a loose thread on his jeans. "I'm okay. Mostly. I feel like an idiot for believing her, though."

My fingers tightened on the wheel. "You aren't an idiot. You thought you could trust her and take her words at face value. I get wanting to have a relationship with all your family members."

Luke turned curious eyes to me. "Are you close with yours?"

I made a humming noise as I thought about how to answer that one. It brought to mind the half a dozen unanswered texts on my phone from my mom. "I'm super close with my brother, Emerson, and his husband, Adrian."

Luke nodded. "Sibs are way easy."

"I agree." I tapped my fingers on the wheel. "My parents are tougher. I wish we were close, but a lot of the time, it feels like they want me to be someone I'm not."

A prickle of guilt swept through me as I thought about those unanswered texts. But if the content was anything to go by, she wasn't interested in getting to know the me I'd become. She'd always want me to be the daughter who played by her rules.

Luke grunted. "That's dumb. You're freaking awesome."

I couldn't help the laugh that bubbled out of me. "Thanks."

He pulled on the thread on his jeans. "I'd get that way with Dad sometimes. Not because he said anything, but because he's just so… perfect. The chief of police. Always does everything right. Everyone loves him. It's hard to live up to."

"I get that. But no one's perfect. He has his struggles. And I'm sure there are plenty of things he wishes he had done differently."

"I don't know. He has it pretty together from where I'm sitting."

I pulled into a parking spot near the deli and turned in my seat so I faced Luke. "You are your own unique brand of awesome. It might look different than your dad, but that doesn't make it any less incredible."

Luke looked doubtful.

"It's true. Want to know one of the things I've admired about you from the moment we met?"

He didn't answer right away but then curiosity won out. "What?"

"How deeply you feel."

Luke's cheeks flushed.

"I'm serious. You feel everything around you. You sense when others are in pain or struggling. You don't just brush it off. You face it. That's incredibly brave in my book."

He stared down at his hands. "Sometimes, it feels like too much."

"I bet. People who feel as deeply as you do have to take really good care of themselves. They need to take time to refill the well and unplug from the world."

"I get that when I read," Luke admitted. "Especially fantasy because it's this whole other world."

"I love that, too. We can go through all the emotions in a book, but it's safe somehow."

He nodded. "I was actually thinking…"

Luke's words trailed off, but I waited.

"Maybe I might be okay at teaching English."

Warmth lit in my chest. "I bet you would be amazing at it."

Luke's gaze lifted. "Really?"

"I can't think of a teacher I would rather have."

"My teacher this year sucks. It's the same boring books. I'd want to make it so the kids could pick at least a few books they *wanted* to read."

"I love that idea." I paused for a moment. "You know, I think there's an after-school program at the elementary school for kids who have fallen behind in their reading. You could see if they need volunteers. I bet kids would be more excited if they were working with a cool high school student."

Luke laughed. "I don't know about *cool*, but that might be a good way to try it out."

"I'll get some more information for you."

He glanced in my direction, his eyes holding mine. "Thanks, Hallie. You're the best."

That warmth was back and spreading. "You make it easy."

The corner of Luke's mouth kicked up as he looked away. "Enough of the ooey-gooey. Let's get some massive sandwiches."

A laugh burst out of me. "Fair enough."

Turning off the SUV, I grabbed my purse, and we headed for the deli. My footsteps slowed as two familiar figures approached, sandwiches in hand.

Bryan Daniels sent a warm smile in our direction. "Hey, Hallie. Luke."

"Hi," I greeted.

"You picking up sandwiches for lunch, too?" he asked.

"That's what we were thinking. Any recommendations?" I could feel Reed's eyes on me as he stood next to his partner, and I fought the urge to squirm.

"I'm a sucker for the club," Daniels said. "Reed usually goes for pastrami."

"It's the best," Reed said, his gaze still roaming. "You doing anything this weekend, Hallie?"

Luke moved closer to my side, ever the protector.

"We've got Drew's birthday party, actually." I'd never been happier for a busy excuse.

Daniels nodded. "All of us who are off duty will be there." He gave me a sheepish smile. "Any gift ideas? I still haven't gotten him anything."

"I think anything video game or lacrosse related will be a winner."

Daniels glanced at Luke. "What's his favorite team?"

"University of Maryland. He's ride or die for them," Luke informed him.

Daniels grinned. "Maryland gear coming up. Thanks, guys. Enjoy your lunch."

As we moved around them to get to the deli, Reed moved into my space, brushing his shoulder against mine. A shiver ran through me that I hurried to cover.

"That guy's a tool," Luke muttered.

I bit my bottom lip, not exactly disagreeing. "Is tool a curse?"

Luke laughed. "Not according to Merriam-Webster."

I just shook my head. "Pays to be creative."

It took over thirty minutes for us to work our way through the deli line—the downside of stopping during the lunch rush—but the sandwiches looked amazing, and we splurged on chips and brownies on top of it.

"I swear I could eat this in two minutes," Luke groaned.

"I'm not far behind you," I admitted.

I paused beside the SUV as a fluttering piece of paper caught my eye. Plucking it from beneath my windshield, everything in me froze. It was a detailed drawing. Not of a person or a landscape but an intricate gemstone. The same one that had been branded onto my hip.

## Chapter Forty

*Lawson*

NASH AND I TOOK IN THE WALL LITTERED WITH PHOTOS. Over fifteen women had gone missing in the last nine months. Twenty in the past five years. Twenty women who all resembled Hallie and the past victims in some respects. There was no way to know if the women were still alive or not. No way to know for sure if they were connected. But there were too many coincidences to ignore.

Nash shifted so he faced me, his gaze boring in. "Say something."

"I don't have anything constructive."

"It doesn't have to be constructive, Law. But you need to let it out. You bottle things up so tightly; I'm worried you'll have a stroke."

That muscle beneath my eye began to flutter. "They all look like Hallie."

"I know," Nash said quietly.

My fingers twitched. The urge to pick up my phone and call her just to make sure she was okay was strong.

"We either have a copycat, or he's back." I tried to keep my voice calm as I spoke, but my throat strangled the words.

"What does the FBI say?" Nash asked.

My jaw clenched. "That they're looking over the files I sent."

"Bureaucrats," he muttered. "What about Anson?"

"He hung up on me the second I mentioned a case."

Nash leaned back against the conference table. "What the hell is his deal? People are dying, and all you wanted was a little insight."

I shook my head as I scrubbed a hand over the stubble on my jaw. "It's not that simple. Not for him. He's been through too much."

Nash blew out a breath. "That was an asshole thing for me to say. I know he lost a lot. I just—you've told me how good he is. We need that kind of brain."

I knew we did. And the fact that it was within reach but not accessible stung. I didn't know a person on this Earth who was smarter than Anson. His mind worked differently than the rest of ours. He saw connections that were out of my reach.

But he'd lived in dark places for a long time. And, eventually, the darkness bit back. No, it more than bit. It shredded.

"I'll call the FBI again." I was sure they had other geniuses at their disposal. I just needed them to lend me one.

My cell phone rang on the conference table, and I swiped it up. Hallie's name flashed on the screen. My heart rate did a stutter step, the beats almost seeming to trip over themselves. A mixture of anticipation and worry filled me.

"Hey. Everything all—?"

Luke's voice cut me off. "Dad? Something happened."

My blood turned to ice at his words.

"Hallie's freaking out. I think she's having a panic attack. We're by the deli. There was a note on the SUV, but it's just a strange drawing. She's shaking and breathing weird."

I was already moving. Running. Nash was on my heels.

"I'm on my way. Stick close to her."

"I won't leave her," Luke said, but his voice trembled. "She's real scared."

I let a curse fly as my feet pounded the pavement. Two blocks. They were only two blocks away. But what could happen in that length of time? Anything.

Someone could be watching. Waiting.

I pushed my muscles harder, my lungs burning.

The first glimpse of them should've brought relief, but it didn't. Hallie was huddled on the curb. I could see her body trembling from twenty feet away. Luke was close, standing guard, and he held a white piece of paper in his hand.

I crouched in front of Hallie, my hands wrapping around her calves. "Hallie. Look at me."

Her eyes had gone completely vacant as if she weren't even present, and her breaths came in quick pants. Her fingers were curled so tightly in on themselves it looked painful.

"Hallie, one thing at a time. What do you see?"

Her hands squeezed tighter.

I took one between mine and gently forced the fingers to unknot. "What do you see?"

"S-see. F-five things." Hallie's voice trembled, but it was something.

"That's right. Five things. List them off for me."

Her eyes lost a bit of their vacant look as she struggled to focus. "Wheel. Bumper." She took a shaky breath. "Street." Her gaze moved to me. "Uniform." Those eyes lifted, locking with mine. "Blue."

The vise around my rib cage loosened the smallest fraction. "There's my girl."

She launched herself at me.

I wrapped my arms around Hallie, holding her tightly as Luke and Nash watched. I got to my feet, Hallie still in my hold. "You're okay." I glanced at Luke. "What happened?"

He held out a piece of paper. I was about to take it when I saw the drawing. "Nash," I clipped, inclining my head toward the note.

His jaw went hard as granite. "Be right back."

Nash jogged toward the deli, and I turned back to Luke. "Keep holding the corner just like that but don't touch anything else."

Luke's eyes widened. "I shouldn't have touched it. I didn't think."

"It's okay. You were trying to help."

Hallie began to tremble again in my arms but tried her best to straighten. "I'm okay. I'm sorry—I—"

"No apologizing," I said gently.

She turned to Luke. "I'm okay."

Nash was back with a pair of prep gloves and a Ziploc bag from the deli.

"Quick thinking," I muttered.

He shrugged and took the piece of paper from Luke, slipping it into the bag. "Should we print the vehicle?"

"Not a bad idea."

The moment the note was free from Luke's hand, he went straight for Hallie, his arms wrapping around her in a hug. She answered instantly in kind, rubbing her hand up and down his back. "I'm so sorry I scared you. These can happen sometimes…"

Hallie glanced at me. There was so much guilt in those beautiful gray eyes.

"No," Luke said, hugging her tighter. "Dad's right. You shouldn't apologize for anything. I'm just sorry you were scared."

Her eyes glistened with unshed tears. "You're the best kid ever. You know that, right?"

Luke released her. "You're the best nanny ever. You know that, right?"

Hallie's lips curved slightly, but I could still see her hands trembling—the aftermath of the panic attack.

I turned to Nash. "I need to get them home. Have the SUV's windshield, hood, and side mirrors printed. Check and see if any of the businesses' cameras reach this far. And tell Clint I want a call about his interview with Len Keller and the guy's lawyer."

Nash jerked his head in a nod and pulled out his phone. But he froze as he scanned the screen.

"What?" I growled.

Nash's gaze locked with mine. "Len Keller was released from his 5150 hold this morning. Clint and the lawyer can't find him anywhere."

## Chapter Forty-One

*Hallie*

I PULLED THE BATHROBE TIGHTER AROUND MYSELF IN THE steam-filled bathroom. It was as if I couldn't get warm. It didn't matter how long I stayed under the scalding-hot spray, the cold had settled into my bones. The kind that was impossible to get out.

Wiping away the condensation on the mirror, I took in my reflection. My skin was a few shades paler than usual, and my eyes were wide, still with that panicked look.

I turned away. I didn't need a reminder of just how badly I'd lost it. And in front of Luke.

My bare feet padded across the tiled floor, and I opened the bathroom door, coming up short. He would've been a vision, sitting on the edge of my bed, his white tee pulled taut across his muscled chest. If that image weren't paired with the lines of worry etched into his face.

"Feel better?" Lawson asked.

I nodded. "Luke okay?"

"He's fine. He's going to hang out with my mom and dad for the afternoon."

Guilt churned in my stomach. "He didn't have to leave because of me."

But maybe it was that Lawson wanted to protect Luke from another of my outbursts. I couldn't blame him.

Lawson was on his feet in a flash, striding toward me. He framed my face in his hands and ducked low so our eyes were level. "There is no one I'd rather have around my kids than you, Hallie. You teach them kindness and compassion. Strength and bravery. But you also deserve to rest when you've had a hard day. I'd say this qualifies."

A tear slipped from my eye, sliding down my cheek before Lawson caught it with his thumb. "I'm so tired of feeling weak, like a burden."

"Little Minx," he crooned, pulling me into him. "You're the furthest thing from those words."

"I was so scared," I admitted.

"Being scared doesn't make you weak, it makes you human. But you keep facing it head-on. You could run, and I wouldn't blame you. But you stay."

I tipped my head back so I could look into his beautiful blue eyes. "I couldn't leave the boys. My friends. You."

Lawson sucked in a breath as he ran his thumb over my bottom lip. "Can't imagine doing life without you. Not now. Hallie, you've ruined me. But I'd burn myself to ash over and over if it meant getting you in the end."

My heart hammered against my ribs, three little words playing at the tip of my tongue. Nerves had me swallowing them back. But I could show him.

I took a step back, my fingers going to the tie of my robe. Tugging on the ends, I drew the robe open. I shrugged my shoulders, and it fell to the floor.

Lawson stared at me, his blue eyes blazing.

"It's you, Blue. You're the one who brought me out of the ashes. It's always been you."

"Hallie," he rasped.

I moved to him, placing a hand on his chest. "I'm ready. I want to know what it feels like to be fully yours."

Lawson's throat worked as he swallowed. "Tell me you're sure."

"Never been more sure of anything in my life." My stomach flipped as heat pooled low. I wanted more with Lawson. I wanted *everything*.

Lawson's fingers skimmed over my collarbone. "So beautiful." His hand trailed to the center of my chest, the rough pads of his fingertips sending a cascade of shivers over my skin. He circled my breast, coming closer and closer to the peak.

"Look how your body responds. So perfect."

My nipples pebbled under his focus, straining to get to him.

Lawson leaned forward, taking a peak into his mouth.

My lips parted, a mewl leaving my throat. My back arched, my body seeking more of the sensation, more of *Lawson*.

His teeth grazed the bud, sending a rush of heat and wetness to my core.

"More," I breathed. Because Lawson made me bold, unafraid to ask for what I wanted, what I *needed*.

Lawson released my breast and pulled back slowly so he could take in my face. He didn't look away as his hand dipped between my legs, his fingers parting me. He let out a pained groan. "So wet."

I fought the urge to squirm as he teased me. My mouth fell open on a pant.

"Like that, Little Minx?"

"Yes." The sound was more breath than a word.

"Tell me what you want." His voice deepened, coated in sandpaper.

"You." It was that simple.

"Be. Specific."

"Stretching me. Filling me."

Ever since I'd stroked his cock with my hand and felt its girth in my fingers, I'd wanted to know what it would be like to take all of him. I'd dreamt about it.

Lawson's fingers slipped inside me.

My lips parted as I sucked in a breath.

"Killing me," he rasped. "But can't rush this."

"Please," I mumbled. I didn't even know what I was asking for, just more of him.

Lawson's thumb circled my clit as he added a third finger. "Are you on the pill?"

"Mmmmm?" I was so lost in sensation that I barely heard him.

He nipped my earlobe. "Need to know if you're on the pill." His fingers stroked my walls, making my legs tremble.

"On. The. Pill." So much feeling washed through me I could barely get the words out.

My eyes fluttered closed as he stroked, a smile curving my lips. But it quickly transformed into a moan as Lawson's fingers curled inside me.

"Tell me you're close," he rasped in my ear.

My legs shook, and my core spasmed. "Close."

His fingers were gone in a flash.

"Wha—?"

Lawson took my mouth in a hungry kiss. "Want you to come on my cock, not on my fingers, Little Minx. Want to feel you pulsing around me. Want to watch your eyes light up as I take you."

My core spasmed again, craving everything he promised.

Lawson released me, shucking his clothes with a speed that would've been comical if I weren't so desperate for his touch. Then he was back, guiding me to the bed.

"Been checked. Would never take chances with you," he whispered.

My throat clogged. "Me, too."

"Need to know you're with me. Every step of the way."

I nodded. "I always have been."

There wasn't even a flicker of nerves, only want. Need. I framed Lawson's face in my hands. "Take me, Blue. Show me how it can be."

That was all he needed. Lawson had me flat on the mattress in a flash. "Legs around me," he commanded.

They moved on instinct, my heels hooking as my breaths came faster.

Lawson's tip bumped against my entrance, a brutal tease. His eyes locked with mine. "It's you and me. Always you and me."

My throat burned. "You and me."

He pushed inside. The stretch nearly took me out as Lawson dropped his forehead to mine.

"Breathe," he said, his thumb stroking my clit, turning the pain into a delicious burn.

"Blue." His nickname was part prayer, part breath.

"That's my girl."

"More," I begged.

Lawson obliged. His thrusts were gentle at first, testing. But my heels dug into his ass, silently asking for more.

"Hallie," he warned.

My fingers tightened on his shoulders. "All of you. I want all of you."

That blue flashed, and Lawson gave in.

His back arched as he thrust deeper, muscles bowing and flexing. It was art—watching him as he painted a masterpiece with my body.

My mouth fell open as he hit a spot that had lights dancing across my vision. Sparks of color.

My hips rose to meet his in a frantic, desperate plea. I wanted him so deep inside me that I could never get him out.

Lawson let out a guttural growl. "With me, Hallie. Need you with me."

His thumb pressed my clit as he pumped into me, and I shattered. A spiral of sensation.

"Eyes on me," Lawson commanded. "Can't lose those eyes."

I struggled to stay focused, not to lose sight of those deep blues as my body rode the wave.

Lawson arched into me, impossibly deeper as he emptied, my walls clamping down in a vicious squeeze. He let out a curse as his forehead dropped to mine. "Hallie…" he breathed. "Never been happier to be utterly ruined."

My hand lifted to his face, his stubble pricking my palm. "That was more than I ever could've imagined."

Lawson slipped from my body, and I couldn't help a slight wince. He frowned. "Hurting?"

"Maybe just a little," I said with a sheepish smile. "Worth it."

His thumb traced my bottom lip. "Gonna run you a bath in my tub. That should help."

My eyes flared. "I like baths."

Lawson chuckled, but the sound of a ringing phone cut it off. He muttered a curse and quickly searched for the device in our pile of clothes.

"Hartley," he clipped.

His back straightened, his shoulders turning to granite. "Where?" There was a pause. "I'll be there in twenty."

Gone was the blissed-out man from moments ago. My stomach clenched as I sat up. "What?"

Lawson slowly turned to me as if it were the last thing he wanted to do. "They found another body."

## Chapter Forty-Two

*Lawson*

A SICK FEELING CHURNED DEEPLY AS I PULLED INTO THE trailhead's parking lot. The scene had become far too familiar: the array of law enforcement vehicles, the coroner's van. All because another life had been lost.

As I climbed out of my SUV, I caught sight of Maddie and Nash, Shadow at their sides. I lifted my chin in greeting, and Shadow quivered next to them. Maddie gave the dog a release command, and she ran over to me.

I bent to scratch behind her ears. "Going to see if she can catch a scent?" I asked.

"We thought it was worth a try," Nash said. "We might be able to tell if he's parking in the lots or has a place in the woods somewhere."

I nodded. "Definitely worth a try."

Holt had been training Wren's dog, Shadow, for search and rescue, and now that Maddie was home, she'd taken the dog's training up a notch. I glanced up at her. "You sure you're up for this?"

It wasn't that long ago that she'd been through her own harrowing ordeal.

Maddie nodded. "I want to help. And Nash'll be with me."

"Like glue," Nash muttered.

I didn't blame him.

"Let's go," I said.

Maddie gave Shadow another command, and she ran right back. Maddie leashed her, and Shadow stayed right at her side.

We made our way up the trail in the twilight. The poor hiker who'd called in the discovery would likely have nightmares for the rest of his life and might never hit a trail again.

Voices sounded from up ahead, and lights peeked out through the trees. The dump site was closer to the parking lot this time.

"Wanted her found fast," Nash muttered.

"It's a more popular trail, too," I added as the group came into view. "Different from the kills five years ago."

That could mean we had a copycat or that our killer was getting off on discovery, maybe thinking he was sending a message by getting his victims found quicker. My brain could make a case for either. What I really needed was Anson's genius to figure it all out.

Gibson, the crime scene photographer, was shooting away, bending over the body to get some close-ups. Reed and Daniels were talking in hushed tones off to the side. Clint and Adams were speaking with Luisa and her assistant.

Daniels looked up at my approach. "Chief."

I lifted my chin in greeting. "You take the hiker's statement?"

He nodded. "Poor guy."

"Poor me," Reed muttered. "He almost puked on my shoes."

I bit my tongue to keep from saying something I'd regret.

"When did he find the body?" I asked.

"About three this afternoon. Called it in. Reed and I got here a little before three-thirty. Rang you right after."

I glanced at Luisa. "How long has she been dead?"

I shifted then, taking in the woman's face—too much like Hallie's. And now her skin was a sickly gray color. My gut churned. Hallie was safe. At my parents' with the boys, Grae, and Caden.

Luisa's lips pursed. "I'd say a few hours, give or take."

Nash moved in closer to my side. "A few hours ago, someone left that note on Hallie's SUV. Could doing that have set this guy off?"

That was the kind of thing I needed Anson for. To understand a dark and deranged mind. But one thing the note today made clear? The killer had Hallie in his sights.

"Clint," I clipped.

He turned to me. "Yeah, boss?"

"Anything on the BOLO for Len Keller?"

He shook his head. "Nothing yet, but we've got all law enforcement agencies in the county and surrounding areas looking."

My jaw worked back and forth. "I want you to get a list of hotels, motels, and rentals. Fax his mugshot and details to all of them. I want him found and now."

Clint nodded, motioning to Abrams. "We'll get on it. Call if you need anything else."

I glanced at Gibson. "I want these uploaded to the case file and email sent to our point person at the FBI."

"S-sure," Gibson stuttered. "What should I say?"

"I'd *like* to tell them this body is on their conscience, but we'll put it nicer than that. Tell them there's been a development. A new confirmed victim."

I looked down at the woman I recognized as a missing person from one town over, now with no color to her skin and clad in a blood-soaked nightgown with flowers in her hair. I didn't need to see her hip to know there would be a brand there.

Maddie cleared her throat. "If there's something I can use for a scent, I'll start the search."

Luisa reached into her pack for an evidence bag. "I need this back. A piece of the nightgown tore when the killer dragged her body."

Maddie nodded. "Of course. I won't let it get contaminated."

I turned to Nash. "Call me with updates. And be careful."

His hand rested on the butt of his service weapon. "Always am."

Daniels shook his head. "Such a shame. She was so young."

That sick feeling was back. Far too young. Way too much life ahead of her.

"I need to call the chief from Brookdale, make the notification. Stay here until Luisa and Gibson are done."

Reed scowled at me but didn't say anything.

Daniels nodded. "Of course, Chief. Let us know if you need anything."

I made my way back down the trail, the image of the woman haunting my every step. Beeping my locks, I climbed into my SUV. I sat there for a moment, gripping the wheel so hard I thought it might break.

Biting the inside of my cheek, I pulled out my phone and hit a contact. It rang and rang. There was no answer until an automated voicemail picked up, then a beep.

"Anson. I need you, man. I know it'll fuck with your head, but I *need* you. There's a woman I care about. A woman I love." My voice hitched at the word. "She's in danger, and if I don't figure out who's after her, I could lose her. You know what it's like to lose someone you love. Help me. Please."

I hit end on the call and prayed it was one he'd return.

## Chapter Forty-Three

*Hallie*

"Luke, will you get Charlie and move all the goody bags to the picnic tables outside the barn? And then I might need your help with the balloon arch."

I frowned down at the enormous array of balloons in Drew-approved colors. Caden and Grae had come to pick him up first thing this morning for a birthday breakfast and to get him out of the way so the party could be a surprise.

"Where did I put the coolers for our drinks?" I mumbled, spinning around.

Charlie laughed at the sight. "They're right behind you, silly."

Luke caught me by the shoulders. "Breathe, Hallie. It's already the best birthday Drew's ever gonna have."

"Bruh, you got fancy potties," Charlie said, throwing his hands wide.

I blinked at him. I had, in fact, gotten fancy port-a-potties so people wouldn't have to trek from the barn to the house to use the restroom. They were heated and had stocked vanities. "Did you just call me bruh?"

He grinned his gap-toothed smile. "I'm playing Drew today!"

I couldn't help but laugh. "How about you play helping Luke get all those goody bags to the barn?"

"Do I get one?" he asked hopefully.

Luke ruffled his hair. "You're not a party guest, doofus."

"I am so," Charlie argued.

"You both get goody bags. Violet, too," I told Luke with a wink.

Violet had been spending quite a lot of time at our house over the past few days. Even though the Bible preached turning the other cheek, Reverend Hooper wasn't quite on that train when it came to his daughter. When he found out that Luke had decked a boy to protect her from an assault, he'd become Luke's number-one fan. Their whole family was coming to the party today.

Luke's cheeks pinked. "She'll like that. She likes the little things."

I grinned at him. "Sometimes, the little things are the best."

Charlie made a gagging noise. "Gross. I saw them kissing on the front porch yesterday."

Luke's face reddened, and he dove for his little brother. "Shut up, Charlie!"

I grabbed Luke by the back of the shirt. "No, no, no. No broken bones before the party."

"What about at the party?" Luke grumbled.

"Not there either."

"Did someone say broken bones?" Lawson muttered as he wandered into the living room. His gray sweatpants were slung low, and his hair was in haphazard disarray.

The sight made me swallow hard. "No broken bones. I promise."

"What time is it? I feel like I got hit by a Mack truck."

Charlie laughed. "It's almost eleven. You slept *all day*, Dad."

Lawson's eyes went comically wide. "Eleven? I set my alarm…"

I winced. "I turned it off this morning."

Lawson had been burning the candle at both ends, trying to find something, *anything* that would get him a break in this case. But he wouldn't get anywhere if he didn't get some rest.

"You turned off my alarm," he echoed.

I nodded, biting the corner of my lip. "You needed sleep. You've gotten what, a couple of hours the past few nights? You aren't going to be any good to anyone if you don't recharge."

"We have the party today," Lawson argued.

"We've got it, Dad. Practically done. But Hallie needs help with the balloon arch." Luke motioned to the array of balloons taking over the sectional.

Lawson's eyes went huge again. "You mean the balloon monstrosity?"

Charlie giggled. "Careful, it could eat you."

"No kidding," Lawson mumbled.

"Come on, little man. Let's get the goody bags over to the barn," Luke said.

They picked up bags and headed for the door. Nash and Maddie were already there, getting the last-minute things in place for the obstacle course after the company had dropped off the gear this morning.

Lawson stared at the balloons. "You made this?"

"It was actually pretty fun. Caden and Grae have Drew, so he'll still be surprised."

Lawson looked at me. "You're amazing."

Heat swept through me, those three little words dying to be set free. "I like doing it."

"Let me get my shoes, and I'll help you get it to the barn."

Lawson moved quickly. Before long, we were carrying the massive balloon arch to the barn and fastening it above the entrance.

"I want to be Drew," Nash muttered.

Maddie laughed. "Only you would be jealous of a soon-to-be fourteen-year-old."

Nash glared at her as he held the ladder steady for Lawson. "He hits on you all the time."

She shook her head. "He's *thirteen*."

"I still don't like it," Nash grumbled.

I tried to hold in my laughter but couldn't. "He is charming."

Maddie sighed. "Don't stir Nash up. He's bad enough already."

Once the final part of the arch was affixed to the barn entrance, I stepped back. I couldn't help it, I squealed. "It's perfect."

"Bro, you been inside yet?" Nash asked Lawson.

"No," he admitted. "I got home late the last few nights."

"Check it out. Hallie made kid dreams come true."

Lawson grabbed my hand and led me into the barn. He stopped dead, taking it all in. Slowly, he turned to me. "You did all of this?"

I scanned the space and had to admit it looked pretty amazing. There were targets, places to hide a flag for the game, people that popped up, and bales of hay I'd stacked and decorated that the kids could hide behind or climb over. Then a company had brought in a series of slides and climbing structures to complete the look.

"Not all of it—"

"All of it," Maddie shouted from the doorway.

Lawson moved before I had a chance to say anything. His mouth hit mine in a kiss that stole my breath. Heat and comfort and what I thought might just be love flooded me.

When he pulled back, I struggled to catch my breath.

"Thank you," he whispered. "Thank you for giving him this."

"Are you gonna be my mom now?" Charlie's voice piped up from the doorway. "Uncle Roan kisses Cady's mom like that, and now he's Cady's dad. Are you gonna be my mom?"

There was so much hope in Charlie's words that I knew we needed to tread carefully.

"Come here, Charlie Bear," Lawson said.

Charlie came running, and Lawson hoisted him into his arms. "I like Hallie a whole lot."

Charlie's face scrunched. "You gotta if you're kissing her. Kissing is *gross*."

Luke tried to disguise a laugh with a cough.

"Someday, you'll change your tune about that, bud," Lawson said with a smile.

"Nuh-uh. So, you gonna marry her?" Charlie asked hopefully. "I want Hallie to be my mom."

My heart cracked then and there, and I knew Lawson's did, too.

He swallowed hard. "There are a lot of steps between dating and getting married, and we don't want to rush them. But we'll let you know if anything changes. How about that?"

Charlie's shoulders slumped. "Okay." He glanced at me. "Could you be my best friend now? Cady won't mind if I have two."

My nose stung. "I'd love to be your best friend."

Charlie threw himself from his dad to me, and I caught him with an *oof*.

"I'm the bestest best friend. I share my candy and everything."

I struggled to keep the tears at bay. "Then I'm pretty lucky."

"You are," Charlie said, nuzzling into my hold.

"Are you sure you're ready for this?" I whispered to Lawson.

He grinned at me. "Been ready since the moment I laid eyes on you again. And now I get to kiss you whenever I want."

And he did just that.

## Chapter Forty-Four

### Hallie

SUNSHINE BEAMED DOWN AS TEENAGE LAUGHTER AND shrieks came from inside the barn. Younger kids raced around outside in another game I couldn't quite figure out. And the adults milled about, chatting and eating.

An arm came around my shoulders, giving me a squeeze. "This is just incredible," Kerry whispered, emotion clogging her voice.

"He's having fun, isn't he?" I asked as I watched Drew let out a war whoop as he let a series of Nerf darts fly.

"Best birthday he's had. Hands down. And it's all thanks to you," Kerry said, giving me another squeeze.

I shook my head. "I had tons of help. Luke, Charlie, Lawson. All your kids and their partners, actually."

Kerry's smile turned soft. "I've surrounded myself with some good ones, haven't I?"

"That you have," I told her honestly. I couldn't imagine a better group. I wanted Emerson and Adrian to come out here to meet them. Some secret part of me hoped they might fall in love with the small mountain town and kiss city life goodbye.

"But it's you who did the lion's share of the work." She held up a hand when I started to speak. "Don't say it's nothing." Her gaze traveled over to Lawson, where he talked to Clint, Reed, and Daniels. "My boy has been struggling."

A look of pain flashed across Kerry's face. "It doesn't matter how old they get. They'll always be your little boy or girl."

"Because you love them," I said quietly. Kerry loved her kids in the way a parent *should*. In a way my parents hadn't quite been able to understand.

"I do. Which is why it kills me when one of them is hurting. Lawson has been burning the candle at both ends for longer than should be possible, never wanting to take too much help from any of us. Not wanting to be a burden."

I glanced up at Kerry. "I think there's a reason they say it takes a village."

She nodded. "I think you helped him realize that. But more than that, you've got them all *talking*, understanding one another better, helping each other. I haven't seen Luke with this much life in him in years."

My gaze pulled to Luke, where he sat at a picnic table with Violet, his hand twined with hers. They were the perfect picture of young love on what felt like more of a spring day than a winter one.

"He just needed time to find his way," I said.

Kerry pinned me with a motherly stare. "He needed someone who really listened. Who understood him. You gave him that."

My heart clenched at her words. "He's easy to give it to."

Her eyes twinkled. "And you've given it to my boy, too. Brought him back to life. He's smiling for *real* now, and I know that's because of you."

My cheeks heated. "I don't know—"

"I do. And I'll be forever grateful, Hallie."

A burn lit behind my eyes. "They've given me more than I ever could've dreamed of in return. I didn't have this kind of family growing up. I had my brother, who would do anything for me, but my parents? They weren't exactly the warm and fuzzy sort. Lawson has reminded me what family can be. You all have."

Kerry pulled me in for a hard hug. "Sweet girl."

"Hey, everything okay?" Lawson's concerned voice wrapped around us.

Kerry pulled back, dabbing at her eyes. "Just us girls having a moment."

His gaze came to me, checking.

I moved to him then, stretching up onto my tiptoes and brushing my lips across his. "We're good."

Lawson's arms wrapped around me. "We're going to be better than good. Because we're about to give an almost fourteen-year-old his dream gift."

Excitement bubbled up in me. "Is Damien here?"

"Just pulled up." Lawson inclined his head toward an SUV parked below. "You ready?"

I nodded, practically bouncing on the balls of my feet.

Kerry grinned. "I can't wait to see this."

Lawson took my hand and led me toward Damien's SUV. He stepped out just as we approached, wearing a wide smile. "Did someone call for a puppy delivery?"

A little yip sounded from the back seat.

Lawson chuckled. "I think that's a yes. We really appreciate you dropping the little guy off."

Damien waved him off. "It's no problem at all. I'm just happy to see him go to a good home."

He opened the back door and unlocked the crate. The puppy practically shot out and into Damien's waiting arms.

"I think he's excited to see you again."

My smile was so wide my cheeks hurt. "I'm not going to mind having him to myself most days, that's for sure."

Damien handed me the puppy, who promptly began licking my face.

Lawson grinned at the dog. "I don't blame you, buddy."

Damien's eyes flared at the acknowledgment, but he smiled. "Enjoy your new family member. Don't forget to bring him in next week for the next round of shots and dewormer."

Lawson nodded. "We will."

With a wave, Damien got back into his SUV, and Lawson and I headed back to the barn.

"I'm going to block you from view," he said, dipping in front of me.

I nuzzled the puppy's soft fur. "I can't wait to see Drew's face."

"Me either."

I could hear the smile in Lawson's voice.

"Where's the birthday boy?" he called. "We've got one more gift."

"Really?" Drew yelled back as his footsteps pounded.

"This one is all Hallie's doing. Just remember that," Lawson said as people gathered around.

"Now I'm scared," Drew said with a laugh.

Lawson stepped to the side and revealed the puppy and me.

Drew froze. His eyes went wide and then filled with tears. "A puppy? You got me a puppy?"

My eyes filled then. "He's gonna need a name and lots of training, but Maddie said she'll help with the second part."

Drew moved then, taking the wriggling ball of fur into his arms. "Hallie," he choked out. "This is the best birthday I've ever had. And I know it's because of you."

"Drew…"

He pushed into me, holding the puppy with one arm and wrapping the other around my waist. "I love you, Hallie. You make everything better. Special."

Everything burned now. In the best possible way. "I love you, too, Drew."

He pulled back, his eyes still watery. "Plus, think about how many babes I'll get with a *puppy*."

I couldn't help it, I burst out laughing.

✦

"Here, let me help you with those," Daniels offered as I picked up paper plates and tossed them into a trash bag.

"Thank you. Who knew kids could eat so much?"

He chuckled. "They decimated that cake."

I smiled. "I was hoping for leftovers tomorrow, but no dice."

"Get two next time."

"Not a bad idea."

Daniels deposited a few more plates and cups into the trash bag as I held it open. "So, you and the boss man, huh?"

My cheeks heated. "I guess the cat's out of the bag."

"Hard to miss the way he looks at you. Happy for you both."

"Thanks. I appreciate that."

Daniels nodded and took the bag from my hands. "I'll get this into the bin."

"Thank you. I need to go check on Thor. He probably needs to go out."

Our new puppy had been quickly named and promptly tuckered out. I'd finally had to put him in his crate in the house.

Daniels waved me off. "Go on ahead. I'll get the rest of this."

"Thanks."

I hurried down to the house and inside. As I peeked into the living room, I found Thor fast asleep in his kennel, letting out tiny puppy woofs in his sleep. Maybe he didn't need a break quite yet.

I straightened and turned, nearly running smack into Reed. "Oh, geez. You scared the heck out of me."

"Sorry," he said with a grin that wasn't all that repentant. "Just wanted to see if you needed any help."

I took a step back. "I'm good, actually."

Reed moved back into my space. "We could hang in here for a while. Just you and me."

My heart rate picked up speed as I tried to sidestep him. "I need to get back to Lawson and the kids—"

Reed caught my wrist in a bruising grip. "Stop being such a cock tease, Hallie. I know you want me. I've seen the way you eye me. How you wear those second-skin leggings when you know you're gonna see me."

I jerked my wrist free from his grasp. "No, I don't. I'm in a relationship with Lawson, and I don't want you to touch me again."

His face mottled red. "Fucking the boss, huh? Maybe I need a taste to see what has him panting after you."

Reed moved faster than I thought possible. One second, he was next to me. The next, he had me shoved up against a wall so hard I saw stars.

Panic dug its icy claws into me as dark spots danced in front of my vision and Reed's laughter echoed in my ears.

## Chapter Forty-Five

### Lawson

"I'D SAY YOU MADE YOUR KID PRETTY DAMN HAPPY TODAY," Holt said as we loaded gifts into large tote bags that Hallie had brought over for exactly this purpose.

"They're all the happiest I've ever seen them." God, that felt good to say. To know without a shadow of a doubt.

Holt grinned at me as we started toward the house. "You look happier, too."

"I am." Despite everything we'd been through recently, I was happier than I'd ever been.

"You love her?"

I glanced at Holt. "Nosy."

"It's a simple question."

Still, it made my chest convulse. "Yeah. I love her."

"She know that?" he asked as we started up the stairs to the house.

"I'm waiting for the right time."

Holt scoffed. "Chicken."

I opened my mouth to argue, but a crash sounded from inside, and Thor started barking like crazy. Panic lit through me, and I dropped the bag of presents, charging up the stairs and inside.

I skidded to a stop as I found Reed rolling around on the floor, crying and cupping his junk.

Hallie shoved her hair out of her eyes, her face red.

"What the hell happened?" I demanded, striding across the living room and pulling her into my arms.

"He's a creep who isn't keen on the word no," she said with a huff.

Rage, hot and fierce, flashed through me as Reed clambered to his feet.

"She's lying. She hit on me. When I said no, she kneed me in the nuts."

"Law," Holt warned, moving to try to get between us.

But he was too late. I whirled on Reed, my fist catching him right across the nose.

Hallie gasped behind me, and Reed crumpled to the floor again.

"You broke my fucking nose."

"Dude, I think you tripped," Holt muttered.

"She's a fucking cock tease," Reed snapped.

I started to charge, but Holt pushed me back, and Hallie caught hold of the back of my shirt.

"Don't," she pleaded. "Remember the son you just grounded for doing the same thing."

My breaths came in ragged pants as I turned into her. "Did he put his hands on you?"

"Barely," she said quietly. "He pushed me against the wall, said some ugly things, and I kneed him in the balls. He was crying."

"She's lying!" Reed yelled.

"Get him out of my sight," I snarled at Holt.

Thankfully, he listened, hauling Reed up and dragging him out the front door.

My hands skimmed over Hallie, checking for injuries. "Are you hurt anywhere? God, Hallie. I'm so sorry."

She gripped my flannel shirt hard. "Blue."

I stilled at the use of my nickname.

A smile spread over her face. "I got him. I was scared at first, but then I thought about you. How much you believe in me. And

I was able to think. To remember all the self-defense lessons I've taken. He went down with one knee."

I dropped my forehead to hers. "Hallie..."

"He was *crying*. Like a freaking baby."

In any other scenario, I would've laughed. "He could've hurt you."

"But he didn't. Because you've reminded me how strong I am. That I can fight back."

"You're the strongest person I know," I whispered and took her mouth in a slow kiss. I pulled back, staring into her gray eyes. "Love you, Hallie. Might not always do it perfectly, but you have all of me. Always. Never thought I'd get that kind of chance again. But you gave it to me."

Tears filled her eyes. "You love me?"

"With everything I have."

A few tears slipped free, sliding down her cheeks. "That comes in handy because I'm head over heels in love with you, and it would be awkward if you didn't feel the same."

This time, I did laugh.

"You're stuck with me now, Little Minx."

She stretched up onto her tiptoes and pressed her lips to mine. "I guess I'll just have to figure out a way to live with that."

---

My family sat sprawled around the sectional while kids' laughter and shouts sounded from the family room down the hall. Remnants of pizza and soda were everywhere, but we'd moved on to brownies that Aspen had insisted she needed to *rage bake*.

"I still think someone should let me use him as a real-life dummy for my knife-throwing practice," Grae grumbled.

Caden pulled her closer to his side. "Dial it back a notch, Gigi. Your girl already burst his balls."

Hallie hadn't, but I wished she had.

Nash shook his head but grinned at Hallie. "He won't be messing with Trouble again."

No, Hall wouldn't. Because I'd talked Hallie into a restraining order. Thankfully, we had a couple of new cameras in the living room, courtesy of Holt beefing up our security system. They had caught everything. Watching it back nearly had me going down to the station to kill Reed myself, but it was the proof I needed to bring charges and fire him from the force.

"I think I'm going to make a GIF out of him dropping like a stone," Nash added.

Maddie shook her head but patted his chest. "I think that's enough." She glanced at Hallie. "You're really feeling all right?"

Hallie smiled as she burrowed deeper into my hold. "I know it sounds weird, but I feel the best I've felt in weeks. Powerful. Maybe even a little badass."

"Damn straight," Wren said, lifting her water glass to toast Hallie.

Roan nodded. "I think I'm going to get you to teach my Cady those moves."

Aspen gaped at him. "She's six."

He shrugged. "That little kid in her dance class looks like he wants to put the moves on her."

Aspen dropped her head and pinched the bridge of her nose. "Lord, help me."

Everyone laughed at that.

A doorbell cut through the noise, and I groaned. Whoever it was could go the hell away.

As if reading my impatience, Nash got to his feet. "I'll get it."

Muted voices sounded from the entryway, and then Nash reappeared. "There's a guy here who looks like he chews nails for a hobby. Says he's here to see you, Law."

I frowned but got to my feet and headed for the door. I stopped a few feet away. He looked a hell of a lot different. Gone was his always clean-shaven face, replaced with thick stubble. Those alert eyes now had dark circles under them.

"Anson?"

A muscle in his jaw ticked. "You were right. You need my help."

## Chapter Forty-Six

### Hallie

I KNOCKED LIGHTLY ON LAWSON'S OFFICE DOOR BUT DIDN'T wait for an answer before pushing it open. I was tired of the doors between us, both physical and emotional. Since Anson had arrived three days ago, Lawson had gone quiet. He still held me at night, kissed me often, and even told me he loved me, but he wasn't letting me in.

The moment I stepped into the office, Lawson flipped closed the file he'd been poring over, sending Anson a glare to do the same.

Anson moved a lot slower, as if he weren't as concerned about my delicate constitution. His gaze lifted to me. Even surrounded by dark circles, the sharpness in his eyes told me he saw things others didn't. But the shadows that swirled in those depths told me that the things he saw haunted him, too.

"Thought you guys might need lunch." I lowered a tray to one of the few empty spots on the folding table Lawson had set up in his office.

They'd been working in here since Anson had arrived. Partially because of Anson's aversion to police stations and a bit because Lawson didn't want me alone. The couple of times they'd left, Lawson had called Holt to stay with me. I understood after the threatening note, but I also knew we couldn't keep it up forever.

"Thanks," Lawson said. "I could've come and gotten it."

I bit the inside of my cheek.

"She's gonna bite your head off one of these days," Anson muttered under his breath.

Lawson reared back. "Excuse me?"

Anson gestured at me without looking. "This protection thing you're so hell-bent on is going to backfire. She's getting more and more pissed by the day."

"Profilers," I muttered as if the word were a curse. I'd been interviewed by half a dozen of them after my kidnapping, and each one thought they could get some information out of me that would help them find the man who'd taken me and the others. They never did.

Lawson's brow furrowed as he stared at me. "I just don't want you to have to look at this stuff. Or talk about it more than you have to."

"It's about me. Isn't it?" I pushed.

They'd been careful about what they'd shared, but Anson had said something about all the victims having a similar profile. One like mine. Blond hair. Early twenties. Petite.

That muscle beneath Lawson's eye began to flutter. "We don't know—"

"Stop," I clipped. "I'm not going to break. I haven't so far."

"She's got a point," Anson mumbled around a sip of black coffee. I swore it was the only thing the man ingested.

Lawson sighed, dropping his head to his hands and pinching the bridge of his nose. "I'm sorry."

The pure exhaustion in his voice had me softening. I rounded the table and took the seat next to him. I lifted a hand and began massaging the knots in his neck. "I miss the man who believes I can do anything. That I'm strong enough to handle whatever life throws at me."

Lawson lifted his head. "I've never stopped believing that. But just because you can doesn't mean you should have to."

"Fair point. But I don't like being shut out. Especially not when what you're hiding is about me."

He leaned in, pressing his forehead to mine. "Understandable."

"If you're going to start making out, I'm going back to the cabin," Anson muttered.

"Shut up, asshole," Lawson shot back.

There wasn't any hint of a grin on Anson's face, but something told me he wanted to smile. He was just too out of practice. That astute gaze swept to me, piercing. "You want to help?"

I sat up straighter. "Yes."

"I don't know—"

I cut off Lawson with a glare.

"Okay, she's helping," Lawson said instantly.

Anson scoffed. "We're building a profile from the current murders, and then we'll compare it to the profile for the murders five years ago."

I clasped my fingers beneath the table. "Do Reed Hall or Len Keller match the profile?"

It was the question I hadn't dared to ask yet but one that had been eating away at me. Len Keller was still completely MIA. No one had laid eyes on him since he left the hospital. And Reed was lying low. He'd made noise about suing Lawson for assault and the department for wrongful termination, but Lawson's lawyer thought they were threats and nothing more.

Anson leaned back in his chair. "They fit the age range, early thirties to mid-fifties, though Keller is on the outskirts."

"You don't sound convinced," I said.

"I'm not. Hall is too disorganized. Lazy. I don't think Keller is mentally stable enough. But they could be covering. I'd need to interview them to be sure."

I was quiet for a moment. "You almost sound like you respect whoever's doing this."

A muscle along Anson's jaw ticked wildly. "Not respect. Understanding. Two very different things."

A yip sounded, and Thor bounded into the office. I scooped him up and cuddled him to my chest. "How did you get out of your pen *again*?"

Lawson grinned. "We should've named him Houdini."

"We should've. I just hope he didn't leave us a present somewhere."

He winced. "I'll do a check."

I glanced at the clock on the wall. "Shoot. I need to get going."

Lawson stiffened. "Where?"

"Thor has his appointment for his shots," I reminded Lawson.

He nodded and got to his feet. "I'll drive you."

"You don't have to. I'll just go straight there and back."

Lawson's expression hardened. "Nowhere alone. Please, Hallie. I need to know you're safe."

My heart ached at the fear in Lawson's voice.

"He's right," Anson said, standing. "Running errands alone isn't worth getting dead over."

Lawson glared at him, but Anson just ignored him.

"We can go over files in the car while Hallie's dealing with the pup."

Lawson grumbled something under his breath, but Anson was already heading for the door.

I turned and burrowed into Lawson's chest. "I'm sorry I was grumpy."

He wrapped his arms around me and kissed the top of my head. "I'm sorry I was an overbearing bastard."

"Bastard might be a bit extreme. But thanks for letting me in."

Lawson's lips ghosted my temple. "I could never keep you

out. You're burned into me, Hallie. Into my goddamned bones. And I wouldn't want it any other way."

"Love you, Blue."

"Love you, too."

He shifted, guiding me toward the door. "Let's get this puppy some shots."

The drive into town was quiet. I couldn't help watching Anson as he scanned the file in his lap. The way his eyes moved rapidly over the typed words. Every moment he spent poring over the information seemed to turn him darker. Yet he stayed. For Lawson.

Lawson pulled into a parking spot right next to the front door. "Are you sure you don't want me to come inside with you?"

"We'll be fine. Right, Thor?"

Thor yipped and slapped a paw on my cheek.

I laughed. "That's his version of yes. We won't be but a few minutes."

As I slid out of the SUV, I glanced up. Thick snowflakes fell from the sky. What a difference from just a few days ago. A shudder ran through me as I hurried into the vet's office. The first snow always put me on edge. Too many memories. And while I knew Cedar Ridge had gotten some earlier in the year, we hadn't had any in Chicago.

A door shut, and I turned to see Lawson moving forward. Before I could say anything, he wrapped Thor and me in his arms and kissed me long and deep. That fluttering low in my belly started up, the telltale sign of heat building.

"What was that for?" I asked, my breathing still not quite back to normal.

"Love you. Want to make sure you know that. I never doubt how strong you are. I'm sorry if my trying to protect you made you feel that way."

I melted against him, brushing my lips against his. "I love you. Thanks for believing in me."

Lawson pressed his forehead to mine. "Always."

Thor let out a bark and nipped Lawson's chin.

Lawson chuckled and pulled back. "I think he's trying to defend his territory."

I grinned. "My little protector."

"Just text if you need me inside," Lawson called as he climbed back into the SUV.

I nodded and turned to the vet's office but stopped short when I saw Katelyn glaring at me. She held a cat carrier in one hand and stood stock-still. It was clear she'd seen the display with Lawson and wasn't happy about it.

I took a deep breath and started for the door. "Katelyn," I greeted.

Her glare only intensified. "It'll never last."

My lips twitched. "Keep telling yourself that."

I gave her a wide berth as I pulled open the door. A blast of warm air hit me as I stepped inside, and Thor's little nose started twitching at all the scents.

Susan smiled widely at me from behind the reception desk. "How's sweet Red doing? I'm sorry, I mean *Thor*."

I grinned. "Just up to mischief, mayhem, and adorableness."

"As all puppies should be. Come on, I've got a room ready for you."

She led me down the hall to an open exam room. "Dr. Miller will be right in."

I nodded and bounced Thor as he sniffed the familiar scents of his first home.

A soft knock sounded on the door opposite where I'd come in. It slid open, and Damien appeared. "Hallie, good to see you." He bent to the pup's level. "And you, too, Thor."

"Thanks for fitting us in during school hours."

"No problem at all. I hear things are pretty busy at the Hartley house. Important company."

I winced. Much to Lawson's and Anson's chagrin, word had spread like wildfire that an ex-profiler was in town to help with the murder cases. "Lawson's friend is here to help out with the case."

Damien made a humming noise as he prepped a syringe. "That's good to hear. I know everyone has been on edge."

I nodded, not sure what else to say.

Damien pushed the needle into a vial and measured out the medicine. Then he started to hum. A sweat broke out along my spine as the tune for Johnny Cash's *Ring of Fire* filled the room.

My vision went hazy as memories battered at the walls of my mind.

Damien looked up from his work. "I always knew you were special, Halston."

And then he lunged.

## Chapter Forty-Seven

*Lawson*

Anson tapped his pen on the edge of a file as the snow fell harder around us, already accumulating on the ground. "I want to compile a list of all the men aged thirty through fifty-five who've had contact with Hallie since she's been back in Cedar Ridge."

That sick feeling was back in my gut. "You think he's in contact with her now?"

Anson looked up, reading the edge to my tone. "Five years ago, the area the women went missing from was much more spread out. The body dump sites, too. Now, everything is more and more zeroed in on Cedar Ridge."

"Because she's here."

He nodded. "I don't think he'd be able to resist having some contact with her. It's too tempting. The note proves it."

My jaw worked back and forth. "Hallie sticks pretty close to home, but even so, there's everyone at the kids' schools, the businesses she frequents in town. It's going to be a long list."

"A long list is better than no list. We slowly whittle it down, person by person."

I knew Anson was right. We had to start somewhere. It just felt like we had nothing. Less than nothing. And people were dying.

The door to the vet's office flew open, and Susan hurried out, Thor in her arms. Her face was pale, her eyes wide.

I was out of my SUV before a single word left my lips. "What happened? Where's Hallie?"

Susan's head jerked one way and then the other. "I-I don't know. I thought I heard a noise. Almost like a scream but not. Then Thor was barking like crazy. I went back to make sure everything was okay. But they were gone."

"Who was gone?" Anson clipped.

"Hallie and Dr. Miller. I can't find them anywhere."

Everything around me slowed. The blood coursing through me felt heavy and cold. Hallie. My Little Minx. She'd trusted me to keep her safe.

"Show us," Anson barked.

His voice snapped me out of my spiraling thoughts, and I strode after Susan into the vet's office. She led us down the hall and into the exam room. Nothing looked out of sorts. But there was a syringe and a vial on the counter.

Anson bent, his eyes tracking the vial's label. Then he turned, looking up at me. "Ketamine."

"That can't be," Susan argued. "We use that for sedation. Thor just needed some shots."

Blood roared in my ears. The steady pulse of my heart sounded like an explosion every couple of seconds.

"Where does Miller park?" My voice didn't sound like mine. No emotion. Empty. Dead.

"Th-through here," Susan said quickly, leading us through the second door into a back area for treatment. There were a couple of dogs and cats in medical crates but nothing out of place. She headed for a back door. "This is always locked. Alarmed, too, since we have prescription drugs on-site. I don't know how someone could've gotten in. Did they take them? Hallie and Dr. Miller?"

Everything in me twisted as I shared a look with Anson.

He glanced away, scanning the space. "Does anyone else work here? A vet tech? Another doctor?"

"N-no. I mean, yes. But our vet tech is out sick today. She got food poisoning yesterday," Susan stammered.

Food poisoning, the day before Hallie was *scheduled* to bring Thor in. It was all a little too convenient.

Anson scanned the small parking lot. There was only space for four vehicles, and it was flanked by thick woods. "Is that your vehicle or Dr. Miller's?"

Susan glanced at the maroon Subaru. "That's mine. His SUV is gone. Did someone steal that, too?"

My throat burned as if someone had poured acid down it. "I need you to cancel appointments for the rest of the day. Don't let anyone else into the building. This is a crime scene."

---

I paced back and forth along the side of the conference room. My skin felt too tight for my body, and my heart beat so hard it felt as though it might rip right out of my chest.

On one side of the table, Anson's fingers flew over a laptop keyboard. The team at Holt's security company had pulled everything they could find on Damien Miller. Anson was combing through it, comparing it to the previous data he'd compiled.

On the other side of the table, Holt, Grae, Caden, and Roan pored over maps of the area, trying to figure out where to start a search. There'd been no sign of Miller at his house, and he had no other properties on record. Crime scene techs were searching his home now, looking for anything that might give us a lead.

Some officers questioned whether someone had taken both Hallie *and* Miller, possibly forcing them into Miller's vehicle. Possible? Sure. Likely? No.

Miller had her. The woman who'd become everything to me in such a short time. And God only knew what he was doing to her.

A hand clamped down on my shoulder. "Law."

My father's deep timbre made everything hurt more.

"I have to keep moving," I muttered. If I stopped, it felt as if my body would explode.

Dad squeezed my shoulder harder. "We're going to find her."

I whirled on him. "You don't know that. Don't make promises you can't keep."

He gripped both my shoulders then, so hard there was a bite of pain. "I know that none of us will stop until we do."

Bile surged in my throat. I knew he was right. I understood my family would never give up on Hallie. But what would we find when we finally located her?

It wasn't just me. Mom had gone to pick up the boys from school to keep them with her and Wren. But I knew they were beside themselves and scared out of their minds because they'd fallen in love with Hallie just as much as I had.

"I can't lose her," I croaked. "I don't think I can do life without her."

My dad's eyes filled. "You won't have to."

"I love her," I whispered.

"I know." Dad pulled me into a hard hug. "I know."

There was a flurry of activity as Nash strode into the conference room, Clint and Abrams on his heels. His face was a mask of stormy fury.

The world dropped away. "What?" I rasped.

Nash's throat worked as he swallowed. "We found trophies in the basement. More than two dozen of them. Jewelry, driver's licenses, clippings of hair. And not just from this past year." His gaze cut to me. "I'm sorry, Law. It's him. It's been him from the beginning."

## Chapter Forty-Eight

*Hallie*

A SHIVER RACKED MY BODY AS I ROLLED TO MY BACK, smacking my lips. My head felt like it was stuffed full of cotton—my mouth, too. The blanket over me felt rough and unfamiliar. I blinked against the faint glow in the room.

It came together in terrifying snapshots, one at a time, each giving me a different piece of the puzzle. A rough, rocky ceiling. A thin mattress on the floor. A chain secured to my ankle with a cuff. And the flimsy white nightgown.

My breaths came in quick pants as horror set in. Not here. Not again.

Dark spots danced in front of my vision as my fingers started to tingle. I couldn't pass out. Not now. Not here.

I still had my bra and underwear on. At least, that was something. I bit back the sob that tried to break free.

I attempted to focus on my breathing, to slow it down. But it was as if the regulation of my lungs was out of my control. They ached and burned as they struggled for oxygen.

I bit the inside of my cheek hard and forced my mind on something else. Anything. It was Lawson's face that filled it. The tender way he touched me. How one corner of his mouth hitched when he called me *Little Minx*. The way his blue eyes sparked when I knew he wanted me.

The ragged sob broke free this time. Lawson. The man who had given me everything. Reminded me just how strong I was. Showed me how joy-filled everyday life could be. Shared the three most amazing boys there were.

My heart squeezed as an image of Luke, Drew, and Charlie materialized in my head. They'd given me everything, too: purpose, laughter, love.

The tingling in my fingers lessened a fraction as my breathing slowed. My fingernails dug into my palms, hard. I wouldn't lose my guys. Not now. Not after just finding them.

I pushed to a sitting position and studied the room—if that was what you could call it. A shiver racked my body again as I took it all in. It was the same place I'd been held five years ago. Where my torture had begun.

The police and FBI had never found the cave where the man had held the women before he killed them. And while the search had continued in earnest for a good six months after I escaped, the consensus was that he had fled the area.

Not him. Not some unknown bogeyman. Damien.

My mouth went painfully dry. None of it made sense. The vet I'd seen be so gentle with animals, so patient with children. How could he be a person who raped, tortured, and brutally murdered?

I'd thought back then that his voice sounded different at various times. But to put on that sort of affect took practice. Lots of it.

My breaths started coming quickly again.

I closed my eyes and pictured Lawson's face. His strong, stubbled jaw. The nose just slightly crooked. The blue eyes that saved me every time I stared into them.

My breathing slowed again.

I opened my eyes and studied the cave around me. I knew there were all sorts of natural rooms carved into the rock. Just like I knew there was a long tunnel that led to the outside world. I could run that tunnel.

Damien had taken my shoes, likely thinking it would make escape harder, but he should've known better. I would rip my feet to ribbons to get away from him.

My hands went to my ankle and the shackle there. It was rusted but made of thick metal. I tested the lock. It held steady. I tried the spot where the chain connected to the cuff. It, too, held strong.

I stood then, the world going a bit topsy-turvy as I did. I pressed a hand to the wall to steady myself. The stone was freezing and damp, as if water trailed down the walls. Another shiver racked my body as if I were just now realizing how cold it was.

I followed the chain toward the rock wall. It was bolted there, just like before. I tried the bolts first, attempting to turn them with my fingers, but they were stuck in. Then I tugged hard on the chain itself. There was no give.

Hot, burning tears built behind my eyes. I would get free. I would find a way. I'd beaten him before. I'd do it again.

Memories of that night slammed into me. How he'd extended my torture session. I'd been so out of it when he took me back to my *room* that he hadn't even bothered to lock me up. He'd thought I was too beaten. That I'd never try for freedom. But he'd been wrong.

"She looks so beautiful back home in her rightful place."

I whirled at the voice as it echoed off the walls. My hands went up in a defensive posture.

Damien laughed, the sound rich and deep. "You always did have the best fight of them all. That's why you're so special."

I didn't say a word. Was unsure if whatever I might let loose would make things worse. I remembered how quickly his temper could turn.

"Oh, Halston. There's no need to be shy. Not with your husband."

"You're not my husband," I spat, so easily forgetting my previous worry. But I knew what *husband* meant to him. I knew what he thought he could take. He could cut me to the bone before I'd ever let him take that.

Damien made a tsking sound. "Now, now. There's no need to

play hard to get anymore, Halston. I'm here. Haven't I proven my dedication? My patience? What else do you need from me?"

I bit down hard on the inside of my cheek. "They'll know it's you. They'll find us."

He laughed again, a sound that wasn't right in any way. "Oh, they'll know I took you. They'll know I had countless imperfect brides before you. But they'll never find us here." His white teeth flashed in the low light. "How long were those bumbling FBI agents looking for this cave? They never found it."

Another shiver coursed through me. "Why?"

I couldn't help the question. So many lives lost. And for what?

Damien stalked slowly toward me. "Don't you think I deserve perfect, Halston? I work hard. I help countless animals. I'm a good steward for my community. But it's always the whores and traitors who try to catch my eye. How else am I supposed to find a bride? I need to test their merit."

"Merit?" I croaked.

His mouth curved. "Beauty and brains, but most of all strength. I need to find a woman who won't give in to temptation. Who won't break. It's always been you."

Another shudder racked me. I'd only broken in secret when I knew he was gone. That was when I'd let the tears of agony come. But never in front of *him*.

"Can't you see it was meant to be? I never thought you'd come back here. Assumed you'd stay living with that brother of yours forever."

Bile surged at the knowledge that he'd been keeping tabs on me. Watching from afar.

"And then you walked right up to me and *smiled*."

This was my greatest fear come to life. That I wouldn't know the man who'd taken me if he walked right across my path.

"You never broke. That's what makes me know you're the one. You don't need to prove yourself anymore, Halston. Now, you can give in to me. I'll take you away from here. I've got fake passports prepared. Mexico? Canada? Wherever you want to go. Just tell me you'll marry me." Damien reached out, stroking my face with the backs of his fingers.

I jerked away from his touch.

Even in the low light, I saw his face mottle red. Damien lashed out, his hands going around my throat and shoving me against the wall. "I offer you the world, and this is how you reward me? Fine," he spat. "I'm happy to make you scream."

## Chapter Forty-Nine

*Lawson*

"Found something," Anson said as he looked up from his computer screen.

I spun my chair to face his. My back teeth felt ground down to nubs. The FBI was on their way, but it was too late. Miller already had her. What we needed was a line on where he could be now.

"Talk," I snapped.

He ignored my tone and looked back at his computer screen. "Damien Miller was married from age twenty-three to twenty-five. He and his wife divorced, and two years later, she went missing. Her body was never found."

My fingers gripped the edge of the conference table. "What good does that do us now?"

Holt shifted in the chair next to me, gripping my shoulder. "We need to know what makes the guy tick. It will help us figure out where he might go."

I knew he was right, but hours had already passed. Time that Miller could have been doing *anything* to Hallie. Everything inside me trembled as if I might shatter if someone simply breathed wrong.

I knew my family and my team were doing everything they could. The county was crawling with law enforcement. They were checking trailheads and campsites, back roads, and rental cabins. So far, we had absolutely nothing.

Anson cleared his throat. "I found an old friend of the ex-Mrs. Miller on Facebook."

I blinked at him. "You're on Facebook?"

He grimaced at me. "I've got a fake account for research. Told her I was a true crime blogger."

"What did she say?" I pressed.

"Reina Miller knew she made a mistake marrying Damien within a couple of months but wasn't quite sure how to get out of it. She tried to suggest separating, but Damien lost it. Eventually, she started up a relationship with a guy she met at the gym."

Roan let out a low whistle. "While she was still married?"

Anson nodded. "Damien came home from work early one day, had a headache, and found his wife and her workout buddy in bed together. Their bed."

"Having your wife cheat on you doesn't turn someone into a serial killer," I ground out.

"No. There's also a history of antisocial behavior. No close friends. Barely talked to his family. I'm still digging, but this friend thought it was weird that Damien was a vet."

"Why?" Grae asked from her spot at the end of the table.

Anson glanced at her. "He refused to get a pet for Reina. Said animals ruin homes."

"Control freak," Nash muttered.

"I'd say he definitely needs control. Based on Hallie's statements from five years ago and looking at the photos of his ex, I think he's trying to replace his wife."

That sick feeling was back in my gut as Anson turned the laptop around. The woman wasn't as beautiful as Hallie, and her eyes were green instead of gray, but there was no denying the resemblance. Young, fair, pale blond hair, and a petite frame. Just like she resembled the other victims from five years ago and the ones from now. The only one who didn't fit was Kimber Anderson.

"Kimber Anderson had red hair. And her death doesn't match the others," I pointed out.

Anson nodded. "My best guess is he needed an outlet for his rage at seeing Hallie again. She didn't fit the mold, so he didn't keep her."

"But he's not just looking for a replacement." My voice was low, unrecognizable. "He's killing her over and over again."

Anson turned his computer back toward himself. "I think they do something that either proves they aren't similar to Reina or indicates they're unworthy. Hallie didn't do that in all the days he had her. She's smart. She'll hang on."

I shoved back from the table, sending my chair flying. "But what the hell is he doing to her in the meantime?"

Anson's face closed down. I knew he understood what it was to have a loved one in the hands of a madman.

Roan stood, stalking around the table to me. "Rein it in. You won't be doing a damned thing for her if you lose it now."

The muscle beneath my eye fluttered wildly. "I can't lose her."

"So, let's all pull our shit together and *find* her," Roan growled. "I'd like a few minutes alone with this asshole. He's been alone with my wife and daughter."

"You need to start where she was found before," Anson said, his voice devoid of emotion.

Dad turned to him. "Why do you say that?"

"He's trying to finish what he started. The pull will be strong to go back to his original hunting grounds."

Holt was already moving, pulling a map out of the pile. "I've got that area marked."

"She was held in a cave, right?" Caden asked.

I nodded. "One big enough to have several rooms. But the authorities never found it back then."

Caden shook his head. "The FBI doesn't know the area as well as we do. There's a massive system of caves just a couple of miles north of where they found her. Some to the west, too."

"They did some searching around there but said they didn't find anything," I argued.

Dad leaned over the maps. "It would've taken a hell of a lot of manpower to search everything they needed to. Especially if they weren't familiar with the area."

Roan traced a finger over the map. "Here. There used to be a forest service road. It's not active anymore, but I bet it's still passable. It'll get us the closest."

Holt pulled out his phone. "The team's ready. I'll have them meet us there. I want search parties of four. Two SAR team members, two law enforcement. Move. Now."

Everyone was on their feet and heading for the door. Roan came up to my side. "You ride with me."

"I'm fine."

"With me," he clipped.

I bit back my retort as I grabbed my gear bag and followed him out to his truck. At least Roan would be quiet on the drive. And he gave me that for a good fifteen minutes. Right until we hit the forest service road.

"You were there for me when I thought I was going to lose Aspen. You kept my head in the game and helped me get her back."

My throat constricted at the memory of how torn up Roan had been.

He pulled to a stop next to the other vehicles. "I'm going to do the same for you. We won't let her fall."

I swallowed down the burning sensation. "Thank you."

He clapped me on the shoulder. "Let's go get your girl."

It only took minutes for the team to assemble. Grae and Dad would work the map and coordinate the search parties. Holt paired himself with Nash, Caden, and Clint. I went with Roan, Daniels, and Maddie. The rest of our group formed the other teams of four.

Shadow barked, happy to be out in the snow, no matter the circumstances.

Maddie grabbed my arm. "Law, look."

She pointed through the dark forest. I didn't see it at first but then a glimmer of silver peeked through the underbrush—Damien's SUV.

Hope surged. "We move now," I clipped. "He's close. Dad, call in a crime scene team to process the truck."

He jerked his head in a nod, and we took off.

My team and Holt's were sent to the caves to the west. We made the mile-and-a-half trek in fifteen minutes, even in the snow. There were four cave openings, and Shadow sniffed the air, pulling Maddie toward the one on the left.

"Our girl has a scent," Maddie said quietly.

Holt and I shared a look.

"You want everyone in that cave or split up?" he asked.

My gut twisted. Splitting up would mean covering more ground, but Shadow was rarely wrong. "We stick together."

"Smart," Holt agreed.

We started toward the mouth of the cave but stopped dead when a scream tore through the air.

## Chapter Fifty

*Hallie*

THE SCREAM CAUGHT IN MY THROAT AS DAMIEN SHOVED me to the ground. I swallowed it down, but as I looked up at him, I saw the hint of pleasure in those green eyes. Pleasure at inflicting pain.

Something jolted in me. "Your eyes. They're green."

He laughed, but everything about it was wrong. "I'm not a moron, Halston. I took precautions. Just in case there was a clever little birdie like you. Colored contacts are easy to procure."

But Damien wasn't using them now. He wasn't even trying to hide his identity from law enforcement. It meant one of two things. He was either delusional or planning for neither of us to make it out of this alive. Maybe both.

Damien strode back toward the entrance and picked up something he'd leaned against the wall.

My stomach bottomed out at the sight of the long metal stick with a red handle.

He grinned down at me. "Just a little reminder for you to behave."

As if I could forget the painful jolt of the cattle prod. The way my muscles had seized and my skin burned.

Damien bent and unlocked my shackle. "Get up."

I didn't move. My heart pounded against my ribs as I stared up at him. The routine had always been the same. Get me out of the room and march me down to his torture chamber. But what if I refused to go? What would he do then?

Damien's eyes went hard. They were finally recognizable. Even though they weren't the brown I remembered, the hatred and rage were there. "I said, *get up*."

I stayed. I didn't open my mouth to speak or give him anything. But I stayed.

He shoved the cattle prod into my side.

My mouth opened on a silent scream, and my muscles seized in a vicious cramp. When he pulled back, I collapsed to the floor. My breaths came in quick pants as tears leaked from my eyes.

"Why do you make me hurt you, Halston? You've already proven yourself to me. All you have to do is say yes. Say you'll marry me. Then it'll be endless pleasure instead of pain."

Bile surged in my throat. "Never," I wheezed.

The cattle prod jammed into my shoulder, harder this time. Longer.

I couldn't help the whimper of pain that escaped my lips. I didn't want to give him the satisfaction, but I could do nothing to stop it.

The acute pain vanished, but echoes of it still coursed through me.

A hand fisted in my hair, hauling me up. "You will submit. You will learn."

The world was fuzzy around me. I knew I should fight to escape Damien's hold, but it was all I could do to stay upright.

"Move!" Damien shoved me forward and out into the cavernous hallway.

Battery-operated lanterns were scattered every ten to twenty feet. He'd prepared. That scared me most of all.

I tried to turn, to run. Damien grabbed my hair again, pulling in a vicious yank. "Don't even think about it. If you try to run, I will cut my losses and slit your pretty little throat."

His finger trailed over my neck. "And what a waste that would be."

Tears burned the backs of my eyes, but I refused to let them fall. Wouldn't give him the satisfaction.

With a few more hard shoves, Damien maneuvered me into the room that haunted my nightmares. "On the table," he commanded as he pushed me forward.

I turned to face him—the man who had stolen so much from me. Even though I'd never told him I'd *marry him*, how many times had I simply obeyed? Too tired to fight. How many times had I simply given in, so sure it would be the time everything ended?

But not now. Not when I had everything to fight for.

I moved before I had a chance to second-guess myself. I charged forward, and my hand came up in a palm strike. There was a satisfying crunch.

Damien howled in pain and dropped the cattle prod.

I didn't wait, I ran. The rough rock tore into my bare feet, but I didn't care. I just kept running.

It felt as if I were moving through molasses. I had the cattle prod to thank for that.

Curses and pounding footsteps sounded behind me.

I pushed harder, trying to create distance, attempting to get out. "Just keep moving."

A hand caught my nightgown, yanking me back hard. "You are going to pay for that."

Damien's voice vibrated with fury, and then I felt a cool blade pressed to my throat. "I'm going to carve a work of art into your skin so you remember how sorry you are."

"No, you aren't." Lawson's voice was colder than I'd ever heard it. Devoid of anything at all. "Cedar Ridge police. Drop the scalpel and step back, hands in the air."

*Lawson.*

He'd come. Just like I'd known he would.

Damien hauled me in front of him like a human shield, the blade still pressing into my throat. "No, no, no. This isn't your place. You aren't allowed here. It's for me. For my brides and me. No one else. It's our place."

"Drop the weapon," Nash ordered. "There's nowhere for you to go."

I could just make them out. Lawson, Nash, Holt, Roan, and a few more behind them. All held guns trained on us. On Damien.

"Leave!" Damien shouted. "She's mine. She always has been."

Lawson stepped forward, his face finally coming into the light. Those beautiful eyes that had kept me safe so many times, even in my dreams. "No, Miller. She'll never be yours."

Those blue orbs locked with my eyes, and I saw it then, the first signs of pain, fear, and fury.

"You can't have her!" Damien screamed, the blade pricking my throat. "You tried to steal her. To confuse her. But she came back to me. She'll always be mine."

Pain flared at my neck. And I could only think to do one thing. "I love you, Blue. It's always been you."

"No!" Damien pulled the scalpel from my neck and jammed it hard into my belly, yanking the blade to the side.

Pain. So much of it, I was drowning.

Shouts sounded. I heard the deafening pops of bullets. And then I was falling.

## Chapter Fifty-One

*Lawson*

THE WORLD SLOWED AROUND ME. MUFFLED SHOUTS. THEN one shot, a second, a third. My bullet among them. I lost count after that.

My eyes locked on Hallie. Her face was twisted in agony as she fell.

I was already moving, charging toward them, my brothers behind me. Some part of me was aware they were checking Miller for a pulse. But I didn't care.

"Hallie." Her name was part plea, part prayer, as blood soaked the flimsy fabric covering her.

"Blue," she croaked. "Love you."

My jaw set as I lifted that damned nightgown, trying to see the damage.

Roan let out a curse as he knelt next to me. "Got a kit." He pulled out a trauma pad and pressed it to the wound.

Hallie cried out.

I took her hand, pressing my face to hers. "I'm sorry. So goddamned sorry. He's trying to help."

"Blue." Her voice was more of a whisper now.

"Call for a medivac," Roan shouted. "There's space to land at the mouth of the cave."

Footsteps pounded on the stone.

I squeezed Hallie's hand hard. "Stay with me, Little Minx. Gotta stay with me."

"So tired," she mumbled.

"No, you don't. You can sleep later, once they've fixed you up. Not now."

"Love…you." The words were drawn out, more of a wheeze. And then the soft puffs of air against my cheek stopped altogether.

---

I stared down at my hands. They were red, the skin raw. But little flecks of dried blood still stained my nail beds and the ridges and whirls of my fingertips. It was the kind of stain that would never leave. And the glaring hospital lights only made it worse.

I wasn't sure if five minutes had passed or five hours. I was just waiting. Alone in this godforsaken room.

Flashes of memory, of my hands pressing down on Hallie's chest, of forcing her to breathe. I'd hurt her. Caused her pain in hopes of keeping her alive, and it all might've been for nothing.

Everything hurt. I felt a kind of pain I hadn't known existed. Because it was as if the most vital part of myself were being ripped out of my soul.

Footsteps sounded. Not just one pair. A herd.

My head jerked up. A herd was right. Mom and Dad came in first. Mom's face was pale, her hand wrapped around Dad's. But they were quickly overtaken. Charlie ran for me, hitting me in the middle and bursting into tears.

I hauled him into my arms. "I've got you, bud."

I couldn't say everything would be okay because I wouldn't lie to my kids. Not about something like this. Not ever.

Charlie clung to my neck. "I want my Hallie!"

My throat constricted. "Me, too, bud. Me, too."

Drew's face was unnaturally pale as he stepped forward. "Is she out of surgery?"

I shook my head. I wouldn't share that Hallie had flatlined on the chopper ride to Seattle. Wouldn't tell him that she'd lost so much blood her skin had taken on a grayish hue. "Still waiting."

Luke's eyes were red, his hand clasped in a vise-like grip by Violet, who was pressed to his side. "Is she going to make it?"

I swallowed hard. "We need to wait for the doctor."

It was all I could say.

"Let's sit," Mom encouraged.

More family piled in. Roan carried Cady, who clung to him like a monkey. She was clearly shaken by Charlie's state and everything going on around her. Aspen rubbed her back as they sat, muttering sweet nothings.

Wren leaned into Holt, his lips sweeping across her temple. The tender action made my heart jerk.

Grae sat right on Caden's lap, curling into him. I knew this had to bring back hard memories for her, as well. But Caden never let her go.

Nash guided Maddie to a chair, kissing her forehead before moving to me. "Can I get you anything? Coffee? Water? Food?"

I shook my head. I wouldn't be able to keep anything down. Not now.

Instead, I sat, letting Charlie cry everything out. Drew sat on my one side. Luke and Violet on the other.

Reverend Hooper and his wife stepped into the waiting room. His face was somber as he crossed to me. "I don't want to intrude, but I couldn't imagine being anywhere else. I'd like to pray for the girl. She has a goodness our world needs."

My throat clogged. "Thank you, Reverend. I'll take all the prayers you've got."

I'd take anything. I'd do battle with the Devil himself for Hallie.

Hooper nodded and bowed his head. The room went silent as he led us in prayer. I wanted to believe that God was listening, that he would intercede. But everything in me was too damn terrified to hope.

The reverend wasn't the last visitor. Slowly, the room filled. Clint and Abrams. Daniels. The only one who hadn't shown was Anson. And I didn't blame him. He'd been down this road already, and a hospital wasn't anywhere he'd ever willingly go again.

Another two hours ticked by as we waited. I straightened as two figures filled the doorway.

I recognized Emerson first. He had the same gray eyes as his sister, his blond hair just a few shades darker. I stood, handing a sleeping Charlie to my mom.

I strode toward Emerson, who had his hand clasped in a darker one I knew had to belong to Adrian. My throat worked. "I'm Lawson."

Emerson's eyes shone. "Any word?"

I shook my head. "Not yet. We're still waiting for the surgeon. I'm so sorry. *So* sorry I didn't protect her."

Emerson dropped his husband's hand and took hold of my shoulders. "You did everything you could. She told me." His eyes shone with unshed tears, even as he tried to smile. "She was annoyed at you for being overbearing."

My chest throbbed. I could practically hear Hallie complaining.

"My sister,"—his voice hitched—"she's strong. She's going to make it through."

I nodded, unable to speak.

"Halston Astor's family?" a voice asked from the hall.

All our eyes instantly went to the woman with golden-brown skin and dark hair. Her expression was kind but carefully masked. "I'm Dr. Dalal. I've been taking care of Halston."

"Hallie," I rasped. "She likes to be called Hallie."

Dr. Dalal's expression softened. "Of course."

Adrian grasped Emerson's hand. "How is she?"

The doctor scanned the room. "She's in serious but stable condition. The wound caused a tremendous amount of blood loss. I'm afraid we lost her for a minute on the table."

My heart jerked as if it could beat double-time for Hallie's.

"We were able to get her back and repair the trauma to her abdomen. Unfortunately, her kidney was beyond repair, and we had to remove it."

"What does that mean?" Emerson asked.

Dr. Dalal turned to him. "Many people live long and healthy lives with just one kidney. As long as there isn't any brain damage from lack of oxygen, I expect a full recovery."

"When will we know?" Dad asked.

"We need to wait for Hallie to wake up. She's breathing on her own now. I can take one of you up to ICU to sit with her."

Emerson and I shared a look. He motioned me forward as he swallowed. "I've always been her person. But that changed when she moved here. You brought her back to life, to fully living. You'll bring her back again."

"Thank you," I choked out, the pressure building behind my eyes.

I followed the doctor out of the waiting room and toward a bank of elevators. Neither of us spoke on the journey. I didn't have words.

She motioned to a hand sanitizer machine, and I quickly cleansed my hands. She punched in a code and led me through a busy room surrounded by other smaller rooms. She stopped in front of an open door.

"Hallie has a few machines tracking her vitals and stitches in her stomach. But you can hold her hand. Talk to her. It'll help."

"Thank you," I whispered.

As I stepped into the room, the first tears fell. She looked so tiny in the hospital bed. So pale it appeared as if she might fade away.

My feet carried me toward her as if they had a mind of their own. I sank into the chair, taking her hand and pressing my lips to her palm. "I'm right here, Hallie. I've got you. And I'm never letting go."

## Chapter Fifty-Two

*Hallie*

THE FAINT BEEPING PULLED AT ME, SHOVING ME OUT OF the sea of nothingness. I let out a garbled moan. A hand squeezed mine.

"Come on, Little Minx. Been telling all the nurses what a fighter you are. Gotta prove me right."

I knew that voice. I wanted to get to it. To reach Lawson.

My eyelids fluttered, the bright lights making me squint.

"There she is."

Lawson's face filled my vision. His scruff was longer than usual, and dark circles rimmed his beautiful eyes.

"Blue," I rasped.

Pain streaked across his face. "Worried I'd never hear you call me that again."

My hand spasmed in his as it all came rushing back. The vet's office. The cave. "Damien?"

That pain morphed into fury. "He's gone. You'll never have to worry about him again."

Relief rushed through me. Blessed relief. Maybe that made me a bad person, but this world would be a better place without Damien Miller in it.

Lawson leaned over me, pressing his forehead to mine. "You're safe."

"I can't believe it was him and not Len Keller."

Something passed over Lawson's eyes.

My stomach knotted. "What?"

"Cops a couple of counties over found Len and got him back to the hospital. It turns out his daughter was one of Miller's victims. It didn't pop at first because she had a different last name. She was newly married."

"Oh, God," I whispered. "That poor man."

Lawson's fingers traced over the back of my hand. "Some part of his broken mind thought he was trying to save you."

I couldn't imagine how tormented he must've been. How much he'd lost. "You won't charge him, right?"

Lawson shook his head. "Not unless you want to. He's getting the help he needs now."

"I don't want to charge him. He's been through enough. We all have."

His lips ghosted across mine. "I love you, Hallie. With everything I have."

"I love you, too."

Lawson pulled back, searching my face. "Are you in pain? Should I get a nurse?"

I squeezed his hand. My stomach throbbed, but I didn't want medicine. "I just need you. A few minutes holding your hand so I know for sure this is real."

Lawson brushed the hair away from my face. "This is real. You fought for it. Battled your way back to me. To us."

My eyes burned. "You were with me. I thought of you and the boys, and I wouldn't give up."

He lifted my hand to his lips, kissing it and then just holding it there so he was speaking against my knuckles. "Don't want to waste any time. I'm already an old man."

I grinned. "You don't look old to me. And you definitely don't feel old."

Lawson chuckled, the sound skating over my skin. "I want every second with you, and I want to live it to the fullest."

That pressure built behind my eyes. "Me, too. I'll never take a moment for granted."

He slipped a hand into his pocket and pulled out something I couldn't see. "My grandmother gave me a ring once. I never knew why I didn't give it to Melody; it just didn't feel right. But I know now. Because it was always meant for you."

My breath hitched as my heart rate sped up.

Lawson slipped a band onto my finger. The metal was warm from being so close to his body. I stared down at the breathtaking ring. A stunning round diamond glittered up at me, set in a delicate rose gold band with flowers woven into the metal.

My gaze snapped to his.

"Marry me, Hallie."

My mouth curved even as tears spilled over and tracked down my cheeks. "That doesn't sound like a question."

"Say yes anyway."

"Yes," I breathed.

Lawson bent, his lips taking mine.

"We brought you a sandwich from the deli down the street. It's better than this awful cafeteria—oh! She's awake! Em, she's awake," Adrian all but cheered as he stepped into the room, his husband behind him.

Emerson's eyes filled. "I can see that. And she's making out with her hunk of a man already."

"Our girl has her priorities in order," Adrian said with a grin, tears shining in his eyes.

And then they were running to my side, peppering me with questions and gentle hugs.

Adrian gripped my hand and held it up to the light. "Um, Em…I think our girl has some news."

Emerson's tears fell now as he glanced at Lawson. "You move quick."

"Not going to miss another second with her."

My heart clenched, but there was no pain, only the kind of joy that left an ache behind. The *real* kind.

Adrian squeezed my hand and grinned. "We are going to have the most fun planning a wedding!"

I smiled back, knowing he was right. And we could all use some happiness.

I glanced at Lawson. "Where are Charlie, Drew, and Luke?"

A shadow passed over his eyes. "You've been in and out for over three days."

My eyes widened. "Three days?"

He nodded. "They wanted to stay, but I finally got Mom to get them back to the hotel. They refused to go back to Cedar Ridge."

Fresh pain washed through me, knowing how scared they must've been. "Where am I?"

"Seattle," Lawson explained. "They airlifted you here, and the family met us."

"Seattle?"

Lawson took my hand again. "It was touch and go for a while. You lost a lot of blood, and there was damage to one of your kidneys. They had to remove it, but the surgeon has assured us that you'll make a full recovery."

I stared down at my torso. No wonder it had been throbbing since I awoke. "But everything else? I'm okay?"

He bent, pressing his lips to my temple. "You're going to have to take it easy for a while, but you'll be just fine."

I breathed out a sigh of relief and glanced at Emerson. "Do Mom and Dad know?"

A look of fury took root on his face, and I steeled myself for whatever was coming. "I called them on my way here." His jaw worked back and forth as if he struggled to get the words out. "They said it was your choice to put yourself at risk by living here. Said these were the ramifications of your actions."

Tears stung the backs of my eyes. "They aren't coming."

"No," Emerson said through gritted teeth.

Lawson pressed his forehead to my temple. "I'm so sorry."

"I'm not," I admitted.

He pulled back, confusion on his face.

"I'm finally free of them. Maybe I just needed them to cut the cord."

Lawson squeezed my hand. He opened his mouth to say something but was cut off.

"Dad, I brought you a milkshake," Charlie called from the hallway. As he entered the room, he skidded to a stop. "Hallie?" Tears filled his eyes. "Hallie!"

He took off at a dead run, launching himself at me.

Emerson caught him around the waist as Adrian caught the milkshake.

"Whoa," Emerson said, amusement lacing his tone.

"Hallie has stitches, remember?" Lawson asked. "We have to be really careful."

Charlie bobbed his head up and down as Emerson set him down. He moved toward the head of the bed, and I instantly reached for his hand.

"I missed you so much," I whispered.

Tears tracked down his cheeks. "I missed you more. Dad said you were gonna be okay, but you weren't waking up. I was so scared."

I pulled Charlie closer. "I'm so sorry, buddy. I'm right here, and I'm not going anywhere."

Drew and Luke crowded closer to the bed. There were dark circles under Drew's eyes. "You're okay? Really?"

I nodded. "Gonna be sore for a while, but I'll be just fine."

Tears shone in Luke's eyes. "Love you, Hallie."

My throat clogged. "I love you, too."

Lawson cleared his throat, glancing at Charlie, who had laid his head on my shoulder. "You know how we talked about me and Hallie? How we were dating and would let you know when things changed?"

Drew and Luke shared a look while Charlie sat up straight.

Lawson grinned. "I have some good news and some bad news…"

"Spill, Pops," Drew demanded.

"Well, Hallie quit as your nanny."

Their gazes all jerked in my direction, and I had to bite my lip to keep from laughing.

"But she said yes to being my wife," Lawson hurried to add.

Hoots filled the room from Wren, Holt, Nash, and Maddie, who had come in behind the boys.

Drew smiled widely as he glanced at my ring. "You don't mess around, bruh. Respect."

Lawson just shook his head.

Charlie looked at me wide-eyed. "Does this mean you can be my real mom? Not just in my heart?"

My eyes filled as I swallowed down the emotion and glanced at Lawson.

He took my hand and squeezed.

"Nothing would make me happier than to be your mom, Charlie," I whispered.

"I wished it from the first day you came," he said with a wide smile. "And when Drew blew out his candles, I wished it then, too." He glanced at Drew. "Sorry, I stole your wish."

Everyone laughed, and Drew just grinned. "No worries, little man. I can't think of a better one." He shuffled his feet. "Maybe I could call you Mom, too? If it's not weird."

The tears started to fall then. "If it's weird, then I'm the biggest weirdo of all because I'd love it."

Luke moved closer, eyes holding so much emotion. "You've been more of a mom than we've ever had."

Lawson leaned in closer, kissing my temple.

"You guys have given me everything I thought I'd never have. More than I ever could've dreamed," I whispered.

Charlie grinned at me. "We're like the best present ever."

He had no idea.

# Epilogue

## Hallie

### ONE YEAR LATER

I cuddled baby Clara to my chest as she cooed. Lawson lowered himself to the spot on the couch next to me. "You look good holding a baby."

My stomach did a series of somersaults that would've been fitting for Cirque du Soleil. "I think Clara here is doing all the work."

I glanced at Grae on my other side, who held Clara's twin, Micah. "You and Caden do good work in this department."

She laughed. "It's crazy how they're a complete mixture of the two of us. Genes are weird."

Lawson's hand ghosted up and down my arm. "Are they sleeping any better?"

"No," Caden answered from his spot next to Grae. "And they rile each other up. I feel like we might be in for it during the teenage years."

Grae's lips twitched. "Caden gets cranky with lack of sleep, but they've got him wrapped around their little fingers."

He leaned over Micah and tickled his belly. Micah let out a bubbly giggle.

"The lack of sleep is *rough*," Adrian said as he bounced his and Emerson's baby boy on his lap. "We should've bought stock in coffee."

Emerson leaned over and pressed a kiss to Adrian's temple. "But you love those silent moments in the middle of the night with our guy."

Adrian's expression turned soft. "I do. But I miss sleep."

My world felt complete when Emerson and Adrian moved from Chicago to Cedar Ridge six months ago. Adopting a baby boy had changed their minds about city life. They wanted a place for Dawson to run and play as he grew up. And Cedar Ridge had a built-in community. They'd quickly become a part of the Hartley family, and I was able to give Emerson the family we'd never had growing up.

And now that we had some distance from our parents, we were finding more of our footing as individuals, too. Emerson had started a nonprofit that provided tutoring for underprivileged children in need, and I had enrolled in a training program to become a victims' rights advocate. I only had a few months on the job, but I already knew it was my calling.

Kerry scooted over and shook a set of plastic keys for Dawson. "But our boy is so cute, the lack of sleep doesn't matter."

Dawson gave her a drooly, gummy grin.

"It gets easier," Wren promised. Her daughter Josephine's hands were wrapped around her fingers as she toddled across Kerry and Nathan's living room.

"How's the birthday girl?" I asked, giving a little wave.

"She's cake drunk," Holt said with a grin.

"It's her first birthday," Nash defended little Jo. "Go big or go home."

Maddie laughed as she rubbed a hand over her swollen belly. "That's what happens when you get her the good stuff. I still can't believe that cake. How did you get it to look like Shadow, Aspen?"

Aspen grinned from her spot perched on Roan's lap. "It took a few tries, but it really was just mixing the right food coloring."

"Shadow is the love of her life," Holt mumbled.

"Sha Sha!" Josephine chanted.

We all laughed.

A hand landed on my shoulder from behind. "Is it okay if Vi and I head out? We wanted to hit the bookstore before it closes."

I looked up into Luke's face. It was older in just a year. Heck, he was *shaving* and driving now.

"Of course. What time do you think you'll be home?" I asked.

Luke glanced at Violet, so much adoration in his eyes. I couldn't help but wonder if they would go the distance. "I'm having dinner at her place. So, eight or nine?"

"Drive safely, please," I warned.

Luke grinned. "Love you even though you're crazy overprotective."

"Love you, too," I called as Violet gave me a wave and a shy smile.

"Mooooooom!" Charlie came running into the living room, Cady on his heels.

Lawson let out a low chuckle next to me as Charlie skidded to a stop in front of us. "Where's the fire?"

"Cady said there's a new reptile store opening in Brookdale. Can we go? Can we?"

Aspen winced. "We have Roan to thank for this news."

Roan shrugged. "I think it would be cool to have a bearded dragon. What's one more animal for the menagerie?"

Lawson groaned. "Thor *just* stopped peeing everywhere."

"Thor is Drew's dog," Charlie complained. "I should get a pet, too, shouldn't I? Plus, my bearded dragon is going to be way better trained."

"Bruh," Drew said, looking up from his phone. "Thor is a wonder dog. Don't throw him under the bus."

Charlie rolled his eyes. "He ate one of your socks and barfed it up yesterday."

My stomach roiled at the memory.

"We'll see about making a visit to the reptile store," Lawson promised. "But pets are a lot of responsibility."

"I'm the responsiblest," Charlie vowed.

Drew just snorted at that.

Charlie whirled on him. "Shut it. You're just mad because Quinn Adams doesn't want anything to do with you."

Drew's jaw went hard. "Stop eavesdropping, you little—"

Nash clamped a hand on Drew's shoulder. "The little Casanova has fallen?"

Drew had fallen—and hard—for a new student in his first-year class. Only Quinn didn't seem to have the first clue Drew existed. His typical cocky smiles and charm weren't doing a thing, and he was floundering. It was adorable to watch.

"She's shy," Drew mumbled.

"Or smart," Charlie muttered.

"Charlie," I warned. "That's not very nice."

"Sorry, Mom."

"How about an apology to Drew?"

Charlie scowled but turned to his brother. "Sorry."

"*Real* heartfelt," Drew shot back.

"I said sorry!"

Nash stood, lifting Charlie into the air. "Come on, little monster. Let's talk about what it means to be a good wingman."

My gaze followed as he flipped Charlie upside down. That was a mistake. My stomach pitched as Charlie did.

I lurched to my feet, quickly handing Clara to Caden. "Be right back."

I was already practically running. *Don't puke, don't puke, don't puke.*

Sliding into the bathroom, I closed the door behind me and breathed deeply. The worst of the nausea had faded, but it had left me with a light-headed feeling that made the world swim around me.

"Hallie?" Lawson's voice cut into my thoughts as he stepped into the bathroom. "Shit. You're white as a ghost."

His hand went to my forehead. "Are you sick? Want me to take you to Doc?"

I couldn't look at him, could only focus on staying upright. "I already went. Yesterday."

Lawson's body stiffened behind me, and he turned me to face him. "Why didn't you say anything? What's wrong?"

My heart hammered in my chest as blood roared in my ears. "I'm okay. I just—um, it's not what we planned. And I don't know if it's going to freak you out. It's a lot, and I know we talked about it, but—"

A huge smile spread across Lawson's face. "You're pregnant?"

"Triplets," I blurted. I had to get the news out before he went down the single-baby train. My head had been swimming since Doc gave me the news yesterday. *Three* babies when we already had three kids at home. It would be mayhem.

Lawson's jaw went slack. "Triplets…"

I winced and nodded. "I know we only talked about one—"

He cut me off, pulling me into his arms. "Hallie. I'd have a football team with you if you wanted."

I sniffed as tears pooled in my eyes. "Really?"

Lawson's hands came up to frame my face. "There's nothing I love more than building a family with you. Three at once will require a zone defense, but I'm up for the challenge if you are."

A laugh bubbled out of me. "The boys will help, too."

He brushed the hair away from my face. "They're gonna be over the moon."

Tears spilled over. "You think?"

"I know." Lawson bent and brushed a kiss over my lips. "You're a miracle, Little Minx. The missing piece that gave us more happiness than I would've thought possible."

I pressed a hand to his chest. "It's you. All of you. You brought me out of the ashes."

# Acknowledgments

How have we come to the end of another series so quickly? Lost & Found has been a truly life-changing journey for me, and it means the world that you've come along for the ride. Maybe it's because this series has been so special that I struggled a bit with this last book. I've had the idea for Lawson and Hallie for years and finally putting them down on paper was both wonderful and terrifying. Thankfully, I had a lot of people helping me along the way.

A huge first thank-you must go to Sam and Elsie for reading early drafts of this book and helping me find the balance I needed and holding my hand when I was feeling a little unsure. I'm beyond lucky to have both of you in my corner on writing projects and beyond.

Rebecca, how many voice memos is too many? Thank you for your friendship, your support, your ear when I'm spiraling or celebrating. Laura and Willow, thank you for making me laugh until I wheeze, for your support, no matter the project or problem, and for the gift that is your friendship. Amy, thank you for the check-ins, the cheering, the laughter, and the pep talks. I'm so very grateful for you.

Second, in my non-writer world. My STS soul sisters: Hollis, Jael, and Paige, thank you for celebrating every new book and milestone. You make me feel celebrated, seen, and cherished. I thank my lucky stars for you every day.

And to all my family and friends near and far. Thank you for supporting me on this crazy journey, even if you don't read "kissing books." But you get extra special bonus points if you picked up one of mine, even if that makes me turn the shade of a tomato when you tell me.

To my fearless beta readers: Crystal, Elle, Kelly, and Trisha, thank you for reading this book in its roughest form and helping me to make it the best it could possibly be!

The crew that helps bring my words to life and gets them out into the world is pretty darn epic. Thank you to Devyn, Margo, Chelle, Jaime, Julie, Hang, Stacey, Katie, and my team at Lyric Audiobooks, Kimberly, Joy, and my team at Brower Literary. Your hard work is so appreciated!

To all the bloggers who have taken a chance on my words… THANK YOU! Your championing of my stories means more than I can say. And to my launch and ARC teams, thank you for your kindness and support, and for sharing my books with the world. An extra special thank-you to Crystal who sails that ship so I can focus on the words.

Ladies of Catherine Cowles Reader Group, you're my favorite place to hang out on the internet! Thank you for your support, encouragement, and willingness to always dish about your latest book boyfriends. You're the freaking best!

Lastly, thank YOU! Yes, YOU. I'm so grateful you're reading this book and making my author dreams come true. I love you for that. A whole lot!

*Also Available from*
# CATHERINE COWLES

### The Lost & Found Series
*Whispers of You*
*Echoes of You*
*Glimmers of You*
*Shadows of You*
*Ashes of You*

### The Tattered & Torn Series
*Tattered Stars*
*Falling Embers*
*Hidden Waters*
*Shattered Sea*
*Fractured Sky*

### The Wrecked Series
*Reckless Memories*
*Perfect Wreckage*
*Wrecked Palace*
*Reckless Refuge*
*Beneath the Wreckage*

### The Sutter Lake Series
*Beautifully Broken Pieces*
*Beautifully Broken Life*
*Beautifully Broken Spirit*
*Beautifully Broken Control*
*Beautifully Broken Redemption*

### Stand-alone Novels
*Further To Fall*

*For a full list of up-to-date Catherine Cowles titles, please visit www.catherinecowles.com.*

*About*

# CATHERINE COWLES

Writer of words. Drinker of Diet Cokes. Lover of all things cute and furry. *USA Today* bestselling author Catherine Cowles has had her nose in a book since the time she could read and finally decided to write down some of her own stories. When she's not writing, she can be found exploring her home state of Oregon, listening to true crime podcasts, or searching for her next book boyfriend.

# Stay Connected

You can find Catherine in all the usual bookish places…

Website:
catherinecowles.com

Facebook:
facebook.com/catherinecowlesauthor

Catherine Cowles Facebook Reader Group:
www.facebook.com/groups/CatherineCowlesReaderGroup

Instagram:
instagram.com/catherinecowlesauthor

Goodreads:
goodreads.com/catherinecowlesauthor

BookBub:
bookbub.com/profile/catherine-cowles

Amazon:
www.amazon.com/author/catherinecowles

Twitter:
twitter.com/catherinecowles

Pinterest:
pinterest.com/catherinecowlesauthor

Made in United States
Orlando, FL
13 May 2025